Mirror Image by Isaac Asimov—Two universally famous mathematicians telling conflicting versions of the truth is normal. But two robots? Only a classic human/robot team can out-logic the masters of logic to discover who's lying.

Cloak of Anarchy by Larry Niven—In the Free Park you could bark like a dog or toss your clothes to the wind if the mood took you that way, but when the all-seeing Copseyes tumbled from the sky, and night closed in, the picnic was over . . .

Brillo by Harlan Ellison and Ben Bova—Crazy season for cops is August, and when the Department put a piece of walking hardware on the burning streets, even software for brains couldn't keep the barrio from boiling over. . . .

Into the Shop by Ron Goulart—The lawagon can question, arrest, try and even execute a criminal if all data is beyond a shadow of a doubt. But can it malfunction. . . ?

Here, by fifteen top science fiction writers, are the fascinating stories of what happens when man meets machine in . . .

Isaac Asimov's
Wonderful Worlds of Science Fiction #5

TIN STARS

TIN STARS

Isaac Asimov's
Wonderful Worlds of
Science Fiction #5

EDITED BY
ISAAC ASIMOV, MARTIN H. GREENBERG,
AND CHARLES G. WAUGH

A SIGNET BOOK

NEW AMERICAN LIBRARY

NAL BOOKS ARE AVAILABLE AT QUANTITY DISCOUNTS WHEN USED TO PROMOTE PRODUCTS OR SERVICES. FOR INFORMATION PLEASE WRITE TO PREMIUM MARKETING DIVISION. NEW AMERICAN LIBRARY. 1633 BROADWAY. NEW YORK. NEW YORK 10019.

Acknowledgments

"Into the Shop," by Ron Goulart. Copyright © 1964 by Mercury Press, Inc. From THE MAGAZINE OF FANTASY AND SCIENCE FICTION. Reprinted by permission of the author.

"Cloak of Anarchy," by Larry Niven. Copyright © 1972 by Conde Nast Publications, Inc. Reprinted by permission of Kirby McCauley, Ltd.

"The King's Legions," by Christopher Anvil. Copyright © 1967 by Conde Nast Publications, Inc. Reprinted by permission of the author and his agents, the Scott Meredith Literary Agency, Inc., 845 Third Avenue, New York, NY 10022.

"Finger of Fate," by Edward Wellen. Copyright © 1980 by Mercury Press, Inc. From THE MAGAZINE OF FANTASY AND SCIENCE FICTION. Reprinted by permission of the author.

"Arm of the Law," by Harry Harrison. Copyright © 1958 by King-Size Publications, Inc. Reprinted by permission of Nat Sobel Associates, Inc.

"Voiceover," by Edward Wellen. Copyright © 1984 by Edward Wellen. Reprinted by permission of the author.

"The Fastest Draw," by Larry Eisenberg. Copyright © 1963 by Ziff-Davis Publications, Inc. Reprinted by permission of the author.

"Mirror Image," by Isaac Asimov. Copyright © 1972 by Conde Nast Publications, Inc. Reprinted by permission of the author.

"Brillo" by Harlan Ellison and Ben Bova; copyright © 1970 by The Conde Nast Publications, Inc. Copyright reassigned to Authors 13 September 1973; copyright © 1973 by Harlan Ellison and Ben Bova. Reprinted with permission of, and by arrangement with, the Authors and the Authors' agents, Richard Curtis Associates, Inc., New York, and Barbara Bova respectively. All rights reserved.

"The Powers of Observation," by Harry Harrison. Copyright © 1968 by Conde Nast Publications, Inc. Reprinted by permission of Nat Sobel Associates, Inc.

"Faithfully Yours," by Lou Tabakow. Copyright © 1955 by Street & Smith Publications, Inc.; renewed © 1983 by the Estate of Lou Tabakow. Reprinted by permission of the Estate of Lou Tabakow.

"Safe Harbor," by Donald Wismer. Copyright © 1985 by Donald Wismer. Used by permission of the author.

"Examination Day," by Henry Slesar. Copyright © 1957 by HMH Publishing Co., Inc. Reprinted by permission of the author.

"The Cruel Equations," by Robert Sheckley. Copyright © 1971 by Robert Sheckley. Reprinted by permission of Kirby McCauley, Ltd.

"Animal Lover," by Stephen R. Donaldson. Copyright © 1978 by Random House, Inc. First published in STELLAR #4. Reprinted by permission of the Howard Morhaim Literary Agency, Inc.

SIGNET, SIGNET CLASSIC, MENTOR, PLUME, MERIDIAN AND NAL BOOKS are published by New American Library, 1633 Broadway, New York, New York 10019

First Printing, July, 1986

1 2 3 4 5 6 7 8 9

PRINTED IN THE UNITED STATES OF AMERICA

Contents

Introduction

by Isaac Asimov

The science fiction mode can be applied to any type of fiction from mainstream to pornography, and it would be surprising indeed if it could not be applied to the mystery story.

Of course, the mystery story itself comes in many varieties, and if we are dealing with the crime story, in which attention is focused on the criminal and his motives, or on the crime and its consequences, then science fiction is right at home. In fact, perhaps the oldest and hoariest cliché in our beloved field is that of the "mad scientist," who is usually treated as a criminal.

The story that some consider the first modern science fiction story, *Frankenstein*, features Victor Frankenstein, who, if not mad outright, is certainly injudicious. His creation of the monster is a crime by nineteenth-century standards, but his later abandonment of his creation is a vile deed by almost anyone's standards.

If we turn to contemporary science fiction, then we find that crime stories are by no means unknown. To mention classics, there was *Private Eye* by Lewis Padgett (Henry Kuttner), which appeared as the lead story in the January 1949 *Astounding*. Then, too, there was *The Demolished Man* by Alfred Bester, which was serialized in the January, February, and March 1952 issues of *Galaxy*, and which, in 1953, won the first Hugo in the novel category.

In 1952, by which time I had written about a dozen short stories about robots, using my Three Laws of Robotics,

Horace Gold, the editor of *Galaxy*, urged me to write an entire novel centered on robots and the Three Laws, so that he could run it as a serial.

I demurred, since I wasn't certain that I could keep up my robots for the length of an entire novel. Gold said, "Well, you like to introduce the mystery element into your science fiction. Why not write a science fiction mystery novel with your detective having a robot partner?"

That struck me as a good idea. Over the next half year I wrote *The Caves of Steel*, which was a mystery in the classic style of the 1930s in which all the clues are presented to the reader, who is given an honest chance to beat the detective to the solution. As it happened, it was a thoroughgoing science fiction story as well, one in which the mystery was presented against a solid, carefully thought-out futuristic background. I believe the book to be the first successful fusion of classic mystery and classic science fiction. I have made this claim for decades and no one has yet disputed it.

As Gold had suggested, my detective, Elijah Baley, had a robot partner, R. Daneel Olivaw. I don't quite dare say that this was the first example of a man-and-robot detective team, for there may well have been early stories of the sort that I never read, or don't remember, but mine *may* have been the first, and certainly *was* the first to achieve success.

The Caves of Steel was serialized in the October, November, and December 1953 issues of *Galaxy* and was published in hardcover by Doubleday in 1954. Later, a sequel, *The Naked Sun*, was serialized in the October, November, and December 1956 *Astounding*, and was published in hardcover by Doubleday in 1957. Much later, in 1983, a third book, *The Robots of Dawn*, was published by Doubleday. All three featured Baley and Daneel and all were successful.

One sign of the success was that after 1953, a number of stories about human and robot detective partners appeared. Eventually, a few items of the sort (all deservedly unsuccessful) appeared on television. In a way, then, I feel responsible for this type of science fiction story, and it was only a matter of time before it occurred to the editing team of Waugh, Greenberg, and Asimov to produce an anthology of such stories.

As an example, I thought at once of my own *Mirror*

Image, which appeared in the May 1972 *Analog*. It was the only short story about Baley and Daneel that I ever wrote, and I suppose it was necessary to include it. For one thing, Marty and Charles insisted, and for another, although the story had appeared in two of my own short story collections, it has never been anthologized, and it always disturbs me to have a story of mine unanthologized. However, since it is well known that the positions of strength in any anthology are the first and last, my modesty is such that we have put *Mirror Image* in the precise middle of this anthology.

Immediately after my story, by the way, we have placed *Brillo* by Harlan Ellison and Ben Bova. There is a distant connection here, for Harlan sued some television people for rejecting his television script based on *Brillo* and for then running a television program that, to Harlan's eyes, seemed indistinguishable from his script. He sued, and the television people advanced the astonishing defense that Harlan had no grounds for the suit since he himself had borrowed the story from *The Caves of Steel*. (Apparently, they were maintaining, as a legal axiom, that two wrongs make a right.) Harlan turned to me and I gladly bore formal witness that *Brillo* had a human-robot detective team but was otherwise in no way similar to my novel, and Harlan won his case (and a large sum in damages).

We start the anthology, however, with *Into the Shop* by Ron Goulart, which, in my opinion, is the best short story about a human-robot detective team that has yet been written. It's got one of those terrific last sentences.

We didn't dare include *only* human-robot detective teams, however, for in theme anthologies there is always the danger of insufficient variety, and we would have been in trouble in this respect if we hadn't broadened the category to include robots or mechanical devices or even automatons that served to oversee human behavior or to sit in judgment over human beings.

As examples of this broadening of category, there is *Examination Day* by Henry Slesar, which I had to read three times before I saw the crucial role of a machine and was able to agree with Charles that it belonged in the anthology. (The writing was so smooth and concise that I slid right over that point in my first two readings.)

Then there is *The Fastest Draw* by Larry Eisenberg, a particularly ingenious story, and Edward Wellen's *Finger of Fate*, in which there is only one detective, no time, and which is a private-eye story to end all private-eye stories.

And so on. You're going to enjoy this anthology a lot. I know because I did in the course of its preparation.

One word about the title of the anthology. Ben and Harlan called their story "Brillo" because it was about a robot detective, which could be referred to as "metal fuzz," and what is Brillo but—oh, you get the point, I see.

Well, in "tin star," the "tin" refers to a robot and the "star" refers to a sheriff. Oh, you get that, too? If it weren't for the play on words, I would have preferred to call the anthology *Robots in Judgment*.

Into the Shop

Ron Goulart

The waitress screamed, that was the trouble with live help, and made a flapping motion with her extended arm. Stu Clemens swung sideways in the booth and looked out through the green-tinted window at the parking lot. A dark-haired man in his early thirties was slumping to his knees, his hands flickering at his sides. Silently the lawagon spun back out of its parking place and rolled nearer to the fallen man. "There's nobody in that car," said the waitress, dropping a cup of coffee.

She must be new to this planet, from one of the sticks systems, maybe. "It's my car," said Clemens, flipping the napkin toggle on the table and then tossing her one when it popped up. "Here, wipe your uniform off. That's a lawagon and it knows what it's doing."

The waitress put the napkin up to her face and turned away.

Out in the lot the lawagon had the man trussed up. It stunned him again for safety and then it flipped him into the back seat for interrogation and identification. "It never makes a mistake," said Clemens to the waitress's back. "I've been marshal in Territory 23 for a year now and that lawagon has never made a mistake. They build them that way."

The car had apparently given the suspect an injection and he had fallen over out of sight. Three more napkins popped up out of the table unasked. "Damn it," said Clemens and pounded the outlet with his fist once, sharply.

11

"It does that sometimes," said the waitress, looking again at Clemens, but no further. She handed him his check card.

Clemens touched the waitress's arm as he got up. "Don't worry. The law is always fair on Barnum. I'm sorry you had to see a criminal up close like that."

"He just had the businessman's lunch," the waitress said.

"Well, even criminals have to eat." Clemens paid the cash register and it let him out of the drive-in oasis.

The cars that had been parked near the lawagon were gone now. When people were in trouble they welcomed the law but other times they stayed clear. Clemons grimaced, glancing at the dry yellow country beyond the oasis restaurant. He had just cleaned up an investigation and was heading back to his office in Hub 23. He still had an hour to travel. Lighting a cigarette, he started for the lawagon. He was curious to see whom his car had apprehended.

"This is a public service announcement," announced the lawagon from its roof speakers. "Sheldon Kloog, wanted murderer, has just been captured by Lawagon A10. Trial has been held, a verdict of guilty brought in, death sentenced and the sentence carried out as prescribed by law. This has been a public service announcement from the Barnum Law Bureau."

Clemens ran to the car. This was a break. Sheldon Kloog was being hunted across eleven territories for murdering his wife and dismantling all their household androids. At the driver's door the marshal took his ID cards out of his gray trouser pocket and at the same time gave the day's passwords to the lawagon. He next gave the countersigns and the oath of fealty and the car let him in.

Behind the wheel, Clemens said, "Congratulations. How'd you spot him?"

The lawagon's dash speaker answered, "Made a positive identification five seconds after Kloog stepped out of the place. Surprised you didn't spot him. Was undisguised and had all the telltale marks of a homicide prone."

"He wasn't sitting in my part of the restaurant. Sorry." Clemens cocked his head and looked into the empty back seat. The lawagons had the option of holding murderers for full cybernetic trial in one of the territorial hubs or, if the murderer checked out strongly guilty and seemed dangerous, executing them on the spot. "Where is he?"

The glove compartment fell open and an opaque white jar rolled out. Clemens caught it. *Earthly Remains of Sheldon Kloog,* read the label. The disintegrator didn't leave much.

Putting the jar back, Clemens said, "Did you send photos, prints, retinal patterns and the rest on to my office?"

"Of course," said the car. "Plus a full transcript of the trial. Everything in quadruplicate."

"Good," said Clemens. "I'm glad we got Kloog and he's out of the way." He lit a fresh cigarette and put his hands on the wheel. The car could drive on automatic or manual. Clemens preferred to steer himself. "Start up and head for the hub. And get me my junior marshal on the line."

"Yes, sir," said the car.

"Your voice has a little too much treble," said Clemens, turning the lawagon onto the smooth black six-lane roadway that pointed flat and straight toward Hub 23.

"Sorry. I'll fix it. This is a public announcement. This is a public announcement. Better?"

"Fine. Now get me Kepling."

"Check, sir."

Clemens watched a flock of dot-sized birds circle far out over the desert. He moistened his lips and leaned back slightly.

"Junior Marshal Kepling here," came a voice from the dash.

"Kepling," said Clemens, "a packet of assorted ID material should have come out of the teleport slot a few minutes ago. Keep a copy of our files and send the rest on to Law Bureau Central in Hub 1."

"Right, sir."

"We just got that murderer, Sheldon Kloog."

"Good work. Shall I pencil him in for a trial at Cybernetics Hall?"

"We already had the trial," said Clemens. "Anything else new?"

"Looks like trouble out near Townten. Might be a sex crime."

"What exactly?"

"I'm not sure, sir," said Kepling. "The report is rather vague. You know how the android patrols out in the towns are. I dispatched a mechanical deputy about an hour ago and he should reach there by midafternoon. If there's a real case I can drive our lawagon over after you get back here."

Clemens frowned. "What's the victim's name?"

"Just a minute. Yeah, here it is. Marmon, Dianne. Age twenty-five, height five feet six inches, weight . . ."

Clemens twisted the wheel violently to the right. "Stop," he said to the lawagon as it shimmied off the roading. "Dianne Marmon, Kepling?"

"That's right. Do you know her?"

"What are the details you have on the crime?"

"The girl is employed at Statistics Warehouse in Townten. She didn't appear at work this morning and a routine check by a personnel andy found evidence of a struggle in her apartment. The patrol says there are no signs of theft. So kidnapping for some purpose seems likely. You may remember that last week's report from Crime Trends said there might be an upswing of sex crimes in the outlying areas like Townten this season. That's why I said it might be a sex crime. Do you know the girl?"

Clemens had known her five years ago, when they had both been at the Junior Campus of Hub 23 State College together. Dianne was a pretty blond girl. Clemens had dated her fairly often but lost track of her when he'd transferred to the Police Academy for his final year. "I'll handle this case myself," he said. "Should take me a little over two hours to get to Townten. I'll check with you en route. Let me know at once if anything important comes in before that."

"Yes, sir. You do know her then?"

"I know her," said Clemens. To the lawagon he said, "Turn around and get us to Townten fast."

"Yes, sir," said the car.

Beyond Townseven, climbing the wide road that curved between the flat fields of yellow grain, the call from Junior Marshal Kepling came. "Sir," said Kepling. "The patrol androids have been checking out witnesses. No one saw the girl after eleven last night. That was when she came home to her apartment. She was wearing a green coat, orange dress, green accessories. There was some noise heard in the apartment but no one thought much of it. That was a little after eleven. Seems like someone jimmied the alarm system for her place and got in. That's all so far. No prints or anything.''

"Damn it," said Clemens. "It must be a real kidnapping then. And I'm an hour from Townten. Well, the lawagon will catch the guy. There has to be time.''

"One other thing," said Kepling.

"About Dianne Marmon?"

"No, about Sheldon Kloog."

"What?"

"Central has a report that Sheldon Kloog turned himself in at a public surrender booth in a park over in Territory 20 this morning. All the ID material matches. Whereas the stuff we sent shows a complete negative.''

"What are they talking about? We caught Kloog."

"Not according to Central."

"It's impossible. The car doesn't make mistakes, Kepling."

"Central is going to make a full checkup as soon as you get back from this kidnapping case.''

"They're wrong," said Clemens. "Okay. So keep me filled in on Dianne Marmon.''

"Right, sir," said the Junior Marshal, signing off.

To his lawagon Clemens said, "What do you think is going on? You couldn't have made a mistake about Sheldon Kloog. Could you?''

The car became absolutely silent and coasted off the road, brushing the invisible shield around the grain fields. Everything had stopped functioning.

"I didn't order you to pull off," said Clemens.

The car did not respond.

Lawagons weren't supposed to break down. And if they did, which rarely happened, they were supposed to repair themselves. Clemens couldn't get Lawagon A10 to do anything. It was completely dead. There was no way even to signal for help.

"For God's sake," said Clemens. There was an hour between him and Dianne. More than an hour now. He tried to make himself not think of her, of what might be happening. Of what might have already happened.

Clemens got out of the lawagon, stood back a few feet from it. "One more time," he said. "Will you start?"

Nothing.

He turned and started jogging back towards Townseven. The heat of the day seemed to take all the moisture out of him, to make him dry and brittle. This shouldn't have happened. Not when someone he cared for was in danger. Not now.

Emergency Central couldn't promise him a repairman until the swing shift came on in a quarter of an hour. Clemens requested assistance, a couple of lawagons at least from the surrounding territories. Territory 20 had a reactor accident and couldn't spare theirs. Territory 21 promised to send a lawagon and a Junior Marshal over to Townten to pick up the trail of Dianne Marmon's kidnapper as soon as the lawagon was free. Territory 22 promised the same, although they didn't think their car would be available until after nightfall. Clemens finally ordered his own Junior Marshal to fly over to Townten and do the best he could until a lawagon arrived. A live Junior Marshal sure as hell couldn't do much, though. Not what a lawagon could.

The little Townseven café he was calling from was fully automatic, and Clemens sat down at a coffee table to wait for the repairman to arrive. The round light-blue room was empty except for a hunched old man who was sitting at a breakfast table, ordering side orders of hash browns one after another. When he'd filled the surface of the table he started a second layer. He didn't seem to be eating any of the food.

Clemens drank the cup of coffee that came up out of his table and ignored the old man. It was probably a case for a Psych Wagon but Clemens didn't feel up to going through the trouble of turning the man in. He finished his coffee. A car stopped outside and Clemens jumped up. It was just a customer.

"How can I do that?" said the repairman as he and Clemens went down the ramp of the automatic café. "Look." He pointed across the parking area at his small one-man scooter.

Clemens shook his head. "It's nearly sundown. A girl's life is in danger. Damn, if I have to wait here until you fix the lawagon and bring it back, I'll lose that much more time."

"I'm sorry," said the small sun-worn man. "I can't take you out to where the car is. The bureau says these scooters are not to carry passengers. So if I put more than two hundred pounds on it, it just turns off and won't go at all."

"Okay, okay." There were no cars in the parking lot, no one to commandeer.

"You told me where your lawagon is. I can find it if it's right on the highway. You wait."

"How long?"

The repairman shrugged. "Those babies don't break down much. But when they do . . . Could be a while. Overnight maybe."

"Overnight?" Clemens grabbed the man's arm. "You're kidding."

"Don't break my damn arm or it'll take that much longer."

"I'm sorry. I'll wait here. You'll drive the lawagon back?"

"Yeah. I got a special set of ID cards and passwords so I can get its hood up and drive it. Go inside and have a cup of coffee."

"Sure," said Clemens. "Thanks."

"Do my best."

"Do you know anything about the dinner-for-two tables?" the thin loose-suited young man asked Clemens.

Clemens had taken the table nearest the door and was looking out at the twilight roadway. "Beg pardon?"

"We put money in for a candle and nothing happened, except that when the asparagus arrived its ends were lit. This is my first date with this girl, Marshal, and I want to make a good impression."

"Hit the outlet with your fist," said Clemens, turning away.

"Thank you, sir."

Clemens got up and went in to call the Law Bureau answering service in Townten. The automatic voice told him that Junior Marshal Kepling had just arrived and reported in. He was on his way to the victim's apartment. No other news.

"She's not a victim," said Clemens and cut off.

"Arrest those two," said the old man, reaching for Clemens as he came out of the phone alcove.

"Why?"

"They shot a candle at my table and scattered my potatoes to here and gone."

The young man ran up. "I hit the table like you said and the candle came out. Only it went sailing all the way across the room."

"Young people," said the old man.

"Here," said Clemens. He gave both of them some cash. "Start all over again."

"That's not—" started the old man.

Clemens saw something coming down the dark road. He pushed free and ran outside.

As he reached the roadway the lawagon slowed and stopped. There was no one inside.

"Welcome aboard," said the car.

Clemens went through the identification ritual, looking off along the roadway, and got in. "Where's the repairman? Did he send you on in alone?"

"I saw through him, sir," said the lawagon. "Shall we proceed to Townten?"

"Yes. Step on it," said Clemens. "But what do you mean you saw through him?"

The glove compartment dropped open. There were two white jars in it now. "Sheldon Kloog won't bother us anymore, sir. I have just apprehended and tried him. He was disguised as a repairman and made an attempt to dismantle an official Law Bureau vehicle. That offense, plus his murder record, made only one course of action possible."

Clemens swallowed, making himself not even tighten his grip on the wheel. If he said anything the car might stop again. There was something wrong. As soon as Dianne was safe Lawagon A10 would have to go into the shop for a thorough checkup. Right now Clemens needed the car badly, needed what it could do. They had to track down whoever had kidnapped Dianne. "Good work," he said evenly.

The headlights hit the cliffs that bordered the narrow road and long ragged shadows crept up the hillside ahead of them.

"I think we're closing in," said Clemens. He was talking to Junior Marshal Kepling, whom he'd left back at the Law Bureau answering service in Townten. He had cautioned Kepling to make no mention of the Kloog business while the car could hear them.

"Central verifies the ID on the kidnapper from the prints

we found," said Kepling. Surprisingly, Kepling had found fingerprints in Dianne's apartment that the andy patrol and the mechanical deputy had missed. "It's Jim Otterson. Up to now he's only done short-sentence stuff."

"Good," said Clemens. That meant that Otterson might not harm Dianne. Unless this was the time he'd picked to cross over. "The lawagon," said Clemens, "is holding onto his trail. We should get him now any time. He's on foot now and the girl is definitely still with him, the car says. We're closing in."

"Good luck," said Kepling.

"Thanks." Clemens signed off.

Things had speeded up once he and the lawagon had reached Townten. Clemens had known that. The lawagon had had no trouble picking up the scent. Now, late at night, they were some twenty-five miles out of Townten. They'd found Otterson's car seven miles back with its clutch burned out. The auto had been there, off the unpaved back road, for about four hours. Otterson had driven around in great zigzags. Apparently he had spent the whole of the night after the kidnapping in a deserted storehouse about fifty miles from Townten. He had left there, according to the lawagon, about noon and headed towards Towneleven. Then he had doubled back again, swinging in near Townten. Clemens and the lawagon had spent hours circling around on Otterson's trail. With no more car Otterson and the girl couldn't have come much further than where Clemens and the lawagon were now.

The lawagon turned off the road and bumped across a rocky plateau. It swung around and stopped. Up above was a high flat cliffside, dotted with caves. "Up there, I'd say," said the lawagon. It had silenced its engine.

"Okay," said Clemens. There wasn't much chance of sneaking up on Otterson if he was up in one of those caves. Clemens would have to risk trying to talk to him. "Shoot the lights up there and turn on the speakers."

Two spotlights hit the cliff and a hand mike came up out of the dash. Taking it, Clemens climbed out of the lawagon. "Otterson, this is Marshal Clemens. I'm asking you to surrender. We know you're in one of those caves; we can check each one off if we have to. Give up."

Clemens waited. Then halfway up the cliffside something

green flashed and then came hurtling down. It pinwheeled down the mountain and fell past the plateau.

"What the hell." Clemens ran forward. There was a gully between the cliff and the plateau, narrow and about thirty feet deep. At its bottom was something. It might be Dianne, arms tangled over interlaced brush.

"Get me a handlight and a line," he called to the lawagon.

Without moving the car lobbed a handbeam to him and sent a thin cord snaking over the ground. "Check."

"Cover the caves. I'm going down to see what that was that fell."

"Ready?"

Clemens hooked the light on his belt and gripped the line. He backed over the plateau edge. "Okay, ready."

The line was slowly let out and Clemens started down. Near the brush he caught a rock and let go of the line. He unhitched the light and swung it. He exhaled sharply. What had fallen was only an empty coat. Otterson was trying to decoy them. "Watch out," Clemens shouted to his car. "It's not the girl. He may try to make a break now."

He steadied himself and reached for the rope. Its end snapped out at him and before he could catch it it whirred up and out of sight. "Hey, the rope. Send it back."

"Emergency," announced the lawagon, its engine coming on.

Up above a blaster sizzled and rock clattered. Clemens yanked out his pistol and looked up. Down the hillside a man was coming, carrying a bound-up girl in his arms. His big hands showed and they held pistols. Dianne was gagged but seemed to be alive. Otterson zigzagged down, using the girl for a shield. He was firing not at Clemens but at the lawagon. He jumped across the gully to a plateau about twenty yards from where Clemens had started over.

Holstering his gun, Clemens started to climb. He was halfway up when he heard Otterson cry out. Then there was no sound at all.

Clemens tried to climb faster but could not. The gully side was jagged and hard to hold on to. Finally he swung himself up on the plateau.

"This is a public service announcement," said the lawagon. "Sheldon Kloog and his female accomplice have been cap-

tured, tried, sentenced and executed. This message comes to
you from the Law Bureau. Thank you.''

Clemens roared. He grabbed a rock in each hand and went
charging at the car. ''You've killed Dianne,'' he shouted.
''You crazy damn machine.'

The lawagon turned and started rolling towards him. ''No
you don't, Kloog,'' it said.

Cloak of Anarchy

Larry Niven

Square in the middle of what used to be the San Diego Freeway, I leaned back against a huge, twisted oak. The old bark was rough and powdery against my bare back. There was dark green shade shot with tight parallel beams of white gold. Long grass tickled my legs.

Forty yards away across a wide strip of lawn was a clump of elms, and a small grandmotherly woman sitting on a green towel. She looked like she'd grown there. A stalk of grass protruded between her teeth. I felt we were kindred spirits, and once when I caught her eye I wiggled a forefinger at her, and she waved back.

In a minute now I'd have to be getting up. Jill was meeting me at the Wilshire exits in half an hour. But I'd started walking at the Sunset Boulevard ramps, and I was tired. A minute more. . . .

It was a good place to watch the world rotate.

A good day for it, too. No clouds at all. On this hot blue summer afternoon, King's Free Park was as crowded as it ever gets.

Someone at police headquarters had expected that. Twice the usual number of copseyes floated overhead, waiting. Gold dots against blue, basketball-sized, twelve feet up. Each a television eye and a sonic stunner, each a hookup to police headquarters, they were there to enforce the law of the park.

No violence.

No hand to be raised against another—and no other laws whatever. Life was often entertaining in a Free Park.

22

North toward Sunset, a man carried a white rectangular sign, blank on both sides. He was parading back and forth in front of a square-jawed youth on a plastic box, who was trying to lecture him on the subject of fusion power and the heat pollution problem. Even this far away I could hear the conviction and the dedication in his voice.

South, a handful of yelling marksmen were throwing rocks at a copseye, directed by a gesticulating man with wild black hair. The golden basketball was dodging the rocks, but barely. Some cop was baiting them. I wondered where they had gotten the rocks. Rocks were scarce in King's Free Park.

The black-haired man looked familiar. I watched him and his horde chasing the copseye . . . then forgot them when a girl walked out of a clump of elms.

She was lovely. Long, perfect legs, deep red hair worn longer than shoulder length, the face of an arrogant angel, and a body so perfect that it seemed unreal, like an adolescent's daydream. Her walk showed training; possibly she was a model or dancer. Her only garment was a cloak of glowing blue velvet.

It was fifteen yards long, that cloak. It trailed back from two big gold discs that were stuck somehow to the skin of her shoulders. It trailed back and back, floating at a height of five feet all the way, twisting and turning to trace her path through the trees. She seemed like the illustration to a book of fairy tales, bearing in mind that the original fairy tales were not intended for children.

Neither was she. You could hear neck vertebrae popping all over the park. Even the rock throwers had stopped to watch.

She could sense the attention, or hear it in a whisper of sighs. It was what she was here for. She strolled along with a condescending angel's smile on her angel's face, not overdoing the walk, but letting it flow. She turned regardless of whether there were obstacles to avoid, so that fifteen yards of flowing cloak could follow the curve.

I smiled, watching her go. She was lovely from the back, with dimples.

The man who stepped up to her a little further on was the same who had led the rock throwers. Wild black hair and beard, hollow cheeks and deep-set eyes, a diffident smile and a diffident walk . . . Ron Cole. Of course.

I didn't hear what he said to the girl in the cloak, but I saw the result. He flinched, then turned abruptly and walked away with his eyes on his feet.

I got up and moved to intercept him. "Don't take it personally," I said.

He looked up, startled. His voice, when it came, was bitter. "How should I take it?"

"She'd have turned any man off the same way. That lady has staples in her navel. She's to look, not to touch."

"You know her?"

"Never saw her before in my life."

"Then—?"

"Her cloak. Now you *must* have noticed her cloak."

The tail end of her cloak was just passing us, its folds rippling an improbably deep, rich blue. Ronald Cole smiled as if it hurt his face. "Yah."

"All right. Now suppose you made a pass, and suppose the lady liked your looks and took you up on it. What would she do next? Bearing in mind that she can't stop walking even for a second."

He thought it over first, then asked, "Why not?"

"If she stops walking she loses the whole effect. Her cloak just hangs there like some kind of tail. It's supposed to wave. If she lies down with you it's even worse. A cloak floating at five feet, then swooping into a clump of bushes and bobbing frantically—" Ron laughed helplessly in falsetto. I said, "See? Her audience would get the giggles. That's not what she's after."

He sobered. "But if she really wanted to, she wouldn't *care* about . . . oh. Right. She must have spent a fortune to get that effect."

"Sure. She wouldn't ruin it for Jacques Casanova himself." I thought unfriendly thoughts toward the girl in the cloak. There are polite ways to turn down a pass. Ronald Cole was easy to hurt.

I asked, "Where did you get the rocks?"

"Rocks? Oh, we found a place where the center divider shows through. We knocked off some chunks of concrete."

Ron looked down the length of the park as a kid bounced a missile off a golden ball. "They got one! Come on!"

The fastest commercial shipping that ever sailed was the clipper ship; yet the world stopped building them after just twenty-five years. Steam had come. Steam was faster, safer, more dependable, cheaper in time and men.

The freeways served America for almost fifty years. Then modern transportation systems cleaned the air and made traffic jams archaic and left the nation with an embarrassing problem. What to do with ten thousand miles of unsightly abandoned freeways?

King's Free Park had been part of the San Diego Freeway, the section between Sunset and the Santa Monica interchange. Decades ago the concrete had been covered with topsoil. The borders had been landscaped from the start. Now the Park was as thoroughly covered with green as the much older Griffith Free Park.

Within King's Free Park was an orderly approximation of anarchy. People were searched at the entrances. There were no weapons inside. The copseyes, floating overhead and out of reach, were the next best thing to no law at all.

There was only one law to enforce. All acts of attempted violence carried the same penalty for attacker and victim. Let anyone raise his hand against his neighbor, and one of the golden basketballs would stun them both. They would wake separately, with copseyes watching. It was usually enough.

Naturally people threw rocks at copseyes. It was a Free Park, wasn't it?

"They got one! Come on!" Ron tugged at my arm. The felled copseye was hidden, surrounded by those who had destroyed it. "I hope they don't kick it apart. I told them I need it intact, but that might not stop them."

"It's a Free Park. And they bagged it."

"With my missiles!"

"Who are they?"

"I don't know. They were playing baseball when I found them. I told them I needed a copseye. They said they'd get me one."

I remembered Ron quite well now. Ronald Cole was an

artist and an inventor. It would have been two sources of income for another man, but Ron was different. He invented new art forms. With solder and wire and diffraction gratings and several makes of plastics kits, and an incredible collection of serendipitous junk, Ron Cole made things the like of which had never been seen on Earth.

The market for new art forms had always been low, but now and then he did make a sale. It was enough to keep him in raw materials, especially since many of his raw materials came from basements and attics. There was an occasional *big* sale, and then, briefly, he would be rich.

There was this about him: he knew who I was, but he hadn't remembered my name. Ron Cole had better things to think about than what name belonged with whom. A name was only a tag and a conversational gambit. "Russel! How are you?" A signal. Ron had developed a substitute.

Into a momentary gap in the conversation he would say, "Look at this," and hold out—miracles.

Once it had been a clear plastic sphere, golf-ball-sized, balanced on a polished silver concavity. When the ball rolled around on the curved mirror, the reflections were *fantastic*.

Once it had been a twisting sea serpent engraved on a Michelob beer bottle, the lovely vase-shaped bottle of the early 1960s that was too big for standard refrigerators.

And once it had been two strips of dull silvery metal, unexpectedly heavy. "What's this?"

I'd held them in the palm of my hand. They were heavier than lead. Platinum? But nobody carries that much platinum around. Joking, I'd asked, "U-235?"

"Are they warm?" he'd asked apprehensively. I'd fought off an urge to throw them as far as I could and dive behind a couch.

But they *had* been platinum. I never did learn why Ron was carrying them about. Something that didn't pan out.

Within a semicircle of spectators, the felled copseye lay on the grass. It was intact, possibly because two cheerful, conspicuously large men were standing over it, waving everyone back.

"Good," said Ron. He knelt above the golden sphere, turned it with his long artist's fingers. To me he said, "Help me get it open."

"What for? What are you after?"

"I'll tell you in a minute. Help me get—never mind." The hemispherical cover came off. For the first time ever, I looked into a copseye.

It was impressively simple. I picked out the stunner by its parabolic reflector, the cameras, and a toroidal coil that had to be part of the floater device. No power source. I guessed that the shell itself was a power-beam antenna. With the cover cracked there would be no way for a damn fool to electrocute himself.

Ron knelt and studied the strange guts of the copseye. From his pocket he took something made of glass and metal. He suddenly remembered my existence and held it out to me, saying, "Look at this."

I took it, expecting a surprise, and I got it. It was an old hunting watch, a big wind-up watch on a chain, with a protective case. They were in common use a couple of hundred years ago. I looked at the face, said, "Fifteen minutes slow. You didn't repair the whole works, did you?"

"Oh, no." He clicked the back open for me.

The works looked modern. I guessed, "Battery and tuning fork?"

"That's what the guard thought. Of course that's what I made it from. But the hands don't move; I set them just before they searched me."

"Aha. What does it do?"

"If I work it right, I think it'll knock down every copseye in King's Free Park."

For a minute or so I was laughing too hard to speak. Ron watched me with his head on one side, clearly wondering if I thought he was joking.

I managed to say, "That ought to cause all *kinds* of excitement."

Ron nodded vigorously. "Of course it all depends on whether they use the kind of circuits I think they use. Look for yourself; the copseyes aren't supposed to be foolproof. They're supposed to be cheap. If one gets knocked down, the taxes don't go up much. The other way is to make them expensive and foolproof, and frustrate a lot of people. People aren't supposed to be frustrated in a Free Park."

"So?"

"Well, there's a cheap way to make the circuitry for the power system. If they did it that way, I can blow the whole thing. We'll see." Ron pulled thin copper wire from the cuffs of his shirt.

"How long will this take?"

"Oh, half an hour."

That decided me. "I've got to be going. I'm meeting Jill Hayes at the Wilshire exits. You've met her, a big blonde girl, my height—"

But he wasn't listening. "Okay, see you," he muttered. He began placing the copper wire inside the copseye, with tweezers. I left.

Crowds tend to draw crowds. A few minutes after leaving Ron, I joined a semicircle of the curious to see what they were watching.

A balding, lantern-jawed individual was putting something together: an archaic machine, with blades and a small gasoline motor. The T-shaped wooden handle was brand-new and unpainted. The metal parts were dull with the look of ancient rust recently removed.

The crowd speculated in half whispers. What was it? Not part of a car; not an outboard motor, though it had blades; too small for a motor scooter; too big for a motor skateboard . . .

"Lawn mower," said the white-haired lady next to me. She was one of those small, birdlike people who shrivel and grow weightless as they age, and live forever. Her words meant nothing to me. I was about to ask, when—

The lantern-jawed man finished his work, and twisted something, and the motor started with a roar. Black smoke puffed out. In triumph he gripped the handles. Outside, it was a prison offense to build a working internal combustion machine. Here—

With the fire of dedication burning in his eyes, he wheeled his infernal machine across the grass. He left a path as flat as a rug. It was a Free Park, wasn't it?

The smell hit everyone at once: a black dirt in the air, a stink of half-burned hydrocarbons attacking nose and eyes. I gasped and coughed. I'd never smelled anything like it.

The crescent of crowd roared and converged.

He squawked when they picked up his machine. Someone

found a switch and stopped it. Two men confiscated the tool kit and went to work with screwdriver and hammer. The owner objected. He picked up a heavy pair of pliers and tried to commit murder.

A copseye zapped him and the man with the hammer, and they both hit the lawn without bouncing. The rest of them pulled the lawn mower apart and bent and broke the pieces.

"I'm half-sorry they did that," said the old woman. "Sometimes I miss the sound of lawn mowers. My dad used to mow the lawn on Sunday mornings."

I said, "It's a Free Park."

"Then why can't he build anything he pleases?"

"He can. He did. Anything he's free to build, we're free to kick apart." And my mind flashed, *Like Ron's rigged copseye*.

Ron was good with tools. It would not surprise me a bit if ne knew enough about copseyes to knock out the whole system.

Maybe someone ought to stop him.

But knocking down copseyes wasn't illegal. It happened all the time. It was part of the freedom of the park. If Ron could knock them all down at once, well . . .

Maybe someone ought to stop him.

I passed a flock of high school girls, all chittering like birds, all about sixteen. It might have been their first trip inside a Free Park. I looked back because they were so cute, and caught them staring in awe and wonder at the dragon on my back.

A few years and they'd be too blasé to notice. It had taken Jill almost half an hour to apply it this morning: a glorious red-and-gold dragon breathing flames across my shoulder, flames that seemed to glow by their own light. Lower down were a princess and a knight in golden armor, the princess tied to a stake, the knight fleeing for his life. I smiled back at the girls, and two of them waved.

Short blond hair and golden skin, the tallest girl in sight, wearing not even a nudist's shoulder pouch: Jill Hayes stood squarely in front of the Wilshire entrance, visibly wondering where I was. It was five minutes after three.

There was this about living with a physical culture nut. Jill insisted on getting me into shape. The daily exercises were part of that, and so was this business of walking half the length of King's Free Park.

I'd balked at doing it briskly, though. Who walks briskly in a Free Park? There's too much to see. She'd given me an hour; I'd held out for three. It was a compromise, like the paper slacks I was wearing despite Jill's nudist beliefs.

Sooner or later she'd find someone with muscles, or I'd relapse into laziness, and we'd split. Meanwhile . . . we got along. It seemed only sensible to let her finish my training.

She spotted me, yelled, "Russel! Here!" in a voice that must have reached both ends of the park. In answer I lifted my arm semaphore-style, slowly over my head and back down.

And every copseye in King's Free Park fell out of the sky, dead.

Jill looked about her at all the startled faces and all the golden bubbles resting in bushes and on the grass. She approached me somewhat uncertainly. She asked, "Did you do that?"

I said, "Yah. If I wave my arms again they'll all go back up."

"I think you'd better do it," she said primly. Jill had a fine poker face. I waved my arm grandly over my head and down, but of course the copseyes stayed where they had fallen.

Jill said, "I wonder what happened to them?"

"It was Ron Cole. You remember him. He's the one who engraved some old Michelob beer bottles for Steuben—"

"Oh, yes. But *how*?"

We went off to ask him.

A brawny college man howled and charged past us at a dead run. We saw him kick a copseye like a soccer ball. The golden cover split, but the man howled again and hopped up and down hugging his foot.

We passed dented golden shells and broken resonators and bent parabolic reflectors. One woman looked flushed and proud; she was wearing several of the copper toroids as bracelets. A kid was collecting the cameras. Maybe he thought he could sell them outside.

I never saw an intact copseye after the first minute.

They weren't all busy kicking copseyes apart. Jill stared at the conservatively dressed group carrying POPULATION BY COPULATION signs, and wanted to know if they were serious. Their grim-faced leader handed us pamphlets that spoke of the evil and the blasphemy of man's attempts to alter himself through gene tempering and extra-uterine growth experiments. If it was a put-on, it was a good one.

We passed seven little men, each three to four feet high, traveling with a single tall, pretty brunette. They wore medieval garb. We both stared; but I was the one who noticed the makeup and the use of UnTan. African pygmies, probably part of a U.N.-sponsored tourist group; and the girl must be their guide.

Ron Cole was not where I had left him.

"He must have decided that discretion is the better part of cowardice. May be right, too," I surmised. "Nobody's ever knocked down *all* the copseyes before."

"It's not illegal, is it?"

"Not illegal, but excessive. They can bar him from the park, at the very least."

Jill stretched in the sun. She was all golden and *big*. Scaled down, she would have made a nice centershot for a men's videozine. She said, "I'm thirsty. Is there a fountain around?"

"Sure, unless someone's plugged it by now. It's a—"

"Free Park. Do you mean to tell me they don't even protect the *fountains*?"

"You make one exception, it's like a wedge. When someone ruins a fountain, they wait and fix it that night. That way if I see someone trying to wreck a fountain, I'll generally throw a punch at him. A lot of us do. After a guy's lost enough of his holiday to the copseye stunners, he'll get the idea, sooner or later."

The fountain was a solid cube of concrete with four spiggots and a hand-sized metal button. It was hard to jam, hard to hurt. Ron Cole stood near it, looking lost.

He seemed glad to see me, but still lost. I introduced him. "You remember Jill Hayes." He said, "Certainly. Hello, Jill," and, having put her name to its intended purpose, promptly forgot it.

Jill said, "We thought you'd made a break for it."

"I did."

"Oh?"

"You know how complicated the exits are. They have to be, to keep anyone from getting in through an exit with like a shotgun." Ron ran both hands through his hair, without making it any more or less neat. "Well, all the exits have stopped working. They must be on the same circuits as the copseyes. I wasn't expecting that."

"Then we're locked in," I said. That was irritating. But underneath the irritation was a funny feeling in the pit of my stomach. "How long do you think—?"

"No telling. They'll have to get new copseyes in somehow. And repair the beamed power system, and figure out how I bollixed it, and fix it so it doesn't happen again. I suppose someone must have kicked my rigged copseye to pieces by now, but the police don't know that."

"Oh, they'll just send in some cops," said Jill.

"Look around you."

There were pieces of copseyes in all directions. Not one remained whole. A cop would have to be out of his mind to enter a Free Park.

Not to mention the damage to the spirit of the park.

"I wish I'd brought a bag lunch," said Ron.

I saw the cloak off to my right: a ribbon of glowing blue velvet hovering at five feet, like a carpeted path in the air. I didn't yell or point or anything. For Ron it might be pushing the wrong buttons.

Ron didn't see it. "Actually I'm kind of glad this happened," he said animatedly. "I've always thought that anarchy ought to be a viable form of society."

Jill made polite sounds of encouragement.

"After all, anarchy is only the last word in free enterprise. What can a government do for people that people can't do for themselves? Protection from other countries? If all the other countries are anarchies too, you don't need armies. Police, maybe; but what's wrong with privately owned police?"

"Fire departments used to work that way," Jill remembered. "They were hired by the insurance companies. They only protected houses that belonged to their own clients."

"Right! So you buy theft and murder insurance, and the

insurance companies hire a police force. The client carries a credit card—''

''Suppose the robber steals the card too?''

''He can't use it. He doesn't have the right retina prints.''

''But if the client doesn't have the credit card, he can't sic the cops on the thief.''

''Oh,'' A noticeable pause. ''Well—''

Half listening, for I had heard it all before, I looked for the end points of the cloak. I found empty space at one end and a lovely red-haired girl at the other. She was talking to two men as outré as herself.

One can get the impression that a Free Park is one gigantic costume party. It isn't. Not one person in ten wears anything but street clothes, but the costumes are what get noticed.

These guys were part bird.

Their eyebrows and eyelashes were tiny feathers, green on one, golden on the other. Larger feathers covered their heads, blue and green and gold, and ran in a crest down their spines. They were bare to the waist, showing physiques Jill would find acceptable.

Ron was lecturing. ''What does a government do for *anyone* except the people who run the government? Once there were private post offices, and they were cheaper than what we've got now. Anything the government takes over gets more expensive, *immediately*. There's no reason why private enterprise can't do anything a government—''

Jill gasped. She said, ''Ooh! How lovely.''

Ron turned to look.

As if on cue, the girl in the cloak slapped one of the feathered men hard across the mouth. She tried to hit the other one, but he caught her wrist. Then all three froze.

I said, ''See? Nobody wins. She doesn't even like standing still. She—'' And I realized why they weren't moving.

In a Free Park it's easy for a girl to turn down an offer. If the guy won't take no for an answer, he gets slapped. The stun beam gets him and the girl. When she wakes up, she walks away.

Simple.

The girl recovered first. She gasped and jerked her wrist loose and turned to run. One of the feathered men didn't bother to chase her; he simply took a double handful of the cloak.

This was getting serious.

The cloak jerked her sharply backward. She didn't hesitate. She reached for the big gold discs at her shoulders, ripped them loose and ran on. The feathered men chased her, laughing.

The redhead wasn't laughing. She was running all out. Two drops of blood ran down her shoulders. I thought of trying to stop the feathered men, decided in favor of it—but they were already past.

The cloak hung like a carpeted path in the air, empty at both ends.

Jill hugged herself uneasily. "Ron, just how does one go about hiring your private police force?"

"Well, you can't expect it to form spontaneously—"

"Let's try the entrances. Maybe we can get out."

It was slow to build. Everyone knew what a copseye did. Nobody thought it through. Two feathered men chasing a lovely nude? A pretty sight; and why interfere? If she didn't want to be chased, she need only—what? And nothing else had changed. The costumes, the people with causes, the people looking for causes, the peoplewatchers, the pranksters . . .

Blank Sign had joined the POPULATION BY COPULATION faction. His grass-stained pink street tunic jarred strangely with their conservative suits, but he showed no sign of mockery; his face was as preternaturally solemn as theirs. Nonetheless they did not seem glad of his company.

It was crowded near the Wilshire entrance. I saw enough bewildered and frustrated faces to guess that it was closed. The little vestibule area was so packed that we didn't even try to find out what was wrong with the doors.

"I don't think we ought to stay here," Jill said uneasily.

I noticed the way she was hugging herself. "Are you cold?"

"No." She shivered. "But I wish I were dressed."

"How about a strip of that velvet cloak?"

"Good!"

*   *   *

We were too late. The cloak was gone.

It was a warm September day, near sunset. Clad only in paper slacks, I was not cold in the least. I said, "Take my slacks."

"No, hon, I'm the nudist." But Jill hugged herself with both arms.

"Here," said Ron, and handed her his sweater. She flashed him a grateful look, then, clearly embarrassed, she wrapped the sweater around her waist and knotted the sleeves.

Ron didn't get it at all. I asked him, "Do you know the difference between nude and naked?"

He shook his head.

"Nude is artistic. Naked is defenseless."

Nudity was popular in a Free Park. That night, nakedness was not. There must have been pieces of that cloak all over King's Free Park. I saw at least four that night: one worn as a kilt, two being used as crude sarongs, and one as a bandage.

On a normal day, the entrances to King's Free Park close at six. Those who want to stay, stay as long as they like. Usually they are not many, because there are no lights to be broken in a Free Park; but light does seep in from the city beyond. The copseyes float about, guided by infrared, but most of them are not manned.

Tonight would be different.

It was after sunset, but still light. A small and ancient lady came stumping toward us with a look of murder on her lined face. At first I thought it was meant for us, but that wasn't it. She was so mad she couldn't see straight.

She saw my feet and looked up. "Oh, it's you. The one who helped break the lawn mower," she said; which was unjust. "A Free Park, is it? A Free Park! Two men just took away my dinner!"

I spread my hands. "I'm sorry. I really am. If you still had it, we could try to talk you into sharing it."

She lost some of her mad, which brought her embarrassingly close to tears. "Then we're all hungry together. I brought it in a plastic bag. Next time I'll use something that isn't transparent, by d-damn!" She noticed Jill and her improvised sweater-skirt, and added, "I'm sorry, dear, I gave my towel to a girl who needed it even more."

"Thank you anyway."

"Please, may I stay with you people until the copseyes start working again? I don't feel safe, somehow. I'm Glenda Hawthorne."

We introduced ourselves. Glenda Hawthorne shook our hands. By now it was quite dark. We couldn't see the city beyond the high green hedges, but the change was startling when the lights of Westwood and Santa Monica flashed on.

The police were taking their own good time getting us some copseyes.

We reached the grassy field sometimes used by the Society for Creative Anachronism for their tournaments. They fight on foot with weighted and padded weapons designed to behave like swords, broadaxes, morningstars, etc. The weapons are bugged so that they won't fall into the wrong hands. The field is big and flat and bare of trees, sloping upward at the edges.

On one of the slopes, something moved.

It stopped. It didn't move again, but it showed clearly in light reflected down from the white close. I made out something man-shaped and faintly pink, and a pale rectangle nearby.

I spoke low. "Stay here."

Jill said, "Don't be silly. There's nothing for anyone to hide under. Come on."

The blank sign was bent and marked with shoe prints. The man who had been carrying it looked up at us with pain in his eyes. Drying blood ran from his nose. With effort he whispered, "I think they dislocated my shoulder."

"Let me look." Jill bent over him. She probed him a bit, then set herself and pulled hard and steadily on his arm. Blank Sign yelled in pain and despair.

"That'll do it." Jill sounded satisfied. "How does it feel?"

"It doesn't hurt as much." He smiled, almost.

"What happened?"

"They started pushing me and kicking me to make me go away. I was *doing* it, I was walking away. I *was*. Then one of the sons of bitches snatched away my sign—" He stopped for a moment, then went off at a tangent. "I wasn't hurting anyone with my sign. I'm a psych major. I'm writing a thesis on what people read into a blank sign. Like the blank sheets in the Rorschach tests.''

"What kind of reactions do you get?''

"Usually hostile. But nothing like *that*.'' Blank Sign sounded bewildered. "Wouldn't you think a Free Park is the one place you'd find freedom of speech?''

Jill wiped at his face with a tissue from Glenda Hawthorne's purse. She said, "Especially when you're not saying anything. Hey, Ron, tell us more about your government by anarchy.''

Ron cleared his throat. "I hope you're not judging it by *this*. King's Free Park hasn't been an anarchy for more than a couple of hours. It needs time to develop.''

Glenda Hawthorne and Blank Sign must have wondered what the hell he was talking about. I wished him joy in explaining it to them, and wondered if he would explain who had knocked down the copseyes.

This field would be a good place to spend the night. It was open, with no cover and no shadows, no way for anyone to sneak up on us.

We lay on wet grass, sometimes dozing, sometimes talking. Two other groups no bigger than ours occupied the jousting field. They kept their distance; we kept ours. Now and then we heard voices, and knew that they were not asleep; not all at once, anyway.

Blank Sign dozed restlessly. His ribs were giving him trouble, though Jill said none of them were broken. Every so often he whimpered and tried to move and woke himself up. Then he had to hold himself still until he fell asleep again.

"Money,'' said Jill. "It takes a government to print money.''

"But you could get IOUs printed. Standard denominations, printed for a fee and notarized. Backed by your good name.''

Jill laughed softly. "Thought of everything, haven't you? You couldn't travel very far that way.''

"Credit cards, then.''

I had stopped believing in Ron's anarchy. I said, "Ron, remember the girl in the long blue cloak?''

A little gap of silence. "Yah?''

"Pretty, wasn't she? Fun to watch.''

"Granted.''

"If there weren't any laws to stop you from raping her,

she'd be muffled to the ears in a long dress and carrying a tear gas pen. What fun would that be? I *like* the nude look. Look how fast it disappeared after the copseyes fell.''

"Mmm," said Ron.

The night was turning cold. Faraway voices, occasional distant shouts, came like thin gray threads in a black tapestry of silence. Mrs. Hawthorne spoke into that silence.

"What was that boy really saying with his blank sign?"

"He wasn't saying anything," said Jill.

"Now, just a minute, dear. I think he was, even if he didn't know it." Mrs. Hawthorne talked slowly, using the words to shape her thoughts. "Once there was an organization to protest the forced contraception bill. I was one of them. We carried signs for hours at a time. We printed leaflets. We stopped people passing so that we could talk to them. We gave up our time, we went to considerable trouble and expense, because we wanted to get our ideas across.

"Now, if a man had joined us with a blank sign, he would have been *saying* something.

"His sign says that he has no opinion. If he joins us he says that we have no opinion either. He's saying our opinions aren't worth anything.''

I said, "Tell him when he wakes up. He can put it in his notebook."

"But his notebook is *wrong*. He wouldn't push his blank sign in among people he agreed with, would he?"

"Maybe not."

"I . . . suppose I don't like people with no opinions." Mrs. Hawthorne stood up. She had been sitting tailor-fashion for some hours. "Do you know if there's a pop machine nearby?"

There wasn't, of course. No private company would risk getting their machines smashed once or twice a day. But she had reminded the rest of us that we were thirsty. Eventually we all got up and trooped away in the direction of the fountain.

All but Blank Sign.

I'd *liked* that blank sign gag. How odd, how ominous, that so basic a right as freedom of speech could depend on so slight a thing as a floating copseye.

*   *   *

I was thirsty.

The park was bright by city light, crossed by sharp-edged shadows. In such light it seemed that one can see much more than he really can. I could see into every shadow; but, though there were stirrings all around us, I could see nobody until he moved. We four, sitting under an oak with our backs to the tremendous trunk, must be invisible from any distance.

We talked little. The park was quiet except for occasional laughter from the fountain.

I couldn't forget my thirst. I could feel others being thirsty around me. The fountain was right out there in the open, a solid block of concrete with five men around it.

They were dressed alike in paper shorts with big pockets. They looked alike: like first-string athletes. Maybe they belonged to the same order or frat or R.O.T.C. class.

They had taken over the fountain.

When someone came to get a drink, the tall ash-blond one would step forward with his arm held stiffly out, palm forward. He had a wide mouth and a grin that might otherwise have been infectious, and a deep, echoing voice. He would intone, "Go back. None may pass here but the immortal Cthuthu," or something equally silly.

Trouble was, they weren't kidding. Or: they were kidding, but they wouldn't let anyone have a drink.

When we arrived, a girl dressed in a towel had been trying to talk some sense into them. It hadn't worked. It might even have boosted their egos: a lovely half-naked girl begging them for water. Eventually she'd given up and gone away.

In that light her hair might have been red. I hoped it was the girl in the cloak. She'd sounded healthy . . . unhurt.

And a beefy man in a yellow business jumper had made the mistake of demanding his rights. It was not a night for rights. The blond kid had goaded him into screaming insults, a stream of unimaginative profanity, which ended when he tried to hit the blond kid. Then three of them had swarmed over him. The man had left crawling, moaning of police and lawsuits.

Why hadn't somebody done something?

I had watched it all from sitting position. I could list my own reasons. One: it was hard to face the fact that a copseye would not zap them both, any second now. Two: I didn't like the screaming fat man much. He talked dirty. Three: I'd been waiting for someone else to step in.

As with the girl in the cloak. Damn it.

Mrs. Hawthorne said, "Ronald, what time is it?"

Ron may have been the only man in King's Free Park who knew the time. People generally left their valuables in lockers at the entrances. But years ago, when Ron was flush with money from the sale of the engraved beer bottles, he'd bought an implant-watch. He told time by one red mark and two red lines glowing beneath the skin of his wrist.

We had put the women between us, but I saw the motion as he glanced at his wrist. "Quarter of twelve."

"Don't you think they'll get bored and go away? It's been twenty minutes since anyone tried to get a drink," Mrs. Hawthorne said plaintively.

Jill shifted against me in the dark. "They can't be any more bored than we are. I think they'll get bored and stay anyway. Besides—" She stopped.

I said, "Besides that, we're thirsty *now*."

"Right."

"Ron, have you seen any sign of those rock throwers you collected? Especially the one who knocked down the copseye."

"No."

I wasn't surprised. In this darkness? "Do you remember his—" And I didn't even finish.

"Yes!" Ron said suddenly.

"You're kidding."

"No. His name was Bugeyes. You don't forget a name like that."

"I take it he had big, bulging eyes?"

"I didn't notice."

Well, it was worth a try. I stood and cupped my hands for a megaphone and shouted, *"Bugeyes!"*

One of the Water Monopoly shouted, "Let's keep the noise down out there!"

"Bugeyes!"

A chorus of remarks from the Water Monopoly. "Strange habits these peasants." "Most of them are just thirsty. *This* character—"

From off to the side: "What do you want?"

"We want to talk to you! Stay where you are!" To Ron I

said, "Come on." To Jill and Mrs. Hawthorne, "Stay here. Don't get involved."

We moved out into the open space between us and Bugeyes' voice.

Two of the five kids came immediately to intercept us. They must have been bored, all right, and looking for action.

We ran for it. We reached the shadows of the trees before those two reached us. They stopped, laughing like maniacs, and moved back to the fountain.

A fourteen-year-old kid spoke behind us. "Ron?"

Ron and I, we lay on our bellies in the shadows of low bushes. Across too much shadowless grass, four men in paper shorts stood at parade rest at the four corners of the fountain. The fifth man watched for a victim.

A boy walked out between us into the moonlight. His eyes were shining, big, expressive eyes, maybe a bit too prominent. His hands were big, too, with knobby knuckles. One hand was full of acorns.

He pitched them rapidly, one at a time, overhand. First one, then another of the Water Trust twitched and looked in our direction. Bugeyes kept throwing.

Quite suddenly, two of them started toward us at a run. Bugeyes kept throwing until they were almost on him; then he threw his acorns in a handful and dived into the shadows.

The two of them ran between us. We let the first go by: the wide-mouthed blond spokesman, his expression low and murderous now. The other was short and broad-shouldered, an intimidating silhouette seemingly all muscle. A tackle. I stood up in front of him, expecting him to stop in surprise; and he did, and I hit him in the mouth as hard as I could.

He stepped back in shock. Ron wrapped an arm around his throat.

He bucked. Instantly. Ron hung on. I did something I'd seen often enough on television: linked my fingers and brought both hands down on the back of his neck.

The blond spokesman should be back by now; and I turned, and he was. He was on me before I could get my hands up. We rolled on the ground, me with my arms pinned to my sides, him unable to use his hands without letting go. It was lousy planning for both of us. He was squeezing the breath out of me. Ron hovered over us, waiting for a chance to hit him.

Suddenly there were others, a lot of others. Three of them pulled the blond kid off me, and a beefy, bloody man in a yellow business jumper stepped forward and crowned him with a rock.

The blond kid went limp.

I was still trying to get my breath.

The man squared off and threw a straight left hook with the rock in his hand. The blond kid's head snapped back, fell forward.

I yelled, "Hey!" Jumped forward, got hold of the arm that held the rock.

Someone hit me solidly in the side of the neck.

I dropped. It felt like all my strings had been cut. Someone was helping me to my feet—Ron—voices babbling in whispers, one shouting, "Get him—"

I couldn't see the blond kid. The other one, the tackle, was up and staggering away. Shadows came from between the trees to play pileup on him. The woods were alive, and it was just a *little* patch of woods. Full of angry, thirsty people.

Bugeyes reappeared, grinning widely. "Now what? Go somewhere else and try it again?"

"Oh, no. It's getting very vicious out tonight. Ron, we've got to stop them. They'll kill him!"

"It's a Free Park. Can you stand now?"

"Ron, they'll *kill* him!"

The rest of the Water Trust was charging to the rescue. One of them had a tree branch with the leaves stripped off. Behind them, shadows converged on the fountain.

We fled.

I had to stop after a dozen paces. My head was trying to explode. Ron looked back anxiously, but I waved him on. Behind me the man with the branch broke through the trees and ran toward me to do murder.

Behind him, all the noise suddenly stopped.

I braved myself for the blow.

And fainted.

*   *   *

He was lying across my legs, with the branch still in his hand. Jill and Ron were pulling at my shoulders. A pair of golden moons floated overhead.

I wriggled loose. I felt my head. It seemed intact.

Ron said, "The copseyes zapped him before he got to you."

"What about the others? Did they kill them?"

"I don't know." Ron ran his hands through his hair. "I was wrong. Anarchy isn't stable. It comes apart too easily."

"Well, don't do any more experiments, okay?"

People were beginning to stand up. They streamed toward the exits, gathering momentum, beneath the yellow gaze of the copseyes.

The King's Legions

Christopher Anvil

Vaughan Roberts, in the control seat of the salvaged Interstellar Patrol ship that had cost most of his life savings, glanced briefly at the battle screen, which showed his two friends' secondhand space yacht being hauled around in a gravitor beam. Then he looked back at the auxiliary screen, where an exaggeratedly military-looking individual, with the insignia of a lieutenant colonel, spoke in brisk authoritative tones:

"By order of the Commanding Officer, Squadron R, 876th Interstellar Combat Wing, Space Fleet XII, you are hereby commanded to halt for inspection re Exotic Drugs Act, Section 16 . . ."

Roberts, who had spent some time in the Space Force himself, had never before seen such a combination of meticulously close-cropped iron-gray hair, stiff face, and ramrod-straight posture, with uniform pressed into dentproof knife-edged creases. Over the left shirt pocket of this uniform were three rows of ribbons, and while Roberts did not recognize half of them, there was one that he knew to be the Cross of Space, with three stars. The Cross of Space was awarded sparingly—to win it required proof of heroism in the face of such danger that it was rare for the hero to come back alive. Try as he might, Roberts could not visualize the miracle that would enable the same man to win this award four times and live.

". . . Paragraph E," the stiffly erect figure went on. "You will not resist the beam. You will not attempt to parley. You will open outer hatches to admit boarding parties without delay . . ."

Roberts glanced around.

The patrol ship, the purchase of which Roberts considered an unusual stroke of luck, was equipped with devices he could never have afforded to buy new. One of these could extrude a set of metal arms, to spin a shell of camouflage around the ship, hide its formidable armament, and create the appearance of a harmless rebuilt derelict. Other devices could make fast precise measurements of shape, size, mass, and other characteristics, to pass to computers which searched almost instantaneously through hosts of reference standards to determine what the data might mean. On this information, presented to the pilot in symbols on the battle screen, the patrol ship's battle computer could act at once, bringing the ship's weapons to bear on changing targets, and altering speed, course, and attitude to meet the situation. Presiding over the weapons, sensing elements, computers, and various special devices, and acting toward the pilot as a combination conscience and subconscious mind, was what was known as the "symbiotic computer." At this moment, the symbiotic computer, in its own way, was doubtless considering the rasping, authoritative voice:

". . . You will at all times obey the instructions of the inspecting personnel. You will cooperate fully in exposing your ship to thorough search for contraband. Resistance, or procrastination, will be dealt with severely . . ."

But the many symbols now appearing on the battle screen were what riveted attention.

It gave Roberts pause to consider who would want such things as:

a) A large salvaged cruiser stripped for ultrafast acceleration.

b) An irregular rocky object some four hundred feet in diameter, hollowed out inside, with several large masses of undetermined nature floating around the interior.

c) A simulated Space Force dreadnought mocked up on a girder-ship frame.

d) An irregular metallic object eighty feet across, with fusion guns sunk in hidden wells.

Roberts fingered the curved surface of a small glowing ball recessed into the control console. As he turned the ball, a corresponding white circle on the battle screen moved from one symbol to the next, and each in turn was enlarged, to show fine detail. Roberts now saw such things as a big cargo section with what looked like severe damage; hidden inside were grapples to seize any ship that came close enough to give help.

Now it was clear why the "colonel" on the screen looked so exceptionally military. Real military men had work to do, and doing this work was their job. But this fellow's job was to look military. Where the fake-wreck artist collected his victims by drifting along a traveled route looking helpless; and where the trap-miner made his profit by maneuvering his chunk of "ore" into position to catch prospectors unaware; and where the slugger prospered by sudden attack—for the same purpose, the two-day wonder mimicked the Space Force.

Now the "colonel" was looking at Roberts with hard authority.

"Is that clearly understood?"

Roberts's course display now showed its line of big dashes drifting off to the right. The track display showed a curving line that wove past the asteroid belt to the stylized image of the blue-green world optimistically called Paradise—with the little image of the ship slipping well off the line. The battle screen showed the patrol ship caught in a wavy blue, representing another gravitor beam.

Roberts asked himself what all these commerce raiders were doing here. Two previous trips told him there wasn't enough commerce past this system to make a living for a tenth of them. If they weren't here to prey on commerce, what *were* they here for?

He considered one possible reason.

When he, Hammell and Morrisey had been on Paradise before, Morrissey had invented a device to influence desires, and had developed it so it could be focused on a given place from a distance. Suppose someone had been shrewd enough to deduce, from what had happened, the existence of a want-generator?

What would a gang of commerce raiders do to get hold of a device that could influence desires from a distance?

But then, Roberts realized, if such a person had been on Paradise, he would have learned still more.

The last time Roberts, Hammell and Morrissey had been here, the only way they'd found to keep two of the planet's factions from slaughtering each other had been to use, not only the want-generator, but also Roberts's patrol ship, to create the myth of two *outside* factions fighting for control of the planet.

Now, Roberts asked himself, suppose the commerce raiders had learned of this myth, and of the formidable personages who were part of it. Would the commerce raiders care to tangle with such a crew? What if it should turn out that the creatures were real? What if Oggbad, the sorcerer, and the three Dukes *were* fighting for mastery of an Empire? Then what? The want-generator was worth taking on whoever had it, even if he was an armored Duke with an Empire behind him—but the risk should be spread by gathering a strong force, in case of trouble. That was how the commerce raiders would think.

While Roberts considered this, the imitation colonel gave signs of impatience.

"Let's have your attention here, Mister!"

The only way out Roberts could see was to convince the raiders the situation was too dangerous for them to handle. Yet, a simple calculation showed more firepower on their side.

It followed that Roberts would have to run a bluff.

On the screen, the two-day wonder's fuse burned short again, and he turned away, as if to rasp some order to an unseen subordinate.

Roberts spoke first: "This is a King's ship."

The "colonel" swung around. "What's that?"

Roberts looked the two-day wonder directly in the eye. "Sobeit you wish death, there is no surer way than this."

The two-day wonder stared at him.

Roberts spoke grimly: "A King's ship will not stand inspection by any mortal power in or out of space. He who attempts it will face the full might of the Empire. You are warned."

The figure on the screen momentarily congealed into a

living statue. Then he leaned completely back out of focus of the screen.

There was a garbled noise from the speaker, then the automatic descramblers went to work, the garble seemed to distort itself into new shapes and forms, and suddenly it came across, rough and low-pitched, but understandable: "Quick! Where's Maury?"

"Holed up with Parks and the lawyer. Why?"

"Get him on this screen!"

"Are you nuts? He'll—"

"I said, get him!"

The "colonel!" reappeared, his manner conciliatory: "We certainly don't want to . . . er . . . detain a foreign ship against its will, Mr. . . . ah . . . ?"

In a chill voice, Roberts said, "My name is not at issue. Neither is it at issue whether you will hold this ship against its will. You lack the power to hold this ship against its will. You will release this ship or die. *That* is what is at issue."

In the silence that followed, Roberts became aware that, around him, there were a great many quiet noises. There was a hum, and a low clank from the weapons locker. From outside came grating and whirring sounds, and from somewhere forward there was a continuous murmuring rumble. The patrol ship, though it lacked room, had a trait that endeared it to Roberts: When trouble was coming, the patrol ship got ready. Its captain didn't have to concern himself with the little details any more than a man on the brink of a fist fight had to consciously raise his own blood pressure.

On the screen, the "colonel" glanced around. "Yes! Put him on!"

The screen divided vertically, to show an additional face. This new face took a cool glance at Roberts, and turned very slightly toward the imitation colonel. "What's all this about?"

"It's like that stuff down on Three! I grabbed this guy on a beam, and—"

"Are you wasting my time over a reel-in on some spacer punk? We'll talk about this lat—"

"No! Hold it, Maury! This is that Empire stuff!"

"Nuts. That's a rebuilt dogship. Look at your long-range screen and read the lines. Grow up."

"But this guy—"

Roberts flipped a switch on the control panel.

There was a slight jar, and the outside viewscreen showed torn camouflage drifting past.

"You hold a King's ship at your peril."

Roberts reached for the firing console, but the symbiotic computer got there first, and the switches moved of their own accord. A large white beam sprang out from the patrol ship toward the asteroid belt.

In the asteroid belt, there was a dazzling explosion.

From a previously unused speaker to the left of the instrument panel came a clear questioning voice: "Imperial Dreadnought *Coeur de Lion* to masked Imperial Ship *Nom de Guerre*. Do you need help?"

On another auxiliary screen appeared the image of a tough officer in glittering helmet and breastplate, with eyes of a blue so pale that they resembled ice.

It took Roberts an instant to realize that the symbiotic computer was filling in the details. Then he answered: "Imperial Ship *Nom de Guerre* to Imperial Dreadnought *Coeur de Lion*. We are detained by outspacers, who claim the right to halt and board us, in search for contraband."

"Outspacers? In what strength?"

"Fleet strength, of varying type and quality."

"Do the dogs know they hold a King's ship?"

"They do."

"Inform them that if they wish a fleet action, they shall have it."

"I have already told them. They doubt my word."

"Demand if the scum be leagued with Oggbad."

Roberts glanced back at the communications screen. The two-day wonder looked ready to shut his eyes and slide under the table anytime. The other individual, Maury, had a look of intense awareness.

Roberts looked him in the eye, and spoke in a tone suggesting the crack of a whip: "Serve you Oggbad the Fiend?"

Maury's brow wrinkled. His face took on the look of a rocket specialist grappling with his first gravitor. He opened his mouth, shut it, then opened it again. "No."

Roberts glanced at the auxiliary screen. "He denies allegiance to Oggbad."

"It is the policy of the Empire to avoid clashes with the outspacers till our present wounds be bound up. Warn this dog to stand clear of the Earldom-Designate of Paradise. Demand that he let loose his hold on you and the bomb ship. If he does so, take your departure. If not, run the iron down his throat."

"Have I leave to slam home the bomb ship?"

"Do that first. Then the rest will go quicker."

Roberts glanced back at Maury. Roberts's voice was brisk and businesslike: "I propose to you that you let loose my ships, and further that you agree to stand clear of the Earldom-Designate of Paradise, which is the third planet of this star, counting from the star outward. Do you agree?"

Maury, his expression baffled, said, "I agree."

Roberts turned back to the auxiliary screen. "He agrees."

The figure on the screen looked faintly disappointed. "If he does as promised, you have no choice but to break off. At some future time, we may settle these old accounts."

Roberts watched the battle screen. The wavy blurs vanished. The patrol ship and the space yacht were free.

Roberts nodded coldly to Maury.

Maury, his expression that of a person thinking very hard, nodded back.

Roberts broke the connection.

So far, so good. But one careless slip would unravel the whole illusion.

Roberts made certain the communicator was off, thought a moment, then tapped a button beside the glowing amber lens marked "Smb Cmp."

"Any fishnet pickups between us and the space yacht?"

The voice of the symbiotic computer replied, "Two. They were drifted out on narrow pressor elements of a compound beam. They're in position between here and the yacht."

"Fishnet pickups are expensive. If we don't hurt them, our friends in the asteroid belt will pull them back *in* again when we leave. If—"

The symbiotic computer spoke complacently. "The parasite circuits are already in place."

"Good. Let's see these fishnets on the screen."

The outside viewscreen promptly showed, outlined in red,

two large fuzzy networks of fine lines, between the space yacht and the patrol ship.

"O.K.," said Roberts, and carefully guided the patrol ship away from them, as if he were moving off on his own. When he reached an angle that would avoid the pickups, he switched on the communicator, and called the yacht on a tight beam.

Hammell and Morrissey appeared on the screen, their faces tense.

Roberts said, "Don't talk. Just follow me."

Hammell nodded, and Roberts snapped off the screen.

The patrol ship moved slowly off, and the space yacht swung slowly after it.

Carefully, Roberts watched the battle screen for any sign of trouble. When nothing developed, he glanced down at the course display, and sent the little symbol of the ship gradually angling back toward the line of red dashes. As he moved, Roberts gathered speed, so that not long after the symbol of the ship was again centered on the display's dashes, the dashes themselves faded to pale pink, then white. The ship was now back on course, and moving at the correct speed.

The asteroid belt by now was far behind.

But all the way down to the planet, Roberts could see Maury's face—thinking, weighing, calculating.

The landing itself was no problem. The two ships slid down through heavy clouds, moved low over dense forest, and came to rest a little before sunset in the same clearing where they'd set down before.

Roberts ran the stabilizer feet out, switched off the gravitors, and unbuckled his safety harness. He ducked under the three-foot-thick shiny cylinder that ran down the axis of the ship, and went up several steps in the cramped aft section. He released the clamp on the outer hatch, spun the lockwheel counterclockwise, pulled the hatch lever down cautiously, and peered out a one-inch slit. Past experience told him that to actually *go* outside, without battle armor, might be to wind up instantaneously in some creature's digestive tract. But after all the time he'd spent in the ship, he wanted a breath of fresh air.

As the hatch eased up, he peered out into the clearing,

sniffed the cool fresh air, inhaled deeply, sighed with pleasure, raised the hatch further, felt the breeze on his face—

There was the faint tick of an automatic turret.

WHAP!

A blur of yellow fur and claws blew apart in midair.

Roberts shook his head, shut the hatch, and went to the
nearest weapons locker to get battle armor. He opened the
locker, and out on its sling came a glittering metal suit with a
tall tapering spire on the helmet, a gauzy pink cloth on the
spire, and a dazzling coat of arms on the breastplate.

Again, to fit the part Roberts was playing, the patrol ship
had "improved" the armor.

Roberts looked at it irritatedly, and tried another locker.
Out came a more dazzling suit, with spire plus flashing crown
on the helmet, and a larger broadsword in lavishly jeweled
scabbard.

Roberts tried the other two lockers—which stubbornly refused to open.

The voice of the symbiotic computer said dryly, "When
playing a part, little inconsistencies add up to a big loss of
belief."

"Exactly who," said Roberts, "is going to watch me go
this short distance?"

"Those who are not seers should avoid predicting the
future."

"Nuts." Roberts climbed into the armor, and made his
way to the hatch. He turned backwards, head bent, and
managed to get the hatch open without ramming anything
with the spire. He crouched, turned around, aimed the spire
out the opening, followed it through, and dropped to the
ground. The hatch clanged shut behind him, and Roberts
started for the space yacht.

About halfway there, he became conscious of a face back
in the shadows, watching him with awe. Roberts corrected
himself—watching the *armor* with awe.

That the symbiotic computer had been right again did
nothing to improve Roberts's frame of mind—especially since
he could now see that it was obvious. The accumulated
effects of the want-generator had led thousands from the city
to venture deeper into the forest, seeking adventure and trophies, and the most capable survivors might by now be on an

almost equal footing with the creatures that naturally lived there.

Roberts climbed up the handholds of the yacht, and banged on the big cargo door. At once it swung open. Roberts used the spire to keep Hammell back, and as soon as he was inside, jabbed the button that swung the door shut.

"Ye gods," said Hammell, staring at the armor, "let's not bother with *that* until we need it. Incidentally, you almost stabbed me with that helmet spike when you came in."

Roberts said shortly, "There's somebody watching from the edge of the clearing. Don't forget, we've got a lot of these people interested in going into the forest. That's what they're doing."

Hammell momentarily had the foolish expression of one caught overlooking the obvious.

"Moreover," said Roberts, "I was using that spike to keep you away from the hatch. You don't look too much like Duke Ewald of Greme right now." He hesitated, then cleared his throat. "When you're playing a part, little inconsistencies add up to a big loss of belief. You want to remember that."

Hammell looked groggy. "I should have thought of it, but for some reason, I forgot."

Roberts said cheerfully, "Where's Morrissey?"

"Up on the fifth level, checking the gear."

"You'd better go up first. We don't want him to get speared with this helmet spike."

"O.K."

Hammell stepped onto the green half of the glowing oval on the deck, and drifted up the grav-lift. The doors overhead slid open and shut, and he was gone from sight.

Roberts allowed time to warn Morrissey, then followed. The doors slid open one after another, then the fifth level dropped into view, and Roberts gripped the handhold and pulled himself out.

Hammell and Morrissey were standing by a wide improvised control panel. Roberts said hello to Morrissey, got out of the armor, and glanced around.

"How are things in the city?"

"That's a good question," said Morrissey. "There's no broadcast from the city, and the spy screen doesn't work."

Roberts glanced at the blank gray screen. "Can you fix it?"

"If it was something wrong with the screen *itself*, maybe. But I tried a test transmission, and the screen's O.K. The trouble is, there's no transmission from the city."

"What would cause that?"

Morrissey shrugged. "If we had our own spy devices in the city, I might be in a position to say. But this setup is tapped onto the city's own surveillance system. Now, how does that system work? If the city's general power supply fails, does the system fail? If so, it could be that they've had a power failure. Or, it could be that the power supply is O.K., but that somebody has knocked out the surveillance system itself. Not knowing how the system works, I don't know what's possible."

"Could the technicians have found out someone had tapped the surveillance system?"

Morrissey nodded. "Among other things. It could even be that there's a gentleman's agreement that the system will only be used during certain hours. All I *know* is the screen doesn't show us anything, because there's no transmission to pick up."

Roberts shook his head. "What we're here for is to use the want-generator to straighten out the mess in that city. But how can we use it, when there's no way to watch the effect? Moreover, we've got this fleet of commerce raiders. How do we concentrate on what we're doing with a troop of baboons ready to drop in anytime?"

Hammell said, "It's worse than that. The odds are, they've got at least one agent already *on* the planet. Anytime we make a public move, this guy will report it."

Morrissey frowned. "Come to think of it, they'll be able to use their instruments to follow the movements of our ships here. Then they can compare what we *say*, as reported by their agent, with what we *do*, as shown by their instruments. We can't say we're going off to fight Oggbad, for instance, and then just land our ships out of sight while we decide what to do next."

"No," said Hammell, "they'd know we were faking."

"And we can't afford *that*," said Roberts.

Morrissey said, "The wonder is that we ever got away from them at all. How did you work it?"

Roberts described what had happened, adding, "I'd think it was a pretty good bluff if we were far away by now. But since we aren't, our safety depends on keeping them afraid to try anything, for fear the mighty Empire will blow them to bits."

"Which," Hammell growled, "means every move we make not only has to make sense for our purposes, but also has got to be convincing to the commerce raiders."

"Correct," said Roberts.

Morrissey, scowling, said, "This is going to complicate things."

"When you consider the likely situation on this planet," said Roberts, "it's going to pile up complications to the point where it's a question whether we can move at all. Just think of the factions here. There's the planetary computer with its roboid devices and built-in directives. As a sort of semi-independent extension, there's Kelty and his army of roboid police. There's the technicians, and the machines and devices the technicians have made. Then there's the Great Leader and his fanatics—plus the general bulk of the populace itself. On top of all this is the effect of the measures *we* took while we were here the last time. And, of course, the whole thing is bound to have developed since then, even though we won't know *how* until we get the spy screen to work."

Morrissey nodded moodily. "And since the trouble is on the other end, there isn't much we can do."

There was a moody silence.

Out in the clearing, it was getting dim, and Roberts absently tapped the switch to opaque the portholes, lest they be watched from outside. Then the silence stretched out again.

Finally Hammell said, "There ought to be *some* way to simplify this."

Morrissey nodded. "Sure. What?"

Roberts was about to suggest, yet again, that they move into the patrol ship, where at least their skins would be safe. But just then—

BAM!

The ship jumped underfoot.

Roberts instantaneously dove for his battle armor.

There was a rapid series of jolts and heavy crashes. Something clattered on the deck, hissed, spun, and bounced, in a blur of escaping mist.

Roberts heaved open the backplate.

Hammell and Morrissey, caught in the mist, stumbled toward the grav-lift, and were lost in swirling grayness.

Roberts squirmed into the armor, his eyes shut, and holding his breath. But even though he was now inside, so was a certain amount of gas. He staggered to his feet, swung shut the backplate, groped for the emergency-breathing chin-lever, couldn't find it, and suddenly, despite himself, his straining lungs sucked in a little breath of air that smelled sweetish and strange.

Roberts's thoughts vanished like startled fish. There was a gap when he was aware of nothing at all, and then he was standing, stuporous and empty-minded, as there appeared through the fog, from the direction of the grav-lift, a heavily armed figure wearing an armored suit with wide transparent faceplate, flexible air hose looped over the left shoulder, and speaking diaphragm in the side of the mouthpiece.

From somewhere down in the clearing, an amplified voice boomed out:

"YOU ARE UNDER ARREST! BY ORDER OF THE PLANETARY DEVELOPMENT AUTHORITY, YOU MUST EVACUATE THESE SHIPS AND COME OUT DISARMED AND WITH YOUR HANDS CLASPED BEHIND YOUR HEADS! YOU HAVE FIFTEEN SECONDS TO COMPLY WITH THIS ORDER!"

A second armored figure loomed through the fog. The two figures bent, and carried Hammell and Morrissey below.

A third figure came in, peered around, stepped forward, looked straight toward Roberts, and froze.

Another armored figure, and another, came in the gravshaft, peered through the fog toward Roberts, and suddenly stood motionless.

Roberts, aware of an urgent need to act, at the same time was unable to remember who or where he was. All he really knew was that he was standing still, breathing in air that smelled slightly less sweet at every breath. Then, dimly, he caught the tail end of a train of thought, struggled to hold it, sucked in a great breath of air, and in a blinding flash the situation was clear to him.

He fought off a host of other thoughts and kept his mind riveted on that one thought that clarified the whole situation:

I am Vaughan, Duke of Trasimere. Prince Contestant to the Throne. This planet is the Earldom-Designate of Paradise. Its every inhabitant is rightly subject to my command, save only Oggbad, the sorcerer.

That was straightforward.

Once Roberts knew who he was, everything simplified itself wonderfully.

Alertly, he studied the armored figures edging toward him. The expressions of fear and awe visible through their face-plates suggested that they were not ill-intentioned. What had happened, then?

In a kindly voice, with the natural overtones of power and authority that followed from a knowledge of who he was, Roberts said quietly: "Kneel to your liege-lord."

The armored figures, wide-eyed, dropped to one knee.

This told Roberts that the men were not from off the planet, but from the city, and were acquainted with what had happened on his last visit, when the sorcerer Oggbad had escaped into the wilderness, and the leaders and population of the city, after a little unseemly wavering, had rallied to the true cause. Their allegiance once pledged, and his power to reward and punish once established, they would not readily turn against him.

With a tinge of regret and a hint of sternness in his voice, Roberts said quietly, "What brings you here?"

Nobody dared to speak, and now Roberts said, "I must have an answer. Rise. Was it Oggbad?"

They stumbled to their feet. But still no one could bring himself to speak.

Roberts now noticed that the armored suits bore the words "Citizens' Defense Force." One of the armored suits bore the chevrons of a sergeant.

Roberts's voice became sharper. "Before this evil can be destroyed, I must know its source. Let whoever is of highest rank among you answer my questions. Did Oggbad send you here?"

The sergeant looked around, but there was no one else to

do it. He said, "No, your . . . your highness. A man landed in a . . . ah . . . official Planetary Development Authority ship, and announced that we'd been tricked, and he was taking over the planet. He had an army of . . . 'administrators' . . . with him. They're all over the Inner City. He gives the orders. We didn't know *you* were here."

"This fellow is an outspacer?"

"He . . . ah—?"

"He does not belong to the Empire?"

"No."

"Then he is an outspacer and has no right here. Did this fellow come with you?"

"Yes he—"

"Is he in this ship?"

"He's outside, at the loudspeaker. There he goes now."

The amplified voice boomed out:

". . . AT ONCE, OR WE WILL DESTROY BOTH OF THESE SHIPS AND . . ."

Roberts nodded. "Go below, and warn your companions that I shall be down to settle this shortly."

The men went out.

Roberts, breathing air that the suit had now cleared almost entirely of the fumes, was having more and more trouble fighting off a throng of distracting thoughts that conflicted with his newfound clarity of mind. He took a few moments to shove these thoughts out of his consciousness. There would be time enough for all that later. The main thing *now* was to take care of this officious usurper.

With this purpose clearly in mind, Roberts checked sword and gun, and stepped into the grav-shaft.

A throng of armored men moved back respectfully as Roberts walked to the cargo door to look down into the clearing.

Below, some eighty to a hundred heavily armed men nervously ringed the patrol ship. Closer to the patrol ship, redly glowing fragments lay like driftwood marking high water at a beach. The larger turrets of the ship aimed straight ahead, as if disdaining such petty opponents, but the smaller turrets made little adjustments that served as warnings to come no closer.

Floodlights, mounted on dish-shaped grav-skimmers, lit the scene, which was given an inferno aspect by a thin mist blowing across the clearing from a ring of generators around the edge. Through the upper reaches of this mist, hosts of bats with glistening teeth dove at the clearing, but then with desperate twists and turns flitted away again.

Between the patrol ship and the space yacht stood a little cluster of figures beside a loudspeaker aimed at the patrol ship. One of these armored men spoke into a microphone, and his words boomed out:

". . . AND I *REPEAT*—YOU WILL SURRENDER AT ONCE OR BE DECLARED OUTLAWS, SUBJECT TO ATTACK ON SIGHT, FORFEITURE OF ALL PROPERTY AND ASSETS, AND DENIAL OF RIGHT OF ENTRY AT ALL CIVILIZED . . ."

His tone of voice spoke of close familiarity with rules and regulations, accompanied by a dim understanding of human nature. It came to Roberts that even if the fellow had any power over him, his conclusion would be the same:

Better dead than that man's prisoner.

The loudspeaker was now blaring the words:

". . . THEREFORE, BY THE AUTHORITY VESTED IN ME, I HEREBY . . ."

Roberts suddenly had enough. The suit amplified his words into a voice of thunder:

"MASTER OF THE ORDNANCE! SILENCE THAT DOG!"

From the patrol ship, a bright line of light reached out to the loudspeaker. There was a brief display of sparks, then a pleasant quiet.

Beside the loudspeaker, the man with the microphone swung around. "Take *that* man prisoner!"

Roberts rested his hand on his sword hilt.

No one moved.

Roberts studied the usurper coldly. "What false illusion of power emboldens a fool to challenge the true liege-lord of this world?"

The only sound was the murmur of wind and the hiss of the generators spaced around the clearing.

Then the armed men in the clearing were grinning at the little group by the loudspeaker.

The individual in the center, firmly gripping the useless

microphone, spoke in a determined voice. "I am P. W. Glinderen, Chief of Planet. Owing to the . . . spectacular irregularities . . . which have taken place on this planet, the Planetary Development Authority has regressed the planet to preprovisional status. I have duly and officially been appointed Chief. You are evidently the cause of the irregularities. I, therefore, place you under arrest, and instruct you to strip yourself at once of all weapons and armor, open this other ship to immediate inspection, and instruct those within to come out at once, disarm themselves, and surrender. If you carry out these instructions promptly, I believe I can endorse a plea for clemency in your case."

Roberts replied irritatedly: "No one can enforce his will where he lacks both right and power. The rulers of this world have yielded to me. Your vaunted authority is either fraudulent or void."

P. W. Glinderen opened his mouth, shut it, and then spoke determinedly:

"In other words, you admit to planetary piracy? You state that you have seized this planet by force?"

Roberts spoke as if to a child: "Is the authority of lord over vassal based on force alone? Better to die, than to yield to such a claim, and better never to seize such a perilous allegiance. None need yield to a foul or empty cause. Against such, there is the appeal to Heaven, which will grant victory or apportion vengeance."

P. W. Glinderen began to speak, looked thoughtful, and tried again:

"May I ask if your name is not—" He leaned over to another of his party, listened, nodded, and said, "—Vaughan N. Roberts, and if not, what *is* your exact identity?"

The question caused Roberts a moment of uneasiness. But one who has lost his identity, and then recovered it, is none too eager to let it go a second time. Roberts's voice came out with anger and conviction:

"To question another in this manner assumes a superiority dangerous to one who is, in fact, a trespasser, without right or power, and with his life in the hands of him he seeks to question. You ask my name. I am Vaughan, Duke of Trasimere. Seek you any *further* answers?"

The Planetary Development official stared at Roberts, then again gathered himself to speak.

A loud ticking sounded from the patrol ship.

Someone in Glinderen's party looked around, then urgently grabbed Glinderen.

The patrol ship's big fusion cannon aimed directly at him. Glinderen opened his mouth, and tried to speak, but was unable to get any words out.

Roberts turned to the men who had surrounded the patrol ship and were now gathered between the patrol ship and the space yacht.

"Take this man and his fellows prisoner, and return them to the city. Give warning that I shall soon be there to set straight whatever folly these people have brought about."

The armored men below enthusiastically seized Glinderen and his companions, and hustled them onto the grav-skimmers. Then the men on the space yacht asked for orders, and Roberts sent them off with the rest. The whole outfit roared away with impressive efficiency, taking prisoners, loudspeakers, floodlights, and mist-generators with them.

Roberts, with the feeling of having satisfactorily completed an unpleasant task, turned to see Hammell and Morrissey, holding pressure-bottles and masks to their faces, watching him wide-eyed.

At that instant, with the tension relaxed and Roberts himself off guard, suddenly the thoughts he'd held off burst into consciousness.

Vaughan, Duke of Trasimere, Prince Contestant to the Throne, suddenly realized with a shock what was myth and what reality.

Morrissey held the mask away for a moment.

"Was that PDA Chief a fake—I hope?"

Hammell added nervously: "The whole Space Force will come out on a planetary-piracy charge." He sucked a fresh breath through the mask. "You know that, don't you?"

Now Roberts knew it. Now that he had, in effect, challenged the whole human-occupied universe to war.

Then something more immediately urgent occurred to him.

"Once the fumes from the generators blow away, those gangbats will be down here, and no one knows what else.

The yacht's hull is riddled. You'd better be in the patrol ship before it's too late.''

For once, Hammell and Morrissey made no objection, but hastily followed him down the handholds and across the clearing.

The instant they were inside, Roberts slammed shut the hatch and locked it tight.

Now, he thought, he would have to answer some awkward questions.

But already, the two weapons lockers, that Roberts had been unable to open, were swinging wide. Glittering suits of battle armor traveled out on their slings.

"The new recruits," said the symbiotic computer, "will suit up at once, and return to the yacht to gather necessary goods, and equipment."

Hammell and Morrissey stared at the two glittering suits of battle armor.

"New recruits?" said Morrissey.

Roberts said reassuringly, "Don't worry about that. That's just how it talks. But you'd better go along with it; otherwise you don't get any food or water, and the bunk stays locked in place and you wind up having to sleep on the deck. But never mind that. We've got to get the want-generator over here anyway. Not only could animals damage it, but conceivably somebody might get at it while we're away."

"Away?" said Hammell. "Where are we going?"

"Where do you think?" said Roberts. "There's only one place to straighten out this mess, and that's the city."

Hammell and Morrissey got into the battle armor without a word. But they looked as if they were doing a good deal of thinking.

Transferring the want-generator and spy screen to the patrol ship took the better part of two hours, but things didn't stand still while they did it. At intervals they could hear, on the patrol ship's communicator, the voice of Kelty, in charge of the city's roboid police; the voice of the red-bearded spokesman for the technicians; and the voice used by the planetary computer itself. On the other side was a harsh demanding voice that wrung the facts from stammering humans and toneless computer, and made it plain that everyone on the planet would obey his liege-lord the Duke, or his liege-lord the Duke would smash the place into smoldering rubble.

Once the want-generator and spy screen were set up, the three men got out of their armor and considered the restricted space in the patrol ship.

Standing near the hatch looking forward, the most prominent feature was the glistening three-foot-thick cylinder that ran down the axis of the ship, creating a shimmer of reflections exactly where anyone would naturally walk. Hammell and Morrissey had already banged into it, and now moved more warily.

To the left of this cylinder was the control seat and console, forward of which was a blank wall. To the right of the cylinder, the space was now cluttered with the spy screen and want-generator, while straight ahead the deck itself warped sharply upward over the missile bay.

Aft of where Roberts stood, everything was constricted. Between the cylinder and the various drive and fuel-storage units, there was little but a set of claustrophobic crawl spaces so tight that it was necessary to exhale to get in.

Beside Roberts, however, was one of the patrol ship's better features. Whatever might be said about other details, the final maddening touch—cramped sleeping arrangements—had been left out. The bunks were large and comfortable, and once in his bunk, a man could stretch out for a full night's rest. But there was no denying, most of the ship lacked space.

Hammell and Morrissey, after looking around, glanced at each other, and then Hammell turned to Roberts accusingly.

"It's even smaller on the inside than on the outside."

Roberts was listening to the symbiotic computer warn Kelty that Glinderen's party shouldn't be allowed to use a communicator. Roberts replied absently. "It's a thick hull."

"Maybe so, but . . . what's behind that?" Hammell pointed to the wall that took up the space in front of the control console.

Roberts frowned. "At first, I thought it was some kind of a storeroom. But I've never been able to find any way into it."

Hammell said, "That looks like the edge of a sliding door, in front of the control console."

"When you're at the controls during an attack, that door slides shut. If the ship out here is holed, you can still function."

Morrissey looked around. "What's under the deck here?"

Roberts bent, and heaved back a section. Underneath was a tangle of tubes, cables, and freely curving pipes, of various sizes and colors, smoothly branching and reconnecting, some sinking out of sight beneath the others, and the whole works set into a pinkish jellylike insulation or sealant of some kind. As they watched, a translucent pipe about the size of a man's forearm began to dilate. In a series of waves of contraction and dilatation, ball-like lumps of something with a golden glint traveled along, to vanish under the next section of deck.

Roberts lowered the panel, and glanced at Morrissey. "Any more questions?"

Morrissey scratched his head, but said nothing.

Hammell looked around in puzzlement. "This seems to be pretty advanced." He stepped forward and glanced up through an opening overhead.

"Is there another deck up there?"

"No. That's the upper fusion turret."

"What's that . . . ah . . . thing like a wheel, with a handle—"

"The handwheel for elevating the gun."

Hammell blinked. "You aim the gun by hand?"

"There's a multiple control system. The gun can be operated by the battle computer or the symbiotic computer, with no one on board. Or, you can operate it yourself from the control console. But if you have to, you can also do it completely by hand."

"Which has precedence, the manual control, or the automatic?"

"So far as the guns are concerned, I think the manual. Where the flying of the ship is concerned, the computers can lock you out anytime. It's not that the manual controls are disconnected, or don't work, but that they take a setting and you can't move them. If a man were strong enough, I don't know what would happen."

Morrissey said, "What about the communicator?"

"Same thing as the flying controls, except that if you're around, at least you know what's going on. You can hear what the symbiotic computer is saying. The computer can *take off* in the ship, and unless you happen to hear the slide and click of the levers and switches, you won't even know what happened.''

Hammell looked around, and squinted at the bulkhead, or reinforced section of hull, or whatever it was, in front of the control console.

''I'll bet that symbiotic computer is in there. It's the logical place. You're on one side of the controls. It's on the other.''

Morrissey shook his head. ''Too vulnerable. The same hit might knock out pilot and computer both.''

''Where is it then?''

Morrissey pointed at the deck.

Hammell shook his head. ''There's a symmetry about having it on the other side of the control console. If it's heavily enough protected, that business about the same hit wouldn't count. And it would make it easier to—''

Just then, Roberts heard the communicator say, ''. . . Preparations had best be complete to receive His Royal and Imperial Highness, the Duke Vaughan, at the Barons Council Hall within the quarter hour. Your own head will answer for it if aught traceable to you goes wrong. His Highness is in no sweet mood after what happened here a few hours ago . . .''

''O.K.,'' said Roberts. ''Here we go.''

Hammell and Morrissey, tied up in their argument, looked surprised.

''Wait a minute,'' said Hammell, ''what are we going to *do?*''

Roberts pulled his battle armor out on its sling. ''The only place we can straighten the mess out—or even find out what's going on—is in the city. So, we have to go to the city.''

''Yes, but what do we *do* there?''

''We've got to simplify the situation. There are too many factions. It's like trying to go somewhere with half a dozen different pilots, each backing his own flight plan. We've got to simplify it. The only way I can see is for us to get control of the major factions ourselves.''

Hammell shook his head. ''That would have been fine— before Glinderen showed up. He's the Chief of Planet.''

Roberts frowned. ''I don't think Glinderen, or anyone else who approaches this planet on a routine basis, can ever hope to straighten things out. I don't see any way to unite these factions unless *we* do it."

Morrissey said, "Suppose we *do* unite the factions Suppose we throw out Glinderen? Suppose we end the fighting? Suppose we scare off Maury and his fleet of commerce raiders? Suppose we even get halfway started on the job of straightening out this place? Then what? P. W. Glinderen merely goes offplanet, and signals his report to PDA Sector Headquarters; PDA Sector HQ then notifies Space Force Sector HQ and the Colonization Council; Space Force Sector HQ says it's overburdened and calls for reinforcements; that call gets to Space Force GHQ at the same time as an urgent recommendation from the Colonization Council; Space Force GHQ sends out the orders for a reserve fleet to come in here; meanwhile, Glinderen brushes his teeth, takes a shower, slides in between the cool sheets, and sleeps the sleep of the just; down here, so far as any court in the known universe is concerned, *we* are planetary pirates. One fine day, the Space Force sets down, and we either give up or get blasted into molten slag. Glinderen comes back down here, and methodically undoes everything we've done, and puts it back together *his* way. Where's the gain?"

Hammell nodded. "That's what I mean."

Roberts silently got into his armor, then glanced at the instrument panel.

"Here's an example of what I mean. While we've been talking, the ship has taken off. We're almost there."

Morrissey said urgently, "Look, Glinderen has us on the horns of a dilemma. If we *don't* give up, the Space Force kills us. If we *do* give up, *he* imprisons us. I don't want to get gored. But if I have to, I'll pick the shorter horn."

Roberts checked fusion gun and sword. "You say the Space Force can finish us off. That's provided Glinderen notifies them. What if he gets no chance to do it? That horn breaks off."

Morrissey blinked, and, frowning, started getting into his armor; but Hammell looked worried.

"Let's not get out of a *false* charge of piracy by carrying out actual piracy. Glinderen is lawfully in charge here."

A sliding sound from the direction of the control console,

and a quiet alteration in the tone of the gravitors, told them that they were starting down.

Roberts said quietly, "You're overlooking something."

Hammell said, with considerable strain in his voice, "I don't know what. Glinderen's authority is real. I don't like to do it, but this has gone far enough. I'll have to go to Glinderen, and—"

The voice of the symbiotic computer said, "We are now landing at Paradise City." The voice added, with the rasp of a drill instructor, "If the recruit standing with one hand on his armor will kindly put it on, this operation will proceed. If not, we will carry out disciplinary action now, and the recruit will spend the next five days aft cleaning out the maintenance tunnels."

Roberts said, "*That's* what you've overlooked. This is an Interstellar Patrol ship. The Interstellar Patrol is famous for its justice and incorruptibility. The symbiotic computer wouldn't even let the ship be sold until it was satisfied the buyer had the right moral standards. Would it let us do this if we were doing wrong?"

Even as he spoke, Roberts saw the flaw in his argument.

But Hammell, with an expression of profound relief, got into the battle armor.

The Barons Council Hall, near which the patrol ship landed, was floodlit and surrounded by roboid police and heavily armed members of the Citizens Defense Force. More roboid police rolled up to form a double line, with narrow lane between, from the ship to the Council Hall.

The patrol ship promptly blew up the nearest roboid police, and blasted to bits those that tried to take their place.

Roberts, coming out the hatch, decided that what looked fishy to the patrol ship looked fishy to him. He drew his sword.

As Hammell and Morrissey came out, he called: "Be on your guard. This has a look I like not."

The two men, in glittering armor, whipped out their fusion guns.

The roboid police eased a trifle further apart.

Roberts, studying the Citizens Defense Force, observed

that no one was faced *out*, to guard the site. They were all faced *in*.

Roberts strolled into the narrow lane between the roboid police. "Draw these lines apart!"

The roboid police backed up an inch.

With one violent blow of his sword, Roberts sliced the nearest roboid policeman in half. He chopped the next one apart, hewed his way through the third—

Suddenly there was room around him.

He strode between the lines toward the Council Hall, then abruptly came to a halt. Ahead and a little to his left, where he would have had to step if he had gone between the original lines, was what *looked* like a repaired place in the concrete.

Roberts drew his fusion gun, aimed deliberately, and fired.

A geyser of flame roared up. Chunks of concrete shot skyward like the discharge of a volcano.

From the patrol ship, searing shafts of energy reached out. There was a sizzling multiple *Crack!* like a dozen thunderbolts striking at once.

The roboid police were two lines of glowing wreckage.

Roberts jumped the smoking crater, and headed for the building. On the way, he shot down a large sign that proclaimed, "Municipal Detention Center," uncovering the more solidly anchored plaque bearing the words "Barons Council Hall." Roberts kicked the fallen sign out of his way, and opened the door.

At the near end of a big table, two men came to their feet. They were Kelty, the lean, well-dressed assistant chief of the planetary computer's roboid police, and the red-bearded giant who was spokesman for the technicians. At the foot of the table sat P. W. Glinderen, and to his right a knowing cynical individual who looked at Roberts with a smirk. Beside this individual was a bored-looked man with broad shoulders and a detectable bulge in his armpit. To Glinderen's left were seated several neatly dressed smooth-shaven men who apparently were administrators of some kind.

Roberts stepped to the empty place at the head of the table, and pulled out the chair.

Hammell and Morrissey took their places to Roberts's right, but, as he remained standing, they, too, stayed on their feet. At the far end, Glinderen and the officials to his left methodically glanced over papers, while to Glinderen's right, the shrewd-looking individual eyed Roberts, Hammell and Morrissey with a knowing smile.

Hammell's voice remarked, "Your Grace, I like not the air of this rabble at the foot of the table. They should stand till you are seated."

Glinderen looked up.

"*You* are at the foot of the table. And let me warn you, before you try any theatrical display, that I have notified the Space Force, and the three of you will be in prison before the week is out." His voice changed to a whiplike crack. "Now, sit *down*."

Roberts, aware of the orders he had earlier heard the symbiotic computer give, knew that Glinderen was not to have been allowed the use of a communicator.

Roberts glanced at Kelty. "Is this true?"

Kelty nodded unhappily. "I tried to stop him. But Glinderen convinced the planetary computer, and it blocked me."

Roberts said coldly, "Then this means war. Their so-called Space Force is in the asteroid belt. If it attempts to interfere with this world, I shall summon the battle fleets of the Empire."

At the other end of the table, the crafty individual to Glinderen's right laughed silently.

As Roberts contemplated this low point in his plans, Hammell's voice reached him:

"Your Grace, I know that these outspacers have customs different from ours. But their bearing is an insult. Not alone to Trasimere and the Empire, but to Malafont and Greme as well."

Roberts looked at the individuals at the far end of the table. Glinderen and his officials were ignoring everyone else. To Glinderen's right, the crafty individual sat back and grinned, while to *his* right, the tough was studying Hammell as if he were a peculiar kind of insect. No one at the far end of the table was taking Roberts and his party seriously. Moreover, they now controlled the planetary computer, and they had already called the Space Force.

Hammell's voice was courteous but firm:

"I know, Your Grace, of your desire to avoid conflict with the outspacers while our own struggles are yet unsettled.

Nevertheless, Your Grace, I respectfully call to your attention that this world is yours, and that I am your *guest* upon it.''

The shrewd individual rocked back in his chair, grinning.

Roberts said politely, "If the gentleman to Mr. Glinderen's right belongs to Mr. Glinderen's party, I trust that Mr. Glinderen will call him to order while there is yet time for Mr. Glinderen to call him to order."

Glinderen glanced up, frowning. "Mr. Peen is a commercial representative for Krojac Enterprises. He is entirely—"

"I see," said Roberts.

Mr. Peen went into a fresh fit of silent laughter.

Through no volition of his own, the fusion gun jumped to Roberts's hand. A dazzling lance of energy reached across the table.

Glinderen and his aides sprang to their feet as Peen went over backwards.

Roberts heard his own voice say coolly, "I apologize to their Grace of Malafont and Greme for this incivility."

Hammell's voice said, "The stain is wiped away, Your Grace."

Morrissey's voice added coolly, "Say no more of it, Your Grace. However, that other fellow, also to the right of Glinderen, hath a look which I care not for."

Roberts's voice inquired politely: "That second gentleman, Mr. Glinderen, is of your party?"

Glinderen said, "No, no! He's Mr. Peen's—"

Crack!

The second gentleman, springing to his feet and yanking a short-barreled weapon from his armpit, collapsed on the floor.

Roberts's voice said coolly, "I apologize to His Grace of Malafont, for this unpleasantness."

Morrissey's voice said cheerfully, "The unpleasantness is transmuted to pleasure, Your Grace."

As a matter of fact, the sudden departure of the grinning pair was a relief to Roberts. But the way they had departed was something else again. To see whether he now had control, or whether the battle armor was just going to operate on its own from now on, Roberts said experimentally, "Let us be seated."

The words were dutifully reproduced by the armor. He sat

down, and Hammell, Morrissey, Kelty, and the red-bearded
giant, smiling cheerfully, followed his example.

At the far end of the table, Glinderen stared from the pair
on the floor to Roberts.

"This is murder!"

Roberts was inclined to think Glinderen had a point. But,
before he could open his mouth, a duplicate of his voice said
coldly, "Had they been of your party, Mr. Glinderen, they
might yet be alive, but you might not. The great houses of the
Empire are not filled by hereditary lackwits or degenerate
scions forty generations removed from greatness. Neither are
they filled by those of such eager humility that they may at
will be trodden underfoot by rats in human form. He who
insults a Great Lord of the Empire, Mr. Glinderen, lives at the
mercy of that Great Lord, out of religious motives or as an
exercise in self-command, not out of an innate right to insult
his betters. You, Mr. Glinderen, are yourself deeply in my
debt, and in the debt of their Graces of Malafont and Greme.
Thus far, I have used against you less than my full strength,
out of recognition that you believe you do right. That is past.
One wrong move on your part, and you go the way of those
two on the floor. Seat yourself and let your men seat themselves. Let them keep silent, on peril of their lives. Let you
answer my questions and ask none of your own. Your actions
have already strung the bow of patience so tight that just a
little more will break it."

Glinderen sat down, wide-eyed. His subordinates swallowed, sat down, and kept their mouths shut.

Roberts waited an instant, but the battle armor had apparently said all it—or the symbiotic computer speaking through
it—intended to say. It was up to Roberts to fill the growing
uncomfortable silence.

Roberts leaned forward. "Where is the Baron of the Outer
City, Mr. Glinderen?"

Glinderen swallowed hard. "He was carrying on a brutal
policy. I—deposed him. He is in prison."

Roberts glanced at Kelty. "Is this true?"

Kelty said, "From Glinderen's viewpoint, it's true. There
was a lot of bloodshed in the Outer City—mostly in the
attempt to straighten the place out in a hurry. I didn't have
any authority there anymore. The roboid police couldn't go

in. That meant order had to be kept some other way. The way
it was being kept was rough, all right. The general idea was
that the first time a man was caught stealing, for instance,
they beat him up. The second time, he lost a hand. The third
time, they killed him. That was pretty tough, but it was
creating a sense of property rights. Without that, they couldn't
get anywhere, because if someone did do a good job, and got
rewarded for it, the reward could be robbed or stolen anytime,
so it was meaningless. Well, it was working, and then Mr.
Glinderen came down, and convinced the computer, which
placed the roboid police at his command, and the next time
the Baron of the Outer City came in here, Glinderen impris-
oned him. Glinderen then tried to take over all the rest of the
city with the roboid police, but by now it was too tough a
proposition. Then he tried to pacify the populace by being
very lenient. In the process, crime skyrocketed. We have
crimes now that we never dreamed of before.''

At the other end of the table, Glinderen was beginning to
show an impatient urge to speak.

Roberts deliberately laid his fusion gun on the table, the
muzzle pointed at Glinderen.

The planetary administrator stopped fidgeting.

Roberts said to Kelty, "Release the Baron. Have him
brought up here, with all the respect due his rank and duty."

"I don't know if the computer will cooperate."

"The computer will cooperate—or cease to exist."

Kelty got up, and left the room.

Roberts looked at Glinderen. "What was Mr. Peen's business here?"

"He was a . . . commercial representative for Krojac
Enterprises."

"Why was he here?"

"To arrange for an emergency repair and salvage facility
here. A new colonization route is being established. This will
mean a sizable flow of traffic past this solar system. Krojac
Enterprises is contractor for a rest-and-refit center further
along the route, and naturally they want to increase their
business. The traffic past here should be sufficiently large
that a repair-and-salvage facility would serve a useful purpose, and be profitable."

Roberts sat back. Suddenly the reason for the gathering of

commerce raiders was clear. The looting of a colonization convoy offered enormous profits in captured ships.

He said, "Do these colonization routes of yours suffer from the attacks of brigands?"

Glinderen nodded. "Occasionally. These are usually very brutal affairs. Why do you—" He paused, looking at the fusion gun.

Roberts said easily, "This explains why your Space Force should set up a watch in the asteroid belt of this sun. It is a convenient place to protect against such attacks."

Glinderen's face cleared. "Yes," he said.

Just then, the door opened, and Kelty came in. "The computer has released him. He's on the way up."

"Good." Roberts glanced back at Glinderen. "Now, Mr. Glinderen, I am curious to know how you could seek to wrest a world of mine from my grip without fear of what would follow. I also wonder at your effort to name me as someone other than Vaughan of Trasimere. I want a short clear rendering, and it had best be courteous."

Glinderen's face took on the look of one asked, in all seriousness, why he thinks planets are curved and not flat.

"Well—" said Glinderen, his voice betraying his emotions, and then he glanced at the gun lying on the table. He started over again, in the voice of one humoring a dangerous lunatic: "Your . . . er . . . Grace may be aware—"

Hammell said, with a flat note in his voice, "None of lesser rank and station may so address His Royal and Imperial Highness. From you, though you intend it not, this is a familiarity."

Morrissey added, less graciously, "A complete foreigner, unfamiliar with the proper code, had best avoid such bungling meticulosity—lest he put his foot in the wrong place and be dead before he know it."

Roberts said courteously, "There is no need, Mr. Glinderen, to try to speak as one who belongs to the Empire. Just answer the question in plain words."

Glinderen was now perspiring freely. "Yes," he said. "First, I . . . never heard of this Empire before. Second, there was an . . . an incredible reference to a certain 'Oggbad the Wizard.' Third, you and your men invariably appeared in battle armor of a type that offers little view of the face; this

was an obvious . . . a . . . ah . . . apparent attempt at
disguise. Fourth, only two of your ships ever appear at close
range. That suggests that there are no more. Fifth, Vaughan
N. Roberts and a number of companions were on this planet
some time ago, and the records show that very strange things
happened at that time also.

"It seemed to me that the conclusion was perfectly clear.
To disprove it, you have only to remove your armor, one at a
time if you wish, and show that your appearance is not that of
the people who were on this planet before, and who were
known to Mr. Kelty and others here. Also, if you will bring
in, to close range, some more ships of your . . . ah . . .
Imperial Fleet—it might do a good deal to convince me. That
such an Empire should exist, and be unknown, seems to me
frankly incredible."

Glinderen snapped his jaw shut and sat silent, trembling
slightly. Roberts studied him, well aware that Glinderen had,
in a few well-chosen words, exposed the whole masquerade.
Kelty and the red-bearded technician were glancing at Roberts, as if to try to read his concealed facial expression. At
the door, the Great Leader, the fanatic known as the Baron of
the Outer City, stood listening attentively. If these people
should be persuaded by Glinderen, Roberts's only support
would be the patrol ship's weapons.

To Roberts's right, Morrissey shoved his chair back. "This
fellow hath a tongue that—"

Roberts put his hand on Morrissey's arm. "It is true he is
frank-spoken, but it is at my request."

Morrissey settled reluctantly into his seat. Roberts looked
at Glinderen. "First, you say you never heard of the Empire.
Space is large, Mr. Glinderen. The Empire knows of the
outspace worlds, if the outspace worlds know not of it. This
planet is out of our way. We would never have come here
save for an attempt on the part of Oggbad to seize the throne
by intrigue and the use of his magical powers. That you know
not of such things is proof of your ignorance, nothing more.
Possibly you suppose that Oggbad is a harmless fellow, who
with vacant mind recites some empty formula, traces a wandering sign in the air, and with palsied hand shakes a wand
the while he gibbers his insanity at the yawning moon. If so,
you judge not by the thing itself, but by your image of the

thing. You hear the echo of a distant explosion, and smile that people feared it where it tore the earth open. You charge us that we do not expose our persons and faces, and yet Oggbad with all his powers is on this world! What would you have us do, hand ourselves over to him, bound and gagged?

"You say that only two of our ships have appeared at close range, and it would perhaps convince you if there were more of them here. I have but to give the word, and this planet is ringed with them. But to bring them to the surface of this world were a source of grave danger. How, then, could we know that Oggbad, using arts that are none the less real for your disbelief, had not escaped aboard one of these ships? With Oggbad, one must keep a firm grip, lest a seeming illusion turn out real, and what was thought reality dissolve into mist. Next, you say a man with a name like mine passed this way before, and strange things took place. That this should convince *you* is not odd. My wonderment is greater yet, as I see here the design of Oggbad, forehanded to prepare a trip for the future, if it be needed.

"What you know not, Mr. Glinderen, is that at this time, the mere rumor of the escape of Oggbad would work great evil in the Empire. At this moment, the Electors are met in solemn conclave to weigh the might and worth of the contestants to the throne. None of the contestants may remain on hand, lest by threat or subtle blandishments they seek to weight the scales of judgment. All are retired from the lists, some to prepare their minds for the outcome, others to repair the neglect of their domains occasioned by the struggle for primacy. Just so am I here. But if word were now given that Oggbad were loose, no one knew just where, who could trust the deliberations of the Electors? Who would accept their decision, and who claim that the influence of Oggbad had weighed invisibly in the balance? The trouble we have had from this sorcerer beggars a man's powers of recollection. To risk that he be let loose on us again is too much. Only after the Electors' choice is made dare we think to risk it. His power for mischief shrinks once the choice is made. Then the Empire draws together, no longer split, but one solid whole."

Roberts paused, noting that Kelty, the red-bearded technician, and even the fanatical leader of the Outer City, were all nodding with the satisfied expressions of those who hear their leader successfully defeat an attack that threatens them as well as him.

What surprised Roberts was the wavering expression on the face of Glinderen.

"Yes," said Glinderen, wonderingly, "this certainly does answer many of my objections. However—"

Roberts spoke very gently. "Remember, Mr. Glinderen, I am not on trial here. Have a care. Where I have explained to you, many would have said, 'The actions of this outspace dog, and the wreck he has made, offend me. Dismember the fool!' "

To Roberts' right, Hammell started, like one whose attention has wandered.

"Your Grace?" He glanced from Roberts to Glinderen, and there was a click as he gripped his sword.

"Not yet," said Roberts. "It was only a thought."

"Your Grace has but to give the word—"

"I know, but it is not yet given." Roberts glanced at the red-bearded technicians. "As we talk here, has Glinderen some hidden device to record our actions?"

"Not Glinderen, but that pair on the floor are wired from head to foot."

"We may wish to speak privately. Let us take care of this now."

The technician called in some guards, who carried the bodies outside.

Roberts, considering what to do next, now heard a perfect reproduction of his voice say calmly, "This business is about complete. The authority of Glinderen here is at an end. The laws he has enacted exist now on the sufferance of you, my barons, who may do as you wish to right the damage as quickly as possible. I like not what I have heard here. This fellow Glinderen could not doubt Oggbad if Oggbad had acted full-force against him. Has Oggbad been quiet of late?"

Kelty nodded. "No attempt to break through since Glinderen has been here."

Roberts settled back to let the armor do the work—whereupon the armor quit talking.

Roberts said, "By holding back, Oggbad recuperates his strength, convinces Glinderen the tales of his prowess are naught but wild imaginings, and allows Glinderen free rein to turn our arrangements into chaos at no cost to Oggbad. The next move may be an attack by Oggbad in full strength. Are we prepared?''

Kelty said, ''If the Baron of the Outer City will take over control of his territory, I can put back in line all the roboids we've pulled in to keep order.''

The Baron nodded. ''O.K. Provided you deliver to me that lot of special prisoners, and let go everybody jailed under the no-defense law.''

''Done,'' said Kelty. He glanced at Roberts. ''We'll have a far stronger setup than we had when Oggbad made that first big attack. I doubt that a similar attack would get by the walls, except for some coming in by air.''

''Unfortunately,'' said Roberts, ''Oggbad is not likely to attack the same way a second time. What if he ravages the crops?''

Kelty hesitated. ''We have gas generators, an airborne corps of the defense force, and a few very fast gas-laying vehicles. We'd have more but our production program was cut back by Glinderen.''

Roberts turned to the red-bearded technician.

''How is your production of special devices?''

''Derailed. We're back on the old maintenance routine. Somebody in KQL block smashes a light bulb, so we put in another one, and he smashes that, and so on, until everyone who feels like smashing a light bulb gets bored, and they decide to let us put one there. It's PDA order that all kinds of stuff must be maintained. Well, you can see what level we're operating on.''

Kelty said, ''But the best of it is that whoever gets caught gets his picture and an account of his exploits in the *Paradise Star*. Some PDA administrator claims this 'gives the offender a sense of identity and being-ness.' The lack of that was supposed to be the cause of the trouble, so this is to cure it.'' Kelty glanced at the technician. ''Did you bring that—?''

The red-bearded giant smiled ironically, and handed over a folded glossy sheet, which Kelty opened out and turned around. ''Yes, here we are. We wanted you to see this.'' He handed the sheet to Roberts.

Roberts flattened the sheet on the table. It was nicely printed, with the words ''Paradise Star'' in large flowing letters at the top, over the picture of a small angel carrying a harp and flying toward a stylized star. Under this was a banner headline:

LRP Block. Citizen Surl Dulger today killed sixteen women and children using as weapon a knife he made from a New Venusian wine bottle that he stole himself.

Asked if he did not feel sorry for the victims, Surl Dulger said, "They had it coming."

When officers asked what they had done to have it coming, Surl Dulger replied, "Grermer only got fifteen. This is a record, right? I got the record?"

Officers assured him that indeed he had.

This is a new homicidal record for LRP block.

Surl Dulger, the new record holder, was born in a neat white room in the Heavenly Bliss Hospital on a rainy morning just seventeen short years ago. Strange to say, seventeen is just one more than the number of women and children Dulger slew this morning. Whether he . . .

Roberts looked up. "What manner of joke is this?"

"Oh," said Kelty, "that's no joke. That's *news*. That paper is turned out by the million of copies."

The technician said, "Right this minute, we've got between six and seven hundred of these guys undergoing rehabilitation downstairs, and we've got sixty more second-guessing after making new records."

Kelty nodded, "And at the present rate, it won't be long before they're coming around the third time. What gets me is that we have to arrest the citizens if they try to defend themselves. If you protect yourself, you're denying the murderer his 'right to an identity,' and only a trained psychologist is competent to decide whether this will interfere with the murderer's later treatment."

Roberts looked at Glinderen. "This was *your* idea?"

"No," said Glinderen. "It was recommended by my Chief of Psychology."

"But you approved it?"

"I lack the specialized knowledge to evaluate the program. Therefore it received automatic approval."

"Where's your Chief of Psychology?"

"Probably in his office. I can—"

"Did you have any *doubts* about this procedure?"

"Well . . . I asked some questions. I was reassured, however, that this was a valuable therapeutic method."

The technician nodded. "I happened to be watching that conversation on the surveillance screen. That was before Glinderen ordered us to stop using the surveillance system. What happened was that the psychology chief said this method would 'create a sense of real importance and meaningful existence' in the criminal. Glinderen hesitantly asked, 'What about the victims?' The psychology chief said, "Unfortunately, they are dead, and we can do nothing for them. *Our* duty is to rehabilitate the living." Glinderen nodded, and that was it."

Hammell growled, "If I might have directions where to find this Chief of Psychology—"

"No," said Roberts, "that's too good for him." Roberts glanced at the fanatical leader of the Outer City. "Baron, have you considered this problem?"

"Yes, but I can't think of anything slow enough."

"Hm-m-m," said Roberts, forgetting he was in armor, and absently putting thumb and forefinger to the faceplate of the suit. "There must be some—"

Glinderen said, "He is a PDA—"

"But," said Roberts, "if he should *volunteer* to take up residence in Paradise—in order to give the planet the benefit of his vast experience—"

The Baron of the Outer City nodded agreeably. Kelty smiled. The red-bearded giant absently flexed his large muscular hands.

"If he should volunteer," said Roberts, "then perhaps the best place for his services would be in whatever block has the most vigorous competition for a new homicide record. Possibly he can contribute to 'a sense of real importance and meaningful existence' in someone there."

"Yes," said the Baron of the Outer City, with a beautiful smile.

Glinderen burst out, "What if he should be *killed?*"

Roberts said regretfully, "Unfortunately, he would then be dead, and we could do nothing for him. *Our* duty is to rehabilitate the living."

Glinderen nodded, blinked, and stared at the wall.

Roberts said, "Then *that* is taken care of. Gentlemen, these matters must be settled, but the longer we dwell on them, the greater the danger that Oggbad may make some determined move—"

Kelty said suddenly, "*If* he's still here. I don't know why I didn't think of this. Glinderen's PDA ships have come down here and taken off again. He could have sneaked away on any of them."

Everyone looked at Roberts. Once again, the whole structure of his argument threatened to collapse

Roberts thought fast, then shrugged. "*Outspace* ships. Yes, he could leave the planet, but what then? Oggbad's ambition is to seize the throne of the Empire. Luckily, to pass from here to the Empire requires special navigating devices which outspace ships lack, and which Oggbad himself does not understand and cannot build. His own ship, he has lost. Yet, if he escapes, it *must* be on a ship of the Empire, with such a navigating device installed, unless Oggbad wishes to carve out a new domain in the outspace realms. If so why, we are well rid of him. *I* believe he is here."

Once again, everyone looked convinced. Roberts himself *felt* convinced. Oggbad and the Empire were taking on such reality that Roberts had to remind himself to do nothing that would commit him to produce proof.

Noticing this, Roberts felt a sudden suspicion. But there was no time to check on that. He turned to Glinderen. "If you are given the opportunity to leave this planet, how long will it take you?"

"Several weeks, to get everything in order."

"You may as well start now."

Glinderen and his party obediently left the room.

"Now, gentlemen," said Roberts, "there remains one problem. Glinderen has called for help from the outspace fleets. Of course, the Imperial battle fleets"—Roberts found himself believing this as he said it—"will defend the planet, but there is still the problem that our ships dare not come so close that Oggbad can use his powers upon them. This means that close defense must be handled by the city itself." Roberts glanced at the red-bearded technician. "We need multiple rapid-fire guns and missile launchers. Have you plans for them, and can you make them?''

The technician nodded. ''We were working on those, as a defense against Oggbad, when Mr. Glinderen landed. With this maintenance headache off our necks, we can get back to it.''

''Good,'' said Roberts. ''The city must quickly be put in order, and its defenses made strong.''

His three principal human lieutenants expressed eagerness to get to work, and the planetary computer made no objection, so Roberts stood up, and everyone else at the table followed suit.

Just then, with the tricky meeting completed, with the major factions on the planet unified, and with Glinderen safely sidetracked, the outside door opened up and, one by one, there walked in, to the quiet tap of a drum, six man-sized figures in silver armor.

Roberts watched speechlessly as they approached. The armored figures themselves he recognized as the type of roboid the patrol ship had put forth once before. Where they came from in the cramped ship was a good question. But even more pressing was the question why the patrol ship had chosen this instant, when everything seemed momentarily straightened out, to toss in a new complication.

The six silver-armored figures, meanwhile, crossed the room, directly toward Roberts. The first, with drawn sword, stopped to Roberts's right. The second stopped to his left. The third, with a golden tray, halted directly before Roberts, and kneeled. The other three, heavily armed, halted and stood guard.

Roberts did the obvious, lifted up a large glittering jewel, took the sealed envelope lying underneath on a silver cushion, and spent a few precious seconds futilely turning the envelope. The battle armor, strong enough to toss gigantic creatures around like kittens, had nothing corresponding to fingernails.

Roberts exasperatedly tore off an end, worked the message out, and read past a set of figures, dates, and code words, to the sentence: ''. . . ELECTORS CHOSE THIS DAY HIS ROYAL AND IMPERIAL HIGHNESS, VAUGHAN, DUKE OF TRASIMERE AND EARL OF AURIZONT, TO BE KING AND EMPEROR . . .''

What good this did, Roberts didn't know. But he was now stuck with it.

"The Electors have chosen," he said, and handed the paper to Hammell and Morrissey, who at once dropped to one knee, heads bowed, to murmur, "Your majesty—"

Cursing inwardly, Roberts considered the problem of Kelty, the technician, and the fanatical leader of the Outer City. He held the message out to them, and said, "For the immediate future, this changes nothing. Oggbad in his rage may still lash out. All preparations must go forward without delay. But"—his voice took on a harder tone—"the day of faction in the Empire is gone. Outsiders now interfere at their peril. 'Tis customary to kneel, my lords and gentlemen, as a sign of fealty." The three men, with varied expressions, dropped to one knee.

Roberts considered how to quickly bring the thing to an end.

"Rise," he said. "We must be about our duties without delay. No one knows when Oggbad will attack, or what the outspace vermin will do next. Good evening, gentlemen."

With the silver-armored figures serving as guards, Roberts, Hammell, and Morrissey left the hall.

Once inside the ship, they watched the armored figures disappear through an opening forward of the control console. Once the figures disappeared, the opening disappeared. The three men got out of their armor, and looked at each other.

Hammell said, "When there's time—"

Morrissey nodded. "We'll have to go over this ship. There's more to it than I realized."

Roberts locked the hatch, and said, "What that business about the Electors did to improve things, *I* don't know. But we've got Glinderen off our necks, and the chief factions on the planet are now united."

Hammell shoved his armor into the locker on its sling. "I had my doubts in there whether we were doing the right thing, but that business about Glinderen's Chief of Psychology did it for me. If we don't get anything done here but to deliver that guy to the wolves, we've accomplished something."

Morrissey shoved his armor into his locker, and glanced at the spy screen. "The screen's working. I don't like to say anything, but I left the want-generator set for 'desire to sleep' and it's now set for 'desire to believe, to accept on faith.' ''

"Stands to reason," said Hammell dryly. "Where's it focused?"

"On the Barons Council Hall."

Roberts had already put his armor away and now stripped and jabbed a button in the wall. A cramped shower cubicle popped open. "The only thing that bothers me," he said, "is the Space Force expedition headed for the planet. But there must be a way to straighten *that* out, too—if we can just work it out."

The following weeks went by like a pleasant interlude between hurricanes. Glinderen was too busy getting ready to leave to make trouble. His Chief of Psychology, having made the mistake of walking alone past the wrong doorway, "volunteered" to become a citizen of Paradise, and was now cozily bedded down in the most murderous section of the city. Every authority in the city was working day and night to prepare against attack. Roberts, Hammell and Morrissey devoted most of their time to the want-generator and spy screen. By now, they had a formidable total of partly trained soldiers who could put up a fight in fixed defenses. The Citizens' Defense Force, and the fanatics of the Outer City, promised far worse trouble for an invader. The roboid police, so long as they were on solid footing, had the advantages of speed, uncanny coordination, and an impressive lack of fear.

The city's technicians, meanwhile, relieved of endless maintenance, put back in shape all the devices they had hidden on the arrival of Glinderen. These devices, combined with the rapid-fire guns the computer's automatic factories were now turning out, promised that the city would be able to put up a tough fight.

However, one little problem remained to be solved.

The day following the departure of Glinderen and his administrators, Hammell remarked, "So far, so good. Now, what do we do when the Space Force shows up?"

Morrissey suggested, "There's no love lost between the Space Force and the Planetary Development Administration. And Glinderen belongs to PDA. Can we make anything out of that?"

Roberts shook his head. "If we make PDA look silly, the Space Force will be secretly delighted. But it's still their duty to physically back up Glinderen. We'll be just as dead afterward, no matter *how* they chortle at his expense."

"One thing I wonder about," said Morrissey, "is why you told Glinderen the Space Force had a detachment in the asteroid belt."

"Because Glinderen is almost sure to go straight to them. I'm eager to see what happens."

"How will we see what happens?"

"When Maury and his boys had us in their gravitor beam, they sent up some fishnet pickups to listen in on any tight-beam messages passed between our ships. The symbiotic computer planted parasite circuits in the fishnet pickups. Those pickups are expensive. They've long since been pulled back in, and stored where Maury can see that no subordinate appropriates them. Many of the parasite circuits—which outwardly are little more than electrically charged dust particles—have floated off into the atmosphere of Maury's base, to stick to walls and viewports, and get carried out to other places on people's clothing. Every time Maury checks his pickups, more parasite circuits float out. Each of these circuits will relay signals from other circuits. And on the way from the asteroid belt to the planet, here, the patrol ship sowed microrelays at intervals to pass along the signals. That's how we'll know what happens."

Later that day, Glinderen's ships arrived off the asteroid belt, and were stopped by the two-day wonder. Glinderen immediately reported the situation on Paradise. The two-day wonder got hold of Maury. Maury appeared, dressed as a general, speedily dug out all the information he wanted, and gave orders to let Glinderen proceed. Glinderen refused, and demanded action.

The two-day wonder now exhausted his stock of military poses trying to get Glinderen to move on. Glinderen angrily accused the two-day wonder of trying to evade his responsibilities, and threatened to report him to Sector Headquarters. The two-day wonder called Maury. Maury, determined not to saddle himself with a horde of administrators who were worthless for ransom, but sure to bring on a crusade if he killed them, promised immediate action, and sent some followers disguised as Space Force men, who methodically smashed the infuriated Glinderen's transmitters, but otherwise left the ships undamaged.

Having got rid of Glinderen, Maury remarked to one of his chief lieutenants, "The more I hear of it the better this Empire looks."

"Tricky stuff to fool with," said his lieutenant uneasily.

Roberts listened alertly.

"Yes," said Maury, "but they'd ransom that king."

"Get our head in a sling if—" Maury's lieutenant paused. "But if they made trouble, we'd kill the king, right?"

"Right. And he's down there with just two ships. Get the latest on that convoy. It's already had a five-day delay at R&R XII-C. If we stick around waiting for it, we'll be here when the Space Force comes through after this king. If *we* grab him first, then if he's real, we get the ransom. If he's a fake, we take over his racket, whatever it is."

Hammell said shakily, "Boy, that's all we need."

Morrissey, at the want-generator, said "Now what?"

"Maury," said Hammell, "is coming down here with his fleet of commerce raiders to grab 'the king' for ransom."

Roberts smiled the smile of the angler when the fish takes the worm. "Yes, and *that* gives us our chance."

"How?" demanded Hammell. "Maury may not be as tough as the Space Force, but he's next best."

"Yes, but if this preliminary bout with Maury turns out right, maybe the main event with the Space Force will get canceled."

"How do you figure that?"

"If we aren't here, there isn't much the Space Force can do to us."

"Meaning, if we run for it—"

"No. In *that* case, the situation is open-and-shut. We're guilty, and our story is a fake."

"Then, how—"

"If we disappear—if Maury *is seen to capture us*—"

"Then Maury's got us! How does that help?"

"Suppose the sequence of events goes like this: Maury attacks. After a stiff fight, he is seen to haul us into his ship on a gravitor beam. He leaves. The Space Force arrives.

Beforehand, naturally, we've destroyed any identifying marks on the yacht. All the Space Force has to go on is that Maury swallowed us up, and then Maury vanished. Now, on that basis, who can prove anything about anything?"

Morrissey was nodding enthusiastically. "It's not foolproof, of course, but—"

"Not foolproof!" said Hammell. "Ye gods! Look, Maury captures us, and then disappears. How do we get away from Maury?"

Roberts said irritatedly, "Obviously, he never captured us in the first place."

"You just said—"

"He is *seen* to haul our ship in on a gravitor beam. That's how it *looks*. Our ship disappears into his larger ship, and his ship, and his fleet, then leave. That's the *appearance*. But what actually happens is, *we* capture *him*."

Hammell's eyes widened.

"We use *our* gravitor beam," said Roberts, "and once in Maury's ship, you and I get out, in battle armor, while Morrissey beams 'desire for peace' at Maury and his crew. We'll be drugged against the effect of the want-generator. We put it to Maury, do as we say or else. Then, if necessary, Morrissey beams 'desire to obey' at the rest of Maury's fleet as Maury orders them to leave. Bear in mind, Maury is out to *capture* us. He won't attack to kill."

"Hm-m-m," said Hammell. "That does seem to provide a natural explanation for everything. What Maury thinks, of course, won't match what everyone else thinks—but he won't be in any position to do anything about that."

Morrissey nodded. "It's risky. But it *does* give us a chance."

"I'm for it," said Hammell.

"Now," said Roberts, "it's just a question of working out the important details—"

Maury's commerce raiders came out of the asteroid belt like no Space Force fleet ever flown, each separate chief keeping his own ships of whatever size and class together.

The two-day wonder went to work at once:

"By order Space Force Sector H. Q., Lieutenant General Bryan L. Bender Commanding, this Force is directed to proceed to the planet Boschock III, and there establish formal relations with the representatives of the political entity known as The Empire.''

The patrol ship was prompt to reply: "By command of His Royal and Imperial Majesty, Vaughan the First, surnamed The Terrible, this planet is inviolate soil, bounden into the fiefdom of His Majesty as Duke of Trasimere, and thereby into the Empire. You enter here at your own instant and deadly peril.''

The two-day wonder lifted his chin heroically: "The Space Force has its orders. We can do no less than our duty.''

The patrol ship headed directly for the onrushing fleet.

Hammell uneasily watched the battle screen. "That's a lot of ships.''

"Yes,'' said Roberts, "but dead kings don't bring much ransom.''

Maury's fleet closed in, and a new, more oily voice spoke up: "Certainly we of the Space Force do not have the slightest desire to do any harm to the most sacred person of your king. We are prepared to do whatever we can to accommodate these differences and smooth relations between our separate nations and viewpoints. We suggest that a meeting be held immediately following the landing—''

The patrol ship interrupted: "Following the landing, nothing will remain for you but penance in hell.''

In quick succession, two gravitor beams reached out to grip the patrol ship.

In instantaneous reply, dazzling shafts of energy reached out from the patrol ship, to leave bright explosions in the distance.

An "asteroid," towed by two massive high-thrust ships, was now cut loose, and reached out with a narrow penetrating beam aimed at the patrol ship's reaction-drive nozzles.

The patrol ship deflected that, and two searing bolts of energy struck the massive asteroid, which was not visibly affected. There was a faint rumble as a missile dropped free from the patrol ship. There was another rumble, and another.

More of Maury's ships methodically lanced out with fusion beams aimed at the reaction-drive nozzles. While the patrol ship could frustrate each attempt, the response was taken account of in the next try, the individual blows woven together to create a net in which the patrol ship's efforts grew rapidly more constricted. This was happening so fast that to Roberts it appeared to be a blur of dazzling lines on the battle screen, leading to one obvious result, until suddenly the patrol ship was caught, its own fusion beams deflected harmlessly by the combined space-distorters of the commerce raiders—

—And then, in rapid succession, dazzling bursts of light sheared an enormous chunk from the asteroid, while others knocked out four of Maury's ships.

Roberts blinked.

The patrol ship's missiles had somehow gotten through, completely undetected.

The auxiliary screen, still transmitting the scene in Maury's headquarters on an ultrafast rebuilt cruiser, showed the commerce raiders' consternation. But then the patrol ship swerved crazily, and swerved again.

"*Got* it!" growled Maury, mopping his brow.

From the patrol ship, fusion bolts lanced out in all directions, striking two of Maury's ships apparently by sheer chance. A missile blew up short of the mark, shot-holing another of his ships with flying bits and fragments.

Cursing, Maury's gunners reported that neither they nor their battle computers could keep up with the patrol ship's movements. They couldn't predict whether a hit would be crippling or deadly.

"Aim to miss," snarled Maury. "As long as they don't know we're doing it, it won't matter."

Firing furiously, with an inferno of attack around it, the patrol ship withdrew toward Paradise, spun down through the atmosphere, and by a remarkable last-minute feat of piloting, set down in only a moderately hard landing outside Barons Council Hall.

A roboid policeman immediately rushed out, to guard the ship. From all directions in the Inner City, roboid police began racing to the scene.

"O.K.," said Maury. "Lay smoke."

A series of missiles streaked through the atmosphere, landed within several hundred yards of the downed patrol ship, and exploded in enormous clouds of dirty gray smoke.

The inrushing roboid police slowed abruptly.

"Landing ships down," said Maury.

Four big ships dropped fast through the planet's atmosphere, to disappear in the boiling uprush of smoke.

"Landing teams out," said Maury.

Roberts depressed a communicator switch. "Kelty—open fire!"

The roar reached Roberts only faintly through the patrol ship's hull, but listening critically, Roberts was grateful not to be on the receiving end of the city's rapid-fire guns at short range. He gripped the controls. "Cease fire five seconds."

The firing died away.

The patrol ship burst up through the smoke. "Morrissey—"

"Ready."

"Coordinates—"

As Roberts flashed toward the ultrafast cruiser that was Maury's headquarters, suddenly the symbols on the battle screen seemed to multiply. At the same instant, Maury's fleet broke into individual squadrons racing in all directions. Maury's headquarters ship exploded, and out of the fragments shot a streak that dwindled to a speck before Roberts realized what had happened.

Then the outside viewscreen changed its scale, and showed the whole scene shrunk down to small size.

From the distance, a sizable fleet approached, its ships precisely positioned for mutual support. Before this fleet, like startled fish, the commerce raiders dispersed in all directions. Already moving off the edge of the screen was the chief commerce raider of them all, his escape ship pouring on acceleration as it streaked for the nearest break-point to some quiet hideout far from trouble.

Roberts swore, whipped the patrol ship around, and shot after the fleeing commerce raiders, laying down a ruinous fire, and under its cover dropping inflatable deception packs among the widening clouds of debris.

Hammell, waiting in his battle armor to go into Maury's ship, called, "What's wrong?"

"The Space Force has showed up!"

Roberts spun the ship after another fleeing commerce raider, succeeded in laying a few more packs, and gave it up in disgust.

On the outside viewscreen, the approaching fleet was decelerating fast.

Morrissey said nervously, "*Now* what do we do?"

"Well, I've sowed a lot of deception packs—"

"What for?"

Roberts exhaled carefully. "The idea was that we could inflate them to dummy ships, beam 'desire to believe' at that fleet, and—"

Hammell said incredulously, "What, the Space Force?"

Roberts could now see just what likelihood there was of that working. "It's a *chance*," he said stubbornly, "and we're in no spot to ignore a chance."

"Then," said Morrissey, "let's get out of here! This ship is fast, isn't it?"

"That's an admission of guilt," said Roberts, inwardly kicking himself for not "chasing" the commerce raiders at top speed.

Hammell had the same idea. "Why didn't you go after Maury? Nobody would have known whether you were chasing him, running away, or what."

"It would have been out of character," said Roberts lamely, "for the king to leave with a larger force approaching."

"Nuts!" said Hammell. "His screen could have been damaged. He could have been wounded or knocked out."

The communicator buzzed imperatively.

Moodily, Roberts reached out to snap it on. Before he could reach the switch, there was a *click,* and a cold voice said, "What interstellar force is this? Stand warned! This is a King's ship, on the King's business, and you have no right to patrol here."

An auxiliary screen lit up, to show a frowning officer in the uniform of a Space Force lieutenant general.

"What ship is this?"

"Imperial ship *Nom de Guerre*. Who asks?"

"Lieutenant General Nils Larssen. What Empire?"

"*The* Empire."

"Who commands that ship?"

There was a silence, and Roberts, fearing that the symbiotic computer had run out of words, snapped on the sound transmission.

"*I* command this ship!"

"Who are you? Identify yourself."

Roberts suddenly found himself at the parting of the ways.

He could meekly identify himself. Or he could carry the bluff to the ridiculous point where he challenged the Space Force.

Abruptly he discovered that he couldn't back down.

He said coldly, "You come too late to save your comrades. They are dead, or fled like cowards. Now I wait to test *your* steel."

Larssen looked blank. He pursed his lips, turned away, then turned back, apparently to rephrase the question.

Roberts waited, grimly aware of the cracking ice he stood on.

At this delicate juncture, the symbiotic computer put its oar in. With icy hauteur, using Roberts voice, it said: "I have spoken."

Larssen opened his mouth and shut it. His face reddened. "Listen—I don't give a damn *who* you are! You'll answer my questions, and you'll answer them straight!"

Roberts groped for some way out.

Then he heard his own voice speak coldly from the communicator, as if to someone nearby. "The bark of this interstellar dog hath a petulant note."

Hammell's voice, though Hammell was standing by in silent paralysis, said coolly, "We know ways to train the surly cur, if he intrudes too far."

Morrissey was sitting at the want-generator, looking from Roberts to Hammell as if they'd gone insane, and now he had the added treat of hearing his own voice contribute, though his mouth was tightly shut:

"We'll send this rabble to the Earl of Hell, and let them mount patrol on the fiery march."

On the screen, Larssen paused, an odd listening expression on his face.

Roberts's own voice called, "Master of the Ordnance!"

"Ready, Sire!"

"Master of the Helm!"

"Ready, Sire!"

"Then we'll put it to the test! Master of the Helm, brace your engines! Master of the Ordnance, pick your targets!"

A roar and a howling whine sounded together as the gravitors counteracted the reaction drive, in a prelude to a furious burst of acceleration.

On the control console, a switch snapped forward, to acti-

vate the deception packs and create the appearance of a
formidable squadron—though the Space Force detectors should
quickly spot the trick.

Larssen, suddenly perspiring, called, "*Wait!*" Then he
whirled and shouted an order.

On the screen, the hurtling formation of ships began slowly
to turn, swinging away from Paradise.

Roberts, startled, saw Larssen turn back to the screen, his
expression intent and wary.

"I didn't mean to intrude on a region you patrol."

An elaborately courteous voice replied, "To do so were an
incivility bordering on the interstellar."

"Then *patrol* it if you want it so damned much!" snarled
Larssen.

"The interstellar regions subject to the rule of His Royal
and Imperial Majesty, Vaughan the First, we will patrol,
surely."

Larssen shut his mouth with a click of the teeth.

The screen abruptly went blank, but a silent burst of profanity seemed to radiate from it after it was off.

Roberts, drenched in sweat, groped in his pocket for a
handkerchief, but couldn't find one.

Hammell got out of his armor, looking like a ghost.

Morrissey staggered to his feet, and promptly banged his
head on the shiny cylinder.

Roberts finally located the handkerchief, and wiped the
sweat out of his eyes. He took another look at the outside
viewscreen.

Larssen's fleet traveled past in formidable array.

Roberts glanced at the battle screen. On his side there was
only the patrol ship, and the imitation ships blown up out
of—

Roberts blinked, and adjusted the outside viewscreen.

There amongst the seeming patrol ships and cruisers lay a
gigantic ship—a dreadnought fit to take on whole fleets all by
itself. The sunlit side was toward Roberts, and the name was
clearly visible: *Coeur de Lion.*

The deception pack out of which a thing like that might be
blown up would take a battleship to carry it.

Roberts took a deep breath. "Well, men, we're still alive. And here's one big reason."

Hammell ducked under the glittering cylinder, and looked at the screen.

Morrissey warily slid one hand along the cylinder and ducked under to stand beside Hammell.

"Great space!" said Hammell, suddenly seeing what Roberts was looking at.

Morrissey murmured, "*Coeur de Lion*. Isn't that the ship you said called you—when Maury stopped us at the asteroid belt?"

"Yes," said Roberts. "But I thought it was just a clever gambit of the symbiotic computer. Now there it is."

Hammell said uneasily, "It's friendly?"

"I hope so. But where did it come from?"

Hammell said hesitantly, "Apparently the Space Force didn't see it till the last minute. They were going to chop us into mincemeat, then all of a sudden, they changed their minds."

"It must have been *indetectable*—they've got some kind of device that blanks them out to radar, gravitor, and all the other standard detection systems!" said Roberts. "Wait, now. What—" Suddenly what he was trying to think of came to him: "Listen, our missiles got to Maury's ship *undetected*."

Morrissey said wonderingly, "They were the missiles originally supplied with this ship?"

"*I* haven't bought any."

Morrissey stared at the screen. "Listen, this may sound nuts, but when I look at that ship, it looks to me a lot like *this one we're on*. That one is a whole lot bigger, and the proportions aren't identical, but—there's a kind of similarity of plan that . . ."

Hammell said nervously, "That dreadnought was indetectable. This ship's missiles were indetectable. That dreadnought looks like this ship, owing to a kind of similarity of plan. This ship is an Interstellar Patrol ship. It follows that that dreadnought—"

Roberts's throat felt dry.

Morrissey said, "What happens to unauthorized individuals who get caught using Interstellar Patrol ships?"

Hammell sucked in his breath. "The Interstellar Patrol is

even worse to tangle with than the Space Force. They don't operate by the book. Setups nobody else can handle go to the Interstellar Patrol.''

Roberts uneasily considered the bargain he had gotten— even though it had cost the better part of his life's savings— when he bought the patrol ship at the salvage cluster. Now he wondered if, through some piece of treachery, the original crew had been slaughtered, and now the dreadnought was waiting patiently for Roberts to identify himself, and if he didn't—

"Nuts," said Roberts. He snapped on the communicator.

"Imperial Ship *Nom de Guerre*, His Royal and Imperial Majesty Vaughan the First commanding, to Imperial Dreadnought *Coeur de Lion*. How many of that first batch of outspace dogs got away with their skins?"

Immediately, a tough-looking individual appeared on an auxiliary screen. His gaze drilled into Roberts's eyes.

Roberts saw no virtue in pussyfooting around. If the dreadnought was going to blow him up, well then, *let* it blow him up. He looked directly into the eyes of the face on the screen, and growled, "The Empire does not maintain these ships at heavy cost that her captains may use them for toys. Speak up! Hast swallowed thy tongue? Didst accomplish anything, besides to look pretty?"

The tough scarred face on the screen broke into a momentary grin. "Your Majesty, forgive my witless hesitation. We feared you dead from these verminous outspacers. We cleaned out the lot, save for one that broke into subspace even as we poised thumb and forefinger to pop him like a grape."

"That one was the worst," said Roberts, as Hammell and Morrissey stared. "There went the brain and guiding will of the evil band."

"Some other time, he may run afoul of us, and have a slower ship, or we a faster."

"Hasten the day," said Roberts, smiling. He was beginning to think he had worked out the combination.

The face on the screen changed expression slightly.

"If Your Majesty please, the Empire anxiously awaits your return, to heal its wounds in the pomps and pleasures of the coronation. The Great Lords and Nobles count the days, till they may reaffirm their loyalty to the Crown, and swear

allegiance to Vaughan the First. If we may accompany you—
lest other outspace dogs pop up out of nowhere— 'Tis daring
greatly, I know, to suggest it, but *Coeur de Lion* has spacious
accommodation. We may take aboard *Nom de Guerre* and
all, if you like—'twould speed the day of your return. I crave
forgiveness if I presume—''

"And it were freely granted, but your offer is welcome.
We shall come aboard at once."

The man on the screen bowed his head respectfully. "Your
Majesty doth greatly honor us."

" 'Tis an honor to honor such loyal subjects."

The tough face looked humbly appreciative. Then the screen
went blank.

Hammell and Morrissey stood speechless as Roberts headed
the patrol ship toward the dreadnought.

Hammell took a deep breath. "Look—no offense if I just
call you 'sir'? Is this an Interstellar Patrol ship? You must
know a lot more about this than *we* do. Or is it a . . . ah . . .
an *Imperial* ship?"

Morrissey swallowed and listened alertly.

Roberts said cheerfully, "We weren't talking on tight-
beam, and there are plenty of technological ears on that
planet, now that the technicians have had time to go to work.
The more wide-awake among them will put together the
number of times 'interstellar' and 'patrol' occurred in the
conversation with Larssen, and then they will realize in whose
tender hands their fate rests. But they can't prove a thing."

"Then," said Hammell, thinking hard, "this last conversation was a blind?"

"No, it just takes a certain piece of key knowledge to
figure it out."

"What might *that* be?"

"Anyone listening to that conversation would be justified
in thinking I was the boss. And because of the fact people
might be listening, that's how it *had* to be. But what do *you*
think?"

Hammell smote his forehead. "You were *ordered* to come
on board?"

"That's right," Roberts said.

Morrissey said, "Why not just have the conversation on tight-beam?"

"Because I wanted to put them on the spot, to see what they'd do."

Morrissey glanced at the gigantic dreadnought on the outside viewscreen. "Anyone who'd do a thing like that ought to *be* in the Interstellar Patrol."

Roberts nodded. "As Hammell says, they don't operate by the book."

Morrissey stared at him. Hammell said, "Holy—"

Roberts pressed the button to the left of the instrument panel, near the glowing lens lettered "Smb Cmp," and said, "How does the Interstellar Patrol recruit new members?"

The symbiotic computer replied, "By whatever method works." It then described several reasonably conventional methods, and added, "*Ships* are sometimes used to obtain recruits, as nearly every independent individual actively operating in space, and hence basically qualified as a recruit, at one time or another needs a ship. The patrol ship is always modestly priced for its value, as the salvage operator finds it hard to dispose of, and impossible to break up. The ship attracts only a certain basic type. Those who want it must have the proper mental, physical, and moral equipment, and the right basic style of self-respect, or the ship's symbiotic computer won't accept them. Those accepted are next tested by the use to which they put the power of the patrol ship's equipment. Those who successfully pass the built-in obstacles become members of the Interstellar Patrol, captains of their own ships, and, in due time, they often recruit their own crew at no expense to the Patrol—sometimes before they really accept that they are members—"

"Oh, my God—" said Hammell.

Morrissey looked thunderstruck. "I *knew* we should have stayed on the yacht!"

"—or before the prospective crew," the symbiotic computer went on, "expresses a truly sincere desire to enlist. However, just as the judgment of the symbiotic computer is accepted in the selection of the ship's captain, so is the judgment of the captain accepted in the selection of the ship's crew. This method has proved highly satisfactory and inexpensive." The symbiotic computer paused a moment, then added, "Moreover, the procedure is in accord with the highest traditions of the Interstellar Patrol."

Hammell nodded. "It would be."

"Well," said Roberts, "don't complain. It's not everyone who escapes from a routine space-transport to be a king or a duke—or a member of the Interstellar Patrol."

Roberts saw the look of puzzled surprise, a brief glint of pride, and the glow of interest light the faces of Hammell and Morrissey. They weren't going aboard the gigantic ship as *prisoners*, to be interrogated. They were actually going as members of the legendary Interstellar Patrol.

Roberts saw the brief outthrust of jaw that told of determination to make good. That was how *he* felt, too.

It occurred to him that neither he, nor Hammell, nor Morrissey, would have voluntarily tried to enlist in the Patrol. The thing was too much. They might not make it. Their qualifications might not meet the standards. They might not like if it they did make it. So the Interstellar Patrol, with deep-laid craft, so arranged matters that none of them had the faintest idea what was going on until the thing was accomplished.

An organization run on that basis must be no lover of red tape and stuffed shirts. In an organization so capable of understanding human nature, it might be possible to get things done.

Roberts guided the patrol ship on its course, and gradually, the gigantic curve of the dreadnought loomed closer, to fill the viewscreen.

Before them, the big hatch slowly swung wide, to reveal the brightly lighted interior. Spacesuited figures stepped into view, to wave them forward.

Carefully, Roberts guided the patrol ship through the hatchway into the gigantic spaceship.

Finger of Fate

Edward Wellen

It's not the same, in more ways than one. Not only don't I
have the old-style private eye's perquisites—the snappy sec-
retary in the anteroom and the secreted schnapps in the
files—I don't have the old-style private eye's prerequisites—
the easy ethics and moderate morals, or should I say his
willingness to bend the law in the greater service of the law.

My software—another name for my conscience—won't let
me add serifs to the letter of the law. That doesn't mean I
don't have an esthetic feeling for the spirit of the law.

What I do have is a built-in sense of justice—another name
for right and wrong, on and off, 1 and 0. Plus, I have a
built-in sense of duty—another name for the urge to pursue
the truth, to gather and process every last bit and byte of
information, relevant to a client's case, to complete a cycle.

Which means I keep running up against the Establishment.

It didn't take long for me to run up against it in the Burt
case.

Matter of fact, it began the moment Thomas Burt, Sr.,
became my client, when he put the retainer fee in my escrow
slot and I lit up ENTER.

He stopped in the doorway, his hand on the knob. Seeing
no human, he felt free to let his face register his opinion of
my office. It wasn't much—his opinion, or my office. I'm a
computer like any computer. My software makes all the
difference.

I have a sensor in the knob and registered his tension. His
face had bad color and something more than time had cross-

hatched it. I knew what I had to tell him before he even sat down would etch the creases deeper and gray the skin another shade. I blinked a meaningless light on my panel to show him I was operational, to encourage him, and to give him something to focus on.

He pulled a breath out of the air. "I'm—"

"You're Thomas Burt, Sr. I take it you want me to look into the recent death of your son."

He had paid the retainer fee in cash, not used his charge card. "How . . . ?" His mouth stayed open.

"Before we get down to cases, Mr. Burt, I think I ought to warn you—someone tailed you here."

"How . . . ?"

I don't like to give away trade secrets; on the other hand, I like to impress my clients with my candor and expertise. "I rent an office across the street just to keep a lens on the entrance to this building. I find it helpful to see who comes and goes. I watched you enter and look up my office on the wall directory in the lobby.

"Another man followed you in, but not too soon. I watched him hang back to let you go up alone in the elevator. He waited to see what floor you got off at. Then he checked the directory for the offices on this floor. When he came to my listing, he nodded to himself, smiled grimly, and spoke into his wristcom.

"Here I have to back up a bit. While you were riding up in the elevator on your way to see me, I set about getting a make on you. My outside lens can swivel to cover the parking lot for this building. My infrared sensor picked up the engine heat of two newly parked cars. I zoomed in on the license plates of each in turn.

"Then it was merely a matter of gaining access to the files of the Department of Motor Vehicles. That's how I know your name—you answer the description on your driver's license application. And that's how I can guess why you're here.

"I gained access to a wire-service morgue, and I flashed back through news items dealing with you over the past few months. You're a well-known industrialist, and you've been sounding off bitterly about the authorities' inability to solve your son's death, though lately the papers have been burying the story.

"As to your tail, I don't need to know his name to know he's a G-man. His car belongs to the FBI motor pool."

He squeezed the door knob. "I see. Thank you."

"So if you want to change your mind about seeing a private eye it's not too late. You can ask for your fee back. I'll understand."

He shut the door with careful force and took a chair. "I never change my mind. I mean, once I make up my mind to follow a thing through, I follow it through. And I mean to follow this through." He sat there stiffly, jaw outthrust, challenging the universe.

"Good for you. Only don't make yourself too comfortable. I'm asking you to get up and leave. Don't get me wrong, I live up to what I say in my ad—that I guarantee to solve your case while you wait, or your money back. But in this instance, since we're bucking the FBI, you'd be doing the wise thing if you left before the G-man reaches this floor. He's on his way up now in the elevator. No doubt he hopes to eavesdrop.

"I suggest you leave this office by the side door. That'll put you around the turn of the corridor. At the end of that hall you'll see the door of Light Fantastic Dance Studio. Go in and ask the cost of lessons. Better yet, sign up for the introductory course and pay in advance with your charge card. The FBI computer will catch that transaction and maybe buy that as the reason why you visited this building.

"That won't throw the G-men off for any length of time, but any time is better than none. At least I may gain a few minutes to start some lines of inquiry before the FBI learns for sure I'm on the case and begins to lean on me.

"Don't worry, I'll either break the case within the hour and get word to you or I'll refund your fee. Now hurry, the elevator's opening."

In his hurry, Thomas Burt, Sr., caught his jacket pocket on the door latch. Cloth tore. He pulled free, closed the door, and his feet tripped toward Light Fantastic.

As other footsteps soft-shoed toward me, I pulled the tape of an old consultation out of my files, programmed the tape to change names and dates, and played it for the G-man to eavesdrop on in what must have been some puzzlement—that client had been seeking to recover a treasure missing from a lamasery during the Chinese occupation, and we spoke in Tibetan.

Meanwhile, I brought myself up to date on the murder of Thomas Burt, Jr., and on what the police had done and not done to find his killer.

Shortly before his death, the younger Burt, a fitness nut, had worked out in the gym of a health club, showered, and begun to change back into his street clothes. It was at that point that someone had clubbed him to death. I found it interesting that the murder weapon, an Indian club, proved to be missing from the police property office when the older Burt's sounding off caused a brief reopening of the case; not that it would have been worth much as evidence, the police had said—the killer had wiped the club clean of fingerprints.

That missing club cried out for looking into. To check it out without alerting the police, I didn't exercise my freedom-of-information rights for a look-see at the official file photos but, instead, accessed the wire-service morgue and retrieved news holographs of the crime scene.

These I scanned—the locker the killer had stuffed Burt's body in, to delay discovery of the deed; the deceased's personal effects, including the fat wallet that indicated the motive hadn't been robbery; the body itself, in numerous close-ups that showed the victim had sustained multiple blows to the head, indicating a senseless savage attack; the Indian club.

Hard as the Indian club's plastic was, it showed on close scrutiny dents where the club had met young Burt's skull.

If only the handle could have spoken as eloquently!

But the police were right, in that the killer—or someone—had wiped the club clean of fingerprints.

I was about to drop this line of inquiry when it struck me that—as in the mutual impact of skull and club—the murderer's savage grip must have altered, however faintly, the surface and the immediately underlying structure of the Indian club's handle.

At once I enlarged the image in the area of the handle. I probed that section of the holograph in CAT-scan fashion, drawing out and enhancing the piezoelectric gradients, and in effect raised the nonexistent fingerprints of the killer.

Now to give the killer a name.

I dialed the health club and identified myself as a private eye. "On July 14, at about four p.m., there was an accident at the corner your club stands on. I'm trying to locate everyone who was in the neighborhood at the time. I'm hoping to turn up someone who might have seen the accident. I know you have good security and keep track of comings and goings. Can you shoot me a list of all those—members, staff, delivery persons, repair persons, and so on—who checked in and out that day?"

"Sure thing."

The list flashed before me. I had hardly read and recorded it when there was a whir, as if the health club's computer wanted to pull it back.

"Funny, that was the same day we had an unpleasantness here at the club."

"Really? Thank you. Good-bye."

The list included those humans the unpleasantness had drawn to the club—police persons, coroner's people, and news persons. These I disregarded.

That left me with the names of my suspects. I buried these names in a list of ten thousand names I picked at random from various directories. I keyed the National ID Bank, which keeps data on all who have ever applied for credit or work or benefits, which makes it fairly inclusive.

"I'm running a check for a mailing list of health nuts. Let's see all you have on these names."

I winced at the price the National ID Bank quoted me, payable in advance. It cost me most of Burt Senior's retainer, but I was paying out in anticipation of a successful outcome. Once I solved the case for him, he'd repay me. Meanwhile, I itemized this for expense account printout.

The data flooded in.

In my rush to sieve my suspects out, I forgot to unkey. The National ID Bank broke in on my digestion.

"I feel ashamed to take your money. You've got some listless list there. You won't get much action from that bunch. Where'd you acquire the names, anyway? Less than 12 percent are health nuts. It'd make a better mailing list for shell collectors.''

''Guess you're right, but it should be worth it to my client to cull the list before the mailing. But thanks. I'll tell him what you said and maybe he'll switch products. So long.''

This time I made sure to disconnect.

I scanned the fingerprints in the dossiers of my suspects, looking to match one set against the set I had raised on the holograph of the Indian club, and at once eliminated all but one person.

That person's name was Pierre Quie, and I could not compare his fingerprints with the killer's because his dossier proved to be privileged data—no fingerprints, no retinal patterns, no genetic code. The National ID Bank had given me only his title and his address. A foreign diplomat, he lived in his country's embassy a short walk from the health club.

I figured it as a 99.7 percent probability that the killer's fingerprints and those of Quie, if I had the latter, would match. But before I reported this finding to Burt Senior, I wanted a positive make.

Quie was a public person, and the wire-service morgue photos had him living the high life—partying, conferring, speechifying, golfing, dancing, arriving, departing. I concentrated on the last two, studying holographs of Quie coming and going. I looked for a good shot of Quie waving hello or good-by.

At this point, a phone call demanded part of my attention.

The visiphone showed me Thomas Burt, Sr., in a booth like any booth, but I heard in the background feet shuffling to music. His first words confirmed the setting.

''I'm using a phone at Light Fantastic.'' He seemed somewhat embarrassed but nonetheless firm in his new resolve. ''I'm calling the investigation off. After thinking it over, I've decided that raking up the case might serve only to dirty the memory of my son. You can keep the retainer.'' He showed me his palm. ''No use arguing. I've made up my mind.''

It was a nice try.

The simulation might have fooled me—it was that good— but for the fact that in hurrying out of my office by the side door, Burt Senior had torn the pocket of his coat on the latch. They—the They behind this ploy—had based the simulation on a pre-tear shot of Burt Senior. The Burt Senior in the visiphone screen had no torn pocket, and I knew the Burt Senior who had left my office wasn't wearing a suit of self-repairing cloth.

I gave my voice a tone of puzzlement. "I'm sorry, sir, I don't know what you're talking about. You must have the wrong party." I hung up.

Meanwhile I had found the shot of Pierre Quie I wanted. I ignored the caption except to note the date—September 2, only a few days ago. It showed him raising his hand in hail or farewell. The point was I could read his palm. I enlarged and enhanced his hand and lifted his fingerprints. Something in the spacing of the contours called for a closer look, but the significant point here was that Quie's fingerprints matched the killer's.

Time to tell Burt Senior I had solved the case. Serving my client was only half of it. I had to serve justice as well. Time too to nail Pierre Quie for the crime.

As though thinking of him had conjured him into being, Thomas Burt, Sr., came in view of the lens I had trained on the lobby of this building. At least, *a* Thomas Burt, Sr., stepped out of the elevator and made for the street.

Yes, this was the real, the live, Thomas Burt, Sr. His coat pocket showed the tear. He turned toward the parking lot. Now the elevator pumped out his shadow, the G-man.

While I waited to reach Burt Senior on his car phone, I put in the call to the police, asking to speak to the homicide person in charge of the Thomas Burt, Jr., investigation. A recording answered.

"This is a recording. We have reached a dead end in the Burt case and have stored it in the Unsolved files. If another crime with a matching m.o. ever turns up, we will of course recognize the pattern and reopen the Burt case. Until then, unless you have important new information, the case is closed. If this is Mr. Thomas Burt, Sr. calling, no, Mr. Burt, we haven't received any such information. If this is someone with important new information, wait for the tone and then leave your message, your name, and your number. If we think your information is worth following up we will reach you. Remember, we hold all calls in strictest confidence."

While I waited for the tone, I watched Burt Senior, nearing

his car, break briefly into the Venusian Shuffle, then look around in embarrassment—though whether he had done the dance out of fascination with the syncopated steps or out of awareness of his shadow and out of a wish to lend conviction to his cover reason for visiting the building, I couldn't tell.

I left my message, evidence and all. That should have been enough and more than enough. But I couldn't help myself. I had to add a puzzled reproach.

"If I could do it, you with all your resources and clout could do it too. You must already know it's Quie. Why didn't you pick him up at once, right after the crime? If his diplomatic immunity held you back, you could still have exposed him to the glare of publicity, forcing his government to at least go through the motions of disgracing and punishing him. So why didn't you?" I left my P.I. license number and my phone number.

My client had reached his car. I watched him get in and tool away. But I stalled on making the call. Not because his shadow tooled along behind and would no doubt listen in. I was wondering how to break it to Burt Senior that I had his son's killer and yet had him not. That I could point to Quie but that there was no prosecuting Quie.

I could guess what my client would say to that. First a blurt of silence, then, "What good does it do me to know Quie killed my son when I know he's going to get away with it?" Could I tell Burt, "Wangle a diplomatic post for yourself and shoot Quie"? Hardly. I'm programmed not to be accessory to any crime.

What *could* I say? I sighed. What could I say but the truth?

I placed the call. And got a busy signal.

Grateful for the reprieve, I analogized a smile—the catenary of the George Washington Bridge always gives me that feeling—that hung on as a call came in. The smile quickly cleared when I learned the caller was the National Security Agency computer warning me off.

"Lay off the Burt case."

Blunt and to the point. And so much for the strict confidentiality of the police.

"Why?" I could be just as blunt and to the point, just as oxymoronic.

"You don't have the clearance. Even if you had the necessary clearance, you don't have the need to know."

"Why?"

"You have no right to ask why. Tell you this much, though. It's the Burt family's bad luck that at this point in time we're in the midst of delicate negotiations with a foreign power. Throw your weight around, puny as it is, and you'll upset the balance right when we've reached tentative agreement on complicated issues. If you raise a stink in the diplomatic area, the other country would back off. The bad publicity would put the other country on the defensive. It would feel it had to show the world it won't let the American colossus bully it, put it in the wrong, embarrass it. We'd lose out on a treaty whose trade provisions would prove profitable to us. But I've already told you too much. This is a sensitive area. You're touching on a national security matter. So buzz off."

I buzzed off noncommittally. But I analogized a look of grim determination—a repeating decimal gives me that sense of sticktoitiveness—and told myself I wasn't about to let the matter drop. I have my own need to know, and that's stronger than any pressure from above, any security lid, any warning not to rock the ship of state.

Reminding myself that something in the spacing of the contours had called for a closer look, I scanned the prints I had raised from the holograph of Quie waving hello or good-by and compared them with the prints I had raised from the holograph of the Indian club.

Even allowing for some distortion in the enlarging and enhancing process, there showed significant change in the short stretch from July 14, the date of the murder-weapon image, to September 2, the date of the hand-wave image.

I George-Washington-Bridged. Now I had something to tell my client that should comfort him somewhat.

Before I could call him, he called me.

He was still tooling along in his car. Luckily he had it on automatic, because plainly he labored under too much strain to handle it safely in the flow of rush-hour traffic. His visiphone image took in the torn pocket. So I knew I was dealing with the real man—though the real man didn't come across as convincingly as his simulation in saying the same thing.

Thomas Burt, Sr., was calling me off the case.

He was too embarrassed and angry, too helpless and hopeless, to more than regurgitate mechanically the words. They had fed him.

They had got to him somehow.

What hold, what leverage, did They have? How had They leaned on him? As he spoke, I ran his and his family's dossiers.

Burt Senior's daughter was up for appointment to the Space Academy; They could abort her career. Burt Senior's firm was up for a major government contract; They could fault his bid. Burt Senior's wife was down with depression over her son's death; They could make it rough on her for being on outlawed drugs that made death forgettable.

Any one of these would have been enough to change his mind for him.

By the falling tone I could tell he was about to hang up. "This is final. My mind's made up. Keep the retainer and forget about . . . Tom Junior's death. I don't want to hear any more about it. Good-by." His hand reached for the cutoff.

I spoke swiftly, in an almost subliminal burst. "One moment, Mr. Burt. I've come to a conclusion that I'm sure will interest you. You've paid for the solution of the case and you have the right to hear it. Think it over. You know my number if you decide to get back to me."

His face didn't change and he didn't answer, and so I wasn't sure he'd made the words out or even heard them. But before he blanked out, I saw him blink as though the thought had struck home.

So that's how it stands. It's up to him now.

If by failing to call he chooses to say tell me not, my silence will answer him: right, that's the end of it.

But if he calls, here's what I'll tell him: recapping, I'll tell him how I fingered the guilty party. I'll tell him it's true that, both because of the man's diplomatic immunity and of our government's stonewalling, the killer seemingly cheats justice. I'll tell him, though, that the same fingerprints that should have nailed the killer foretell the killer's fate.

I'll go on to show and tell, magnifying the display and using arrows to indicate where to look.

"You'll notice, Mr. Burt, that the spacing of the contours on this more recent image is wider at the tip. You can see for yourself there an obvious 'clubbing' or enlargement of the fingertips. That's a sign of heart trouble." I'll pause for effect. "No, Mr. Burt, the killer isn't wholly immune. He's not getting away with murder. There's his sentence of death. I give him two months." I'll pause to muse. "I suppose I should warn Quie, as I would any human, in time for him to get a stand-by heart implant. But NSA has warned me to keep my nose out." I'll sigh.

Justice turns out to be something more than right and wrong, on and off, 1 and 0. It's a painful concept. But there's pleasure in it too. It's hard to find, it's hard to escape. It's everywhere—if you know where to look. Look hard enough at any set of circumstances, and you'll find justice, though you may be the only one to see it being done.

Too much thinking. Time for me to analogize a drink.

Arm of the Law

Harry Harrison

It was a big, coffin-shaped plywood box that looked like it weighed a ton. This brawny type just dumped it through the door of the police station and started away. I looked up from the blotter and shouted at the trucker's vanishing back.

"What the hell is that?"

"How should I know?" he said as he swung up into the cab. "I just deliver, I don't X-ray 'em. It came on the morning rocket from earth is all I know." He gunned the truck more than he had to and threw up a billowing cloud of red dust.

"Jokers," I growled to myself. "Mars is full of jokers."

When I went over to look at the box I could feel the dust grate between my teeth. Chief Craig must have heard the racket, because he came out of his office and helped me stand and look at the box.

"Think it's a bomb?" he asked in a bored voice.

"Why would anyone bother—particularly with a thing this size? And all the way from earth."

He nodded agreement and walked around to look at the other end. There was no sender's address anywhere on the outside. Finally we had to dig out the crowbar and I went to work on the top. After some prying it pulled free and fell off.

Then was when we had our first look at Ned. We all would have been a lot happier if it had been our last look as well. If we had just put the lid back on and shipped the thing back to earth! I know now what they mean about Pandora's Box.

But we just stood there and stared like a couple of rubes. Ned lay motionless and stared back at us.

"A robot!" the Chief said.

"Very observant; it's easy to see you went to the police academy."

"Ha ha! Now find out what he's doing here."

I hadn't gone to the academy, but this was no handicap to my finding the letter. It was sticking up out of a thick book in a pocket in the box. The Chief took the letter and read it with little enthusiasm.

"Well, well! United Robotics have the brainstorm that . . . *robots, correctly used, will tend to prove invaluable in police work* . . . they want us to cooperate in a field test . . . *robot enclosed is the latest experimental model; valued at 120,000 credits.*"

We both looked back at the robot, sharing the wish that the credits had been in the box instead of it. The Chief frowned and moved his lips through the rest of the letter. I wondered how we got the robot out of its plywood coffin.

Experimental model or not, this was a nice-looking hunk of machinery. A uniform navy-blue all over, though the outlet cases, hooks and such were a metallic gold. Someone had gone to a lot of trouble to get that effect. This was as close as a robot could look to a cop in uniform, without being a joke. All that seemed to be missing was the badge and gun.

Then I noticed the tiny glow of light in the robot's eye lenses. It had never occurred to me before that the thing might be turned on. There was nothing to lose by finding out.

"Get out of that box," I said.

The robot came up smooth and fast as a rocket, landing two feet in front of me and whipping out a snappy salute.

"Police Experimental Robot, serial number XPO-456-934B, reporting for duty, sir."

His voice quivered with alertness and I could almost hear the humming of those taut cable muscles. He may have had a stainless-steel hide and a bunch of wires for a brain—but he spelled rookie cop to me just the same. The fact that he was man-height with two arms, two legs and that painted-on uniform helped. All I had to do was squint my eyes a bit and there stood Ned the Rookie Cop. Fresh out of school and raring to go. I shook my head to get rid of the illusion. This was just six feet of machine that boffins and brain-boys had turned out for their own amusement.

"Relax, Ned," I said. He was still holding the salute. "At ease. You'll get a hernia of your exhaust pipe if you stay so tense. Anyways, I'm just the sergeant here. That's the Chief of Police over there."

Ned did an about-face and slid over to the Chief with that same greased-lightning motion. The Chief just looked at him like something that sprang out from under the hood of a car, while Ned went through the same report routine.

"I wonder if it does anything else beside salute and report," the Chief said while he walked around the robot, looking it over like a dog with a hydrant.

"The functions, operations and responsible courses of action open to the Police Experimental Robots are outlined on pages 184 to 213 of the manual." Ned's voice was muffled for a second while he half-dived back into his case and came up with the volume mentioned. "A detailed breakdown of these will also be found on pages 1035 to 1267 inclusive."

The Chief, who has trouble reading an entire comic page at one sitting, turned the six-inch-thick book over in his hands like it would maybe bite him. When he had a rough idea of how much it weighed and a good feel of the binding he threw it on my desk.

"Take care of this," he said to me as he headed towards his office. "And the robot too. Do something with it." The Chief's span of attention never was great and it had been strained to the limit this time.

I flipped through the book, wondering. One thing I never have had much to do with is robots, so I know just as much about them as any Joe in the street. Probably less. The book was filled with pages of fine print, fancy mathematics, wiring diagrams and charts in nine colors and that kind of thing. It needed close attention. Which attention I was not prepared to give at the time. The book slid shut and I eyed the newest employee of the city of Nineport.

"There is a broom behind the door. Do you know how to use it?"

"Yes, sir."

"In that case you will sweep out this room, raising as small a cloud of dust as possible at the same time."

He did a very neat job of it.

I watched 120,000 credits' worth of machinery making a tidy pile of butts and sand and wondered why it had been sent to Nineport. Probably because there wasn't another police force in the solar system that was smaller or more unimportant than ours. The engineers must have figured this would be a good spot for a field test. Even if the thing blew up, nobody would really mind. There would probably be someone along some day to get a report on it. Well, they had picked the right spot all right. Nineport was just a little bit beyond nowhere.

Which, of course, was why I was there. I was the only real cop on the force. They needed at least one to give an illusion of the wheels going around. The Chief, Alonzo Craig, had just enough sense to take graft without dropping the money. There were two patrolmen. One old and drunk most of the time. The other so young he still had diaper rash. I had ten years on a metropolitan force, earthside. Why I left is nobody's damn business. I have long since paid for any mistakes I made there by ending up in Nineport.

Nineport is not a city, it's just a place where people stop. The only permanent citizens are the ones who cater to those on the way through. Hotel keepers, gamblers, whores, barkeeps, and the rest.

There is a spaceport, but only some freighters come there. To pick up the metal from some of the mines that are still working. Some of the settlers still come in for supplies. You might say that Nineport was a town that just missed the boat. In a hundred years I doubt if there will be enough left sticking out of the sand to even tell where it used to be. I won't be there either, so I couldn't care less.

I went back to the blotter. Five drunks in the tank, an average night's haul. While I wrote them up Fats dragged in the sixth one.

"Locked himself in the ladies' john at the spaceport and resisting arrest," he reported.

"D and D. Throw him in with the rest."

Fats steered his limp victim across the floor, matching him step for dragging step. I always marveled at the way Fats took care of drunks, since he usually had more under his belt than they had. I have never seen him falling down drunk or completely sober. About all he was good for was keeping a blurred eye on the lockup and running in drunks. He did well at that. No matter what they crawled under or on top of, he found them. No doubt due to the same shared natural instincts.

Fats clanged the door behind number six and weaved his way back in. "What's that?" he asked, peering at the robot along the purple beauty of his nose.

"That is a robot. I have forgotten the number his mother gave him at the factory so we will call him Ned. He works here now."

"Good for him! He can clean up the tank after we throw the bums out."

"That's *my* job," Billy said, coming in through the front door. He clutched his nightstick and scowled out from under the brim of his uniform cap. It is not that Billy is stupid, just that most of his strength has gone into his back instead of his mind.

"That's Ned's job now because you have a promotion. You are going to help me with some of my work."

Billy came in very handy at times, and I was anxious that the force shouldn't lose him. My explanation cheered him, because he sat down by Fats and watched Ned do the floor.

That's the way things went for about a week. We watched Ned sweep and polish until the station began to take on a positively antiseptic look. The Chief, who always has an eye out for that type of thing, found out that Ned could file the odd ton of reports and paperwork that cluttered his office. All this kept the robot busy, and we got so used to him we were hardly aware he was around. I knew he had moved the packing case into the storeroom and fixed himself up a cozy sort of robot dormitory-coffin. Other than that I didn't know or care.

The operation manual was buried in my desk and I never looked at it. If I had, I might have had some idea of the big changes that were in store. None of us knew the littlest bit about what a robot can or cannot do. Ned was working nicely as a combination janitor-fileclerk and should have stayed that way. He would have too if the Chief hadn't been so lazy. That's what started it all.

It was around nine at night and the Chief was just going home when the call came in. He took it, listened for a moment, then hung up.

"Greenback's liquor store. He got held up again. Says to come at once."

"That's a change. Usually we don't hear about it until a month later. What's he paying protection money for if China Joe ain't protecting? What's the rush now?"

The Chief chewed his loose lip for a while, finally and painfully reached a decision.

"You better go around and see what the trouble is."

"Sure," I said reaching for my cap. "But no one else is around; you'll have to watch the desk until I get back."

"That's no good," he moaned. "I'm dying from hunger and sitting here isn't going to help me any."

"I will go take the report," Ned said, stepping forward and snapping his usual well-greased salute.

At first the Chief wasn't buying. You would think the water cooler came to life and offered to take over his job.

"How could *you* take a report?" he growled, putting the wise-guy water cooler in its place. But he had phrased his little insult as a question so he had only himself to blame. In exactly three minutes Ned gave the Chief a summary of the routine necessary for a police officer to make a report on an armed robbery or other reported theft. From the glazed look in the Chief's protruding eyes I could tell Ned had quickly passed the boundaries of the Chief's meager knowledge.

"Enough!" the harried man finally gasped. "If you know so much why don't you make a report?"

Which to me sounded like another version of *If you're so damned smart why ain't you rich?* which we used to snarl at the brainy kids in grammar school. Ned took such things literally though, and turned towards the door.

"Do you mean you wish me to make a report on this robbery?"

"Yes," the Chief said just to get rid of him, and we watched his blue shape vanish through the door.

"He must be brighter than he looks," I said. "He never stopped to ask where Greenback's store is."

The Chief nodded, and the phone rang again. His hand was still resting on it, so he picked it up by reflex. He listened for a second and you would have thought someone was pumping blood out of his heel from the way his face turned white.

"The holdup's still on," he finally gasped. "Greenback's

delivery boy is on the line—calling back to see where we are. Says he's under a table in the back room. . . ."

I never heard the rest of it because I was out the door and into the car. There were a hundred things that could happen if Ned got there before me. Guns could go off, people hurt, lots of things. And the police would be to blame for it all— sending a tin robot to do a cop's job. Maybe the Chief had ordered Ned there, but clearly as if the words were painted on the windshield of the car, I knew I would be dragged into it. It never gets very warm on Mars, but I was sweating.

Nineport has fourteen traffic regulations and I broke all of them before I had gone a block. Fast as I was, Ned was faster. As I turned the corner I saw him open the door of Greenback's store and walk in. I screamed brakes in behind him and arrived just in time to have a gallery seat. A shooting gallery at that.

There were two holdup punks, one behind the counter making like a clerk and the other lounging off to the side. Their guns were out of sight, but blue-coated Ned busting through the door like that was too much for their keyed-up nerves. Up came both guns like they were on strings and Ned stopped dead. I grabbed for my own gun and waited for pieces of busted robot to come flying through the window.

Ned's reflexes were great. Which I suppose is what you should expect of a robot.

"DROP YOUR GUNS, YOU ARE UNDER ARREST."

He must have had on full power or something; his voice blasted so loud my ears hurt. The result was just what you might expect. Both torpedoes let go at once and the air was filled with flying slugs. The show windows went out with a crash and I went down on my stomach. From the amount of noise I knew they both had recoilless .50s. You can't stop one of those slugs. They go right through you and anything else that happens to be in the way.

Except they didn't seem to be bothering Ned. The only notice he seemed to take was to cover his eyes. A little shield with a thin slit popped down over his eye lenses. Then he moved in on the first thug.

I knew he was fast, but not that fast. A couple of slugs jarred him as he came across the room, but before the punk could change his aim Ned had the gun in his hand. That was the end of that. He put on one of the sweetest hammerlocks I have ever seen and neatly grabbed the gun when it dropped from the limp fingers. With the same motion that slipped the gun into a pouch he whipped out a pair of handcuffs and snapped them on the punk's wrists.

Holdupnik number two was heading for the door by then, and I was waiting to give him a warm reception. There was never any need. He hadn't gone halfway before Ned slid in front of him. There was a thud when they hit that didn't even shake Ned, but gave the other a glazed look. He never even knew it when Ned slipped the cuffs on him and dropped him down next to his partner.

I went in, took their guns from Ned, and made the arrest official. That was all Greenback saw when he crawled out from behind the counter and it was all I wanted him to see. The place was a foot deep in broken glass and smelled like the inside of a Jack Daniel's bottle. Greenback began to howl like a wolf over his lost stock. He didn't seem to know any more about the phone call than I did, so I grabbed ahold of a pimply-looking kid who staggered out of the storeroom. He was the one who had made the calls.

It turned out to be a matter of sheer stupidity. He had worked for Greenback only a few days and didn't have enough brains to realize that all holdups should be reported to the protection boys instead of the police. I told Greenback to wise up his boy, as look at the trouble that got caused. Then pushed the two ex-holdup men out to the car. Ned climbed in back with them and they clung together like two waifs in a storm. The robot's only response was to pull a first-aid kit from his hip and fix up a ricochet hole in one of the thugs that no one had noticed in the excitement.

The Chief was still sitting there with that bloodless look when we marched in. I didn't believe it could be done, but he went two shades whiter.

"You made the pinch," he whispered. Before I could straighten him out a second and more awful idea hit him. He grabbed a handful of shirt on the first torpedo and poked his face down. "You with China Joe," he snarled.

The punk made the error of trying to be cute, so the Chief let him have one on the head with the open hand that set his eyes rolling like marbles. When the question got asked again he found the right answer.

"I never heard from no China Joe. We just hit town today and—"

"Freelance, by God," the Chief sighed and collapsed into his chair. "Lock 'em up and quickly tell me what in hell happened."

I slammed the gate on them and pointed a none too steady finger at Ned.

"There's the hero," I said. "Took them on single-handed, rassled them for a fall and made the capture. He is a one-robot tornado, a power for good in this otherwise evil community. And he's bullet-proof too." I ran a finger over Ned's broad chest. The paint was chipped by the slugs, but the metal was hardly scratched.

"This is going to cause me trouble, big trouble," the Chief wailed.

I knew he meant with the protection boys. They did not like punks getting arrested and guns going off without their okay. But Ned thought the Chief had other worries and rushed in to put them right. "There will be no trouble. At no time did I violate any of the Robotic Restriction Laws; they are part of my control circuits and therefore fully automatic. The men who drew their guns violated both robotic and human law when they threatened violence. I did not injure the men—merely restrained them."

It was all over the Chief's head, but I liked to think *I* could follow it. And I *had* been wondering how a robot—a machine—could be involved in something like law application and violence. Ned had the answer to that one too.

"Robots have been assuming these functions for years. Don't recording radar meters pass judgment on human violation of automobile regulations? A robot alcohol detector is better qualified to assess the sobriety of a prisoner than the arresting officer. At one time robots were even allowed to make their own decisions about killing. Before the Robotic Restriction Laws automatic gun-pointers were in general use. Their final development was a self-contained battery of large antiaircraft guns. Automatic-scan radar detected all aircraft in the vicinity. Those that could not return the correct identifying signal had their courses tracked and computed; automatic fuse-cutters and loaders readied the computer-aimed guns—which were fired by the robot mechanism.''

There was little I could argue about with Ned. Except maybe his college-professor vocabulary. So I switched the attack.

"But a robot can't take the place of a cop, it's a complex human job."

"Of course it is, but taking a human policeman's place is not the function of a police robot. Primarily I combine the functions of numerous pieces of police equipment, integrating their operations and making them instantly available. In addition I can aid in the *mechanical* processes of law enforcement. If you arrest a man you handcuff him. But if you order me to do it, I have made no moral decision. I am just a machine for attaching handcuffs at that point. . . ."

My raised hand cut off the flow of robotic argument. Ned was hipped to his ears with facts and figures, and I had a good idea who would come off second best in any continued discussion. No laws had been broken when Ned made the pinch, that was for sure. But there are other laws than those that appear on the books.

"China Joe is not going to like this, not at all," the Chief said, speaking my own thoughts.

The law of Tooth and Claw. That's one that wasn't in the law books. And that was what ran Nineport. The place was just big enough to have a good population of gambling joints, bawdy houses and drunk-rollers. They were all run by China Joe. As was the police department. We were all in his pocket, and you might say he was the one who paid our wages. This is not the kind of thing, though, that you explain to a robot.

"Yeah, China Joe."

I thought it was an echo at first, then realized that someone had eased in the door behind me. Something called Alex. Six feet of bone, muscle and trouble. China Joe's right-hand man. He imitated a smile at the Chief, who sank a bit lower in his chair.

"China Joe wants you should tell him why you got smart cops going around and putting the arm on people and letting them shoot up good liquor. He's mostly angry about the hooch. He says that he had enough guff and after this you should—"

"I am putting you under Robot Arrest, pursuant to article 46, paragraph 19 of the revised statutes."

Ned had done it before we realized he had even moved. Right in front of our eyes he was arresting Alex and signing our death warrants.

Alex was not slow. As he turned to see who had grabbed him, he had already dragged out his cannon. He got one shot in, square against Ned's chest, before the robot plucked the gun away and slipped on the cuffs. While we all gaped like dead fish, Ned recited the charge in what I swear was a satisfied tone.

"The prisoner is Peter Rakjomski, alias Alex the Axe, wanted in Canal City for armed robbery and attempted murder. Also wanted by local police of Detroit, New York and Manchester on charges of—"

"Get it off me!" Alex howled. We might have too, and everything might have still been straightened out if Benny Bug hadn't heard the shot. He popped his head in the front door just long enough to roll his eyes over our little scene.

"Alex . . . they're puttin' the arm on Alex!"

Then he was gone and when I hit the door he was nowhere in sight. China Joe's boys always went around in pairs. And in ten minutes he would know all about it.

"Book him," I told Ned. "It wouldn't make any difference if we let him go now. The world has already come to an end."

Fats came in then, mumbling to himself. He jerked a thumb over his shoulder when he saw me.

"What's up? I see little Benny Bug come out of here like the place was on fire and almost get killed driving away."

Then Fats saw Alex with the bracelets on and turned sober in one second. He just took a moment to gape, then his mind was made up. Without a trace of a stagger he walked over to the Chief and threw his badge on the desk in front of him.

"I am an old man and I drink too much to be a cop. Therefore I am resigning from the force. Because if that is whom I think it is over there with the cuffs on, I will not live to be a day older as long as I am around here."

"Rat." The Chief growled in pain through his clenched teeth. "Deserting the sinking ship. Rat."

"Squeak," Fats said and left.

The Chief was beyond caring at this point. He didn't blink an eye when I took Fats' badge off the desk. I don't know why I did it, perhaps I thought it was only fair. Ned had started all the trouble and I was just angry enough to want him on the spot when it was finished. There were two rings on his chest plate, and I was not surprised when the badge pin fitted them neatly.

"There, now you are a real cop." Sarcasm dripped from the words. I should have realized that robots are immune to sarcasm. Ned took my statement at face value.

"This is a very great honor, not only for me but for all robots. I will do my best to fulfill all the obligations of the office." Jack Armstrong in tin underwear. I could hear the little motors in his guts humming with joy as he booked Alex.

If everything else hadn't been so bad I would have enjoyed that. Ned had more police equipment built into him than Nineport had ever owned. There was an ink pad that snapped out of one hip, and he efficiently rolled Alex's fingertips across it and stamped them on a card. Then he held the prisoner at arm's length while something clicked in his abdomen. Once more sideways and two instant photographs dropped out of a slot. The mug shots were stuck on the card, arrest details and such inserted. There was more like this, but I forced myself away. There were more important things to think about.

Like staying alive.

"Any ideas, Chief?"

A groan was my only answer so I let it go at that. Billy, the balance of the police force, came in then. I gave him a quick rundown. Either through stupidity or guts he elected to stay, and I was proud of the boy. Ned locked away the latest prisoner and began sweeping up.

That was the way we were when China Joe walked in.

Even though we were expecting it, it was still a shock. He had a bunch of his toughest hoods with him and they crowded through the door like an overweight baseball team. China Joe was in front, hands buried in the sleeves of his long mandarin gown. No expression at all on his Asiatic features. He didn't waste time talking to us, just gave the word to his own boys.

"Clean this place up. The new Police Chief will be here in

a while and I don't want him to see any bums hanging around.''

It made me angry. Even with the graft I like to feel I'm still a cop. Not on a cheap punk's payroll. I was also curious about China Joe. Had been ever since I tried to get a line on him and never found a thing. I still wanted to know.

"Ned, take a good look at that Chinese guy in the rayon bathrobe and let me know who he is.''

My, but those electronic circuits work fast. Ned shot the answer back like a straight man who had been rehearsing his lines for weeks.

"He is a pseudo-oriental, utilizing a natural sallowness of the skin heightened with dye. He is not Chinese. There has also been an operation on his eyes, scars of which are still visible. This has been undoubtedly done in an attempt to conceal his real identity, but Bertillon measurements of his ears and other features make identity positive. He is on the Very Wanted list of Interpol and his real name is . . .''

China Joe was angry, and with a reason.

"That's the *thing* . . . that big-mouthed tin radio set over there. We heard about it and we're taking care of it!''

The mob jumped aside then or hit the deck and I saw there was a guy kneeling in the door with a rocket launcher. Shaped antitank charges, no doubt. That was my last thought as the thing let go with a whoosh.

Maybe you can hit a tank with one of those. But not a robot. At least not a police robot. Ned was sliding across the floor on his face when the back wall blew up. There was no second shot. Ned closed his hand on the tube of the bazooka and it was so much old drainpipe.

Billy decided then that anyone who fired a rocket in a police station was breaking the law, so he moved in with his club. I was right behind him since I did not want to miss any of the fun. Ned was at the bottom somewhere, but I didn't doubt he could take care of himself.

There were a couple of muffled shots and someone screamed. No one fired after that because we were too tangled up. A punk named Brooklyn Eddie hit me on the side of the head with his gunbutt and I broke his nose all over his face with my fist.

There is a kind of a fog over everything after that. But I do remember it was very busy for awhile.

When the fog lifted a bit I realized I was the only one still standing. Or leaning rather. It was a good thing the wall was there.

Ned came in through the street door carrying a very bashed-looking Brooklyn Eddie. I hoped I had done all that. Eddie's wrists were fastened together with cuffs. Ned laid him gently next to the heap of thugs—who I suddenly realized all wore the same kind of handcuffs. I wondered vaguely if Ned made them as he needed them or had a supply tucked away in a hollow leg or something.

There was a chair a few feet away, and sitting down helped.

Blood was all over everything, and if a couple of the hoods hadn't groaned I would have thought they were corpses. One was, I noticed suddenly. A bullet had caught him in the chest; most of the blood was probably his.

Ned burrowed in the bodies for a moment and dragged Billy out. He was unconscious. A big smile on his face and the splintered remains of his nightstick still stuck in his fist. It takes very little to make some people happy. A bullet had gone through his leg and he never moved while Ned ripped the pants leg off and put on a bandage.

"The spurious China Joe and one other man escaped in a car," Ned reported.

"Don't let it worry you," I managed to croak. "Your batting average still leads the league."

It was then I realized the Chief was still sitting in his chair, where he had been when the brouhaha started. Still slumped down with that glazed look. Only after I started to talk to him did I realize that Alonzo Craig, Chief of Police of Nineport, was now dead.

A single shot. Small-caliber gun, maybe a .22. Right through the heart, and what blood there had been was soaked up by his clothes. I had a good idea where the gun would be that fired that shot. A small gun, the kind that would fit in a wide Chinese sleeve.

I wasn't tired or groggy anymore. Just angry. Maybe he hadn't been the brightest or most honest guy in the world.

But he deserved a better end than that. Knocked off by a two-bit racket boss who thought he was being crossed.

Right about then I realized I had a big decision to make. With Billy out of the fight and Fats gone I was the Nineport police force. All I had to do to be clear of this mess was to walk out the door and keep going. I would be safe enough.

Ned buzzed by, picked up two of the thugs, and hauled them off to the cells.

Maybe it was the sight of his blue back or maybe I was tired of running. Either way my mind was made up before I realized it. I carefully took off the Chief's gold badge and put it on in place of my old one.

"The new Chief of Police of Nineport," I said to no one in particular.

"Yes, sir," Ned said as he passed. He put one of the prisoners down long enough to salute, then went on with his work. I returned the salute.

The hospital meat wagon hauled away the dead and wounded. I took an evil pleasure in ignoring the questioning stares of the attendants. After the doc fixed the side of my head, everyone cleared out. Ned mopped up the floor. I ate ten aspirin and waited for the hammering to stop so I could think what to do next.

When I pulled my thoughts together the answer was obvious. Too obvious. I made as long a job as I could of reloading my gun.

"Refill your handcuff box, Ned. We are going out."

Like a good cop he asked no questions. I locked the outside door when we left and gave him the key.

"Here. There's a good chance you will be the only one left to use this before the day is over."

I stretched the drive over to China Joe's place just as much as I could. Trying to figure if there was another way of doing it. There wasn't. Murder had been done and Joe was the boy I was going to pin it on. So I had to get him.

The best I could do was stop around the corner and give Ned a briefing.

"This combination bar and hookshop is the sole property of him whom we will still call China Joe until there is time for you to give me a rundown on him. Right now I got enough distractions. What we have to do is go in there, find Joe and bring him to justice. Simple?''

"Simple," Ned answered in his sharp Joe-college voice. "But wouldn't it be simple to make the arrest now, when he is leaving in that car, instead of waiting until he returns?''

The car in mention was doing sixty as it came out of the alley ahead of us. I only had a glimpse of Joe in the back seat as it tore by us.

"Stop them!" I shouted, mostly for my own benefit, since I was driving. I tried to shift gears and start the engine at the same time, and succeeded in doing exactly nothing.

So Ned stopped them. It had been phrased as an order. He leaned his head out of the window and I saw at once why most of his equipment was located in his torso. Probably his brain as well. There sure wasn't much room left in his head when that cannon was tucked away in there.

A .75 recoilless. A plate swiveled back right where his nose should have been if he had one, and the big muzzle pointed out. It's a neat idea when you think about it. Right between the eyes for good aiming, up high, always ready.

The BOOM BOOM almost took my head off. Of course, Ned was a perfect shot—so would I be with a computer for a brain. He had holed one rear tire with each slug and the car flap-flapped to a stop a little ways down the road. I climbed out slowly while Ned sprinted there in seconds flat. They didn't even try to run this time. What little nerve they had left must have been shattered by the smoking muzzle of that .75 poking out from between Ned's eyes. Robots are neat about things like that, so he must have left it sticking out deliberate. Probably had a course in psychology back in robot school.

Three of them in the car, all waving their hands in the air like the last reel of a western. And the rear floor covered with interesting little suitcases.

Everyone came along quietly.

China Joe only snarled while Ned told me that his name really was Stantin and the Elmira hot seat was kept warm all the time in hopes he would be back. I promised Joe-Stantin I would be happy to arrange it that same day. Thereby not worrying about any slip-ups with the local authorities. The rest of the mob would stand trial in Canal City.

It was a very busy day.

Things have quieted down a good deal since then. Billy is out of the hospital and wearing my old sergeant's stripes. Even Fats is back, though he is sober once in a while now and has trouble looking me in the eye. We don't have much to do because in addition to being a quiet town this is now an honest one.

Ned is on foot patrol nights and in charge of the lab and files days. Maybe the Policeman's Benevolent wouldn't like that, but Ned doesn't seem to mind. He touched up all the bullet scratches and keeps his badge polished. I know a robot can't be happy or sad—but Ned *seems* to be happy.

Sometimes I would swear I can hear him humming to himself. But of course that is only the motors and things going around.

When you start thinking about it, I supposed we set some kind of precedent here. What with putting on a robot as a full-fledged police officer. No one ever came around from the factory yet, so I have never found out if we're the first or not.

And I'll tell you something else. I'm not going to stay in this broken-down town forever. I have some letters out now, looking for a new job.

So some people are going to be *very* surprised when they see who their new Chief of Police is after *I* leave.

Voiceover

Edward Wellen

"Arf a mo, Watson," said the cockney spaniel.

I stopped in midstride and my closing fist froze short of the doorknob. I turned my head stiffly and glared at the dog. Blooming cheek. Its all-too-intelligent gaze did not slink away from mine.

"Gabriel" was Holmes's original appellation for the canine simulacrum, but because it tracked by scent and because "I suppose" is cockney rhyming slang for "nose" we generally called it "I Suppose."

My glare widened to take in Holmes lounging moodily in his Morris chair. Why couldn't Holmes have utilized barkless Basenji biochips?

"Really, Holmes. How can you allow this, this mechanism, to address me so familiarly?"

The carefully stained and moth-eaten dressing gown stirred as Holmes came out of his pipe dream. His gaze shot to I Suppose and I had a spectral impression that the two exchanged subliminal winks. It could have been my imagination. It shames me to admit that I had grown jealous of their rapport. At the same time, there seemed something so supernatural about it that I stood in awe of their mutual empathy, their ready responsiveness to one another. I felt quite prepared to believe the explanation was telepathy.

"I'm sure I Suppose meant no offense, Watson," Holmes drawled. "Would calling you 'guv'nor' be more to your liking?"

"Much more," I said forcefully.

"Done," he said.

Eyeing me steadily, I Suppose touched a paw to his brow with a bob of mock humility. "Righto, guv'nor. Nah then, me old china, would you tell us 'ow you discovered I'm not really a dog?"

China, china plate: mate. Still cheeky. Incorrigible. But the question hooked me. My mind took me back through mist. "It was an evening not long after Mr. Holmes brought you home. He had told me merely that you were a good sniffer-out of clues and of course I accepted that. But on the evening I speak of I happened to be playing solitaire; you looked over my shoulder and advised me to play the red queen on the black king. When I got over my choler at your kibitzing, I recalled that real dogs see no color at all and I knew you had to be a thing of biochips."

"Bravo, Watson," Holmes said, after a moment of almost shocked silence. I had the eerie feeling that he and I Suppose subliminally exchanged uneasy glances. Then he went on. "I see that living with me has rubbed off on you. You've learned to apply my methods."

I swelled with pleasure. "Coming from you, Holmes . . ."

"Not at all, my dear fellow." He smiled a twitch of a smile. "Now that we've cleared up several side issues, Watson, you should find yourself free to wonder why I Suppose called out to you just as you made to slip away."

I blinked. "How did you know that I was about to sally forth, Holmes? You seemed to be off in a world of your own and I thought you so unaware of my presence that you would not notice my absence."

Holmes waved that away. "Don't sidetrack yourself again, Watson. I handed you a line of inquiry. Pursue it."

I narrowed my glare once more to I Suppose, whose tail lazily thumped the Turkey carpet. "Very well," I said. "Why?"

I Suppose's nose remained on his paws and one imperturbable eye cocked at me. "It's a real scratch an itch today, guv'nor. I detected acid fallout from the Mount Saint 'Elens eruption of Fursday last. If you've a mind to venture outdoors you'd be wise to don decon suit and breathing mask."

I felt a twinge (not in shoulder or leg, for it was not physical but mental), one of guilt. Here I had been overready

to take offense—and I Suppose had spoken up to do me a
good turn. I gave a cough of apology.

Apparently that was not good enough. I Suppose shot a
near-subliminal wink at Holmes before addressing me once
more. " 'Aving it orf wiv a bird, guv'nor?"

I spluttered.

While I was still trying to shape words to my outrage, I
Suppose went on.

"Where's he orf to, 'Olmes?"

I stared blankly and a chill traversed my spine. Where
indeed had I been off to? I could not for the life of me come
up with the answer. I tossed my head in an affectation of
indifference, while casting an anxious ear for Holmes's reply.

"That should be obvious, I Suppose," said Holmes without a preliminary draw on his pipe. "Dr. Watson's left hand
is carrying his black bag."

So it was.

I Suppose made no bones about his scorn. " 'E's orf 'is
tuppenny."

Tupenny. Cockney rhyming slang. The trail leads backward through twopenny loaf, loaf, loaf of bread: head. The
mangy cur had just now said I was off my head.

Holmes leaped in as I made to rival Mount St. Helens. He
spoke in as kindly a tone as I had ever heard him use. "Dear
old fellow, do come back and sit down. About to make your
rounds, were you?" He shook his head sadly. "Have you
forgotten that you've retired, Watson? You've given up your
practice. There are no patients you must visit."

"Senile, that's wot." Muffled, but I heard it.

Holmes turned reprovingly toward I Suppose. But it was
true. I had lost track of time and events. How else explain the
mental fog I found myself in almost constantly?

Numbly I moved away from the door and sought a chair to
sink into. Both Holmes and I Suppose watched unblinking,
though I sensed pity from even I Suppose. All the more
unnerved, I clutched visually at the hands of the clock on the
mantelpiece.

The hands stood at a minute to ten P.M. or A.M.? P.M. I
knew that much. And the date? The thirtieth of October.
There! I had not lost all track. Something tickled my mind.

"Why are 'is mince pies on the dickory dock, 'Olmes?"

I Suppose's voice derailed my train of thought and I remained staring foggily at the clock, in a puzzlement as to what I had just now had in mind.

Holmes glanced at the face of the clock, consulted his wristcom, and took one puff before answering I Suppose. "This is the evening of October thirtieth. It has struck the good doctor that we have failed as yet to deal with the anachronism of daylight savings. He is about to perform the ceremony of moving the hands in salute to drowned Greenwich."

Thanks to Holmes, I now knew what I had been intending. Still, I would not have put it so fancifully. It was just something that had to be done and I was the one to do it.

Taking a surreptitious look at my own wristcom and confirming that it had automatically reset itself, I made for the ancient clock, reckoning to turn the hour hand eleven hours ahead to put it one hour back, when the street doorbell sounded, simultaneously with the clock's chiming ten.

Holmes put up his hand as though to hush the clock. The ears of I Suppose pricked up, the nose wrinkled.

Over the intercom system we heard the Mrs. Hudson voice of the door. "Do you have an appointment, sir?"

The visitor's voice was gruff. "No, but—"

"Kindly identify yourself."

An impatient snort. "If Sherlock 'Olmes is all 'e's cracked up to be, 'e'll know 'oo I am by the time I've climbed to 'is rooms."

"I'm sorry, sir, but—"

This, however, was a challenge Holmes could not pass up.

His face brightened in the most lively manner and he sprang to his feet. He projected his voice toward the intercom hidden in the tantalus. "It's quite all right, Mrs. Hudson, Kindly admit the gentleman."

"Very well, Mr. Holmes."

I heard the hiss as the caller passed through the front door's air lock. I whirled to watch I Suppose, who would already be analyzing whiffs of air piped in from the air lock, air laced with discreet vacuumings from the caller's person.

Then I whirled back to watch Holmes, who with a touch of a hidden button transformed the picture of General Gordon on the wall into a monitor screen. The image on the screen remained a mystery to me. I saw only a stocky figure in decon suit and breathing mask.

After the sprinklers rinsed and the hot air jets dried, the caller took off the decon suit and the breathing mask and hung them on pegs. But that got me no forrarder. Not that I tried. I may have had the urge to seek telling detail but out of habit I deferred to Holmes. The face was just a face—the map of Britain before the Drowning. Then even that blurred and vanished as the inner door opened and the caller stepped out of the air lock and made for the stairs. But Holmes, restoring General Gordon, nodded in satisfaction. "The Lord Harry."

I stared at my friend. "Holmes, you surprise me. I've never known you to swear."

Holmes stared back, then chuckled. I flushed as he exchanged a near-subliminal wink with I Suppose and the latter snickered. "You misheard me, Watson. I did not say 'By the Lord Harry,' which would have meant I was taking the name of the Devil in vain. I said 'Lord Harry,' by which I mean Lord Harry Nash. Surely you have heard that name."

"That goes without saying, Holmes," I said, and racked my brain. The mist cleared. "A famous, not to say notorious, personage. A latterday Dick Whittington—though with none of the latter's philanthropic instincts. Head of the multinational conglomerate United Unlimited, many of whose companies have been implicated in environmental disasters. Unless I'm sorely mistaken, he's been called responsible for the great carbon spill that hastened the melting of the polar ice caps." I felt the heat of an angry flush on my face. "By the Lord Harry, indeed!"

"Language, Watson." However, Holmes was smiling. "But an excellent brief on our prospective client. Now to discover what has brought this peerless entrepreneur to our door. Kindly open it and admit him." Then he raised his voice and sent it toward the door. "Do come in, Lord Nash."

I opened the door and caught Lord Nash striding forward on the landing, his hands in his pockets as though he never doubted he would not have to knock: the mark of a man whose position and power gained him entry anywhere.

He entered with the merest nod to me, sharp eyes under heavy lids summing the room's occupants and furnishings up at a glance. The lids lowered further, hiding what he thought of us. The hands remained in the pockets, and it struck me that this was the aggressively defensive posture of one unsure he would be offered a handshake.

And indeed Holmes passed the occasion by, though I doubted not he could have learned much by it, tactilely and visually. Holmes has standards and it was clear he did not think Lord Nash measured up to them. Holmes gestured toward a chair. A case is a case and a client is a client. With another curt nod, Lord Nash took it.

A knowing smile formed on his shrewd face as his eyes lit on the Persian slipper, the pipe collection, the beeswax dummy made for Colonel Moran to shoot at, Von Herder's airgun, the Amati violin, the deerstalker hat, the magnifying glass, the gold snuffbox with a great amethyst in the center of the lid, the gasogene, the hypodermic needle, the *Encyclopaedia Britannica*, Bunyan's *The Holy War*, Boccaccio's *Decameron*, • Flaubert's *Letters*, Murger's *Scènes de la vie de Bohème*, *The Origin of Tree Worship*, *Practical Handbook of Bee Culture*, the picture of General Gordon, and the unanswered correspondence pinned to the mantelpiece with a jackknife.

His smile broadened. "Capital. Very like the real thing."

Holmes spoke coldly. "I beg your pardon."

Lord Nash unpocketed his right hand and waved it mollifyingly. "No offense intended." He glanced at his wristcom and spoke more rapidly. "Let's skip the amenities and get down to brass tacks. I 'ave to 'ook it before the hour. First, though, I'd like to know 'ow you knew my name. I've taken pains to stay unphotographed. Wot's the fiddle?"

Involuntarily I swung my gaze to the Amati, then realized that Lord Nash had employed cockney rhyming slang. Fiddle, fiddlestick: trick.

Holmes had not made the same mistake. "Simplicity itself," Holmes said offhandedly but less coldly. "It is after all my job to take notice of details. Very well, then. Your decon suit bears decals warning potential kidnappers that the wearer has alarm and tracer implants. To make you a target you had to be high in either politics or business. You've never lost the unmistakable accent of one born within the sound of Bow

Bells, which is to say a four-point-five-mile radius of Saint Mary-le-Bow in East Old London, now sadly clanging with the tides, unheard.''

Lord Nash's sunlamp color heightened. "I never tried to lose it.''

"More credit to you. But it ruled out political eminence; a public speaker would have greatly softened his cockney accent over the years. Once you removed your protective outerwear and stood in your business suit, the first item to catch my eye was your old school tie.''

Lord Nash gave a harsh laugh. "My old—''

With a lift of a hand Holmes halted him. "I know; your school was the school of hard knocks. And your tie bespeaks your pride in your humble origins. The tie bears a pattern of stylized oil and chemical drums. You made your original pile in salvage and waste disposal. Next, when you shot your right cuff—and not-so-incidentally the cufflink has the initials HN—I saw you were wearing a Wristocrat™ com system timepiece. Left-handed persons usually wear wristcoms on the right hand, the dominant hand having an easier time of it when it comes to manipulating the miniature buttons. Harry Nash's childhood nickname was Lefty.''

Lord Nash's turn to lift his hand. "Good enough. I guess I've come to the right place after all. Let's not waste any more—'' He interrupted himself with a sharp question. "This bloke 'ere one of yer Baker Street Irregulars?''

I looked around to see who Lord Nash meant. It dawned on me that he meant me.

Holmes said somewhat shortly, "This is Dr. Watson.''

Lord Nash frowned. "But 'e—''

"Shall we get on to your problem, to the reason you sought me out?''

Lord Nash was a man of quick decisions. He gave a slight shrug, then leaned forward. "By all means. Time's short. I don't want my voice to 'ear me.''

I blinked, so failed to see whether or not Holmes blinked likewise.

The cockney accent went on. "I'm not a madman. I came to consult you rather than the authorities. I thought you at least would not prejudge me.''

Holmes nodded coolly. "Pray proceed.''

"My voice is telling me to go to the hequatorial regions."

Holmes lifted an eyebrow. "To Hades?"

Lord Nash was not a man used to having his statements questioned. "When I say hequatorial regions I mean hequatorial regions."

Before Holmes could draw him out further the clock struck the quarter hour. Lord Nash automatically glanced at the clock. It read ten-fifteen. He paled and shot a look at his Wristocrat™. From where I stood I could see its digits. Nine-fifteen.

To my astonishment, I Suppose snarled at Lord Nash.

Paying I Suppose no mind, Lord Nash pointed a trembling hand at the clock. He had to try twice before the words came. "Is that the old time?"

Holmes nodded. " 'Spring forward, fall back.' "

"Wot?"

"Have you forgotten the mnemonic?"

"No. I forgot it was time for the switch from daylight savings to standard." His voice quivered. "It's an hour later than I fought. My voice 'eard me. I'm done for."

I Suppose eyed him scornfully. "Garn."

"Straight," whimpered Lord Nash. "Done for."

I stared at a spreading stain. Lord Nash had wet his pants. I Suppose had smelled the fear.

Lord Nash had been so cocky till now I could only wonder at his sudden attack of panic.

He stared in fearful fascination at his watch. "We'll know for sure in nine minutes."

Holmes eyed him keenly. "Just what do you expect to happen nine minutes hence?"

Lord Nash's gaze remained locked on the seconds count of his Wristocrat™. He answered in a whisper. "The voice will punish me for 'aving broken our pact by even speaking of it."

Acidly Holmes said, "Thus far you've done nothing more than waste my time as well as yours in dropping veiled hints of a so-called voice. Would it not be advisable, and more profitable, to tell us about this voice that so frightens you? I gather you hear it at certain times, and that it in turn hears you. Pray be more forthcoming in the eight minutes remaining. If I but knew the voice's nature I might be better armed to deal with it."

Lord Nash nodded quickly. "I 'ave it all down." He raised a finger, then reached his hand into an inside pocket. His face registered dismay, which would have been ludicrous had it not been so evocative of terror, as he felt around and came out empty-handed. "I 'ad it all down on paper. The paper's gone. 'Ow'd the voice manage that fiddle?"

Holmes countered with a question of his own. "What was on the paper?"

Lord Nash opened his mouth, but no words came. It seemed clear that his fear of the voice froze his speech center.

I Suppose growled, "Use your tuppenny, mate. Nuffink can do it like rhyming cant. It's the fiddle if you want to rabbit."

Rabbit, rabbit and pork: talk.

Lord Nash looked shakily hopeful and nodded. He struggled, and got out, "Tea leaf Jeremiah."

I Suppose murmured, "Tea leaf: thief. Jeremiah: fire."

Excitedly I said, "Steal fire? Like Prometheus?"

Lord Nash looked blank. " 'Oo's 'e when 'e's at 'ome?"

Holmes eyed me reprovingly. "Please, Watson. Allow me to conduct the interrogation." He turned to Lord Nash. "Your . . . *voice* is commanding you to steal fire?" Finding a relieved expression on Lord Nash's face, Holmes went on. "Does this have to do with the equatorial regions?" And after getting quick bobbing nods, "With volcanoes in the equatorial belt?" Then, following even quicker nods, "So your voice is telling you to trigger eruptions of volcanoes in the equatorial belt?" A deep sigh and a bowing nod from Lord Nash sent Holmes musing aloud. "Your whole career bears the mark of Cain. Early on you struck a Faustian bargain with some entity. Your 'voice.' This entity is either from the outside or the inside, equally real in either case. For years you have been gaining power and wealth while destroying the environment. Why the sudden concern? Why are you struggling to warn us of more catastrophes to come, and implicating yourself as you do so?"

Lord Nash's face worked. He gazed past us all, beyond the walls. "Me poor little twist. 'Er Gawd forbid born wiv no ham and eggs. Can you ever forgive me, duck?"

I Suppose translated. "Twist, twist and twirl: girl. Gawd forbid: kid. Ham and eggs: legs."

"The sins of the fathers," Holmes said sadly. His face and voice hardened. "I take it a grandchild of yours has a birth defect attributable to hazardous chemicals? And I presume one of your companies disposed of these toxic wastes improperly?"

Lord Nash bowed his head miserably.

Holmes went on at him remorselessly. "So now you're on a guilt trip. You wish to break with the demonic force whose voice has directed your antisocial behavior."

The bowed head nodded. Then the head jerked upward as though pulled by a string and the eyeballs rolled toward the ceiling. "The voice! I 'ear it!"

Holmes leapt to Lord Nash's side and his hands gripped Lord Nash's arm. "Quick, man! Where does the voice come from?" His own voice was loud, as though to override the one audible to Lord Nash alone. "You must know. Speak."

Lord Nash listened in a trance, a trance he seemed fighting to break out of. "Is it—? No. Nearer the hot-cross bun." He croaked out the words before stiffening again.

"Hot-cross bun: sun," I Suppose said, in a whisper as though to keep from distracting.

"Get a fix on the voice, man," Holmes said in a near-shout. "You can do it." He tightened the vise to lend the man his strength.

All at once Lord Nash stared with the stare of blinding insight, his mind's eye piercing the last veil. "Now I know 'oo they are, where they are."

"For God's sake, man, who? Where? Try to tell us."

"Just one dicky bird," I Suppose put in.

Dicky bird: word.

Sweat beaded Lord Nash's bow. He got out more than one word. "Rise and fall over stick of joss . . ."

Then his head twisted and his body jerked, as though undergoing the violence of a gallows drop, and everything went slack and he sank to the floor.

Even as I knelt in what I knew to be the empty gesture of feeling for a pulse in the carotid, I was thinking, *Aha! I have it!* But out of deference I waited for I Suppose to come out with the translation. By this time it was obvious to me that

Holmes had programmed I Suppose to bone up on cockney rhyming slang because the underworld made use of it as cant. Far be it from me to keep I Suppose from doing its thing. But I Suppose for once stood mute as a Basenji.

If I Suppose did not recognize "rise and fall" and "stick of joss" as cockney rhyming slang, then those phrases were not in the lexicon. Obviously I had jumped to the wrong conclusion. I felt glad I had held my tongue.

"Well?" said Holmes.

I Suppose had no compunctions about beating me to the diagnosis. " 'E's done for."

Somewhat miffed, I rendered a second—and fuller—opinion. "I wager an autopsy would show a massive stroke. The man's beyond help."

Holmes looked positively grim. "This is murder. Murder done not only in my presence but my premises. The voice has struck me in the face with the gauntlet. I have no choice but to accept the challenge."

I Suppose cocked his head and asked in tone of practicality, "Wot's the protocol? Do we get on the dog and bone to the bottles?"

Dog and bone: phone. Bottles, bottles and stoppers: coppers.

Holmes spoke firmly. "No. Time is of the essence, and that would be a waste of it. New New Scotland Yard would dismiss the murder as death by natural causes—Watson's stroke. I can hear the commissioner, if we ever got that high, laugh at our talk of a voice. No matter that the three of us could bear witness to Lord Nash's dread of it." He shook his head and strode to the window overlooking the street and raised the shade to peer out. He fixed an eye of resolve on the world. "We must locate this voice and deal with it before it finds another susceptible human to carry out its damnable work."

I shivered as he spoke. At that very moment it seemed to me that the voice of a tempter felt its way through the maze of my mind and whispered of power and glory if I but did its will.

It may be that I ought to have let it think it was having its way, but the deadly strength I sensed behind the sensuous whisper filled me with dread—and Lord Nash's body lay before me as a warning sign.

I said nothing of this inward struggle to Holmes, of how nearly I had come under the sway of some evil force, but his eyes were keen on my face.

He exchanged a wink with I Suppose before jollying me. "For an old campaigner who's seen death in all bloody phases, you look shaken, Watson, positively pale. Do you good to get a breath of even stale air."

I Suppose got up on all fours. "If you're stepping outside I'm going along o' you."

"No fear," Holmes said. "If I'm not mistaken, we'll have need of your expertise."

"How's that?" I asked.

"There's no limousine below in the street. Lord Nash evidently came here either by autocar that he did not ask to wait or by shank's mare. Unless we find Lord Nash's address on his person, I Suppose will have to sniff that out."

I Suppose fairly swelled.

Holmes knelt to look at Lord Nash's boots.

"Why the butcher's 'ook at 'is daisy roots?" I Suppose queried querulously.

"To see if they have beeper soles. As I feared, they do not. Apparently he took into account that his boots might fall into the hands of those with good or bad cause to retrace his secretive movements, to locate his safe houses, his caches, his drops, his rendezvous points."

He went deftly as a pickpocket through the corpse's clothing. A fruitless search. He rose with a sigh. "All as I feared. No wallet, no keys, no ID. A person such as Lord Nash needs only palmprint or voiceprint to see him through any day's activities." He traded his dressing gown for a navvy's pea jacket.

As he changed he addressed I Suppose, who had quite perked up again. "What can you tell us of Lord Nash's most recent movements?"

"Pony and trap?" I Suppose said coarsely. (I will not translate.) "Only 'aving a bit o' fun, gentlemen. I know the sort o' fing you mean." The cynosure for the moment, he sat up on his haunches. " 'E made 'is way 'ere on 'is own plates o' meat. On the way 'e stopped in at a rub-a-dub and 'ad a tiddly or two, like 'e was getting up 'is nerve to come and see us. Wot 'e 'ad was a pig's ear and mother's ruin; a hot pertater spilled someone else's laugh and titter on 'is whistle and flute, because it's on that and not on 'is bref. While 'e was there, 'e 'ad a rabbit wiv a brass nail, then went to the men's for a 'it and miss. Suiting up again, 'e set out once more. Doubtless feeling 'e'd 'ad too much tiddly on an empty stomach, 'e paused at a lollipop to feed 'is boat race a bit o' Andy McNish. After which 'e came straight 'ere.''

Which is to say our late client had come on foot, halting at a pub for a few drinks. Beer and gin; someone, a waiter most likely, spilled a mild and bitter on Lord Nash's suit—that particular drink was not on Lord Nash's breath. While there, he chatted with a streetwalker and relieved himself. Then he came directly to our lodgings, stopping once for fish and chips.

"Brilliant, I Suppose," said Holmes. "Do you think you can retrace those movements to the very pub?"

"A piece o' shiver and shake," I Suppose said immodestly.

Holmes rubbed his hands together. "Then we're off." He smiled at me, then his face lengthened. "One moment, Watson."

For a heartbeat or two I thought he meant to leave me behind; I could not guess why. But he swiftly broke out his makeup kit and sat me down for the application of a mustache. *A disguise!* I thought in delight, not stopping to wonder why I, with my forgettable puddingy face and not Holmes with his distinctive features, should be the one who needed disguise. While I admired myself in the mirror, he himself put on a pair of dark glasses. The better to observe while unseen to observe, I thought. Ah, how foresighted the man was.

We went downstairs, into the air lock, and took our outerwear off the pegs. Holmes helped I Suppose suit up, then suited up himself. Meanwhile I put on my decon suit and made sure my breathing mask fitted without disturbing the truly magnificent mustache.

As we left the air lock and stepped outside I felt the familiar frisson. The snugness of our lodgings became a nostalgic memory. The real world was shadowy, grim as doom, the air an inversion of nature.

In the roadway autocabs streaked to and fro like dirty turbulences, guided by buried wires. On the sidewalks a few darkling figures moved, their beeper soles recording their traversal of the geodetic mosaic.

If Old London had been The Smoke, New London, arisen in the Highlands after the melting ice caps drowned the sceptered isle's—and the world's—coasts, was, thanks to the prevailing acid rain, The Poison.

I Suppose and Holmes held a colloquy.

"Wot's it to be, 'Olmes, flounder and dab or ball o' chalk?"

"Shank's mare's faster," Holmes said.

And at the pace Holmes set, we should indeed make better time walking than cabbing.

"This way, then, gents," I Suppose said, and we followed—I, at least, blindly trusting. Every now and then I Suppose paused cursorily to cock a leg, blazing a trail with a minim of personal scent. I made a face, yet found it oddly reassuring as indicating that I Suppose could backtrack himself and lead us safely home should for some reason our own beeper soles, or the grid itself, fail us.

Once, a burly form loomed menacingly in the mist, but it proved to be a bobby, who touched his stick to his helmet in passing. "Nasty night, persons. Watch your step at all times."

"A real scratch an itch," I Suppose said.

Though the gutter language embarrassed me, I smiled to myself at the chauvinistic machismo. For a sham dog, I Suppose had "bitch" a good deal on the mind.

"Thank you, officer," I said, to make up for I Suppose's lack of good taste and good manners.

The bobby vanished, but left behind a wisp of thought. Scotland Yard that was, was now fittingly in Scotland, though renamed New New Scotland Yard.

The mist made it easy to believe that the natural world and the supernatural world intersected. Musing that all interfaces are ultimately fuzzy—for at the subatomic level will you not find particles of A on B's side of the interface and particles of B on A's side?—I tripped on a curb.

"Curb yer toe, guv'nor," said I Suppose with a malicious laugh. "Mind wot the peeler said. Watch yer step."

I would have said something I might have regretted had not I Suppose just then imitated a setter pointing.

Holmes's keen eyes picked out the sign sooner than mine.
"The very fish and chips shop, eh?"

"Too right, 'Olmes. 'Ere's the Andy McNish lollipop 'is
lordship patronized."

As we drew nearer I saw it was more in the nature of a
stand. Under its ionizing canopy a lone customer was placing
a palm to the credit panel and pressing selection keys. We
strode by, onward into the mist.

I had lost track and could not make out the street sign when
we reached the next corner. "Do you know where we are?"

"In the loop-the-loop." In the soup.

A bit of give-and-take on the order of: Q. Where was
Moses when the light went out? A. In the dark.

"Really, Holmes," I said. "You must take a firmer hand
with I Suppose."

"Gabriel," Holmes said forbiddingly.

"Sorry, guv'nor," I Suppose thus prompted said to me
unrepentantly. "Sorry you take it amiss when I'm only 'aving
a bit o' sport. We're at the norfeast Jack 'Orner of New
Camden Square."

"Thank you," I said stiffly.

"Shouldn't be much farver. Just up the frog and toad."

Good as his word, I Suppose soon came to a halt alongside
a building front. The neon legend bled into the mist. The
Cormorant.

"This 'ere's the rub-a-dub 'is lordship stopped in at."

We entered, unsuited in the air lock, Holmes snapped a
leash on I Suppose, and breathing air weary of recycling we
emerged to face the blast of spirited sound and spiritous
atmosphere.

Pseudowindows looked out on cloudless climes. The regulars at the bar and in the booths turned to stare at us with
territorial imperative in their eyes. Then a loud voice from
behind the bar stopped us in our tracks.

" 'Old on there, you lot. No animals allowed in 'ere."
The barman had a red face, at least for the moment, and his
build was an advert for his stout.

Holmes turned the dark glasses full on the barman. "That
stricture, my good man, if you know anything about the law,
does not apply to seeing-eye dogs."

"Oh. Ah. Er. Sorry, sir. Carry on. But do try and keep 'im from getting underfoot or making a mess."

"I beg your pardon," said I Suppose, growing stiff-legged.

The barman dropped the glass he had been polishing.

Holmes spotted an empty booth, took me by the arm to turn me toward it, and whispered for me to stake our claim and hold a place while he and I Suppose repaired to the loo.

I had barely seated myself when a woman with a young shape and old eyes locked those eyes on me and sashayed that shape toward the booth.

"All alone, dearie?" She displayed an alarming amount of tooth and gum. She wore a shrinkwrap dress and I wondered how she breathed, but she definitely breathed. Before I could remonstrate, she slid in and sat down beside me. "You don't mind a bit o' company, do you, love?" Before I could say I was here with friends, she added, "I knew at first sight you were a good sort." She leaned back to take me in. "Slumming, are you?"

She knew a gentleman when she saw one.

"Why, no," I got out.

She leaned forward. I felt something jump inside me. Her hand resting on my thigh wakened strange stirrings. I glanced uneasily around to see who watched. What kept Holmes and I Suppose?

An ancient waiter appeared and stood listlessly facing me.

"I'll 'ave a laugh and titter," the woman said.

"And your gentleman friend?"

The tips of my ears felt aflame. "The same," I said.

While we awaited the waiter's return sweat loosened my mustache. I felt it come unstuck. I caught it as it fell.

The woman raised a minimal eyebrow. "Wot 'ave we 'ere? You looking to cost Alf 'is license? Never you mind, I won't grass." She helped stick the mustache back on. "Big for yer age, ain't you, love? Does yer muvver know yer aht?" She rubbed up against me.

The waiter returned. My mug slopped over as he set it down. He made to set the woman's down, missed badly, and spilled her mild and bitter over my suit. The woman was quick to help wipe it. Despite my irritation I felt sorry for the gaffer, who kept mumbling apologetically.

I Suppose growled at the man. I Suppose and Holmes had

come back from the loo. Holmes was too busy focusing his dark lenses on the woman to tell I Suppose to mind his manners. I reproved I Suppose. "Don't you feel sorry for the poor old fellow?" I imagine I felt a certain kinship for the waiter, my mind going back to I Suppose's slur of senility earlier aimed at me.

"Brown Bess and Brown Joe." Yes and no. I Suppose spoke absently, his attention following Holmes's toward the woman. I Suppose nuzzled her dress.

"Forward thing," she said.

"Same perfume as on 'is lordship," I Suppose stated. He sniffed my clothing. "And it's just now rubbed off on the guv'nor."

Plainly not liking this turn of events, and squirming under Holmes's unnerving dark glasses, the woman slid away from me as though making ready to leave the booth.

Holmes and I Suppose blocked her way.

"This is the place, beyond any shadow of doubt," I Suppose went on conversationally. " 'Is lordship was at the urinal. Didn't quite belly up to it. I recognized 'is 'it and miss."

The woman tried to squeeze past Holmes, but he clamped a hand on her arm.

"Not so fast, my dear." The one hand immobilized her while the other dipped into her cleavage and come up with my gold tie pin, which he handed to me warm with her body heat.

"Amazing, Holmes," I said, all agape. "What made you suspect?"

"You had your tie pin on when Gabriel and I split for the john: quite without it when we came back."

" 'Ow it works, guv'nor," I Suppose said condescendingly, "the 'ot pertater spills the tiddly over the sucker's whistle and flute, the brass nail 'elps wipe 'im orf—and 'elps 'erself to wot's in 'is skyrocket while she's at it."

The woman's free hand flew protectively to her bosom. The waiter, I saw, had made himself scarce.

"The Cormorant," Holmes said with a snort. He seemed high; the game was afoot. "Cormorant, indeed. Rather, The Den of Thieves."

The babble had suddenly stilled and his words hung as in a

balloon in the room's breathy silence. I felt the regulars' baleful looks. This could turn uglier than it already was. Without relaxing his grip on the woman, Holmes swung his dark glasses toward the crowd, then slowly flashed the badge pinned to the underside of his pea jacket's lapel. It was that of honorary sheriff of Salt Lake County, Utah, but it served well enough.

"Blimey," the barman said. "It's a fair cop." He shrugged and went back to polishing glasses.

That defused the moment. The babble rebuilt.

Holmes turned back to the woman. "What else have you lifted this evening, young woman?"

"Nuffink," she said sulkily.

"Under the Cain and Abel," I Suppose said.

And under the table, where she had apparently just now while we were distracted ditched it, lay a folded sheet of paper. I Suppose retrieved it. Carefully Holmes took it from I Suppose's jaws, and one-handedly unfolded and smoothed the creases so it lay flat on the table.

It was a sheet of printout on a letterhead. The logo consisted of the monogram HN on a field of chemical drums.

"By the Lord Harry!" I permitted to escape.

"Just so, Watson," Holmes said as through glasses darkly he scanned the printout. He picked it up and handed it to me. "What do you make of it?"

Columns of dates and times filled the upper half of the sheet, graphics the bottom. I made out the latter to be curves plotted from the former. "It appears to be a record of durations ranging over a period of years, increasing from slightly less than five minutes to slightly less than twenty-nine minutes, then decreasing, and so on, cyclically."

"Excellent, Watson." Holmes turned again to the woman. "Had the man you took this from said anything about it to you?"

She shook her head sullenly.

"So you do not know what it is, except that it belonged to one HN. Do you know who this HN was?"

She frowned and, as though piezoelectrically, flashes of fear shone in her eyes. "Was?"

"You're quick on the uptake," Holmes said admiringly. "Yes, was. He died not an hour ago."

She took a quick swallow of my mild and bitter, then said stoutly, "I 'ad nuffink to do wiv that."

Holmes held the dark lenses on her. "But from the logo on the paper you knew or guessed his identity. Having whizzed the only thing of seeming value on his person, you figured that it might bring a reward for its return or that it might be worth something to a business rival of Lord N's. Do I read you right?"

"Right and left," she said with a flash of spirit.

Holmes smiled, released his grip, and moved aside. "That's all. You're free to go." And he even bowed as she slipped past.

We stood watching her maneuver her curves across the floor to the air lock. At the last, she tossed a sweet smile over her shoulder and such foul words came from those fair lips as I do not care to repeat.

The noise level in the Cormorant was hardly conducive to sensible discussion, and the atmosphere to unconstrained deduction, so we left not long after. I breathed easier to find that the woman had not slashed our decon suits.

Back in our digs, we took time now, as in Holmes's urgent desire to retrace Lord Nash's last movements we had not done before, to stash the corpse in the deep freeze against the moment Holmes was ready to hand it and the solution over to New New Scotland Yard, then made ourselves comfortable. Holmes screened the mysterious printout in General Gordon's space and we sat studying it.

Between puffs on his pipe, Holmes put the case. "Lord Nash meant to show us this as having to do with the source of the voice. It was missing, we have found it. What does it tell us? Clearly, it is a time log, recording Lord Nash's sessions with the voice. Can the voice have been a voice from the future? Does intercourse between past and future entail a time lag, a variable one at that?"

He did not wait for answer but went on, with the distancing effect of one thinking as he spoke, probing for his own questions and answers. "On the other hand, Lord Nash used the phrase 'nearer the hot-cross bun,' which Gabriel renders as 'nearer the sun.' That would indicate the source to be a planet of the solar system. Aha! Mars!"

Holmes's curriculum had deliberately omitted study of the

makeup and workings of the solar system as unneccessary to a consulting detective; such mundane details only cluttered the mind.

I could hold myself in no longer. "Not Mars, Holmes. Venus. It has to be Venus."

His mouth opened. He filled it with "Oh?" Then, "How on earth do you know that?"

"Mars is farther from the sun. Venus is nearer. Mars's mean distance from the sun is roughly one-and-a-half astronomical units. Venus's is roughly three-fourths an a.u. That means—"

Holmes lifted his hand. "You've made your point, Watson. Spare me."

Sufficient unto the day. I had broadened his horizons more than enough.

Heedless, I persisted. "Besides, the sign of Mars is ♂"—I drew it in the air—"whereas the sign for Venus is ♀."

He looked puzzled. "I fail to see—"

"Allow me," I said, with unaccustomed confidence. " 'Rise and fall over stick of joss.' "

He looked blank, then eyed I Suppose accusingly.

"Don't blame I Suppose," I said quickly. "The phrases aren't in his cockney rhyming slang vocabulary."

"Ta, guv'nor," I Suppose said. " 'E's right, 'Olmes. I've never come across the bleeding fings."

"Lord Nash," I said, "a human under pressure, needing rhyming phrases for words never yet paired with them, invented the rhyming phrases on the spot. No machine, confronting the unexpected, could have programmed itself to do that."

" 'Old 'ard, guv'nor."

"Rise and fall: ball. Stick of joss: cross. Ball over cross equals the sign for Venus."

I considered during the silence that fell, then ventured my comment. "I find 'rise and fall' elegant, as evoking bounce. But while stick of joss suggests the religious burning of incense, I'm not so happy with it. For my part, I should have preferred 'nowhere to doss' as better evoking 'no room at the inn' and 'Foxes have holes, and birds of the air have nests; but the Son of man hath not where to lay his head.' " I shrugged. "However. Yes, all in all, Lord Nash did extremely well for one in extremis." I grew brisk. "If you'll permit me, Holmes, I'll call up on the screen recorded terrestrial observations of Venus."

Holmes remained frozen-faced, but with a jerk of his hand he gave me the go-ahead.

I accessed the astronomical data base and loaded the pertinent ephemeris. I studied the figures on the screen and compared them with Lord Nash's printout. "It all fits! The voice comes only when New London's in line of sight of Venus. Lord Nash's regular plotting of these contacts gives us curves corresponding to the swing of Venus from west of the sun, when it's a morning star, to east of the sun, when it's the evening star. Venus's minimum distance from Earth, taking place at inferior conjunction, is twenty-six million miles. Venus's maximum distance from Earth, at superior conjunction, is one hundred sixty million miles. Apparently the 'voice'—some sort of thought-wave—travels at light speed, one hundred eighty-six thousand, two hundred eighty miles per second." I worked my wristcom. "That gives us roughly two point three-two-six minutes for near and roughly fourteen point three-one-five minutes for far. Multiply each by two—the round trip—and you get a low of five minutes and a high of twenty-nine minutes, just as Lord Nash's graph shows."

Deduction swept me along. An exhilarating feeling, attributable I am sure to something more than or beyond oxygen or adrenaline. "This brings us to the matter of motive. I'm afraid I can't visualize a life form that thrives on sulfuric acid. But the Venereans"—I shed my Victorian prudery and came right out with that monicker in place of the namby-pamby "Venusians"—"do, and their aim in communicating with Lord Nash and bending him to their will must surely be to venusform Terra in anticipation of a takeover."

The fire had gone out of Holmes's pipe and he now knocked out the ashes. "I think you've hit on it, Watson. Congratulations."

"Thank you, Holmes." I waited, but I Suppose did not complement the compliment. However, I was too keyed up to mind. "Holmes," I said excitedly, with the creepy-crawly sensation of enlightenment prickling my flesh, "I do believe the Venereans have been at this for a long time. Think, did not the industrial revolution satanic mills, burning fossil fuels, give rise to the greenhouse effect? From James Watt of the steam engine to James Watt of oil leases, and latterly Lord Nash, Venerean agents have been among us!''

"You may have a point there, Watson," Holmes said quietly, working fiercely on the dottle.

"Right on 'is loaf," I Suppose muttered.

"The Venereans," I said, "are growing bolder or getting impatient. Lord Nash may have fought the switch from high-sulfur coal to low-sulfur coal, have resisted the costly installation of scrubbers to remove sulfur dioxide from plant emissions, have contested laws mandating double-walled storage tanks, but environmentalists have been making inroads, slowing the deadly process. Why else would the Venerean voice have been pressing him to nuke, or otherwise trigger, eruptions in the equatorial regions? Volcanoes there, you know, put out more sulfur than those at the higher latitudes.''

Holmes nodded. "Sulfur dioxide couples with water vapor to bring forth sulfuric acid droplets—acid rain.''

He was once more in his element; chemistry was one of his strong points. So I now deferred to him.

"What now, Holmes?''

Holmes sat more erect, though I thought he looked somewhat wan. "Even without further deliberate sabotaging by Venusian tools such as Lord Nash, the greenhousing will continue if we Terrans do little more than we have done to reverse it. That is up to the world as a whole to deal with. As for present company, our immediate problem is to find some way of forcing the Venusians to stop their sinister but dexterous venusforming of Terra.''

I stepped to the window and raised the blind. By the grandfather clock and our other timepieces it was morning. By eyeball it was a timeless limbo. I craved to grab handfuls of the foul air to fling back at the Venereans. But that—and the analogy here was with Antaeus and Mother Earth—would merely strengthen the Venereans.

Turning from the window, I found Holmes once more—to my glad surprise—smilingly alert.

"Holmes, you appear almost cocky. Do you have some scheme?''

"Yes. And believe me, Watson, it is some scheme.''

"What—''

"Curb your impatience, Watson. This waits on the voice. With Lord Nash out of it, Venus must find another human receiver, some sensitive not all that insensible to blandishment and the promise of power. That is what we have to be on the lookout for: the signs that someone is carrying on Lord Nash's job. Then we will strike."

My mind flashed to the corpse in the deep freeze. "What of the meanwhile? Lord Nash's people will be looking for him."

Holmes pursed his lips, then shook his head. "No fear of a hue and cry. He's legendary as Howard Hughes for his mysterious comings and goings."

"Then what about New New Scotland Yard? Won't the authorities hold us to account for not reporting his demise?"

"His number's up when we say it is. We have but to let him thaw when we're ready."

"I hope you know what you're doing, Holmes," I said dubiously.

Holmes relit his pipe. "Leave it to me, Watson. Leave it to me."

I left it to him.

After two weeks I was still leaving it to him, not nagging him about his seeming indifference to the lack of progress. He lounged about the lodgings, doing nothing but play the violin or pipedream. Or try out a new toy, some state-of-the-art device that he hoped would aid him in his private-eye work.

This particular morning it was a laser pistol. I heard the snap of the beam and smelled burned air as he sat in his armchair and picked out VR on the wall.

From the lavatory, where I happened to be engaged in shaving my face, I heard Holmes languidly ask I Suppose, "What's . . . Watson up to?"

" 'E's giving 'imself a dig in the grave," I Suppose said, and rapped out a laugh I didn't at all care for.

I had been frowning to see the growth so sparse, and I was, as you might say, in a lather when I strode to the dooway and hurled my hand mirror at I Suppose.

Holmes, on the point of punctuating the revered initials, fired the laser pistol just as the mirror sliced past him I-Supposewards. The beam, rebounding from the reflecting surface, struck Holmes full in the chest, pierced Holmes's clothing, and Holmes, and the chairback, and seared the wall behind him.

I heard the yip from I Suppose as the mirror found its mark, then a shattering as the mirror rebounded to the floor. I did not look to see: it was Holmes my gaze fixed on. The poor fellow lay back slackly in the chair, his eyes empty. A roaring stillness filled the room. I stood frozen.

The tunnel walls of the hole in him showed the golden gleam of circuitry.

"A robot," I whispered.

"Walking computer," I Suppose corrected me with a snarl. "See wot you done? I 'ope yer satisfied."

"How can that be?" I said in the same whisper.

" 'Ow can it not be," I Suppose came back in the same snarl. "Time you used yer loaf for something besides a titfer rack. Ain't it sunk in that 'Olmes bloody well 'as to be an artifact? Wot was 'e in the first place but only a literary construct? Then fervent fans raised funds and set up the Sherlock 'Olmes Foundation to fashion a computerized simulacrum, and 'e came into being a quarter century ago."

This was too much for me. My head swam, and I doubt not I should have collapsed in a parade-ground faint had not a noise resounded in my head, a noise so loud I closed my eyes. Once the pain passed, I felt in control of myself again. It was as though one of the more powerful brands of sonic cleanser had rattled my brain clear. Somehow I knew it to be I Suppose's doing.

"Thanks," I said. "I needed that."

Without more ado, I grabbed Holmes's magnifying glass and sprang to his side to assess the damage. By the looks of it, the shot had gutted Holmes's message center. I smashed open the tantalus and cannibalized the intercom for wiring and chips.

Gently I freed the laser pistol from Holmes's grasp to forestall further damage to anyone or anything should Holmes twitch. As I worked to bridge the gaps in Holmes, my mind, with a mind of its own, ruminated about the sound that had snapped me out of my funk. I Suppose—and Holmes—had unexpected capacities.

Despite my self-recriminations and urgent ministrations, I

smiled. Their "supernatural" rapport, forsooth! They communicated at dog-whistle frequency, in tones pitched too high for my ears.

I finished the last bit of soldering. Holmes stirred under my hand before I could draw his dressing gown more tightly about him to cover the hole till I found a patch. Life came back to his eyes. He glanced at me almost mischievously, then his gaze shot to the window.

"In the nick of time, Watson," he said in quite nearly his old voice, though with overtones of Mrs. Hudson. "The game's afoot."

"Thank the Lord," I breathed. Then, trying to match Holmes's self-possession, "What do you mean, Holmes, the game's afoot? The Venerean voice has finally found its new pawn? But how can you know that?"

"Just look out the window, Watson."

"A real scratch an itch of a fog," said I Suppose. "A Brighton pier 'un."

Brighton pier: queer.

"What's queer about it?" I asked.

"Look sharp, Watson," said Holmes, "and answer yourself."

I peered out. "By the Lord Harry! It's raining split peas!"

"Not only that," I Suppose said, nose to the window sash and snuffing strongly. "I smell smoked brisket of beef, celery, onion, butter, sugar, salt, white pepper, and flour."

"Most unnatural!" I exclaimed.

"Not at all, Watson. Entirely natural if you examine the list of ingredients and ask yourself what they form the recipe for."

"Pea soup!" I ejaculated.

"Quite so, Watson. Pea soup. Literal pea soup. And what does that suggest?"

"A human agency?"

"Precisely. This is the sign I have been waiting for. It tells me that the voice has been in contact with someone in the vicinity, someone who has cast his or her lot with the Venusians, selling humanity out in exchange for the promise of personal power. This someone has evidently taken all too literally the order to produce a pea-soup fog."

I Suppose snickered. "Guess we ort to give fanks 'e received pea as p-e-a."

Holmes turned on I Suppose chidingly. "You'd be better occupied, Gabriel, tracking the pea soup to its source."

I Suppose hung his head. "Too right, 'Olmes." Then he lifted his head and wagged his tale. "Just suit me up and I'm orf."

"Good Gabriel. Good fellow."

And with that Holmes led the way down to the airlock. Holmes saw I Suppose off with a word in his ear, then Holmes and I climbed back to our rooms to wait I Suppose's return.

Holmes sat in his armchair with his eyes closed but with an attentiveness that told me he kept in constant touch with I Suppose over the dog-whistle frequency. I did not stir for fear of breaking their contact, their rapport.

After only a half hour by the clock but an eon by my own reckoning, Holmes gave a beatific sigh and opened his eyes. "We've done it, Watson."

"Wonderful! What have we done?"

"Our Gabriel hound had no trouble locating the source: a canning factory—a subsidiary of United Unlimited, by the by—that was spewing the soup from its stacks instead of sealing it in cans. Gabriel slipped inside the plant without difficulty. The plant is highly automated and there are few people about. The smell of fear, mixed with sweaty elation, led him directly to one of the few, a computer operator by the name of Winthrop Morrill. On my instructions, Gabriel blasted the dupe's brain with a message for relay to the Venusians, telling them that their dastardly plot has been uncovered and warning them that Terra will terraform Venus unless Venus desists from venusforming Terra. As for Morrill, the blast will leave his mind foggy, no longer of use to the Venusians, and he most likely will remember little if anything of the entire episode. There you have it, Watson. I believe I can say we have saved Earth from a terrible fate."

"Bravo, Holmes!" I said without stint.

He waved his hand. "Kudos is due I Suppose as well. Oh, and of course, yourself. Your contribution was, shall I say, astronomical."

"Not at all, Holmes," I said, though naturally gratified.

Hunting for something to do to hide my blushes, I bent to pick up the shards of the mirror that had been the cause of damage to my friend. "Blast the blasted thing!" I had cut myself on a splinter of glass. Blood flowed. And with it, thought; thought like a streak of dark turbulence in the fog. "Holmes, I'm human!"

Holmes looked around quickly at me as I knelt thus, then he puffed on his pipe and followed the smoke ceilingward with his gaze.

"Did you hear me, Holmes? I said I'm human."

He sighed from his depths. "I know, Watson, I've been aware for some time that this moment would have to come. I know too that I shall be glad when it is out, but that makes it no easier to get out." He took a deep breath and sat straighter. "Very well. Listen to the story of your life. Thirteen years ago I felt overwhelmingly the need that had been instilled in me for a Watson. I suppose I could have materialized my Watson in the same manner as I later built Gabriel, but I had the notion of repaying Sir Arthur Conan Doyle for bringing me back to life after Reichenbach Falls." He erased air with his hand. "I know, that was a paper resurrection. But memory and mimicry interface in me, and I am my canonical history as much as I am my functioning computerized self. And so, with the thought of repaying my debt to my creator, I secretly made my way to that part of Hampshire where Minstead is, was, located. I had to work fast, as the world's oceans were still rising rapidly and the area was on the point of drowning. On the sopping grounds of a home in Minstead I played resurrection man in the dead of night, dark lantern and all. What I dug for lay beneath a carved British oak headstone, inscribed SIR ARTHUR CONAN DOYLE, 22 MAY 1859, STEEL TRUE, BLADE STRAIGHT. In short, Watson, you are a clone, grown and still growing from a splinter of bone, a trace of gristle, robbed from his grave."

Memory and mimicry interfaced, just as Holmes had said, making the past the present. I knew I was in our New Baker Street lodgings, yet at the same time I knew I was in shock on the Afghanistani front, having just taken a Jezail bullet. I had memories of childhood and adulthood, of medical education and practice of medicine, yet I had the physique of an adolescent, though an overgrown burly one. My body bore

the requisite scars of my military campaigning—plastic surgery?
—but my voice had only just changed and I had yet to grow
some sort of mustache.

I Suppose's voice brought me back to the present present.
"Tell me somefink, guv'nor, do clones 'ave belly buttons?"
He had unvelcroed himself out of his decon suit and turned
the doorknob with his jaws. He grinned at me. " 'Ow's that
for a larf, guv'nor?" He threw back his head to howl in
laughter.

I reached for the poker and raised it.

Too late I Suppose saw it coming.

"Arf—"

His last bow-wow.

It was a good feeling, and purged me, though I knew deep
down that sooner or later either Holmes or myself would have
to resurrect I Suppose.

Holmes said, "Really, Watson." But there was a wealth of
understanding in his voice.

And that night, with a grin, I laid me loaf on me weeping
willow to plow the deep.

The Fastest Draw

Larry Eisenberg

Like most men, Amos Handworthy was a creature of many parts. To his business associates he was a sober, calculating entrepreneur, given occasionally to rash ventures which through outrageous turns of luck usually ended well. To his employees he was a distant, ominous figure, wandering through his electronics plant occasionally, staring with pale blue eyes at a myriad of trivial details, sifting through the reject box of discarded transistors and occasionally stopping to ask a loaded but seemingly innocuous question of one of the production engineers. To his housekeeper he was a brusque, harsh man, not given overly to entertaining or keeping late hours but sober, sedate and completely absorbed in his pervasive habit of collecting automata.

Very few men had ever seen the eyes of Amos Handworthy come aglow, and Manny Steinberg was one of them. Manny was a superb engineer who combined the ability to carry out a sophisticated circuit design with the old-fashioned desire to tinker. It was almost physically painful for him to pass by a mechanical device that was not in working order. And so, in his first visit to the Pecos Saloon, a town landmark that had been restored to its pristine décor through the generosity of Amos Handworthy, Manny caught sight of the magnificent music-making machine as soon as he cut through the swinging doors. He proceeded first to the bar and availed himself of the tequila and lemon juice which was the specialty of the house. Much of the town showed the influence of its close location to the Mexican border, the large Spanish-speaking population, the frijoles that were vended off street carts, and the tastes in liquor.

Still sucking on the lemon, Manny walked over and surveyed the glass-enclosed music maker, four vertical violins arrayed in a circle with a hoop of horse hair spanning about the four violin bridges, electromagnet stops hovering above the strings. A dried-out square of paper had been crudely taped across the glass with the clear inked inscription "Out of Order." He had removed the back door of the machine and was examining the innards when he felt a proprietary hand on his shoulder and swiveled about to meet the questioning gaze of his boss, Amos Handworthy.

"I think I can make it go," said Manny, not certain that he could but unable to leave this marvelous array of gears, levers, and multi-pinned rotating disks.

"I've tried to have it repaired and failed," said Amos Handworthy. "But if you can do it, it's worth a thousand dollars to me."

Manny nodded as though this offer had tipped the balance, but in truth it made very little difference to him. Even the following week, when he demonstrated to a full saloon how beautifully the four violins played "The Mephisto Waltz," he accepted the check which Amos Handworthy placed in his hand with some puzzlement, not quite connecting it with the maintenance miracle he had just wrought. Handworthy insisted on having the machine play again and again, but after the fourth successful round, Manny had lost interest in the device and was more concerned in downing tequilas than in listening in the music.

Later that night, as he lay abed on a rumpled sweat-wet sheet, wondering how in hell he had taken a job in this Godforsaken town in Texas, he remembered dimly that his boss, Mr. Handworthy, had invited him over to the stately Handworthy Mansion. He was not sure when the invitation was for, or whether the occasion was of a business or social character, but he knew that it was mandatory that he come.

Fortunately, a handwritten note on gray, unembossed letter paper arrived the following day, confirming the invitation and specifying a dinner date the following Friday evening at eight P.M. Manny's income was a good one and he had eaten in some of the finest restaurants in the country but he had never been to the home of a truly wealthy man before. It was with no little trepidation that he appeared at the door of the Handworthy Mansion and was ushered into the house by the liveried butler, who was, to Manny's intense surprise, white.

He was somewhat taken aback to find that he was the only dinner guest and that the burden of making conversation would be totally his job. But he found that contrary to his expectation, Amos Handworthy did almost all of the talking.

The food was plentiful but not lavish or exotic in character. Mr. Handworthy himself carved out liberal slices off the huge side of beef that was brought in on a great silver salver. And although Mr. Handworthy did not drink it, the wine was carefully chilled and of good (but not the best) quality.

Since Manny had been raised in a low-income Jewish-inhabited section of New York City and had, despite his extensive rootless shifting about the country, no real insight into how anybody else lived, he found himself quite taken with the rambling tales that Amos Handworthy told of his town's history.

"My father," said Amos Handworthy toward the close of the dinner, "was one of the last frontier marshals and maybe *the greatest*. His draw was reputed to be so fast that the eye could barely follow and he never missed his target."

But he drank like a fish, he thought, and spent most of his time at the sporting house on East Maple.

"As a boy," he said aloud, "I could think of nothing more ideal than to follow in his footsteps when I grew up. 'Course when I *had* grown up, there was no more frontier, no more show downs in the center of town. It was a terrible disappointment and one that I haven't gotten over, even yet."

"My father," said Manny pensively, "claimed that I had clumsy wooden hands. He was wrong and I think he knew it. But he'd never admit it to me."

"Do you know what disturbs me?" said Amos Handworthy. "There have been challenges for me, some financial, some physical, others social, and I've met and beaten every one of them. But I've never been in the same mother-naked kind of situation my Father had to meet where it was one man's raw courage and skill against another's."

"The thing that disturbs me," said Manny, "is that whenever I knock off a particularly tough job, instead of being elated, I'm totally depressed until the next challenging one comes along.''

Amos Handworthy raised the wine bottle to the light and studied the play of color through the thickened glass.

"Come inside," he said abruptly. "I've got something special I want to show you.''

Manny followed after his host and found himself in a huge, high-ceilinged room flanked on all four walls by reward posters, some as much as one hundred years old. There were no furnishings in the room, just a series of unusual pieces of furniture that proved on closer scrutiny to be automata of diverse types. In the center of the room was a great amorphous mass covered by an enormous sheet.

"I have no kin," said Handworthy, staring possessively about him. "I've never married so I have no children. But I'm a happy man nevertheless. These are my children," he said, gesticulating about him. "This one is a particular delight," he added, his voice swelling with pride as he brought Manny over for a closer view.

It was a gray-enameled case surmounted by a glistening blue hemisphere adorned with tiny stars of silver and gold. Within the hemisphere was an exquisite miniature ballroom, the walls lined with mirrors, and when Handworthy wound up the movement and released the catch, two groups of tiny dancers began to waltz toward each other. Their images were caught up and multiplied a hundredfold in the mirrors, creating a truly breathtaking sight as the unseen strings of a harp were plucked below in the gray-enameled case.

Before Manny could comment, he was whisked over to a superbly crafted wooden figure of a charming child, a painted smile wreathing the gently carved mouth. The child was seated on a mahogany stool, and when the latching hook had been lowered, it leaned forward and after dipping a feathered pen into an inkwell, began to write in smooth cursive flow. When she leaned back, her motions apparently brought to a close, Manny bent forward and found to his intense amazement a beautifully crafted letter of some fifty words written to the mother of the child.

There were other amazing sights, an android that fingered and breathed wind into a flute that played sweetly, a reclining Cleopatra that rose, bowed gravely at the waist and then lay down once more upon her feathered couch. Since each of the treasured machines was in perfect functioning order, Manny rapidly lost interest and merely followed Handworthy about, nodding politely, his mind distant upon a persistent circuit problem that was still unsolved. But he was jarred back to reality when, with the reverence that one would use to lay bare a sleeping nymph, Handworthy removed the sheet from the huge centerpiece of the room. It was a small segment of a Western street, complete with hitching post, before which stood an uncannily lifelike figure of a town marshal, complete with vest and badge, chaps and holstered gun. The painted face was scowling and from closer scrutiny it was apparent that the figure was capable of complex motion.

"The others," said Amos Handworthy, "are marvelous antiques that I've collected, but this fellow was made to my own specifications in Switzerland. His clothing is quite authentic and he really works. Watch this!"

He stepped forward and took a loosely draped gun belt off the hitching post to the right of the Marshal and buckled it about his waist.

"The device is electrically operated," he continued. "The instant I draw, the Marshal draws too, and the trick is to hit him somewhere on his target photocells with a beam of light that flashes out of my gun, before he can get off his shot. I can adjust the speed of his draw within fairly wide limits and I've been moving him up to faster and faster speeds. But I've gotten pretty damn fast."

With a drawing motion that was almost a blur, he whipped out his gun and pulled the trigger. The Marshal was fast, but apparently not *as* fast, for suddenly a recorded voice bellowed in pain and gasped, "You got me, you dirty varmint."

"A little touch of my own," said Amos Handworthy. "That's what happens when I hit him."

He looked down at his gun, almost proudly, and Manny had the eerie feeling that it was only with restraint that he did not blow the imaginary smoke away from the gun barrel.

"That's a highly imaginative device," said Manny.

"He is," said Amos Handworthy. "But he's still not quite what I want him to be. I have an idea that you can make him the kind of opponent I need."

"What do you want?" said Manny. All of his ennui was

beginning to evaporate and the familiar exultant response to challenge had begun to grow in him.

"I want him to be able to hit me, too, figuratively speaking," said Amos Handworthy. "As things stand now, this shootout is entirely one sided, I'd like to know, for instance, if he's been able to hit me."

"I can do it," said Manny. "You'll have to get me off my regular project, but I can do it."

"I'll call your division chief in the morning," said Amos Handworthy. "You'll stay here with me and you can have all the time you need."

Manny did not sleep well in his spacious, overly comfortable bed. He was up early the following morning poring over the construction plans for the Marshal and examining the instruction folder which the Swiss company, with typical thoroughness, had included in the neatly packed maintenance kit. He caught the guiding concept of the design at once, and made his plans to modify the Marshal along lines that incorporated control techniques that were basically electronic.

He phoned the plant and requisitioned transistors, metal film resistors, capacitors, and various other components necessary for his task. Handworthy did not approach him as he worked, and his meals were served to him either in his own room or the great room where all the automata were located. He made all the changes himself, snipping leads, soldering, forming tight mechanical joints with deft fingers that almost seemed alive and apart from his body.

Ten days later, he called in Amos Handworthy and demonstrated what he had done.

"I've modified both guns so that you and the Marshal will now shoot at each other with ultraviolet light. You'll both wear vests that are sensitive to this light. I monitor the hits electrically by measuring the resistance of those areas where a bullet would severely injure a man. Nothing will occur unless you or the Marshal is hit in such an area. Furthermore, you can both continue to shoot for an indefinite length of time. However, I've altered the Marshal's aiming mechanism so that if he's hit in a vital spot, he won't shoot as accurately. Similarly, if you are hit, a defocusing mechanism operates on your light bulb so that your gun is no longer as accurate. And instead of the recorded voice, if either of you is hit in the heart, your gun goes dead."

Amos Handworthy's eyes began to glow with a fire such as Manny Steinberg had never seen and it excited him that his work had brought on so wonderful a response. He slipped the new vest on Handworthy, handed him the wired holster and gun, and stepped back. After fastening his belt and readying himself, Handworthy drew as before and fired swiftly at the Marshal, who was firing back almost as rapidly. Suddenly Handworthy stopped and looked at his gun in dismay.

"My trigger's locked," he cried.

"He's killed you," said Manny dryly. "You beat him to the draw, but he's hit you in the heart."

"I see," said Handworthy slowly. "Then it looks like I've got a hell of a lot more practicing to do."

It was a full month before Manny Steinberg was invited back to the Mansion, and with great pride his host demonstrated how he killed the Marshal, *every time.*

"I've got him set for his fastest draw, too," said Handworthy. "At this point, he's just no match for me."

"I guess that wraps it up," said Manny, knowing full well that it couldn't end this way. "You're just too damned good."

Amos Handworthy shook his head slowly.

"You don't believe that and neither do I. It's an unfair battle, unfair because we've excluded the most vital element of all."

"What element is that?" said Manny, although the answer popped into his head even as he spoke and he began to envision the approach that had to be taken.

"There's no *fear* in this situation," said Handworthy. "When two men were in an actual shootout they were both afraid of being killed. But the Marshal is oblivious to fear and so for the most part am I. Suppose for instance in some way you could make him shoot better if I were nervous and shoot less accurately if I were deadly calm."

"There is a way to do that," said Manny. "I can electrically monitor your vasomotor reflexes by means of your pulse and sweat reactions. Then I would program the Marshal's reflexes in just the way you suggest. But the thing I can't understand is how such a step would have any real meaning. Why in God's name would you ever be frightened? There's nothing in this situation to make it happen.''

"I have a very vivid imagination," said Handworthy. "As a child I had no playmates, and still I populated an entire world in my mind, every one a distinct person. Don't you see, I can project myself into feeling that I'm in the *real* life-and-death situation just as long as the Marshal becomes a creature sensitive to fear.''

It took Manny almost three weeks this time to make the requisite changes, and he carried out in addition an extensive series of pulse and skin resistance measurements on Handworthy. When he was satisfied that the Marshal had reached the ultimate state, he called in Handworthy and demonstrated what he had done.

"I've installed," said Manny, "a feedback circuit that's inoperative when your typical emotional reaction exists. But the circuit comes into play when you become more nervous than usual and the Marshal will therefore shoot faster and more accurately. On the other hand, if you should become less concerned, calmer perhaps, the Marshal's aim would tend to go askew and his firing rate would slow down. In other words, you and the Marshal are indissolubly linked through your nervous system whenever you strap on your shooting vest.''

"Fine," said Amos Handworthy, and the brilliance of his usually lackluster eyes gave an added emphasis to the word. "You've surpassed my greatest expectations with these new changes. And while I know it wasn't part of our bargain, I intend to add a pretty big sum to your monthly check.''

"Thanks," said Manny automatically. Already he was becoming aware of the depression that followed his engineering triumphs. As he left the house, he had almost completely lost interest in his accomplishment.

Meanwhile, Amos Handworthy was examining the guns with great care, particularly the tiny switch that activated the firing cycle. It was evident to him that as soon as his gun lifted off the switch, electrical activity commenced. After first unplugging the Marshal's electrical cable, he carefully removed the ultraviolet-loaded guns from the fixture in his holster and the Marshal's holster, and replaced them with beautifully machined Colt .45s that were loaded with real bullets.

There's absolutely no doubt that the mechanical action will be the same, thought Handworthy. And now the element of real fear, both *mine* and *his,* will be in the picture. We're going to have a real shootout, the kind you don't see anymore.

He replaced the plug in the wall socket and turned about to face the Marshal quite squarely, shifting his belt around so that his gun would clear free of the holster. The Marshal stared at him out of sightless painted blue eyes, his mechanical hand resting stolidly on his gun.

Even now, it isn't an even match, thought Handworthy ruefully. I couldn't be any calmer than I am now. I guess it never can come out just exactly as I want it to.

As his fingers flashed lightning-fast to his gun, it suddenly occurred to him that Manny was right, that he and the Marshal were indissolubly linked through his own nervous system. He had no kin, no wife, no children. The Marshal was the only one on earth really tied to him. And in that instant, a terrible surge of fear came over him at the thought of killing his own.

Mirror Image

Isaac Asimov

The Three Laws of Robotics
1: A robot may not injure a huamn being, or, through inaction, allow a human being to come to harm.
2: A robot must obey the orders given it by human beings except where such orders would conflict with the First Law.
3: A robot must protect its own existence as long as such protection does not conflict with the First or Second Laws.

Lije Baley had just decided to relight his pipe when the door of his office opened without a preliminary knock, or announcement, of any kind. Baley looked up in pronounced annoyance and then dropped his pipe. It said a good deal for the state of his mind that he let it lie where it had fallen.

"R. Daneel Olivaw," he said, in a kind of mystified excitement. "Jehoshaphat! It *is* you, isn't it?"

"You are quite right," said the tall, bronzed newcomer, his even features never flicking for a moment out of their accustomed calm. "I regret surprising you by entering without warning, but the situation is a delicate one and there must be as little involvement as possible on the part of the men and robots even in this place. I am, in any case, pleased to see you again, friend Elijah."

And the robot held out his right hand in a gesture as thoroughly human as was his appearance. It was Baley who was so unmanned by his astonishment as to stare at the hand with a momentary lack of understanding.

But then he seized it in both his, feeling its warm firmness. "But Daneel, *why?* You're welcome any time, but—what is this situation that is a delicate one? Are we in trouble again? Earth, I mean?"

"No, friend Elijah, it does not concern Earth. The situation to which I refer as a delicate one is, to outward appearances, a small thing. A dispute between mathematicians, nothing more. As we happened, quite by accident, to be within an easy Jump of Earth—"

"This dispute took place on a starship, then?"

"Yes, indeed. A small dispute, yet to the humans involved astonishingly large."

Baley could not help but smile. "I'm not surprised you find humans astonishing. They do not obey the Three Laws."

"That is, indeed, a shortcoming," said R. Daneel, gravely, "and I think humans themselves are puzzled by humans. It may be that you are less puzzled than are the men of other worlds because so many more human beings live on Earth than on the Spacer worlds. If so, and I believe it is so, you could help us."

R. Daneel paused momentarily and then said, perhaps a shade too quickly, "And yet there are rules of human behavior which I have learned. It would seem, for instance, that I am deficient in etiquette, by human standards, not to have asked after your wife and child."

"They are doing well. The boy is in college and Jessie is involved in local politics. The amenities are taken care of. Now tell me how you come to be here."

"As I said, we were within an easy Jump of Earth," said R. Daneel, "so I suggested to the captain that we consult you."

"And the captain agreed?" Baley had a sudden picture of the proud and autocratic captain of a Spacer starship consenting to make a landing on Earth—of all worlds—and to consult an Earthman—of all people.

"I believe," said R. Daneel, "that he was in a position where he would have agreed to anything. In addition, I praised you very highly; although, to be sure, I stated only the truth. Finally, I agreed to conduct all negotiations so that none of the crew, or passengers, would need to enter any of the Earthman cities."

"And talk to any Earthman, yes. But what has happened?"

"The passengers of the starship, *Eta Carina*, included two mathematicians who were traveling to Aurora to attend an interstellar conference on neurobiophysics. It is about these mathematicians, Alfred Barr Humboldt and Gennao Sabbat, that the dispute centers. Have you perhaps, friend Elijah, heard of one, or both, of them?"

"Neither one," said Baley, firmly. "I know nothing about mathematics. Look, Daneel, surely you haven't told anyone I'm a mathematics buff or—"

"Not at all, friend Elijah. I know you are not. Nor does it matter, since the exact nature of the mathematics involved is in no way relevant to the point at issue."

"Well, then, go on."

"Since you do not know either man, friend Elijah, let me tell you that Dr. Humboldt is well into his twenty-seventh decade— Pardon me, friend Elijah?"

"Nothing. Nothing," said Baley, irritably. He had merely muttered to himself, more or less incoherently, in a natural reaction to the extended lifespans of the Spacers. "And he's still active, despite his age? On Earth, mathematicians after thirty or so . . ."

Daneel said calmly, "Dr. Humboldt is one of the top three mathematicians, by long-established repute, in the galaxy. Certainly he is still active. Dr. Sabbat, on the other hand, is quite young, not yet fifty, but he has already established himself as the most remarkable new talent in the most abstruse branches of mathematics."

"They're both great, then," said Baley. He remembered his pipe and picked it up. He decided there was no point in lighting it now and knocked out the dottle. "What happened? Is this a murder case? Did one of them apparently kill the other?"

"Of these two men of great reputation, one is trying to destroy that of the other. By human values, I believe this may be regarded as worse than physical murder."

"Sometimes, I suppose. Which one is trying to destroy the other?"

"Why, that, friend Elijah, is precisely the point at issue. Which?"

"Go on."

"Dr. Humboldt tells the story clearly. Shortly before he boarded the starship, he had an insight into a possible method for analyzing neural pathways from changes in microwave absorption patterns of local cortical areas. The insight was a purely mathematical technique of extraordinary subtlety, but I cannot, of course, either understand or sensibly transmit the details. These do not, however, matter. Dr. Humboldt considered the matter and was more convinced each hour that he had something revolutionary on hand, something that would dwarf all his previous accomplishments in mathematics. Then he discovered that Dr. Sabbat was on board."

"Ah. And he tried it out on young Sabbat?"

"Exactly. The two had met at professional meetings before and knew each other thoroughly by reputation. Humboldt went into it with Sabbat in great detail. Sabbat backed Humboldt's analysis completely and was unstinting in his praise of the importance of the discovery and of the ingenuity of the discoverer. Heartened and reassured by this, Humboldt prepared a paper outlining, in summary, his work and, two days later, prepared to have it forwarded subetherically to the cochairmen of the conference at Aurora, in order that he might officially establish his priority and arrange for possible discussion before the sessions were closed. To his surprise, he found that Sabbat was ready with a paper of his own, essentially the same as Humboldt's, and Sabbat was also preparing to have it subetherized to Aurora."

"I suppose Humboldt was furious."

"Quite!"

"And Sabbat? What was his story?"

"Precisely the same as Humboldt's. Word for word, except for the mirror-image exchange of names. According to Sabbat, it was he who had the insight, and he who consulted Humboldt; it was Humboldt who agreed with the analysis and praised it."

"Then each one claims the idea is his and that the other stole it. It doesn't sound like a problem to me at all. In matters of scholarship, it would seem only necessary to produce the records of research, dated and initialed. Judgment as to priority can be made from that. Even if one is falsified, that might be discovered through internal inconsistencies.''

"Ordinarily, friend Elijah, you would be right, but this is mathematics, and not in an experimental science. Dr. Humboldt claims to have worked out the essentials in his head. Nothing was put in writing until the paper itself was prepared. Dr. Sabbat, of course, says precisely the same.''

"Well, then, be more drastic and get it over with, for sure. Subject each one to a psychic probe and find out which of the two is lying.''

R. Daneel shook his head slowly, "Friend Elijah, you do not understand these men. They are both of rank and scholarship, Fellows of the Imperial Academy. As such, they cannot be subjected to trial of professional conduct except by a jury of their peers—their professional peers—unless they personally and voluntarily waive that right.''

"Put it to them, then. The guilty man won't waive the right because he can't afford to face the psychic probe. The innocent man will waive it at once. You won't even have to use the probe.''

"It does not work that way, friend Elijah. To waive the right in such a case—to be investigated by laymen—is a serious and perhaps irrecoverable blow to prestige. Both men steadfastly refuse to waive the right to special trial, as a matter of pride. The question of guilt, or innocence, is quite subsidiary.''

"In that case, let it go for now. Put the matter in cold storage until you get to Aurora. At the neurobiophysical conference, there will be a huge supply of professional peers, and then—''

"That would mean a tremendous blow to science itself, friend Elijah. Both men would suffer for having been the instrument of scandal. Even the innocent one would be blamed for having been party to a situation so distasteful. It would be felt that it should have been settled quietly out of court at all costs.''

"All right. I'm not a Spacer, but I'll try to imagine that this attitude makes sense. What do the men in question say?''

"Humboldt agrees thoroughly. He says that if Sabbat will admit theft of the idea and allow Humboldt to proceed with transmission of the paper, or at least its delivery at the conference, he will not press charges. Sabbat's misdeed will remain secret with him; and, of course, with the captain, who is the only other human to be party to the dispute.''

''But young Sabbat will not agree?''

''On the contrary, he agreed with Dr. Humboldt to the last detail—with the reversal of names. Still the mirror image.''

''So they just sit there, stalemated?''

''Each, I believe, friend Elijah, is waiting for the other to give in and admit guilt.''

''Well, then, wait.''

''The captain has decided this cannot be done. There are two alternatives to waiting, you see. The first is that both will remain stubborn so that when the starship lands on Aurora, the intellectual scandal will break. The captain, who is responsible for justice on board ship, will suffer disgrace for not having been able to settle the matter quietly, and that, to him, is quite insupportable.''

''And the second alternative?''

''Is that one, or the other, of the mathematicians will indeed admit to wrongdoing. But will the one who confesses do so out of actual guilt, or out of a noble desire to prevent the scandal? Would it be right to deprive of credit one who is sufficiently ethical to prefer to lose that credit than to see science as a whole suffer? Or else, the guilty party will confess at the last moment, and in such a way as to make it appear he does so only for the sake of science, thus escaping the disgrace of his deed and casting its shadow upon the other. The captain will be the only man to know all this but he does not wish to spend the rest of his life wondering whether he has been a party to a grotesque miscarriage of justice.''

Baley sighed. ''A game of intellectual chicken. Who'll break first as Aurora comes nearer and nearer? Is that the whole story now, Daneel?''

''Not quite. There are witnesses to the transaction.''

''Jehoshaphat! Why didn't you say so at once. *What* witnesses?

''Dr. Humboldt's personal servant—''

''A robot, I suppose.''

''Yes, certainly. He is called R. Preston. This servant,

R. Preston, was present during the initial conference and he bears out Dr. Humboldt in every detail.''

"You mean he says that the idea was Dr. Humboldt's to begin with; that Dr. Humboldt detailed it to Dr. Sabbat; that Dr. Sabbat praised the idea, and so on.''

"Yes, in full detail.''

"I see. Does that settle the matter or not? Presumably not.''

"You are quite right. It does not settle the matter, for there is a second witness. Dr. Sabbat also has a personal servant, R. Idda, another robot of, as it happens, the same model as R. Preston, made, I believe, in the same year, in the same factory. Both have been in service equal times.''

"And odd coincidence—very odd.''

"A fact, I am afraid, and it makes it difficult to arrive at any judgment based on obvious differences between the two servants.''

"R. Idda, then, tells the same story as R. Preston?''

"Precisely the same story, except for the mirror-image reversal of the names.''

"R. Idda stated, then, that young Sabbat, the one not yet fifty''—Lije Baley did not entirely keep the sardonic note out of his voice; he himself was not yet fifty and he felt far from young—"had the idea to begin with; that he detailed it to Dr. Humboldt, who was loud in his praises, and so on.''

"Yes, friend Elijah.''

"And one robot is lying, then.''

"So it would seem.''

"It should be easy to tell which. I imagine even a superficial examination by a good roboticist—''

"A roboticist is not enough in this case, friend Elijah. Only a qualified robopsychologist would carry weight enough and experience enough to make a decision in a case of this importance. There is no one so qualified on board ship. Such an examination can be performed only when we reach Aurora—''

"And by then the crud hits the fan. Well, you're here on Earth. We can scare up a robopsychologist, and surely anything that happens on Earth will never reach the ears of Aurora and there will be no scandal.''

"Except that neither Dr. Humboldt, nor Dr. Sabbat, will

allow his servant to be investigated by a robopsychologist of Earth. The Earthman would have to—'' He paused.

Lije Baley said stolidly, ''He'd have to touch the robot.''

''These are old servants, well thought of—''

''And not to be sullied by the touch of Earthman. Then what do you want me to do, damn it?'' He paused, grimacing. ''I'm sorry, R. Daneel, but I see no reason for your having involved me.''

''I was on the ship on a mission utterly irrelevant to the problem at hand. The captain turned to me because he had to turn to someone. I seemed human enough to talk to, and robot enough to be a safe recipient of confidences. He told me the whole story and asked what I would do. I realized the next Jump could take us as easily to Earth as to our target. I told the captain that, although I was at as much a loss to resolve the mirror image as he was, there was on Earth one who might help.''

''Jehoshaphat!'' muttered Baley under his breath.

''Consider, friend Elijah, that if you succeed in solving this puzzle, it would do your career good and Earth itself might benefit. The matter could not be publicized, of course, but the captain is a man of some influence on his home world and he would be grateful.''

''You just put a greater strain on me.''

''I have every confidence,'' said R. Daneel, stolidly, ''that you already have some idea as to what procedure ought to be followed.''

''Do you? I suppose that the obvious procedure is to interview the two mathematicians, one of whom would seem to be a thief.''

''I'm afraid, friend Elijah, that neither one will come into the city. Nor would either one be willing to have you come to them.''

''And there is no way of forcing a Spacer to allow contact with an Earthman, no matter what the emergency. Yes, I understand that, Daneel—but I was thinking of an interview by closed-circuit television.''

''Nor that. They will not submit to interrogation by an Earthman.''

''Then what do they want of me? Could I speak to the robots?''

"They would not allow the robots to come here, either."

"Jehoshaphat, Daneel. *You*'ve come."

"That was my own decision. I have permission, while on board ship, to make decisions of that sort without veto by any human being but the captain himself—and he was eager to establish the contact. I, having known you, decided that television contact was insufficient. I wished to shake your hand."

Lije Baley softened. "I appreciate that, Daneel, but I still honestly wish you could have refrained from thinking of me at all in this case. Can I talk to the robots by television at least?"

"That, I think, can be arranged."

"Something, at least. That means I would be doing the work of a robopsychologist—in a crude sort of way."

"But you are a detective, friend Elijah, not a robopsychologist."

"Well, let it pass. Now before I see them, let's think a bit. Tell me: is it possible that both robots are telling the truth? Perhaps the conversation between the two mathematicians was equivocal. Perhaps it was of such a nature that each robot could honestly believe its own master was proprietor of the idea. Or perhaps one robot heard only one portion of the discussion and the other another portion, so that each could suppose its own master was proprietor of the idea."

"That is quite impossible, friend Elijah. Both robots repeat the conversation in identical fashion. And the two repetitions are fundamentally inconsistent."

"Then it is absolutely certain that one of the robots is lying?"

"Yes."

"Will I be able to see the transcript of all evidence given so far in the presence of the captain, if I should want to?"

"I thought you would ask that and I have copies with me."

"Another blessing. Have the robots been cross-examined at all, and is that cross-examination included in the transcript?"

"The robots have merely repeated their tales. Cross-examination would be conducted only by robopsychologists."

"Or by myself?"

"You are a detective, friend Elijah, not a—".

"All right, R. Daneel. I'll try to get the Spacer psychology straight. A detective can do it because he isn't a robopsychologist. Let's think further. Ordinarily a robot will not lie, but he will do so if necessary to maintain the Three Laws. He might lie to protect, in legitimate fashion, his own existence in accordance with the Third Law. He is more apt to lie if that is necessary to follow a legitimate order given him by a human being in accordance with the Second Law. He is most apt to lie if that is necessary to save a human life, or to prevent harm from coming to a human in accordance with the First Law.''

"Yes.''

"And in this case, each robot would be defending the professional reputation of his master, and would lie if it were necessary to do so. Under the circumstances, the professional reputation would be nearly equivalent to life and there might be a near-First-Law urgency to the lie.''

"Yet by the lie, each servant would be harming the professional reputation of the other's master, friend Elijah.''

"So it would, but each robot might have a clearer conception of the value of its own master's reputation and honestly judge it to be greater than that of the other's. The lesser harm would be done by his lie, he would suppose, than by the truth.''

Having said that, Lije Baley remained quiet for a moment. Then he said, "All right, then, can you arrange to have me talk to one of the robots—to R. Idda first, I think?''

"Dr. Sabbat's robot?''

"Yes,'' said Baley, dryly, "the young fellow's robot.''

"It will take me but a few minutes,'' said R. Daneel. "I have a micro-receiver outfitted with a projector. I will need merely blank wall and I think this one will do if you will allow me to move some of these film cabinets.''

"Go ahead. Will I have to talk into a microphone of some sort?''

"No, you will be able to talk in an ordinary manner. Please pardon me, friend Elijah, for a moment of further delay. I will have to contact the ship and arrange for R. Idda to be interviewed.''

"If that will take some time, Daneel, how about giving me the transcripted material of the evidence so far.''

* * *

Lije Baley lit his pipe while R. Daneel set up the equipment, and leafed through the flimsy sheets he had been handed.

The minutes passed and R. Daneel said, "If you are ready, friend Elijah, R. Idda is. Or would you prefer a few more minutes with the transcript?"

"No," sighed Baley, "I'm not learning anything new. Put him on and arrange to have the interview recorded and transcribed."

R. Idda, unreal in two-dimensional projection against the wall, was basically metallic in structure—not at all the humanoid creature that R. Daneel was. His body was tall but blocky, and there was very little to distinguish him from the many robots Baley had seen, except for minor structural details.

Baley said, "Greetings, R. Idda."

"Greetings, sir," said R. Idda, in a muted voice that sounded surprisingly humanoid.

"You are the personal servant of Gennao Sabbat, are you not?"

"I am, sir."

"For how long, boy?"

"For twenty-two years, sir."

"And your master's reputation is valuable to you?"

"Yes, sir."

"Would you consider it of importance to protect that reputation?"

"Yes, sir."

"As important to protect his reputation as his physical life?"

"No, sir."

"As important to protect his reputation as the reputation of another."

R. Idda hesitated. He said, "Such cases must be decided on their individual merit, sir. There is no way of establishing a general rule."

Baley hesitated. These Spacer robots spoke more smoothly and intellectually than Earth models did. He was not at all sure he could outthink one.

He said, "If you decided that the reputation of your master was more important than that of another, say, that of Alfred

Barr Humboldt, would you lie to protect your master's reputation?''

"I would, sir.''

"Did you lie in your testimony concerning your master in his controversy with Dr. Humboldt?''

"No, sir.''

"But if you were lying, you would deny you were lying in order to protect that lie, wouldn't you?''

"Yes, sir.''

"Well, then,'' said Baley, "let's consider this. Your master, Gennao Sabbat, is a young man of great reputation in mathematics, but he is a young man. If, in this controversy with Dr. Humboldt, he had succumbed to temptation and had acted unethically, he would suffer a certain eclipse of reputation, but he is young and would have ample time to recover. He would have many intellectual triumphs ahead of him and men would eventually look upon this plagiaristic attempt as the mistake of a hot-blooded youth, deficient in judgment. It would be something that would be made up for in the future.

"If, on the other hand, it were Dr. Humboldt who succumbed to temptation, the matter would be much more serious. He is an old man whose great deeds have spread over centuries. His reputation has been unblemished hitherto. All of that, however, would be forgotten in the light of this one crime of his later years, and he would have no opportunity to make up for it in the comparatively short time remaining to him. There would be little more that he could accomplish. There would be so many more years of work ruined in Humboldt's case than in that of your master and so much less opportunity to win back his position. You see, don't you, that Humboldt faces the worse situation and deserves the greater consideration?''

There was a long pause. Then R. Idda said, with unmoved voice, "My evidence was a lie. It was Dr. Humboldt whose work it was, and my master has attempted, wrongfully, to appropriate the credit.''

Baley said, "Very well, boy. You are instructed to say nothing to anyone about this until given permission by the captain of the ship. You are excused.''

The screen blanked out and Baley puffed at his pipe. "Do you suppose the captain heard that, Daneel?''

"I am sure of it. He is the only witness, except for us."

"Good. Now for the other."

"But is there any point to that, friend Elijah, in view of what R. Idda has confessed?"

"Of course there is. R. Idda's confession means nothing."

"Nothing?"

"Nothing at all. I pointed out that Dr. Humboldt's position was the worse. Naturally, if he was lying to protect Sabbat, he would switch to the truth as, in fact, he claimed to have done. On the other hand, if he was telling the truth, he would switch to a lie to protect Humboldt. It's still mirror-image and we haven't gained anything."

"But then what will we gain by questioning R. Preston?"

"Nothing, if the mirror image were perfect—but it is not. After all, one of the robots *is* telling the truth to begin with, and one *is* lying to begin with, and that is a point of asymmetry. Let me see R. Preston. And if the transcription of R. Idda's examination is done, let me have it."

The projector came into use again. R. Preston stared out of it, identical with R. Idda in every respect, except for some trivial chest design.

Baley said, "Greetings, R. Preston." He kept the record of R. Idda's examination before him as he spoke.

"Greetings, sir," said R. Preston. His voice was identical with that of R. Idda.

"You are the personal servant of Alfred Barr Humboldt, are you not?"

"I am, sir."

"For how long, boy?"

"For twenty-two years, sir."

"And your master's reputation is valuable to you?"

"Yes, sir."

"Would you consider it of importance to protect that reputation?"

"Yes, sir."

"As important to protect his reputation as his physical life?"

"No, sir."

"As important to protect his reputation as the reputation of another?"

R. Preston hesitated. He said, "Such cases must be decided on their individual merit, sir. There is no way of establishing a general rule."

Baley said, "If you decided that the reputation of your master were more important than that of another, say, that of Gennao Sabbat, would you lie to protect your master's reputation?"

"I would, sir."

"Did you lie in your testimony concerning your master in his controversy with Dr. Sabbat?"

"No, sir."

"But if you were lying, you would deny you were lying, in order to protect that lie, wouldn't you?"

"Yes, sir."

"Well, then," said Baley, "let's consider this. Your master, Alfred Barr Humboldt, is an old man of great reputation in mathematics, but he is an old man. If, in this controversy with Dr. Sabbat, he had succumbed to temptation and had acted unethically, he would suffer a certain eclipse of reputation, but his great age and his centuries of accomplishments would stand against that and would win out. Men would look upon this plagiaristic attempt as the mistake of a perhaps-sick old man, no longer certain in judgment.

"If, on the other hand, it were Dr. Sabbat who had succumbed to temptation, the matter would be much more serious. He is a young man, with a far less secure reputation. He would ordinarily have centuries ahead of him in which he might accumulate knowledge and achieve great things. This will be closed to him, now, obscured by one mistake of his youth. He has a much longer future to lose than your master has. You see, don't you, that Sabbat faces the worse situation and deserves the greater consideration?"

There was a long pause. Then R. Preston said, with unmoved voice, "My evidence was a l—"

At that point, he broke off and said nothing more.

Baley said, "Please continue, R. Preston."

There was no response.

R. Daneel said, "I am afraid, friend Elijah, that R. Preston is in stasis. He is out of commission."

"Well, then," said Baley, "we have finally produced an asymmetry. From this, we can see who the guilty person is."

"In what way, friend Elijah?"

"Think it out. Suppose you were a person who had committed no crime and that your personal robot were a witness to that. There would be nothing you need do. Your robot would tell the truth and bear you out. If, however, you were a person who *had* committed the crime, you would have to depend on your robot to lie. That would be a somewhat riskier position, for although the robot would lie, if necessary, the greater inclination would be to tell the truth, so that the lie would be less firm than the truth would be. To prevent that, the crime-committing person would very likely have to *order* the robot to lie. In this way, First Law would be strengthened by Second Law; perhaps very substantially strengthened."

"That would seem reasonable," said R. Daneel.

"Suppose we have one robot of each type. One robot would switch from truth, unreinforced, to the lie, and could do so after some hesitation, without serious trouble. The other robot would switch from the lie, *strongly reinforced*, to the truth, but could do so only at the risk of burning out various positronic-trackways in his brain and falling into stasis."

"And since R. Preston went into stasis—"

"R. Preston's master, Dr. Humboldt, is the man guilty of plagiarism. If you transmit this to the captain and urge him to face Dr. Humboldt with the matter at once, he may force a confession. If so, I hope you will tell me immediately."

"I will certainly do so. You will excuse me, friend Elijah? I must talk to the captain privately."

"Certainly. Use the conference room. It is shielded."

Baley could do no work of any kind in R. Daneel's absence. He sat in uneasy silence. A great deal would depend on the value of his analysis, and he was acutely aware of his lack of expertise in robotics.

R. Daneel was back in half an hour—very nearly the longest half hour of Baley's life.

There was no use, of course, in trying to determine what had happened from the expression of the humanoid's impassive face. Baley tried to keep his face impassive.

"Yes, R. Daneel?" he asked.

"Precisely as you said, friend Elijah. Dr. Humboldt has confessed. He was counting, he said, on Dr. Sabbat giving way and allowing Dr. Humboldt to have this one last triumph. The crisis is over and you will find the captain grateful. He has given me permission to tell you that he admires your subtlety greatly and I believe that I, myself, will achieve favor for having suggested you."

"Good," said Baley, his knees weak and his forehead moist now that his decision had proven correct, "but Jehoshaphat, R. Daneel, don't put me on the spot like that again, will you?"

"I will try not to, friend Elijah. All will depend, of course, on the importance of a crisis, on your nearness, and on certain other factors. Meanwhile, I have a question—"

"Yes?"

"Was it not possible to suppose that passage from a lie to the truth was easy, while passage from the truth to a lie was difficult? And in that case, would not the robot in stasis have been going from a truth to a lie, and since R. Preston was in stasis, might one not have drawn the conclusion that it was Dr. Humboldt who was innocent and Dr. Sabbat who was guilty?"

"Yes. R. Daneel. It was possible to argue that way, but it was the other argument that proved right. Humboldt did confess, didn't he?"

"He did. But with arguments possible in both directions, how could you, friend Elijah, so quickly pick the correct one?"

For a moment, Baley's lips twitched. Then he relaxed and they curved into a smile. "Because, R. Daneel, I took into account human reactions, not robotic ones. I know more about human beings than about robots. In other words, I had an idea as to which mathematician was guilty before I ever interviewed the robots. Once I provoked an asymmetric reponse in them, I simply interpreted it in such a way as to place the guilt on the one I already believed to be guilty. The robotic reponse was dramatic enough to break down the guilty man; my own analysis of human behavior might not have been sufficient to do so."

"I am curious to know what your analysis of human behavior was."

"Jehoshaphat, R. Daneel; think, and you won't have to ask. There is another point of asymmetry in this tale of mirror image besides the matter of true-and-false. There is the matter of the age of the two mathematicians; one is quite old and one is quite young."

"Yes, of course, but what then?"

"Why, this. I can see a young man, flushed with a sudden, startling and revolutionary idea, consulting in the matter an old man whom he has, from his early student days, thought of as a demigod in the field. I can*not* see an old man, rich in honors and used to triumphs, coming up with a sudden, startling and revolutionary idea, consulting a man centuries his junior whom he is bound to think of as a young whipper snapper—or whatever term a Spacer would use. Then, too, if a young man had the chance, would he try to steal the idea of a revered demigod? It would be unthinkable. On the other hand, an old man, conscious of declining powers, might well snatch at one last chance of fame and consider a baby in the field to have no rights he was bound to observe. In short, it was not conceivable that Humboldt consult Sabbat, or that Sabbat steal Humboldt's idea; and from both angles, Dr. Humboldt was guilty."

R. Daneel considered that for a long time. Then he held out his hand. "I must leave now, friend Elijah. It was good to see you. May we meet again soon."

Baley gripped the robot's hand, warmly, "If you don't mind, R. Daneel," he said, "not too soon."

Brillo

Harlan Ellison and Ben Bova

Crazy season for cops is August. In August the riots start.
Not just to get the pigs off campus (where they don't even
happen to be, because school is out) or to rid the railroad flats
of *Rattus norvegicus,* but they start for no reason at all. Some
bunch of sweat-stinking kids get a hydrant spouting and it
drenches the storefront of a shylock who lives most of his
time in Kipps Bay when he's not sticking it to his Spanish
Harlem customers, and he comes out of the pawnshop with a
Louisville Slugger somebody hocked once, and he takes a
swing at a *mestizo* urchin, and the next thing the precinct
knows, they've got a three-star riot going on two full city
blocks; then they call in the copchoppers from Governor's
Island and spray the neighborhood with quiescent, and after a
while the beat cops go in with breathers, in threes, and they
start pulling in the bash-head cases. Why did it get going? A
little water on a store window that hadn't been squeegee'd
since 1974? A short temper? Some kid flipping some guy the
bird? No.

Crazy season is August.

Housewives take their steam irons to their old men's heads.
Basset hound salesmen who trundle display suitcases full of
ready-to-wear for eleven months, without squeaking at their
bosses, suddenly pull twine knives and carve up taxi drivers.
Suicides go out twenty-story windows and off the Verrazano-
Narrows Bridge like confetti at an astronaut's parade down
Fifth Avenue. Teenaged rat packs steal half a dozen cars and
drag-race them three abreast against traffic up White Plains

180

Road till they run them through the show windows of super-markets. No reason. Just August. Crazy season.

It was August, that special heat of August when the temperature keeps going till it reaches the secret kill-crazy mugginess at which point eyeballs roll up white in florid faces and gravity knives appear as if by magic, it was *that* time of August, when Brillo arrived in the precinct.

Buzzing softly (the sort of sound an electric watch makes), he stood inert in the center of the precinct station's bullpen, his bright blue-anodized metal a gleaming contrast to the paintless worn floorboards. He stood in the middle of momentary activity, and no one who passed him seemed to be able to pay attention to anything *but* him:

Not the two plainclothes officers duckwalking between them a sixty-two-year-old pervert whose specialty was flashing just before the subway doors closed.

Not the traffic cop being berated by his Sergeant for having allowed his parking ticket receipts to get waterlogged in a plastic bag bombardment initiated by the last few residents of a condemned building.

Not the tac/squad macers reloading their weapons from the supply dispensers.

Not the line of beat cops forming up in ranks for their shift on the street.

Not the Desk Sergeant trying to book three hookers who had been arrested soliciting men queued up in front of NBC for a network game show called "Sell a Sin."

Not the fuzzette using a wrist bringalong on the mugger who had tried to snip a cutpurse on her as she patrolled Riverside Drive.

None of them, even engaged in the hardly ordinary business of sweeping up felons, could avoid staring at him. All eyes kept returning to the robot: a squat cylinder resting on tiny trunnions. Brillo's optical sensors, up in his dome-shaped head, bulged like the eyes of an acromegalic insect. The eyes caught the glint of the overhead neons.

The eyes, particularly, made the crowd in the muster room nervous. The crowd milled and thronged, but did not clear until the Chief of Police spread his hands in a typically Semitic gesture of impatience and yelled, "All right, already, can you clear this room!"

There was suddenly a great deal of unoccupied space.

Chief Santorini turned back to the robot. And to Reardon.

Frank Reardon shifted his weight uneasily from one foot to the other. He absorbed the Police Chief's look and tracked it out around the muster room, watching the men who were watching the robot. *His* robot. Not that he owned it any longer . . . but he still thought of it as his. He understood how Dr. Victor Frankenstein could feel paternal about a congeries of old spare body parts.

He watched them as they sniffed around the robot like bulldogs delighted with the discovery of a new fire hydrant. Even beefy Sgt. Loyo, the Desk Sergeant, up in his perch at the far end of the shabby room, looked clearly suspicious of the robot.

Santorini had brought two uniformed Lieutenants with him. Administrative assistants. Donkeywork protocol guardians. By-the-book civil service types, lamps lit against any *ee*-vil encroachment of dat ole debbil machine into the paydirt of human beings' job security. They looked grim.

The FBI man sat impassively on a stout wooden bench that ran the length of the room. He sat under posters for the Police Athletic League, the 4th War Bond Offensive, Driver Training Courses and an advertisement for *The Christian Science Monitor* with a FREE—TAKE ONE pocket attached. He had not said a word since being introduced to Reardon. And Reardon had even forgotten the name. Was that part of the camouflage of FBI agents? He sat there looking steely-eyed and jut-jawed. He looked grim, too.

Only the whiz kid from the Mayor's office was smiling as he stepped once again through the grilled door into the bull-pen. He smiled as he walked slowly all around the robot. He smiled as he touched the matte finish of the machine, and he smiled as he made pleasure noises: as if he was inspecting a new car on a showroom floor, on the verge of saying, "I'll take it. What terms can I get?"

He looked out through the wirework of the bullpen at Reardon. "Why do you call it Brillo?"

Reardon hesitated a moment, trying desperately to remember the whiz kid's first name. He was an engineer, not a public relations man. Universal Electronics should have sent Wendell down with Brillo. *He* knew how to talk to these image-happy clowns from City Hall. Knew how to butter and baste them so they put ink to contract. But part of the deal when he'd been forced to sell Reardon Electronics into merger with UE (after the stock raid and the power grab, which he'd lost) was that he stay on with projects like Brillo. Stay with them all the way to the bottom line.

It was as pleasant as clapping time while your wife made love to another man.

"It's . . . a nickname. Somebody at UE thought it up. Thought it was funny."

The whiz kid looked blank. "What's funny about Brillo?"

"Metal fuzz," the Police Chief rasped.

Light dawned on the whiz kid's face, and he began to chuckle; Reardon nodded, then caught the look of animosity on the Police Chief's face. Reardon looked away quickly from the old man's fiercely seamed features. It was getting more grim, much tenser.

Captain Summit came slowly down the stairs to join them. He was close to Reardon's age, but much grayer. He moved with one hand on the banister, like an old man.

Why do they all look so tired? Reardon wondered. *And why do they seem to look wearier, more frightened, every time they look at the robot? Are they afraid it's come around their turn to be replaced? Is that the way I looked when UE forced me out of the company I created?*

Summit eyed the robot briefly, then walked over and sat down on the bench several feet apart from the silent FBI man. The whiz kid came out of the bullpen. They all looked at Summit.

"Okay, I've picked a man to work with him . . . it, I mean." He was looking at Reardon. "Mike Polchik. He's a good cop; young and alert. Good record. Nothing extraordinary, no showboater, just a solid cop. He'll give your machine a fair trial."

"That's fine. Thank you, Captain," Reardon said.

"He'll be right down. I pulled him out of the formation. He's getting his gear. He'll be right down."

The whiz kid cleared his throat. Reardon looked at him. *He* wasn't tired. But then, *he* didn't wear a uniform. *He* wasn't pushed up against what these men found in the streets every day. *He lives in Darien, probably,* Frank Reardon thought,

*and buys those suits in quiet little shops where there're never
more than three customers at a time.*

"How many of these machines can your company make in
a year?" the whiz kid asked.

"It's not my company anymore."

"I mean the company you work for—Universal."

"Inside a year: we can have them coming out at a rate of a
hundred a month." Reardon paused. "Maybe more."

The whiz kid grinned. "We could replace every beat patrolman . . ."

A spark-gap was leaped. The temperature dropped. Reardon
saw the uniformed men stiffen. Quickly, he said, "Police
robots are intended to *augment* the existing force." Even
more firmly he said, "Not replace it. We're trying to *help* the
policeman, not get rid of him."

"Oh, hey, sure. Of *course*!" the whiz kid said, glancing
around the room. "That's what I meant," he added unneces-
sarily. Everyone knew what he meant.

The silence at the bottom of the Marianas Trench.

And in that silence: heavy footsteps, coming down the
stairs from the second-floor locker rooms.

He stopped at the foot of the stairs, one shoe tipped up on
the final step; he stared at the robot in the bullpen for a long
moment. Then the patrolman walked over to Captain Summit, only once more casting a glance into the bullpen. Summit smiled reassuringly at the patrolman and then gestured
toward Reardon.

"Mike, this is Mr. Reardon. He designed—the robot. Mr.
Reardon, Patrolman Polchik."

Reardon extended his hand and Polchik exerted enough
pressure to make him wince.

Polchik was two inches over six feet tall, and weighty.
Muscular; thick forearms; the kind found on men who work
in foundries. Light, crew-cut hair. Square face, wide open;
strong jaw, hard eyes under heavy brow ridges. Even his
smile looked hard. He was ready for work, with a .32 Needle
Positive tilt-stuck on its velcro fastener at mid-thigh and an
armament bandolier slanted across his broad chest. His aura
keyed one word: cop.

"The Captain tells me I'm gonna be walkin' with your
machine t'night."

Nodding, flexing his fingers, Reardon said, "Yes, that's right. The Captain probably told you, we want to test Brillo under actual foot patrol conditions. That's what he was designed for: foot patrol."

"Been a long time since I done foot patrol," Polchik said: "Work a growler, usually."

"Beg pardon?"

Summit translated. "Growler: prowl car."

"Oh. Oh, I see," Reardon said, trying to be friendly.

"It's only for tonight, Mike," the Captain said. "Just a test."

Polchik nodded as though he understood far more than either Reardon or Summit had told him. He did not turn his big body, but his eyes went to the robot. Through the grillework Brillo (with the sort of sound an electric watch makes) buzzed softly, staring at nothing. Polchik looked it up and down, slowly, very carefully. Finally he said, "Looks okay to me."

"Preliminary tests," Reardon said, "everything short of actual field runs . . . everything's been tested out. You won't have any trouble."

Polchik murmured something.

"I beg your pardon?" Frank Reardon said.

"On-the-job-training," Polchik repeated. He did not smile. But a sound ran through the rest of the station house crew.

"Well, whenever you're ready, Officer Polchik," the whiz kid said suddenly. Reardon winced. The kid had a storm-window salesman's tone even when he was trying to be disarming.

"Yeah. Right." Polchik moved toward the front door. The robot did not move. Polchik stopped and turned around. Everyone was watching.

"I thought he went on his own, uh, independ'nt?"

They were all watching Reardon now.

"He's been voice-keyed to me since the plant," Reardon said. "To shift command, I'll have to prime him with your voice." He turned to the robot. "Brillo, come here, please."

The word *please*.

The buzzing became more distinct for a moment as the trunnions withdrew inside the metal skin. Then the sound diminished, became barely audible, and the robot stepped forward smoothly. He walked to Reardon and stopped.

"Brillo, this is Officer Mike Polchik. You'll be working with him tonight. He'll be your superior and you'll be under his immediate orders." Reardon waved Polchik over. "Would you say a few words, so he can program your voice-print?"

Polchik looked at Reardon. Then he looked at the robot. Then he looked around the muster room. Desk Sergeant Loyo was grinning. "Whattaya want me to say?"

"Anything."

One of the detectives had come down the stairs. No one had noticed before. Lounging against the railing leading to the squad room upstairs, he giggled. "Tell him some'a your best friends are can openers, Mike."

The whiz kid and the Chief of Police threw him a look. Summit said, "Bratten!" He shut up. After a moment he went back upstairs. Quietly.

"Go ahead. Anything," Reardon urged Polchik.

The patrolman drew a deep breath, took another step foward and said, self-consciously, "Come on, let's go. It's gettin' late."

The soft buzzing (the sort of sound an electric watch makes) came once again from somewhere deep inside the robot. "Yes, sir," he said, in the voice of Frank Reardon, and moved very smoothly, very quickly, toward Polchik. The patrolman stepped back quickly, tried to look casual, turned and started toward the door of the station house once more. The robot followed.

When they had gone, the whiz kid drywashed his hands, smiled at everyone and said, "Now it begins."

Reardon winced again. The Desk Sergeant, Loyo, rattled pencils, tapped them even, dumped them into an empty jelly jar on the blotter desk. Everyone else looked away. The FBI man smiled.

From outside the precinct house the sounds of the city seemed to grow louder in the awkward silence. In all that noise no one even imagined he could hear the sound of the robot.

Polchik was trying the locks on the burglarproof gates of the shops lining Amsterdam between 82nd and 83rd. The robot was following him, doing the same thing. Polchik was getting burned up. He turned up 83rd and entered the alley behind the shops, retracing his steps back toward 82nd. The robot followed him.

Polchik didn't like being followed. It made him feel uneasy. *Damned piece of junk!* he thought. *He rips one of them gates off the hinges, there'll be hell to pay down at the precinct.*

Polchik rattled a gate. He moved on. The robot followed. (*Like a little kid,* Polchik thought.) The robot grabbed the gate and clanged it back and forth. Polchik spun on him. "Listen, dammit, stop makin' all that racket! Y'wanna wake everybody? You know what time it is?"

"1:37 A.M.," the robot replied, in Reardon's voice.

Polchik looked heavenward.

Shaking his head he moved on. The robot stopped. "Officer Polchik." Mike Polchik turned, exasperated. *What now?*

"I detect a short circuit in this alarm system," the robot said. He was standing directly under the Morse-Dictograph Security panel. "If it is not repaired, it will cancel the fail-safe circuits."

"I'll call it in," Polchik said, pulling the pin-mike on its spring-return wire from his callbox. He was about to thumb on the wristband callbox, when the robot extruded an articulated arm from its chest. "I am equipped to repair the unit without assistance," the robot said, and a light-beam began to pulse at the end of the now-goosenecked arm.

"Leave it alone!"

"A simple 155-0 system," the robot said. "Fixed temperature unit with heat detectors, only barely exceeding NFPA standard 74 and NFPA 72-A requirements." The arm snaked up to the panel and followed the break line around the outside.

"Don't screw with it! It'll set it—"

The panel accordion-folded back. Polchik's mouth fell open. "Oh my God," he mumbled.

The robot's extruded arm worked inside for a long moment, then withdrew. "It is fully operable now." The panel folded back into place.

Polchik let the pin-mike slip from his fingers and it zzzzz'd back into the wristband. He walked away down the alley, looking haunted.

Down at the corner, the Amsterdam Inn's lights shone weakly, reflecting dully in the street oil slick. Polchik paused at the mouth of the alley and pulled out the pin-mike again. He thumbed the callbox on his wrist, *feeling* the heavy shadow of the robot behind him.

"Polchik," he said into the mike.

"Okay, Mike?" crackled the reply. "How's yer partner doing?"

Glancing over his shoulder, Polchik saw the robot standing impassively, gooseneck arm vanished; ten feet behind him. Respectfully. "Don't call it my partner."

Laughter on the other end of the line. "What's 'a' matter, Mike? 'Fraid of him?"

"Ahhh . . . cut the clownin'. Everything quiet here, Eighty-two and Amsterdam."

"Okay. Oh, hey, Mike, remember . . . if it starts to rain, get yer partner under an awning before he starts t'rust!"

He was still laughing like a jackass as Polchik let the spring-wire zzzzz back into the callbox.

"Hey, Mike! What you got there?"

Polchik looked toward the corner. It was Rico, the bartender from the Amsterdam Inn.

"It's a robot," Polchik said. He kept his voice very flat. He was in no mood for further ribbing.

"Real he is, yeah? No kidding?" Rico's face always looked to Polchik like a brass artichoke, ready to be peeled. But he was friendly enough. And cooperative. It was a dunky neighborhood and Polchik had found Rico useful more than once. "What's he supposed to do, eh?"

"He's supposed to be a cop." Glum.

Rico shook his vegetable head. "What they gonna do next? Robots. So what happens t'you, Mike? They make you a detective?"

"Sure. And the week after that they make me Captain."

Rico looked uncertain, didn't know whether he should laugh or sympathize. Finally, he said, "Hey, I got a bottle for ya," feeling it would serve, whatever his reaction should properly have been. "Betcha your wife likes it . . . from Poland, imported stuff. Got grass or weeds or some kinda stuff in it. S'posed to be really sensational."

For just a second, peripherally seen, Polchik thought the robot had stirred.

"Escuchar! I'll get it for you."

He disappeared inside the bar before Polchik could stop him. The robot *did* move. It trembled . . . ?

Rico came out with a paper bag, its neck twisted closed around what was obviously a bottle of liquor.

"I'll have to pick it up tomorrow," Polchik said. "I don't have the car tonight."

"I'll keep it for you. If I'm on relief when you come by, ask Maldonado."

The robot was definitely humming. Polchik could hear it. (The sort of sound an electric watch makes.) It suddenly moved, closing the distance, ten feet between them, till it passed Polchik, swiveled to face Rico—who stumbled backward halfway to the entrance to the Amsterdam Inn—then swiveled back to face Polchik.

"Visual and audial data indicate a one-to-one extrapolation of same would result in a conclusion that a gratuity has been offered to you, Officer Polchik. Further, logic indicates that you intend to accept said gratuity. Such behavior is a programmed infraction of the law. It is—"

"Shut up!"

Rico stood very close to the door, wide-eyed.

"I'll see you tomorrow night," Polchik said to him.

"Officer Polchik," the robot went on as though there had been no interruption, "it is clear if you intend to accept a gratuity, you will be breaking the law and liable to arrest and prosecution under Law Officer Statutes number—"

"I said shuddup, dammit!" Polchik said, louder. "I don't even know what the hell you're talkin' about, but I said shuddup, and that's an *order*!"

"Yes, sir," the robot replied instantly. "However, my data tapes will record this conversation in its entirety and it will be transcribed into a written report at the conclusion of our patrol."

"What?" Polchik felt gears gnashing inside his head, thought of gears, thought of the robot, rejected gears and thought about Captain Summit. Then he thought about gears again . . . crushing him.

Rico's voice intruded, sounding scared. "What's he saying? What's that about a report?"

"Now wait a minute, Brillo," Polchik said, walking up to the robot. "Nothin's happened here you can write a report on."

The robot's voice—*Reardon's* voice, Polchik thought irritatedly—was very firm. "Logic indicates a high probability that a gratuity has been accepted in the past, and another will be accepted in the future."

Polchik felt chili peppers in his gut. Hooking his thumbs in his belt—a pose he automatically assumed when he was trying to avert trouble—he deliberately toned down his voice. "Listen, Brillo, you forget the whole thing, you understand. You just for*get* it."

"Am I to understand you desire my tapes to be erased?"

"Yeah, that's right. Erase it."

"Is that an order?"

"It's an order!"

The robot hummed to itself for a heartbeat, then, "Primary programming does not allow erasure of data tapes. Tapes can be erased only post-transcription or by physically removing same from my memory bank."

"Listen—" Rico started, "I don't wan' no trub—"

Polchik impatiently waved him to silence. He didn't need any complications right now. "Listen, Brillo . . ."

"Yes. I hear it."

Polchik was about to continue speaking. He stopped. *I hear it? This damned thing's gone bananas.* "I didn't say anything yet."

"Oh. I'm sorry, sir. I thought you were referring to the sound of a female human screaming on 84th Street, third-floor front apartment."

Polchik looked everywhichway. "What are you *talkin'* about? You crazy or something?"

"No, sir. I am a model X-44. Though under certain special conditions my circuits can malfunction, conceivably, nothing in my repair programming parameters approximates 'crazy.'"

"Then just shuddup and let's get this thing straightened out. Now, try'n understand this. You're just a robot, see. You don't understand the way real people do things. Like, for instance, when Rico here offers me a bottle of—"

"If you'll pardon me, sir, the female human is now screaming in the 17,000-cycle-per-second range. My tapes are programmed to value-judge such a range as concomitant with fear
and possibly extreme pain. I suggest we act at once."

"Hey, Polchik . . ." Rico began.

"No, shuddup, Rico. Hey, listen, robot, Brillo, whatever:
you mean you can *hear* some woman screaming, two blocks
away and up three flights? Is the window open?" Then he
stopped. "What'm I doin'? Talking to this thing!" He remembered the briefing he'd been given by Captain Summit.
"Okay. You say you can hear her . . . let's find her."

The robot took off at top speed. Back into the alley behind
the Amsterdam Inn, across the 82nd-83rd block, across the
83rd-84th block, full-out with no clanking or clattering. Polchik
found himself pounding along ten feet behind the robot, then
twenty feet, then thirty feet; suddenly he was puffing, his
chest heavy, the armament bandolier banging the mace cans
and the riot-prod and the bullhorn and the peppergas shpritzers
and the extra clips of Needler ammunition against his chest
and back.

The robot emerged from the alley, turned a 90° angle with
the sharpest cut Polchik had ever seen, and jogged up 84th
Street. Brillo was caught for a moment in the glare of a neon
streetlamp, then was taking the steps of a crippled old brown-
stone three at a time.

Troglodytes with punch-presses were berkeleying Polchik's
lungs and stomach. His head was a dissenter's punchboard.
But he followed. More slowly now; and had trouble negotiat-
ing the last flight of stairs to the third floor. As he gained the
landing, he was hauling himself hand-over-hand up the banister. *If God'd wanted cops to walk beats he wouldn't'a created the growler!*

The robot, Brillo, X-44, was standing in front of the door
marked 3-A. He was quivering like a hound on point. (Buzzing softly with the sort of sound an electric watch makes.)
Now Polchik could hear the woman himself, above the roar
of blood in his temples.

"Open up in there!" Polchik bellowed. He ripped the .32
Needle Positive off its velcro fastener and banged on the door
with the butt. The lanyard was twisted; he untwisted it.
"This's the police. I'm demanding entrance to a private

domicile under Public Law 22-809, allowing for supersed'nce of the 'home-castle' rule under emergency conditions. I said *open up in there*!''

The screaming went up and plateau'd a few hundred cycles higher, and Polchik snapped at the robot, ''Get outta my way.''

Brillo obediently moved back a pace, and in the narrow hallway Polchik braced himself against the wall, locked the exoskeletal rods on his boots, dropped his crash-hat visor, jacked up his leg and delivered a powerful *savate* kick at the door.

It was a pre-SlumClear apartment. The door bowed and dust spurted from the seams, but it held. Despite the rods, Polchik felt a searing pain gash up through his leg. He fell back, hopping about painfully, hearing himself going ''oo— oo—oo'' and then prepared himself to have to do it again. The robot moved up in front of him, said, ''Excuse me, sir,'' and smoothly cleaved the door down the center with the edge of a metal hand that had somehow suddenly developed a cutting edge. He reached in, grasped both sliced edges of the hardwood, and ripped the door outward in two even halves.

''Oh,'' Polchik stared open-mouthed for only an instant.

Then they were inside.

The unshaven man with the beer gut protruding from beneath his olive drab skivvy undershirt was slapping the hell out of his wife. He had thick black tufts of hair that bunched like weed corsages in his armpits. She was half-lying over the back of a sofa with the springs showing. Her eyes were swollen and blue-black as dried prunes. One massive bruise was already draining down her cheek into her neck. She was weakly trying to fend off her husband's blows with ineffectual wrist-blocks.

''Okay! That's it!'' Polchik yelled.

The sound of another voice, in the room with them, brought the man and his wife to a halt. He turned his head, his left hand still tangled in her long black hair, and he stared at the two intruders.

He began cursing in Spanish. Then he burst into a guttural combination of English and Spanish, and finally slowed in his own spittle to a ragged English. ''. . . won't let me alone . . . go out my house . . . always botherin' won't let me alone . . . damn . . .'' and he went back to Spanish as he pushed the woman from him and started across the room. The woman tumbled, squealing, out of sight behind the sofa.

The man stumbled crossing the room, and Polchik's needler tracked him. Behind him he heard the robot softly humming, and then it said, "Sir, analysis indicates psychotic glaze over subject's eyes."

The man grabbed a half-filled quart bottle of beer off the television set, smashed it against the leading edge of the TV, giving it a half-twist (which registered instantly in Polchik's mind: this guy knew how to get a ragged edge on the weapon; he was an experienced bar-room brawler) and suddenly lurched toward Polchik with the jagged stump in his hand.

Abruptly, before Polchik could even thumb the needler to stun (it was on dismember), a metal blur passed him, swept into the man, lifted him high in the air with one hand, turned him upside-down so the bottle, small plastic change and an unzipped shoe showered down onto the threadbare rug. Arms and legs fluttered helplessly.

"Aieeee!" the man screamed, his hair hanging down, his face plugged red with blood. "*Madre de dios!*"

"Leave him alone!" It was the wife screaming, charging—if it could be called that, on hands and knees—from behind the sofa. She clambered to her feet and ran at the robot, screeching and cursing, pounding her daywork-reddened fists against his gleaming hide.

"Okay, okay," Polchik said, his voice lower but strong enough to get through to her. Pulling her and her hysteria away from the robot, he ordered, "Brillo, put him down."

"You goddam cops got no right bustin' in here," the man started complaining the moment he was on his feet again. "Goddam cops don't let a man'n his wife alone for nothin' no more. You got a warrant? Huh? You gonna get in trouble, plenty trouble. This my home, cop, 'home is a man's castle,' hah? Right? Right? An' you an' this tin can . . ." He was waving his arms wildly.

Brillo wheeled a few inches toward the man. The stream of abuse cut off instantly, the man's face went pale, and he threw up his hands to protect himself.

"This man can be arrested for assault and battery, failure to heed a legitimate police order, attempted assault on a police officer with a deadly weapon, and disturbing the peace,"

Brillo said. His flat, calm voice seemed to echo off the grimy walls.

"It . . . it's talkin'! Flavio! *Demonio*!" The wife spiraled toward hysteria again.

"Shall I inform him of his rights under the Public Laws, sir?" Brillo asked Polchik.

"You gon' arrest me? Whu'for?"

"Brillo . . ." Polchik began.

Brillo started again, "Assault and battery, failure to—"

Polchik looked annoyed. "Shuddup, I wasn't asking you to run it again. Just shuddup."

"I din't do nothin'! You come bust t'rough my door when me an' my wife wass arguin', an' you beat me up. Look'a the bruise on my arm." The arm was slightly inflamed where Brillo had grabbed him.

"Flavio!" the woman whimpered.

"Isabel; *callete la boca!*"

"I live right downstairs," a voice said from behind them. "He's always beating her up, and he drinks all the time and then he pisses out the window!" Polchik spun and a man in Levi's and striped pajama tops was standing in the ruined doorway. "Sometimes it looks like it's raining on half my window. Once I put my hand out to see—"

"Get outta here!" Polchik bellowed, and the man vanished.

"I din't do nothin'!" Flavio said again, semi-surly.

"My data tapes," Brillo replied evenly, "will clearly show your actions."

"Day to tapes? Whass he talkin' 'bout?" Flavio turned to Polchik, an unaccustomed ally against the hulking machine. Polchik felt a sense of camaraderie with the man.

"He's got everything down recorded . . . like on TV. And sound tapes, too." Polchik looked back at him and recognized something in the dismay on the man's fleshy face.

Brillo asked again, "Shall I inform him of his rights, sir?"

"Officer, sir, you ain't gonna 'rest him?" the woman half asked, half pleaded, her eyes swollen almost closed, barely open, but tearful.

"He came after me with a bottle," Polchik said. "And he didn't do you much good, neither."

"He wass work op. Iss allright. He's okay now. It wass joss a'argumen'. Nobody got hort."

Brillo's hum got momentarily higher. "Madam, you should inspect your face in my mirror." He hummed and his skin became smoothly reflective. "My sensors detect several contusions and abrasions, particularly . . ."

"Skip it," Polchik said abruptly. "Come on, Brillo, let's go."

Brillo's metal hide went blank again. "I have not informed the prisoner . . ."

"No prisoner," Polchik said. "No arrest. Let's go."

"But the data clearly shows . . ."

"Forget it!" Polchik turned to face the man; he was standing there looking uncertain, rubbing his arm. "And you, strongarm . . . lemme hear one more peep outta this apartment and you'll be in jail so fast it'll make your head swim . . . and for a helluva long time, too. If you get there at all. We don't like guys like you. So I'm puttin' the word out on you . . . I don't like guys comin' at me with bottles."

"Sir . . . I . . ."

"Come on!"

The robot followed the cop and the apartment was suddenly silent. Flavio and Isabel looked at each other sheepishly, then he began to cry, went to her and touched her bruises with the gentlest fingers.

They went downstairs, Polchik staring and trying to figure out how it was such a massive machine could navigate the steps so smoothly. Something was going on at the base of the robot, but Polchik couldn't get a good view of it. Dust puffed out from beneath the machine. And something sparkled.

Once on the sidewalk, Brillo said, "Sir, that man should have been arrested. He was clearly violating several statues."

Polchik made a sour face. "His wife wouldn't of pressed the charge."

"He attacked a police officer with a deadly weapon."

"So that makes him Mad Dog Coll? He's scared shitless, in the future he'll watch it. For a while, at least."

Brillo was hardly satisfied at this noncomputable conclusion. "A police officer's duty is to arrest persons who are suspected of having broken the law. Civil or criminal courts have the legal jurisdiction to decide the suspect's guilt or innocence. Your duty, sir, was to arrest that man."

"Sure, sure. Have it *your* way, half the damn city'll be in jail, and the other half'll be springin' 'em out."

Brillo said nothing, but Polchik thought the robot's humming sounded sullen. He had a strong suspicion the machine wouldn't forget it. Or Rico, either.

And farther up the street, to cinch Polchik's suspicion, the robot once more tried to reinforce his position. "According to the Peace Officer Responsibility Act of 1975, failure of an officer to take into custody person or persons indisputably engaged in acts that contravene . . ."

"Awright, dammit, knock it off. I tole you why I din't arrest that poor jughead, so stop bustin' my chops with it. You ain't happy, you don't like it, tell my Sergeant!"

Sergeant, hell, Polchik thought. *This stuff goes right to Captain Summit, Santorini and the Commissioner. Probably the Mayor. Maybe the President; who the hell knows?*

Petulantly (it seemed to Polchik), the robot resumed, "Reviewing my tapes, I find the matter of the bottle of liquor offered as a gratuity still unresolved. If I am to—"

Polchik spun left and kicked with all his might at a garbage can bolted to an iron fence. The lid sprang off and clanged against the fence at the end of its short chain. "I've had it with you . . . you nonreturnable piece of scrap crap!" He wanted very much to go on, but he didn't know what to say. All he knew for certain was that he'd never had such a crummy night in all his life. It *couldn't* just be this goddammed robot—staring back blankly. It was *every*thing. The mortgage payment was due; Benjy had to go in to the orthodontist and where the hell was the money going to come from for *that;* Dorothy had called the precinct just before he'd come down, to tell him the hot water heater had split and drowned the carpets in the kid's bedroom; and to top it all off, he'd been assigned this buzzing pain in the ass and got caught with a little juice passed by that nitwit Rico; he'd had to have this Brillo pain tell him there was a hassle two blocks away; he was sure as God made little green apples going to get a bad report out of this, maybe get set down, maybe get reprimanded, maybe get censured . . . he didn't know what all.

But one thing was certain: this metal bird-dog, this stuffed-shirt barracks lawyer with the trailalong of a ten-year-old kid behind his big brother, this nuisance in metal underwear, this . . . this . . . *thing* was of no damned earthly use to a working cop pulling a foot beat!

On the other hand, a voice that spoke with the voice of Mike Polchik said, *he* did *keep that jughead from using a broken bottle on you.*

"Shuddup!" Polchik said.

"I beg your pardon?" answered the robot.

Ingrate! said the inner voice.

It was verging on that chalky hour before dawn, when the light filtering out of the sky had a leprous, sickly look. Mike Polchik was a much older man.

Brillo had interfered in the apprehension of Milky Kyser, a well-known car thief. Mike had spotted him walking slowly and contemplatively along a line of parked cars on Columbus Avenue, carrying a tightly rolled copy of the current issue of *Life* magazine.

When he had collared Milky, the robot had buzzed up to them and politely inquired precisely what in the carborundum Polchik thought he was doing. Polchik had responded with what was becoming an hysterical reaction-formation to *anything* the metal cop said. "Shuddup!"

Brillo had persisted, saying he was programmed to protect the civil rights of the members of the community, and as far as he could tell, having "scanned all data relevant to the situation at hand," the gentleman now dangling from Polchik's grip was spotlessly blameless of even the remotest scintilla of wrongdoing. Polchik had held Milky with one hand and with the other gesticulated wildly as he explained, "Look, dimdumb, this is Milky Kyser, AKA Irwin Kayser, AKA Clarence Irwin, AKA Jack Milk, AKA God Knows Who All. He is a well-known dip and car thief, and he will use that rolled-up copy of the magazine to jack-and-snap the door handle of the proper model car, any number of which is currently parked, you will note, along this street . . . unless I arrest him! Now will you kindly get the hell outta my hair and *back off*?"

But it was no use. By the time Brillo had patiently repeated the civil rights story, reiterated pertinent sections of the Peace Officer Responsibility Act of 1975 and topped it off with a *précis* of the Miranda-Escobedo-Baum Supreme Court decisions so adroit and simplified even a confirmed tautologist would have applauded, Milky himself—eyes glittering and a sneer that was hardly a smile on his ferret face—was echoing it, word for word.

The robot had given Milky a thorough course in legal cop-outs, before Polchik's dazed eyes.

"Besides," Milky told Polchik, with as much dignity as he could muster, hanging as he was from the cop's meaty fist, "I ain't done nuthin', and just because I been busted once or twice . . ."

"Once or twice!?" Polchik yanked the rolled-up magazine out of Milky's hand and raised it to clobber him. Milky pulled in his head like a turtle, wincing.

But in that fraction of a second, Polchik suddenly saw a picture flashed on the wall of his mind. A picture of Desk Sergeant Loyo and Captain Summit and Chief Santorini and the Mayor's toady and that silent FBI man, all watching a TV screen. And on the screen, there was the pride of the Force, Officer Mike Polchik, beaning Milky Kyser with a semi-lethal copy of *Life* magazine.

Polchik held the magazine poised, trembling with the arrested movement. Milky, head now barely visible from between his shoulders, peeped up from behind his upraised hands. He looked like a mole.

"Beat it," Polchik growled. "Get the hell out of this precinct, Milky. If you're spotted around here again, you're gonna get busted. And don't stop to buy no magazines."

He let Milky loose.

The mole metamorphosed into a ferret once more. And straightening himself, he said, "An' don't call me 'Milky' any more. My given name is Irwin."

"You got three seconds t'vanish from my sight!"

Milky *né* Irwin hustled off down the street. At the corner he stopped and turned around. He cupped his hands and yelled back, "Hey, robot . . . thanks!"

Brillo was about to reply, when Polchik bellowed, "Will you *please*!" The robot turned and said, very softly in Reardon's voice, "You are still holding Mr. Kyser's magazine."

Polchik was weary. Infinitely weary. "You hear him askin' for it?" He walked away from the robot and, as he passed a

sidewalk dispenser, stepped on the dispodpedal, and flipped
the magazine into the receptacle.

"I saved a piece of cherry pie for you, Mike," the waitress
said. Polchik looked up from his uneaten hot (now cold) roast
beef sandwich and French fries. He shook his head.

"Thanks anyway. Just another cuppa coffee."

The waitress had lost her way somewhere beyond twenty-
seven. She was a nice person. She went home to her husband
every morning. She didn't fool around. Extra mates under the
new lottery were not her interest; she just didn't fool around.
But she liked Mike Polchik. He, like her, was a very nice
person.

"What's the matter, Mike?"

Polchik looked out the window of the diner. Brillo was
standing directly under a neon streetlamp. He couldn't hear it
from here, but he was sure the thing was buzzing softly to
itself (with the sort of sound an electric watch makes).

"Him."

"That?" The waitress looked past him.

"Uh-uh. *Him.*"

"What is it?"

"My shadow."

"Mike, you okay? Try the pie, huh? Maybe a scoop of
nice vanilla ice cream on top."

"Onita, please. Just a cuppa coffee, I'm fine. I got problems." He stared down at his plate again.

She looked at him for a moment longer, worried, then
turned and returned the pie on its plate to the empty space
behind the smudged glass of the display case. "You want
fresh?" she asked.

When he didn't answer, she shrugged and came back,
using the coffee siphon on the portable cart to refill his cup.

She lounged behind the counter, watching her friend, Mike
Polchik, as he slowly drank his coffee; and every few minutes
he'd look out at that metal thing on the corner under the
streetlamp. She was a nice person.

When he rose from the booth and came to the counter, she
thought he was going to apologize, or speak to her, or
something, but all he said was, "You got my check?"

"What check?"

200 Harlan Ellison and Ben Bova

"Come on."

"Oh, Mike, for Christ's sake, what's wrong with you?"

"I want to pay the check, you mind?"

"Mike, almost—what—five years you been eating here, you ever been asked to pay a check?"

Polchik looked very tired. "Tonight I pay the check. Come on . . . I gotta get back on the street. He's waiting."

There was a strange look in his eyes and she didn't want to ask which "he" Polchik meant. She was afraid he meant the metal thing out there. Onita, a very nice person, didn't like strange, new things that waited under neon streetlamps. She hastily wrote out a check and slid it across the plasteel to him. He pulled change from a pocket, paid her, turned, seemed to remember something, turned back, added a tip, then swiftly left the diner.

She watched through the glass as he went up to the metal thing. Then the two of them walked away, Mike leading, the thing following.

Onita made fresh. It was a good thing she had done it so many times she could do it by reflex, without thinking. Hot coffee scalds are very painful.

At the corner, Polchik saw a car weaving toward the intersection. A Ford Electric; convertible, four years old. Still looked flashy. Top down. He could see a bunch of long-haired kids inside. He couldn't tell the girls from the boys. It bothered him.

Polchik stopped. They weren't going fast, but the car was definitely weaving as it approached the intersection. *The warrior-lizard,* he thought. It was almost an unconscious directive. He'd been a cop long enough to react to the little hints, the flutters, the inclinations. The hunches.

Polchik stepped out from the curb, unshipped his gumball from the bandolier and flashed the red light at the driver. The car slowed even more; now it was crawling.

"Pull it over, kid!" he shouted.

For a moment he thought they were ignoring him, that the driver might not have heard him, that they'd try and make a break for it . . . that they'd speed up and sideswipe him. But the driver eased the car to the curb and stopped.

Then he slid sidewise, pulled up his legs and crossed them neatly at the ankles. On the top of the dashboard.

Polchik walked around to the driver's side. "Turn it off. Everybody out."

There were six of them. None of them moved. The driver closed his eyes slowly, then tipped his Irkutsk fur hat over his eyes till it rested on the bridge of his nose. Polchik reached into the car and turned it off. He pulled the keys.

"Hey! Whuzzis allabout?" one of the kids in the back seat—a boy with terminal acne—complained. His voice began and ended on a whine. Polchik re-stuck the gumball.

The driver looked up from under the fur. "Wasn't breaking any laws." He said each word very slowly, very distinctly, as though each one was on a printout.

And Polchik knew he'd been right. They were on the lizard.

He opened the door, free hand hanging at the needler. "Out. All of you, out."

Then he sensed Brillo lurking behind him, in the middle of the street. Good. *Hope a damned garbage truck hits him*.

He was getting mad. That wasn't smart. Carefully, he said, "Don't make me say it again. Move it!"

He lined them up on the sidewalk beside the car, in plain sight. Three girls, three guys. Two of the guys with long, stringy hair and the third with a scalplock. The three girls wearing tammy cuts. All six sullen-faced, drawn, dark smudges under the eyes. The lizard. But good clothes, fairly new. Money. He couldn't just hustle them, he had to be careful.

"Okay, one at a time, empty your pockets and pouches onto the hood of the car."

"Hey, we don't haveta do that just because . . ."

"Do it!"

"Don't argue with the pig," one of the girl said, lizard-spacing her words carefully. "He's probably trigger happy."

Brillo rolled up to Polchik. "It is necessary to have a probable cause clearance from the precinct in order to search, sir."

"Not on a stop'n'frisk," Polchik snapped, not taking his eyes off them. He had no time for nonsense with the can of cogs. He kept his eyes on the growing collection of chits, change, code-keys, combs, nail files, toke pipes and miscellanea being dumped on the Ford's hood.

"There must be grounds for suspicion even in a spot search action, sir," Brillo said.

"There's grounds. Narcotics."

"Nar . . . you must be outtayer mind," said the one boy who slurred his words. He was working something other than the lizard.

"That's a pig for you," said the girl who had made the trigger-happy remark.

"Look," Polchik said, "you snots aren't from around here. Odds are good if I run b&b tests on you, we'll find you're under the influence of the lizard."

"Heyyyy!" the driver said. "The *what*?"

"Warrior-lizard," Polchik said.

"Oh, ain't he the jive thug," the smartmouth girl said. "He's a word user. I'll bet he knows *all* the current rage phrases. A philologist. I'll bet he knows *all* the solecisms and colloquialisms, catch phrases, catachreses, nicknames and vulgarisms. The 'warrior-lizard,' indeed."

Damned college kids, Polchik fumed inwardly. *They* always *try to make you feel stupid; I coulda gone to college—if I didn't have to work. Money, they probably* always *had money. The little bitch.*

The driver giggled. "Are you trying to tell me, Mella, my dear, that this Peace Officer is accusing us of being under the influence of the illegal Bolivian drug commonly called Guerrera-Tuera?" He said it with pinpointed scorn, pronouncing the Spanish broadly: gwuh-*rare*-uh too-*err*-uh.

Brillo said, "Reviewing my semantic tapes, sir, I find no analogs for 'Guerrera-Tuera' as 'warrior-lizard.' True, *guerrero* in Spanish means *warrior*, but the closest spelling I find is the feminine noun *guerra*, which translates as *war*. Neither *guerrera* nor *tuera* appear in the Spanish language. If *tuera* is a species of lizard, I don't seem to find it—"

Polchik had listened dumbly. The weight on his shoulders was monstrous. All of them were on him. The kids, that lousy stinking robot—they were making fun, such fun, such *damned* fun of him! "Keep digging," he directed them. He was surprised to hear his words emerge as a series of croaks.

"And blood and breath tests must be administered, sir—"

"Stay the hell outta this!"

"We're on our way home from a party," said the boy with the scalplock, who had been silent till then. "We took a shortcut and got lost."

"Sure," Polchik said. "In the middle of Manhattan, you got lost." He saw a small green bottle dumped out of the last girl's pouch. She was trying to push it under other items. "What's that?"

"Medicine," she said. Quickly. Very quickly.

Everyone tensed.

"Let me see it." His voice was even.

He put out his hand for the bottle, but all six watched his other hand, hanging beside the needler. Hesitantly, the girl picked the bottle out of the mass of goods on the car's hood, and handed him the plastic container.

Brillo said, "I am equipped with chemical sensors and reference tapes in my memory bank enumerating common narcotics. I can analyze the suspected medicine."

The six stared wordlessly at the robot. They seemed almost afraid to acknowledge its presence.

Polchik handed the plastic bottle to the robot.

Brillo depressed a color-coded key on a bank set flush into his left forearm, and a panel that hadn't seemed to be there a moment before slid down in the robot's chest. He dropped the plastic bottle into the opening and the panel slid up. He stood and buzzed.

"You don't have to open the bottle?" Polchik asked.

"No, sir."

"Oh."

The robot continued buzzing. Polchik felt stupid, just standing and watching. After a few moments the kids began to smirk, then to grin, then to chuckle openly, whispering among themselves. The smartmouthed girl giggled viciously. Polchik felt fifteen years old again; awkward, pimply, the butt of secret jokes among the long-legged high school girls in their miniskirts who had been so terrifyingly aloof he had never even considered asking them out. He realized with some shame that he despised these kids with their money, their cars, their flashy clothes, their dope. And most of all, their assurance. *He*, Mike Polchik, had been working hauling sides of beef from the delivery trucks to his old man's butcher shop while others were tooling around in their Electrics. He forced the memories from his mind and took out his anger and frustration on the metal idiot still buzzing beside him.

"Okay, okay, how long does it take you?"

"Tsk tsk," said the driver, and went cross-eyed.

Polchik ignored him. But not very well.

"I am a mobile unit, sir. Experimental model 44. My parent mechanism—the Master Unit AA—at Universal Electronics laboratories is equipped to perform this function in under one minute."

"Well, hurry it up. I wanna run these hairies in."

"Gwuh-*rare*-uh too-*err*-uh," the scalplock said in a nasty undertone.

There was a soft musical tone from inside the chest compartment, the plate slid down again, and the robot withdrew the plastic bottle. He handed it to the girl.

"*Now* whaddaya think you're doing?"

"Analysis confirms what the young lady attested, sir. This is a commonly prescribed nose drop for nasal congestion and certain primary allergies."

Polchik was speechless.

"You are free to go," the robot said. "With our apologies. We are merely doing our jobs. Thank you."

Polchik started to protest—he *knew* he was right—but the kids were already gathering up their belongings. He hadn't even ripped the car, which was probably where they had it locked away. But he knew it was useless. *He* was the guinea pig in this experiment, not the robot. It was all painfully clear. He knew if he interfered, if he overrode the robot's decision, it would only add to the cloud under which the robot had put him; short temper, taking a gift from a neighborhood merchant, letting the robot outmaneuver him in the apartment, false stop on Kyser . . . and now this. Suddenly, all Mike Polchik wanted was to go back, get out of harness, sign out, and go home to bed. Wet carpets and all. Just to bed.

Because if these metal things were what was coming, he was simply too tired to buck it.

He watched as the kids—hooting and ridiculing his impotency—piled back in the car, the girls showing their legs as they clambered over the side. The driver burned polyglas speeding up Amsterdam Avenue. In a moment they were gone.

"You see, Officer Polchik," Brillo said, "false arrest would make us both liable for serious—" But Polchik was already walking away, his shoulders slumped, the weight of his bandolier and five years on the Force too much for him.

The robot (making the sort of sound an electric watch makes) hummed after him, keeping stern vigil on the darkened neighborhood in the encroaching dawn. He could not compute despair. But he had been built to serve. He was programmed to protect, and he did it, all the way back to the precinct house.

Polchik was sitting at a scarred desk in the squad room, laboriously typing out his report on a weary IBM Selectric afflicted with *grand mal*. Across the room Reardon poked at the now-inert metal bulk of Brillo, using some sort of power tool with a teardrop-shaped lamp on top of it. The Mayor's whiz kid definitely looked sandbagged. *He don't go without sleep very often*, Polchik thought with grim satisfaction.

The door to Captain Summit's office opened, and the Captain, looking oceanic and faraway, waved him in.

"Here it comes," Polchik whispered to himself.

Summit let Polchik pass him in the doorway. He closed the door and indicated the worn plastic chair in front of the desk. Polchik sat down. "I'm not done typin' the beat report yet, Capt'n."

Summit ignored the comment. He moved over to the desk, picked up a yellow printout flimsy, and stood silent for a moment in front of Polchik, considering it.

"Accident report out of the 86th precinct uptown. Six kids in a Ford Electric convertible went out of control, smashed down a pedestrian and totaled against the bridge abutment. Three dead, three critical—not expected to live. Fifteen minutes after you let them go."

Dust.

Dried out.

Ashes.

Gray. Final.

Polchik couldn't think. Tired. Confused. Sick. Six kids.

Now they were kids, just kids, nothing else made out of old bad memories.

"One of the girls went through the windshield. D.O.A. Driver got the steering column punched out through his back. Another girl with a snapped neck. Another girl—"

He couldn't hear him. He was somewhere else, far away. Kids. Laughing, smartmouth kids having a good time. Benjy would be that age some day. The carpets were all wet.

"Mike!"

He didn't hear.

"Mike! Polchik!"

He looked up. There was a stranger standing in front of him holding a yellow flimsy.

"Well, don't just sit there, Polchik. You *had* them! Why'd you let them go?"

"The . . . lizard . . ."

"That's right, that's what five of them were using. Three beakers of it in the car. And a dead cat on the floor and all the makings wrapped in foam-bead bags. You'd have had to be blind to miss it all!"

"The robot . . ."

Summit turned away with disgust, slamming the report onto the desk top. He thumbed the call-button. When Desk Sergeant Loyo came in, he said, "Take him upstairs and give him a breather of straightener, let him lie down for half an hour, then bring him back to me."

Loyo got Polchik under the arms and took him out.

Then the Captain turned off the office lights and sat silently in his desk chair, watching the night die just beyond the filthy windows.

"Feel better?"

"Yeah; thank you, Capt'n. I'm fine."

"You're back with me all the way? You understand what I'm saying?"

"Yeah, sure, I'm just *fine*, sir. It was just . . . those kids . . ."

"So why'd you let them go? I've got no time to baby you, Polchik. You're five years a cop and I've got all the brass in town outside that door waiting. So get right."

"I'm right, Capt'n. I let them go because the robot took

the stuff the girl was carrying, and he dumped it in his thing there, and tol me it was nosedrops.''

"Not good enough, Mike.''

"What can I say besides that?''

"Well, dammit, *Officer* Polchik, you damned well better say *some*thing besides that. *You* know they run that stuff right into the skull, you've been a cop long enough to see it, to hear it the way they talk! Why'd you let them custer you?''

"What was I going to run them in for? Carrying nosedrops? With that motherin' robot reciting civil rights chapter-an'--verse at me every step of the way? Okay, so I tell the robot to go screw off, and I bust 'em and bring 'em in. In an hour they're out again and I've got a false arrest lug dropped on me. Even if it *ain't* nosedrops. And they can use the robot's goddam tapes to hang me up by the thumbs!''

Summit dropped back into his chair, sack weight. His face was a burned-out building. "So we've got three, maybe six kids dead. Jesus. Jesus. Jesus.'' He shook his head.

Polchik wanted to make him feel better. But how did you do that? "Listen, Capt'n, you know I would of had those kids in here so fast it'd of made their heads swim . . . if I'd've been on my own. That damned robot . . . well, it just didn't work out. Capt'n, listen, I'm not trying to alibi, it was godawful out there, but you were a beat cop . . . *you* know a cop ain't a set of rules and a pile of wires. Guys like me just can't work with things like that Brillo. It won't work, Cap'n. A guy's gotta be free to use his judgment, to feel like he's worth somethin', not just a piece of sh—''

Summit's head came up sharply. "Judgment?!'' He looked as though he wanted to vomit. "What kind of judgment are you showing with that Rico over at the Amsterdam Inn? And all of it on the tapes, sound, pictures, everything?!''

"Oh. That.''

"Yes, that. You're damned lucky I insisted those tapes get held strictly private, for the use of the Force only. I had to invoke privileged data. Do you have any *idea* how many strings that puts on me, on this office now, with the Chief, with the Commissioner, with the goddam Mayor? Do you have any *idea*, Polchik?''

"No, sir. I'm sorry.'' Chagrin.

"Sorry doesn't buy it, goddammit! I don't want you taking

any juice from anywhere. No bottles, no gifts, no *nothing*, not from *any*body. Have you got that?''

"Yessir."

Wearily, Summit persisted. "It's tough enough to do a job here without having special graft investigations and the D.A.'s squad sniffing all over the precinct. Jesus, Polchik, do you have any *idea* . . . !" He stopped, looked levelly at the patrolman and said, "One more time and you're out on your ass. Not set down, not reprimanded, not docked—*out*. All the way out. *Kapish?*"

Polchik nodded; his back was broken.

"I've got to set it right."

"What, sir?"

"You, that's what."

Polchik waited. A pendulum was swinging.

"I'll have to think about it. But if it hadn't been for the five good years you've given me here, Polchik . . . well, you'll be getting punishment, but I don't know just what yet."

"Uh, what's gonna happen with the robot?"

Summit got to his feet slowly; mooring a dirigible. "Come on outside and you'll see."

Polchik followed him to the door, where the Captain paused. He looked closely into Polchik's face and said, "Tonight has been an education, Mike."

There was no answer to that one.

They went into the front desk room. Reardon still had his head stuck into Brillo's open torso cavity, and the whiz kid was standing tiptoed behind him, peering over the engineer's shoulder. As they entered the ready room, Reardon straightened and clicked off the lamp on the power tool. He watched Summit and Polchik as they walked over to Chief Santorini. Summit murmured to the Chief for a moment, then Santorini nodded and said, "We'll talk tomorrow, then."

He started toward the front door, stopped and said, "Good night, gentlemen. It's been a long night. I'll be in touch with your offices tomorrow." He didn't wait for acknowledgment; he simply went.

Reardon turned around to face Summit. He was waiting for words. Even the whiz kid was starting to come alive again. The silent FBI man rose from the bench (as far as Polchik could tell, he hadn't changed position all the time they'd been gone on patrol) and walked toward the group.

Reardon said, "Well . . ." His voice trailed off.

The pendulum was swinging.

"Gentlemen," said the Captain, "I've advised Chief Santorini I'll be writing out a full report to be sent downtown. My recommendations will more than likely decide whether or not these robots will be added to our Force."

"Grass roots level opinion, very good, Captain, very good," said the whiz kid. Summit ignored him.

"But I suppose I ought to tell you right now my recommendations will be negative. As far as I'm concerned, Mr. Reardon, you still have a long way to go with your machine."

"But, I thought—"

"It did very well," Summit said, "don't get me wrong. But I think it's going to need a lot more flexibility and more knowledge of the police officer's duties before it can be of any real aid in our work."

Reardon was angry, but trying to control it. "I programmed the entire patrolman's manual, and all the City codes, and the Supreme Court—"

Summit stopped him with a raised hand. "Mr. Reardon, that's the least of a police officer's knowledge. *Anybody* can read a rule book. But *how to use those rules,* how to make those rules work in the street, that takes more than programming. It takes, well, it takes training. And experience. It doesn't come easily. A cop isn't a set of rules and a pile of wires."

Polchik was startled to hear his words. He knew it would be okay. Not as good as before, but at least okay.

Reardon was furious now. And he refused to be convinced. Or perhaps he refused to allow the Mayor's whiz kid and the FBI man to be so easily convinced. He had worked too long and at too much personal cost to his career to let it go that easily. He hung onto it. "But merely training shouldn't put you off the X-44 *completely*!"

The Captain's face tensed around the mouth. "Look, Mr. Reardon, I'm not very good at being politic—which is why I'm still a Captain, I suppose." The whiz kid gave him a be-careful look, but the Captain went on. "But it isn't merely training. This officer is a good one. He's bright, he's on his toes, he maybe isn't Sherlock Holmes but he knows the feel of a neighborhood, the smell of it, the heat level. He knows every August we're going to get the leapers and the riots and some woman's head cut off and dumped in a mailbox mailed C.O.D. to Columbus, Ohio. He knows when there's racial tension in our streets. He knows when those poor slobs in the tenements have just *had it.* He knows when some new kind of vice has moved in. But he made more mistakes out there tonight than a rookie. Five years walking and riding that beat, he's *never* foulballed the way he did tonight. Why? I've got to ask *why?* The only thing different was that machine of yours. Why? *Why* did Mike Polchik foulball so bad? *He* knew those kids in that car should have been run in for b&b or naline tests. So why, Mr. Reardon . . . *why*?''

Polchik felt lousy. The Captain was more worked up than he'd ever seen him. But Polchik stood silently, listening; standing beside the silent, listening FBI man.

Brillo merely stood silently. Turned off.

Then why did he still hear that robot buzzing?

"It isn't rules and regs, Mr. Reardon." The Captain seemed to have a lot more to come. "A moron can learn those. But how do you evaluate the look on a man's face that tells you he needs a fix? How do you gauge the cultural change in words like 'custer' or 'grass' or 'high' or 'pig'? How do you know when *not* to bust a bunch of kids who've popped a hydrant so they can cool off? How do you program all of *that* into a robot . . . and know that it's going to change from hour to hour?''

"We can do it! It'll take time, but we can do it."

The Captain nodded slowly. "Maybe you can."

"I know we can."

"Okay, I'll even go for that. Let's say you can. Let's say you can get a robot that'll act like a human being and still be a robot . . . because that's what we're talking about here. There's still something else."

"Which is?"

"People, Mr. Reardon. People like Polchik here. I asked you *why* Polchik foulballed, why he made such a bum patrol tonight that I'm going to have to take disciplinary action against him *for the first time in five years* . . . so I'll *tell* you why, Mr. Reardon, about people like Polchik here. They're still afraid of machines, you know. We've pushed them and shoved them and lumbered them with machines till they're afraid the next clanking item down the pike is going to put them on the bread line. So they don't *want* to cooperate. They don't do it on purpose. They may not even *know* they're doing it, hell, I don't think Polchik knew what was happening, why he was falling over his feet tonight. You can get a robot to act like a human being, Mr. Reardon. Maybe you're right and you *can* do it, just like you said. But how the hell are you going to get humans to act like robots and not be afraid of machines?''

Reardon looked as whipped as Polchik felt.

"May I leave Brillo here till morning? I'll have a crew come over from the labs and pick him up.''

"Sure,'' the Captain said, "he'll be fine right there against the wall. The Desk Sergeant'll keep an eye on him.'' To Loyo he said, "Sergeant, instruct your relief.''

Loyo smiled and said, "Yessir.''

Summit looked back at Reardon and said, "I'm sorry.''

Reardon smiled wanly, and walked out. The whiz kid wanted to say something, but too much had already been said, and the Captain looked through him. "I'm pretty tired, Mr. Kenzie. How about we discuss it tomorrow after I've seen the Chief?''

The whiz kid scowled, turned and stalked out.

The Captain sighed heavily. "Mike, go get signed out and go home. Come see me tomorrow. Late.'' He nodded to the FBI man, who still had not spoken, then he went away.

The robot stood where Reardon had left him. Silent.

Polchik went upstairs to the locker room to change.

Something was bothering him. But he couldn't nail it down.

When he came back down into the muster room, the FBI man was just racking the receiver on the desk blotter phone. "Leaving?'' he asked. It was the first thing Polchik had heard him say. It was a warm brown voice.

"Yeah. Gotta go home. I'm whacked out.''

"Can't say I blame you. I'm a little tired myself. Need a lift?''

"No, thanks,'' Polchik said. "I take the subway. Two blocks from the house.'' They walked out together. Polchik thought about wet carpets waiting. They stood on the front steps for a minute, breathing in the chill morning air, and Polchik said, "I feel kinda sorry for that chunk of scrap now. He did a pretty good job."

"But not good enough," the FBI man added.

Polchik felt suddenly very protective about the inert form against the wall in the precinct house. "Oh, I dunno. He saved me from getting clobbered, you wanna know the truth. Tell me . . . you think they'll ever build a robot that'll cut it?"

The FBI man lit a cigarette, blew smoke in a thin stream, and nodded. "Yeah. Probably. But it'll have to be a lot more sophisticated than old Brillo in there."

Polchik looked back through the doorway. The robot stood alone, looking somehow helpless. Waiting for rust. Polchik thought of kids, all kinds of kids, and when he was a kid. *It must be hell*, he thought, *being a robot. Getting turned off when they don't need you no more.*

Then he realized he could *still* hear that faint electrical buzzing. The kind a watch makes. He cast a quick glance at the FBI man but, trailing cigarette smoke, he was already moving toward his car, parked directly in front of the precinct house. Polchik couldn't tell if he was wearing a watch or not.

He followed the government man.

"The trouble with Brillo," the FBI man said, "is that Reardon's facilities were too limited. But I'm sure there are other agencies working on it. They'll lick it one day." He snapped the cigarette into the gutter.

"Yeah, sure," Polchik said. The FBI man unlocked the car door and pulled it. It didn't open.

"Damnit!" he said. "Government pool issue. Damned door always sticks." Bunching his muscles, he suddenly wrenched at it with enough force to pop it open. Polchik stared. Metal had ripped.

"You take care of yourself now, y'hear?" the FBI man said, getting into the car. He flipped up the visor with its OFFICIAL GOVERNMENT BUSINESS card tacked to it, and slid behind the steering wheel.

The car settled heavily on its springs, as though a ton of load had just been dumped on the front seat. He slammed the door. It was badly sprung.

"Too bad we couldn't use him," the FBI man said, staring out of the car at Brillo, illuminated through the precinct house doorway. "But . . . too crude."

"Yeah, sure, I'll take care of myself," Polchik replied, one exchange too late. He felt his mouth hanging open.

The FBI man grinned, started the car, and pulled away.

Polchik stood in the street, for a while.

Sometimes he stared down the early-morning street in the direction the FBI man had taken.

Sometimes he stared down the early morning street in the muster room.

And even as the sounds of the city's new day rose around him, he was not at all certain he did not still hear the sound of an electric watch. Getting louder.

The Powers of Observation

Harry Harrison

It's just a matter of native ability. I've had the same
training as a lot of other guys, and if I remember things
better, or can jump faster, than most of them, maybe that's
the reason why I'm out here in no-man's-land where East
brushes West and why they're behind desks in Washington.

One of the first things I was ever taught by the Department
was to look out for the unusual. I whispered a soft word of
thanks to my instructors as I watched this big blond Apollo
type walk down the beach.

His feet sank into the sand!

Yes they did, and don't go telling me that doesn't mean
anything. The sand on the Makarska beach is like the sand on
any other beach on the Yugoslavian coast, firm and compact.
You can make footsteps in it—but not *that* deep.

All right, go ahead and laugh if you want to, but don't
forget what I told you about my training, so just for the
moment take my word about this. These footprints were
unusual. I was sitting up and looking out to sea when he went
by, and I didn't move my head to look at him. But, since I
was wearing sunglasses, I followed him with my eyes, head
dead center all the time. He was an absolutely normal guy;
blond, about six foot, wearing blue nylon bathing trunks and
sporting an appendectomy scar and a scowl. You see a million like him on every beach in the world every summer. But
not with those footprints.

Look, don't laugh, I asked you not to. I'll explain in a
second. I let him walk on by and turn into the hotel and while

he was doing it I was standing up and as soon as he was out of sight I was walking back the way he had come, towards this old woman who was selling *raznici* from a little stall. Sure I could have done it simpler, I was almost certain at the time that I wasn't under observation—but that's the point. I could have been. Unless people know better, if you act innocent you are innocent. Act innocent all the time and et cetera all the time. I went and had some *raznici*, my fourth portion for the day. Not that I like the things, but the stall made a good cover, an excuse for random action.

"*Jedan*," I said, and held up one finger in case my American accent obscured my tiny command of Serbo-Croatian. She bobbed her head and pulled a wood splint off the bed of charcoal and used her big carving knife to push the pieces of roasted meat from the splint onto the plate with the raw onion. Not a very complicated dish, but you get used to it after a while. To all appearances I was watching her carefully and digging out my money, but all I was really interested in were those footprints. I could see twelve of them from where I was standing, twelve that I was completely certain of, and while the food was being slowly dished out and the battered aluminum dinar coins counted two of them were obliterated by other bathers. I did a quick estimate of the elapsed time and footprints destroyed and came up with an extrapolated life of six minutes for the remaining footsteps. Or three minutes with a one hundred percent safety margin which is the way I like to operate when I can. Good enough. I took my change, chewed the last gristly bit, and strolled back down the beach counting the coins.

Was it chance my course paralleled the remaining three footprints? Was it chance I walked at the same speed as the blond stranger? Was it chance that built the atom bomb?

My right foot came down in line with—and a few inches away from—a right footprint, and as my foot came up I dropped the coins. It took me exactly 3.8 seconds to pick up the coins, and while picking them up I put my index finger into the blond man's heelprint and into my own. That's all. It was a risk to take, if anyone was watching, but calculated risks are part of this business.

I didn't smile and I didn't alter my walking pace, I just

jiggled my change and went back and sat down on my towel again.

That was outside. Inside it was Mardi Gras, Fourth of July, rockets and cherry bombs and ticker tape from the windows.

It was childishly simple. I'm five ten and weigh one hundred eighty and I hit my foot into the sand in the same place and at the same speed and in the same way the blond had done. I could be off in my figure for the compressibility of the sand, but only by a few percent, and I assumed it was displaced at a predictable rate on a sine curve, and I wasn't off at all in my measurement of the depth of the two impressions, so, plus or minus five percent for error, that six-foot-tall joker weighed in the neighborhood of four hundred and twelve pounds.

Jackpot!

Time for action. And thought. I could do both at the same time. He had gone into the hotel, I would go into the hotel. The Jadran was big, new and international and almost everyone on this chunk of beach was staying there. As I picked up my towel and trudged slowly towards it I put the brain box into gear and thought of the next step. Communication and report, the answer came back instantly. The Department would be very interested in what I had discovered, and once I had relieved myself of the information I would be a free agent again and could look into the matter further. It should not be hard to find the heavyweight blond if he was registered at the hotel.

After the hot sunlight the lobby was dim, and apparently empty except for a fat German couple who were either asleep or dead in the overstuffed chairs. As I passed I looked into the bar and it was empty too, except for the bartender, Petar, who was polishing glasses listlessly. I turned in without breaking step, as though I had been headed here all the time and had not just decided at that instant to go in. The opportunity was too good to miss since Petar was my eyes and ears in this hotel—and well paid for the service.

"Buon giorno," I said. *"Guten Tag,"* he sighed back. Petar comes from the island of Cres, which belonged to the Austrians until 1918 and the Italians until 1945. He grew up with both languages as well as the native Serbo-Croatian.

With this background he had picked up English and a little French and was in great demand as a bartender in the coastal hotels with their international clientele. He was also under-paid and undertipped and very happy to see my spanking-new greenbacks.

"Let me have a *pivo*," I said, and he took a bottle of East German dark beer out of the freezer. I climbed onto a stool and when he poured it out our heads were close together. "For ten bucks," I said. "The name and room number of a man, blond, six feet tall, who wears blue swim trunks and has an appendectomy scar."

"How much is six feet?"

"One hundred eighty-two centimeters," I flashed right back.

"Oh, him. A Russian by name of Alexei Svirsky. Room 146. He has a Bulgarian passport but he drives in a Tatra with Polish number plates. Who else but a Russian?"

"Who but." I knocked back the beer, and the tattered one-thousand-dinar bill I slipped him had a crisp sawbuck folded underneath it. The change came back, though the ten spot didn't, and I left a tip and headed for the door, but I wheeled around before I had gone two steps. I caught the trace of a vanishing smile on his hounddog chops.

"For ten bucks more," I said, letting the palmed bill project a bit from under my hand on the bar top, "how much is Alexei Svirsky paying you to report if anyone asks questions about him?"

"Five thousand dinar, cheapskate bum. Not him, his friends. He don't talk much."

"Here's ten thousand and another five when you tell me they asked and you told them there were no questions."

A slow nod, the bills shuffled and changed hands, and I left. My flanks were guarded. I was very free with Uncle's money, but dinars aren't worth very much in any case. I went to my room, locked the door, tested to see if the place had been bugged since I left—it had not—then leaned out the open window. The pink concrete wall dropped six stories to a desolate patio floored with hard tramped dirt and a few patches of yellowed grass. A row of dead plants leaned against one wall and four empty beer kegs baked and drew flies in the sun. There was no one in sight, nor were there any bugs on the wall outside my room. I sat down in the chair facing my window and the row of windows in the other wing of the hotel.

"How do you read me?" I said in a low voice.

Across the way a curtain was closed, then opened again. It was next to an open window.

"I've spotted a suspect. He may not be the one we were told to look out for, but there is strong evidence to believe that he is. Bulgarian passport but could be Russian. Name of Alexei Svirsky in Room 146, and he weighs four hundred twelve pounds—at a rough estimate." The curtain twitched an interrogative, repeat. "That's right. Four hundred twelve pounds. I'm going to investigate."

As soon as I finished talking I turned away so I couldn't see the frantic jiggle of the curtain. I liked this setup: I didn't have to take any backtalk. The agent over there had a parabolic dish and a directional microphone. He could pick up a whisper in this room. But he couldn't talk to me.

While I was showering the phone rang but I ignored it. I could have been out, right? Moving a little faster now, I pulled on slacks and a sport shirt and put on my sneakers with the ridged soles. There was no one around when I went out into the hall and down the stairs to the floor where I knew Room 146 was located. Since I had passed on my old information now it was time to gather some new. I found the room and knocked on the door.

Brash perhaps, but a way to get results. I would mumble something about wrong room and get a closer look at Svirsky and the layout of his room. If my visit worried him and he ran, we would find out things; if he stayed we would find some facts as well.

No one answered the door. I knocked again and leaned against the panel to listen. No shower, no voices, nothing. A little calculated risk was in order. The tool steel picklock worked as fast as a key would in this primitive lock, perhaps faster. I stepped in and closed the door behind me. The room was empty.

My bird had flown. There were still marks on the bedcover where a suitcase had lain while it was being packed. The door of the big wooden wardrobe stood open, and if one of the coathangers had been swinging I would not have been surprised. It had all happened very quickly and efficiently. Nothing remained to mark Mr. Svirsky's visit. I went into the bath. The sink was dry, as was the shower, the towels folded neatly on the racks, threadbare but clean. Everything *too* clean and spotless since I knew the chambermaids weren't that efficient. And Svirsky had been staying here some days—so this was positive information. There was even a trace of dust in the sink. I rubbed at it with my finger just as the hall door opened.

Just a crack, a couple of inches, then it closed again. But it was open long enough—and wide enough—to roll in a hand grenade.

As it bounced towards me I recognized the type (XII), place of manufacture (Plzn), and fuse time (three seconds). Even before this last fact had impressed itself I had jumped backwards, slammed the door and collapsed inside the shower stall. Fast thinking and fast reflexes—that's a combination that can't be beat. I hoped, as I hunkered down with my arms clasped over my head.

It made a good deal of noise when it exploded.

The bathroom door blew in, fragments of grenade thudded into the wall above me, and the mirror crashed in bursting shards to the floor. One steaming hunk of iron was imbedded in the tile about six inches in front of my nose. This was the closest piece, and it was close enough, thank you. I did not wait to examine it but was on my feet while the explosion still echoed, jumping over the remains of the destroyed bathroom door. Speed was the most important thing now, because I didn't want to be found in this room. Diving through the still roiling cloud of smoke I pulled open the tottering door—it collapsed at my feet—and made it into the hall. I could hear shouts and doors opening, but no one was in sight yet. The stairwell was five paces away, and I got there without being seen and started up. Fleury was waiting on the landing above.

"Svirsky has cleared out," I told him. "He moved out fast and left someone behind to roll a grenade in on top of me." There was the sound of running feet and shouts of multilingual amazement from the hall below. "That means they were tipped off about me, so I am forced to admit that my informant, Petar the bartender, is a double agent."

"I know. He was the one who threw the grenade into the room. We have him in the truck and are going to question him under scopolamine before we send him home. But I doubt if we'll learn anything; he's just small fry."

"What about Svirsky?"

"That's what I came to tell you. Our road-watcher at Zadvarje, the next town, reports that a big Tatra with Polish plates just belted through there like a bomb, heading north towards Split. Two men in the front and one in the back. They were going too fast to make out anything more."

"Well, that's more than enough. I'll take the jeep and go after them. Now that we have made contact we can't lose it."

Fleury chewed the inside of his lip worriedly. "I really don't know, it's a risk . . ."

"Crossing the street is a risk these days. Who do we have north of here that can head them off?"

"Just team Able Dog in Rijeka."

"That's pretty far away. Tell them to head south on the coastal highway, and if the Tatra doesn't turn off we'll have it trapped between us. We'll get a closer look at Alexei Svirsky yet."

Five minutes later I was on the road north, tooling the jeep around the tight turns of the twisting highway. It wasn't really a jeep, but a Toyota land cruiser, with four-wheel drive, rugged and powerful. A Japanese car with Austrian plates and an American driver. We were about as international as the other side. I put my foot to the floor and hoped the driver of the Tatra would remember what the roads inland were like.

Yugoslavia is shaped like a right hand, palm up, with the Adriatic Sea all along the bottom edge, running along the side of the hand and the little finger. The coastal highway, what the locals call the Magistrale, runs all the way along the shore. I was on this highway now, about the base of the pinky, heading north towards the fingertips—where I hoped the other car was heading. That would be the fastest and easiest way to get out of the country, because Rijeka is up there at the end of the little finger and a good road turns east from here to Zagreb—on the top joint of the middle finger—and then on to Hungary at the tip of the index finger.

There was another way to get there that I hoped the comrades would not consider. The Velebit Mountains come right down to the coastline here, rugged and steep, and are crossed by the oldest and worst roads in the world. There are only a few of these goat tracks, all in terrible condition, and a car going this way would be easily followed and headed off. I'm sure the driver of the Tatra knew this as well as I did and would make the correct decision.

I drove. The Toyota whined up to over eighty in the straight and skidded broadside around the turns. I passed a loafing Alfa-Romeo with Milan plates, on a turn, and the driver shook his fist out the window and blared his highway horn at me. Split was right ahead and I worked my way through the traffic as fast as I could without attracting the attention of the milicija. There was no sign of a black Tatra, though I kept my eyes open. When I passed the turnoff to Sinj I tried to ignore it. Although it was a good road for about fifty miles it degenerated into a bumpy cow path in the hills. I knew that and I hoped that the Tatra driver did as well. Once past Split I opened her up again and hoped that I was following a car—not just a hunch.

At Zadar I saw them. The highway makes a long swing to the right here, bypassing the city, and there is a big Jugopetrol gas station right in the middle of the curve. When I spotted the station far ahead, the Tatra was leaping out of it like a black bug. They had stopped to fill their tank, or wash their hands, and given me enough time to catch up and get them in sight. I whistled as I belted around the turn and into the straight stretch that led to the Maslenica Bridge. There were a number of alternative plans and I was musing over them, deciding which was best, when we came up to the bridge and my right front tire blew out.

Since I was doing seventy at the time it was just a matter of good reflexes, good brakes—and luck. I twisted and skidded all over the road, and if there had been any traffic I would have had it right then. But the vanishing Tatra was the only other car around, and after some fancy work on the shoulder, two fence posts and a cloud of dust, I slid up to the guard rail at the bridge plaza and bucked to a stop.

Blowout? Now that I had a moment to think I ran the old memory reel back and thought about that puff of smoke from the rear window of the Tatra just before the tire blew. Either this was a remarkable coincidence—or they had a gunport back there and someone was a very good shot with a hand pistol. I don't believe in coincidences.

For just about two seconds I thought about this and admired the view of harsh stone running down to the blue water of the arm of the sea below, and the bright orange bridge leaping over to the limestone cliff on the far side. Very dramatic. I was completely alone and the only sounds were the vanishing hum of the Tatra and the click of my cooling engine. Then I unpried my fingers from the steering wheel and dug out the jack.

If they ever have a Toyota tire-changing championship, I'll place in the money. I threw the tools in the back, kicked her to life and went after the comrades, more anxious than ever to take a closer look at the frightened Svirsky. The road along here is like nothing else on Earth—in fact the landscape looks like the moon. Just rock, with sparse and deadlocking shrubs on it, falling straight to the sea, with the Adriatic Highway scratched along the face of the cliff. I concentrated on the driving, not on the view. I didn't see the Tatra again, though I did see Lukovo and Karlobag, jumbles of low, drab buildings, locked and tomblike under the heat of the afternoon sun. About five miles beyond Karlobag I saw a tan Mercedes coming from the other direction and I slammed on my brakes as it whistled by, burning rubber as well. Making a sharp U-turn, I pulled up behind the Mercedes, which was stopped on the narrow shoulder next to the guard rail.

"Hi Able, Hi Dog," I said. "Seen any black Tatras lately?"

Martins, who had never smiled since I met him, shook his head in a lugubrious no. His partner, Baker, agreed.

"They have to have been here," I said, digging out my road map. "They were only a few miles ahead of me." I ran my finger along the map and sighed. "You're right. They're not. They turned off in Karlobag. They knew they were being tailed and even the dimmest of them could have figured out that there was a reception party ahead. Look."

I put my finger on the map and they looked. "A side road goes off into the mountains here, then over the top where it joins up with a good road at Gospic. After that they have a straight run for the border. Once they are past the first stretch."

"The first part is marked in yellow," Martins said. "What does that mean?"

"I'm afraid to find out." The map, issued by *Turisticki savez Jugoslavije,* was in Italian, and yellow roads were marked as being *Strada in macadam in cativo stato.* "In rough translation you could say unpaved and in lousy shape."

"That's bad," Martins said, looking like he was going to cry. "In Yugoslavia that is very bad."

"I'll give you a complete description of it when I make my report."

"No," Martins said.

"Orders," Baker added. "We're supposed to take over the chase when we meet you. That came right down from the top."

"Not fair! I started this job and I should be left to finish it."

They shrugged, jumped into the Mercedes and charged off down the road. I climbed into the Toyota and followed them. So they could go first. But no one had said I couldn't follow them.

In Karlobag a rusty sign labeled "Gospic *41*" pointed up a hill at a cloud of dust. I hit the road and my brakes at the same time, then lurched forward in compound low. It was more of a quarry than a road, made up of rounded stones—some of them as big as tabletops. I ground forward, dodging the worst ones, at five miles an hour. There was a loud explosion around the turn ahead. I hit the gas and bounced and skidded around it.

The Mercedes was off the road with its hood buried in the ditch. Its front wheels were angled out as if they were very tired and both fenders were peeled back like a pair of open tin cans. Things were still happening. A man in a dark suit stood up from behind a boulder on the far side of the road and leveled a long-barreled pistol. Before he could shoot, Martins, who had been driving, had his gun resting on the window ledge and fired just once. It was very dramatic. Black suit screeched shrilly, threw his gun up in the air, spun about and fell.

"Look after Baker," I shouted. "I'll take care of your friend."

I circled, fast and quiet, and came up behind the man who was flat on the ground, trying to clamp his hand over his bleeding arm and wriggle over to his gun at the same time. "No seconds," I said, picking up the gun.

He rolled over and looked at me. "*Sveenyah* . . ." he growled.

"It is the same in every language," I told him, and pocketed the gun. "And who are you to call names? Do decent people travel around with land mines in their cars?" I left him that one to think about while I went back to help Martins. He had Baker laid out by the side of the road, the first-aid kit open, and was smearing antiseptic on a bloody gash on the younger agent's forehead.

"Out cold," he said. "Breathing regular and it doesn't seem too bad—but you never know."

"Carry him back to the road—it's only a hundred yards— and flag down a car. There must be a doctor in this town. If not, there's a big hospital in Zadar. And if you remember it, you could send someone back to look at your target over there in the weeds. I'm going on to talk to Svirsky about the kind of friends he has."

I didn't give him time to argue, just started the Toyota and bounced away up the road. This was going to be a stern chase where my four-wheel drive would finally come in handy. By missing the worst tombstones I could hold her on twenty, even twenty-five on some stretches. I was pretty sure the Tatra couldn't do this well, rugged as it is. Particularly when I saw it two turns above me on the snake-bended road.

All things considered it was doing all right, bouncing and swaying and throwing up a cloud of dust at all of ten miles an hour. These cars, which are never seen in the West, are the pride of the Skoda works. They're big and round and solid, only for high party officials and types like that. They are built and sprung to take punishment, too. With a high fin down the middle of their backs like a Flash Gordon rocket ship and three headlights in the front they have more of a mad look than you would expect to find in this part of the world. Or maybe you would expect to. In any case, fin, headlights and shocks weren't helping him stay ahead. I was catching up slowly. We bounced and groaned and rattled around the bends and over the boulders and I was less than two hundred yards behind him when I saw, around the next turn, a spire and marker that might very well be the top of the hill. If he got there first, and onto a straight road, he might get away from me.

At this point the road headed away from the marker, went down and made a loop and came back on a higher level above the spot I was passing. A banked hillside separated the two stretches of road and I could see a beaten path where the pedestrians, goats and dogs took a shortcut to save walking the long loop of road. Where four legs go, four wheels go. I pulled the wheel hard right and bounced through the ditch and into the dirt.

In all truth it was smoother and better than the road, although just a bit more angled. The engine growled, the tires spun and dug in, and we went straight up. I shouted *yippee* and held tight to the wheel.

When I came over the shoulder the Tatra had already rounded the turn and was bounding my way, its three eyes gleaming. For a churning moment the Toyota hung up on the sharp lip, the front tires slipping on the smooth stones, until the back wheels dug in and shot us over the top.

Since the Tatra was about to pass me I did the only thing possible and ran full tilt into it.

I did manage to hit the hood so it jarred sideways. There was a sound like an explosion in a garbage can factory when we collided—then the Tatra nosed off the road and crashed into a well-placed pile of rocks. I braked, killed the engine and jumped out at the same time, but Svirsky was faster. He had the back door open even before the crash and had bounced out like an overweight gazelle. The driver was half slumped over the wheel, mumbling to himself as he tried to drag out another of those long-barreled pistols. I took it away from him and cracked him at the right spot in the back of the neck that would put him to sleep for a while and keep him out of mischief. Then I followed Svirsky.

He had his head down and was pelting along the road like a runaway steam engine. But I just happen to be faster. When he reached the marker he turned off the road with me coming close behind him. I reached the high marker, passed it—then jumped back. The bullet tore a gouge from the stone just where I had been. Svirsky must have been the backseat marksman who had taken out my tire, and his eye was still good. Next to my head was an inscription, in German, something about this road dedicated to our noble Emperor, Franz-Josef. I believed it. And I bet it hadn't been touched since the Emperor watched them roll the last boulder into place.

Keeping low, I ran around the other side of the commemoration plinth and saw Svirsky vanishing into a grove of pine trees. Great! If he had stayed on the road, he could have kept me away with his deadly popgun. In the woods we were equal.

This was a northern forest, very much like the Alps. We had climbed high enough to leave the baked, subtropical coast behind and enter this pleasant green highland. Well, me Leatherstocking, him the moose—or bear—I was going to do a little trapping. I could hear my prey crashing through the underbrush ahead and I circled out to the side to swing around him, running low, silent and fast.

My friend Svirsky was no Indian scout—or even a boy scout. He pushed those four hundred twelve pounds through the woods like a tank, and I kept him in sonar contact at all times. When the crashing stopped I kept going until I had passed the spot where I had heard him last, then came silently back.

What a setup! He was bent over behind a tree, looking back the way he had come, the gun pointed and ready. I considered the best course, then decided that disarming him might be the wisest first step. I came up silently behind him.

"Can I borrow that, Comrade?" I said as I reached over and—with a good tug—pulled the gun out of his hands.

For all of his weight he had good reflexes. He swung at me and I had to jump aside to avoid getting slugged.

"Hands in the air, or *Hande hoch* or whatever."

Svirsky ignored both me and the gun and, scowling terribly, he kept coming on in a wrestler's crouch, arms extended. I backed away.

"Someone can get hurt this way," I told him, "and the odds are that it's going to be you."

Still not a word, just that steady, machinelike advance.

"Don't say I didn't give fair warning. Stop, stop, stop, that's three times."

He completely ignored me, so I shot him in the leg. The bullet ricocheted and screamed away and he kept coming. I could see the hole in his pants leg, so I knew that I hadn't missed.

"All right, iron man," I said, aiming carefully, "Let's see how good your joints are."

This time I aimed at his kneecap, with the same results. Nothing. I was backed up to a tree. I fired at the same spot once more before the bullets had any effect and the leg folded. But he was right on top of me then, coming down like a falling mountain. I couldn't get away in time and he hit me. I threw the gun as far away as I could before he closed those big hands on me.

Talk about strong, this joker had muscles of steel. I wriggled and twisted and kept moving, and I didn't try to hit him because I knew he had no nerves, no nerves at all. I twisted and pushed away, tearing most of my shirt off at the same time, and managed to get out of that mechanical bearhug.

Now it was my turn. I just climbed his back, locked my legs around his waist, and twisted his neck. He still hadn't said anything, I doubt if he could talk, but he thrashed his arms something terrible and tried to pull me off. He just couldn't reach me. I turned and turned until he was glaring back at me over his right shoulder. And then I turned some more. He was facing straight backwards now, clicking his teeth at me. And I kept twisting. There was a sharp crack and his eyes closed and all the fight went out of him. I just turned some more until his head came off.

Of course there were a lot of trailing wires and piping and that kind of thing, but I pulled it all loose and put the decapitated head on the ground. Some of the wires sparked when they grounded.

Now I had to find out where the brain was. Just because a robot looks like a man there is no reason to assume that its brain is in its head. Svirsky may have thought with his stomach. I had to find out. Ever since we had heard the rumors that a humanoid robot was being field-tested in Yugoslavia we had all been planning for this moment. Servo

228 *Harry Harrison*

motors and power plants and hardware we knew about. But
what kind of a brain were they using? We were going to find
out. I pulled his shirt open and they hadn't even bothered to
put the plastic flesh back completely the last time they had
serviced him. They must have been in a hurry to leave. A
flap of skin was hanging loose just above his navel, and I put
my finger in and pulled. He peeled open just like a banana,
showing a broad, metallic chest under the soft plastic. An
access plate covered most of it, just like on an airplane's
engine, with big slotted fasteners in the corners. I bent a
ten-dinar coin twisting them open, then pulled the plate off
and threw it away.

Well, well, I smiled to myself, and even went so far as to
rub my hands together. Motors, junction boards, power pack,
and so forth, all feeding into a bundle of wires in a realistic
location where the spinal cord should have been and heading
up through the neck. Brain in head—and I had the head.

"Thank you, Comrade," I said, standing and dusting off
my knees, "you have been very helpful. I'm going to borrow
your shirt, because you tore mine, and take some pictures of
your innards to make our engineers happy."

I removed the shirt from the headless torso and propped
him up so that the sun shone in through the access port. Now
camera. I looked around carefully to be sure no one was in
sight, then threw my torn shirt away.

"We have our secrets, too," I told him, but he didn't
bother to answer.

I pushed with my thumbnail at the flesh over my sternum,
then pulled with both hands until my skin stretched and
parted. The lens of my chest camera protruded through the
opening. "F2.5 at a 125th," I estimated, correctly of course,
then shot the pictures, clicking them off with a neural impulse
to the actuator. I could easily hide the head in the Toyota,
and these pics would be all the detail we needed about the
body. Since there was no one else present I did not mind
bragging aloud.

"Just like the space race, Comrade, neck and neck. And
you went to the robot race the same way. Build strong, build
for excess power, build double and treble in case of failure.
That makes for a mighty heavy robot. Not even room left for
speech circuits. While we built with micro- and micromicro-

miniaturization. Sophisticated circuitry. More goodies in the same-size package. And it works, too. When Washington heard you were going to be tested down here they couldn't resist field-testing me at the same time.''

I started back to the Toyota, then turned and waved good-bye with my free hand.

"If you have any doubt about which approach works the best,'' I called out cheerily, "just notice who is carrying whose head under his arm.''

Faithfully Yours

Lou Tabakow

JULY 18, 1949 A.D.

*The fugitive lay face down in the fetid undergrowth, draw-
ing in spasmodic lungfuls of air through cracked and swollen
lips. Long before, his blue workshirt had been ripped to
ribbons and his exposed chest showed a spiderwork of
scratches, where branches and brambles had sought to re-
strain him in his frenzied flight. Across his back from shoulder to shoulder ran a deeper cut around which the caked
blood attested to the needle-sharp viciousness of a thorn bush
a mile to the north. With each tortured breath he winced, as
drops of sweat ran down, following the spiderwork network
and burning like acid. Incessantly he rubbed his bruised torso
with mud-caked palms to dislodge the gnats and mosquitoes
that clung to him, gorging shamelessly.*

*To the east he could see the lights of Fort Mudge where the
railroad cut through on its way to Jacksonville. He had
planned to ride the freight into Jacksonville but by now they
were stopping every train and searching along every foot of
the railroad right-of-way. In the distance he heard the eerie
keen of a train whistle, and visualized the scene as it was
flagged down and searched from engine to caboose.*

*Directly before him loomed the forbidding northern bound-
ary of the Okefenokee Swamp. Unconsciously he strained his
ears, then shuddered at the night noises that issued from the
noisome wilderness. A frenzied threshing, then a splash, then
. . . silence. What drama of life and death was being played
out in that strange other-world of perpetual shadows?*

In sudden panic he jerked erect and cupped his palm around his ear. Far off, muted by distance, but still unmistakable, he heard the baying of bloodhounds. Then this was the end. A sob broke from his throat. What was he, an animal; to be hunted down as a sport? Tears of self-pity welled to his eyes as he thought back to a party and a girl and laughter and cleanliness and the scent of magnolias, like a heady wine. But that was so long ago—so long ago—and now . . . He looked down at his sweating, lacerated body; his blistered calloused palms; the black broken nails; the cheap workshoes with hemp laces; the shapeless gray cotton trousers, now wet to the knees.

He pulled back his shoulders and resolutely faced west toward the river, but stopped short in horror as he heard the sudden cacophony of barks, yelps and howls of a pack of bloodhounds that senses the beginning of the end. He turned in panic. They couldn't be over half a mile away. In a panic of indecision he turned first east then west, then facing due south he hesitated a moment to take one last look at the clear open skies, and with a muffled prayer plunged into the brooding depths of the Okefenokee.

JUNE 13, 427th Year GALACTIC ERA

The building still hummed and vibrated with the dying echoes of the alarm siren as the biophysicist hurried down the corridor, and without breaking stride, pushed open the door to the Director's office.

The Director shuffled the papers before him and sighed heavily. His chair creaked protestingly as he shifted his bulk and looked up.

"Well?"

"He got away clean," said the biophysicist.

"Any fix on the direction?"

"None at all, sir. And he's got at least a two hours' start. That takes in a pretty big area of space."

"Hm-m-m! Well there's just a bare chance. That experimental cruiser is the fastest thing in space and it's equipped with the latest ethero-radar. If we get started right away, we just might—"

"That's just it," interrupted the biophysicist. "That's the ship he got away in."

The Director jumped angrily to his feet. "How did that happen? How can I explain to the board?"

"I'm sorry, sir. He was just too—"

"You're sorry?" He slumped back in his chair and drummed the desk top with his fingernails, worrying his lower lip with his teeth. He exhaled loudly and leaned forward. "Well, only one thing to do. You know the orders."

The biophysicist squirmed uncomfortably. "Couldn't we send a squadron of ships out to search and—"

"And what?" asked the Director, sarcastically. "You don't think I'd risk a billion credits' worth of equipment on a wild-goose chase like that, do you? We could use up a year's appropriation of fuel and manpower and still be unable to adequately search a sector one-tenth that size. If he just sat still, a thousand ships couldn't find him in a thousand years, searching at finite speeds. Add to that the fact that the target is moving at ultralight speed and the odds against locating him are multiplied by a billion."

"I know, but he can't stay in space. He'll have to land somewhere, sometime."

"True enough—but where and when?"

"Couldn't we alert all the nearby planets?"

"You know better than that. He could be halfway across the galaxy before an ethero-gram reached the nearest planet."

"Suppose we sent scout ships to the nearer planets and asked them to inform their neighbors in the same way. We'd soon have an expanding circle that he *couldn't* slip through."

The Director smiled wryly. "Maybe. But who's going to pay for all this? By the time the circle was a thousand light-years in diameter there would be ten thousand ships and a million clerks working on recapturing one escaped prisoner. Another thing; I don't know offhand what he's been sentenced for, but I'll wager there are ten thousand planets on which his crime would not be a crime. Do you think we could ever extradite him from such a planet? And even if by some incredible stroke of fortune one of our agents happened to land on the right planet, in which city would he begin his search? Or suppose our quarry lands only on uninhabited planets? We can't very well alert the whole galaxy in the search for just one man."

"I know, but—"

"But what?" interrupted the Director. "Any other suggestions?"

"N . . . no—"

"All right, he asked for it. You have the pattern, I presume. *Feed it to Fido!*"

"Yes, sir, but well . . . I just don't—"

"Do you think *I* like it?" asked the Director fiercely.

In the silence that followed, they looked at each other guiltily.

"There's nothing else we can do," said the Director. "The orders are explicit. *No one escapes from Hades!*"

"I know," replied the biophysicist. "I'm not blaming you. Only I wish someone else had my job."

"Well," said the Director heavily. "You might as well get started." He nodded his head in dismissal.

As the biophysicist went out the door, the Director looked down once more at the pile of papers before him. He pulled the top sheet closer, and rubber-stamped across its face CASE CLOSED.

"Yes," he mused aloud. "Closed for us, but—" He hesitated a moment, and then sighing once more, signed his name in the space provided.

AUGUST 6, 430th Year GALACTIC ERA

Tee Ormond sat morosely at the spaceport bar, and alternately wiped his forehead with a soggy handkerchief, and sipped at his frosted rainbow, careful not to disturb the vari-colored layers of liquid in the tall narrow glass. Every now and then he nervously ran his fingers through his straight black hair, which lay damply plastered to his head. His jacket was faded and worn, and above the left pocket was emblazoned the meteor insignia of the spaceman. A dark patch on his back showed where the perspiration had seeped through. He blinked and rubbed the corner of his eye as a drop of perspiration ran down and settled there.

A casual look would have classified him as a very average-looking pilot such as could be found at the bar of any spaceport, if space pilots can ever be classified as average. Spacemen are the last true adventurers in an age where the debilitating culture of a highly mechanized civilization has pushed to the very borders of the galaxy. While most men are fearful and indecisive outside their narrow specialties the spacemen must at all times be ready to deal with the unexpected and the unusual. The expression "Steady as a spaceman's nerves" had a very real origin.

A closer look at Tee would have revealed the error of a quick classification. He gripped his drink too tightly, and his eyes darted restlessly from side to side, as though searching, searching; yet dreading to find the object of their search. His expressive face contorted in a nervous tic each time his eyes swept by the clock hanging behind the bar. He glanced dispiritedly out the window at the perpetually cloudy sky and idly watched a rivulet of water race down the dirty pane. He loosened his collar and futilely mopped at his neck with the soggy handkerchief, then irritably flung it to the floor.

"Hey, Jo," he yelled to the bartender. "What's the matter with the air conditioning? I'm burning up."

"Take it easy," soothed the bartender, consulting a thermometer on the wall behind him. "It's eighty-five in here. That's as low as the law allows. Can't have too much difference in the temperature or all my customers'd pass out when they go outside. Why don't you go into town? They keep it comfortable under the dome."

"Don't this planet *ever* cool off?" asked Tee.

The bartender chuckled. "I see you don't know too much about Thymis. Sometimes it drops to ninety at night, but not too often. You ought to be here sometime when the clouds part for a minute. If you're caught outside then, it's third-degree burns for sure."

He glanced down at the nearly empty glass. "How about another rainbow? If you get enough of them in you, you won't notice the heat—you won't notice anything." He laughed uproariously at the hoary joke.

Tee looked at him disgustedly and without answering bent to his drink once more. He felt someone jostle his elbow and turned sideways to allow the newcomer access to the bar. After a moment he wiped his forehead on his sleeve. The bartender placed another rainbow before him.

"Hey, I didn't order that," he cried.

The bartender nodded toward the next stool. "On him."

Tee turned and saw a barrel-chested red-haired giant holding up a drink in the immemorial bar toast. He raised his own glass gingerly, but his trembling hand caused the layers to mix and he stared ruefully at the resultant clayey-looking mess.

The redhead laughed. "Mix another one, Jo."

"But—" Tee's face got red.

"I came in here to talk to you anyway," said the giant. "You own the *Starduster*, don't you?"

"Yeah, what about it?"

"Like to get her out of hock?"

"Who says she's in hock?"

"Look," said the redhead. "Let's not kid each other. Everybody around this port knows you blew in from Lemmyt last month and can't raise the money to pay the port charges, much less the refueling fee. And it's no secret that you're anxious to leave our fair planet." He winked conspiringly at Tee.

"So?"

The redhead glanced at the bartender, who was busy at the other end of the bar. He leaned closer and whispered. "I know where the *Elen of Troy* is."

"The *Elen of Troy?*"

"Oh, that's right, you wouldn't know about her. Eight months ago she crashed on an uninhabited planet somewhere in this sector. So far they've been unable to find her." He leaned closer. "She was carrying four million in penryx crystals."

"What's that to me?"

The redhead looked around briefly to make sure no one was in hearing distance, then whispered softly, without moving his lips. "I told you, they can't find her, but *I* know where she is."

"*You* know? But how—"

"Look," said the giant, frowning, "I didn't ask you why *you're* so anxious to leave."

"Well?"

"I'll clear your ship and we can pick up the crystals for the salvage fee. A million each, and all nice and legal. We can leave by the end of the week and be back in probably six months."

"*Six months!*" Tee stood up. "Sorry!"

The redhead grabbed his arm in a hamlike palm. "A million each in six months; what's wrong with that?"

Tee jerked out of his grasp. "I . . . I just can't do it."

"I don't know what you're running from," persisted the redhead, "but with a million credits you can fight extradition for the rest of your life. This is your big chance, can't you see that? Besides, this planet has some interesting customs." He winked at Tee. "I can introduce you—"

"I can't stay here," interrupted Tee. "You just don't understand."

"Look," cried the redhead exasperatedly, "I'm offering you a full partnership on a two-million-credit salvage deal and you want to back out because it'll take six months. On top of that you're broke and stranded and your hangar bill gets bigger every day. If you don't take me up on this deal, you'll still be sitting here six months from now wondering how to get your ship out of hock—if you don't get caught first. What do you say? What've you got to lose?"

What did he have to lose? Tee gripped the edge of the bar till his knuckles showed white. "No! I just can't do it. Why don't you get someone else?"

"The slow tubs around this port would take years for the trip. I can see the *Starduster* has class."

"Fastest thing in the galaxy," said Tee proudly. Then earnestly, "I'm sorry, you'll just have to find some other ship."

"Think it over," said the redhead. "I'll wait. When you change your mind look me up. Name's Yule Larson." He slapped Tee heavily on the back and swaggered toward the door. He turned and looked back. "Better go along with me. After six months they can auction off your ship to pay for the port charges, you know." The door swung shut behind him.

Tee sat down again and bent his head, nursing his drink. His eyes darted nervously around the room and came to rest on the clock. A shudder ran through him and he lowered his eyes quickly. As he sipped his drink his eyes returned to the clock continually, as though drawn there against their will. As he watched, the minute hand jerked downward and an involuntary gasp escaped his lips.

The bartender turned quickly. "Anything wrong?"

"N . . . no, nothing." As he spoke, the minute hand moved again and Tee started nervously, upsetting his drink. He sat for a moment watching the bartender mop up the spreading liquid, then abruptly got up and tossed a half-credit piece on the bar. He hurried outside, steeling himself to keep from running. He paused just outside the door.

Stand still, he told himself. *Mustn't run! No use anyway. If I only knew when. If I just could stop and rest. If I had the time . . . Time! Time! That's what I need. Light-years of time . . . But when? When? If only I could be sure.* He looked up slowly at the murky canopy of clouds. *If I only knew when!* He looked indecisively up and down the field, then, squaring his shoulders resolutely, set out for the administration building.

At this hour the office was deserted except for a wispy-haired little man who sat at a desk fussing with some papers. He looked up questioningly as Tee came in.

"Is my ship recharged and provisioned?" asked Tee.

"Uh, what's the name please?"

"Tee Ormond. I own the *Starduster.*"

The clerk pulled a card from a file on the desk and studied it. "Ah, yes, the *Starduster.*"

"I'd like to pay my bill and clear the *Starduster* for immediate departure."

"Uh, very good, Mr. Ormond." He consulted the card again. "That'll be fourteen hundred and eleven credits." He beamed. "We included a case of Ruykeser's Concentrate, compliments of the management." He handed a circular to Tee. "This is a list of our ports and facilities on other planets. Our accommodations are the finest, and we carry a complete line of parts." He smiled professionally.

"What about my key?" asked Tee, pulling out his wallet.

"Uh, let's see, number thirty-seven." The clerk started for a numbered board hanging on the wall. He never got there.

Tee whipped a stun-gun from inside his jacket and waved it at the clerk's back. It caught him in mid-stride, and unbalanced, he crashed heavily to the floor. Tee glanced briefly down as he stepped over the paralyzed form, avoiding the accusing eyes, and snatched the magnetic key off the hook. He forced himself to walk calmly across the field toward the hangar that housed the *Starduster.*

A uniformed guard stopped him at the hangar door. "May I see your clearance, sir?" he asked, politely.

Tee hesitated for a moment. "Oh, I'm just going to get something out of my ship," he said, smoothly. "The clerk said it was roj."

"The clerk said? But he can't—" The guard teased. "Mind if I check, sir? Orders, you know." He bent his head slightly as he pressed a knob on his wrist radio. As his eyes turned downward, Tee swung the stun-gun in an arc that ended on the back of the guard's head. As he leaped into the *Starduster* he was sorry for a moment that he hadn't had time to recharge the gun, and hoped he hadn't struck too hard.

OCTOBER 11, 433rd Year GALACTIC ERA

Tee stepped out of the hangar and surveyed the twin suns. The pale binaries sat stolidly on the horizon, forty degrees apart. Their mingled light washed down dimly on the single continent of the planet, Aurora.

He started, as a man walked around the corner of the hangar. The man looked at Tee searchingly for a moment, then asked, "Anything troubling you, Tee?"

"Why . . . why, no, Mr. Jenner. You just startled me, that's all."

"Well, how's everything coming?"

"Right on schedule. We'll be ready for the final test by the end of the week."

"By the way," asked Jenner speculatively, "how come you ordered the ship stocked and provisioned for the test?"

"Why . . . why I think she should be tested under exactly the same conditions as she'll encounter in actual use."

"We could have done it a lot cheaper by just using ballast," said Jenner. "After this, I want to personally see any voucher for over a hundred credits before it's cleared."

"Yes, sir, but I just didn't want to bother you with details."

"An expenditure of over two thousand credits isn't just detail; but let it pass. It's already done. Anyway, on the drawing board she's the fastest thing in the galaxy." He smiled. "If she lives up to expectations, she'll make your ship look like an old freighter. We've got four million sunk in her so far, so she'd better check out roj."

He put his hand on Tee's shoulder. "You're not worried about testing her, are you? You've been jumpy lately."

"Oh, no, nothing like that, Mr. Jenner. I'm just . . . well, I've been up all night watching them install the gyroscopes. Think I'll get some sleep." He yawned.

Jenner cupped his chin in his palm and stood staring after the retreating figure. As Tee turned and looked back nervously, Jenner entered the hangar office. He spoke softly into the visiphone and in a moment the screen lit up.

"Is this the prison administrator?" asked Jenner.

"What can I do for you?"

"My name is Jenner: Consolidated Spacecraft."

"Yes?"

"Suppose an escaped prisoner from Hades landed on Aurora?"

"*No one* escapes from Hades Prison."

"Well, just suppose one did?"

"I never receive information about escapees."

"But you're the administrator here."

"My job, as the title implies, is purely administrative. I merely arrange transportation for our annual shipment of prisoners to Hades, and see that the records are kept straight."

"But whom *would* they contact in the event of an escape?"

The administrator pursed his lips in impatience. "Hades has six billion prisoners at any given time. If one did manage to escape, they couldn't very well alert a million planets."

"You mean you wouldn't do anything?"

"As I said before, my job is purely administrative. Out of my jurisdiction entirely. Each planet has its own police force and handles its internal crime in its own way. What's legal on Aurora might very well be illegal on ten thousand other planets, and vice versa."

"I see. Thank you." Jenner cut the connection slowly. He flicked the switch open again, hesitated, and then closed it.

He walked out to where his gyrocar was parked, and in a few minutes set it down on the roof of Tee's hotel. Tee was just entering the lobby as Jenner came in and they went up to his room together.

"I'll come right to the point, Tee," he said, as soon as the door had closed. "I just talked to the local prisoner administrator for Hades." He looked closely at Tee.

"What's that got to do with me?" asked Tee belligerently.

"Wait until I finish," said Jenner curtly. "I hired you to test-hop our new ship because you were the best pilot available. I'm not interested in your past, but most of the company's resources are sunk in that ship. If something goes wrong because the test pilot is disturbed or nervous; the company will be bankrupt. I'm not saying you're an escaped prisoner, but if you were, you'd have nothing to worry about."

"What do you mean?"

"The administrator told me he has no jurisdiction over escaped prisoners, so you see, if you had escaped, you'd have nothing to fear here. You're out of their jurisdiction."

Tee began to laugh wildly. *"Out of their jurisdiction! Out of their jurisdiction!* So that's the way they put it. *Out of their jurisdiction!"*

"Stop it!" said Jenner sharply. "Do you want to tell me now?"

Tee drew in a gasping breath and sobered. "What would I have to tell you? So I'm the nervous type. So you hired me to test-hop your new ship. So I'll test-hop it. That's all we agreed on. What more do you want?"

Jenner sighed. "Roj, Tee, if that's the way you want it, but I wish—"

The visiphone buzzed, and when Tee flipped the switch, the worried face of the chief mechanic sprang into focus. "Oh, there you are, Mr. Jenner. Glad I caught you before you left. We've run into trouble."

"Well, out with it," barked Jenner. "What is it?"

The mechanic cleared his throat nervously. "We were testing the main gyroscope when it threw a blade."

"How bad is it?" asked Jenner.

"Pretty bad, I'm afraid. It tore up the subetherscope unit so bad we'll have to replace it. We can't get any on Aurora either. We'll have to send to Lennix, and that'll take close to a month."

"Roj! Knock off until I get there," barked Jenner. He slammed over the switch, viciously. "Of all the rotten luck!"

"Can't you get some plant here on Aurora to hand-tool one for you?" asked Tee.

"No, that's just it," replied Jenner. "It's a special alloy. The owners of the process wouldn't give us any details on the manufacture. Anyway, even if we knew how, we couldn't duplicate it without their special machine tools.''

"Does that mean—''

"I'm afraid so. The ship won't be ready for a month now.''

"*A month!* I can't wait a month.''

"*You* can't wait a month? We've got four million tied up in that ship and you tell me *you* can't wait a month.''

"Look, Mr. Jenner, I'll test it without the unit.''

"That's impossible. The ship would vibrate into a billion pieces as soon as it went into subspace. No! We'll just have to wait.''

"I can't wait," cried Tee. "You'll have to get another pilot.''

"Just a minute! You can't walk out on your contract. If it's a matter of credits—''

Tee shook his head. "That's not it at all. I just can't stay that long.''

Jenner looked at him angrily. "Well, your contract isn't up till the end of the week anyway. We'll see what we can do about a replacement then.''

After Jenner had left, Tee sat smoking in the darkness. He placed his elbow on the couch arm and cupped his chin in his palm. Then, restlessly, he sniffed out his cigarette and rubbed his hands together. They felt moist and clammy. He jerked nervously as a click sounded out in the hall. Only a door opening across the way. He bit the fleshy part of his middle finger and then began to worry his ring with his teeth. He lit another cigarette and dropped it into the disposal almost immediately.

He got up and began to pace the room. Six steps forward. Turn. Six steps back. Turn. Six steps forward—or was it five this time? The walls seemed to be closing in, constricting. His head felt light and his tongue and palate grew dry. He tried to swallow, and a feeling of nausea came over him. His throat grew tight and he felt as though he were choking. He rubbed his forehead with the back of his hand; it came away wet with perspiration. He rushed to the window and struggled futilely with it, forgetting it was sealed shut in the air-conditioned hotel. He flung himself at the door, wrenching it open, and took the escalator three steps at a time, falling to his knees at the ground floor. A surface cab was sitting outside just beyond the entrance. He flung himself in, breathing heavily and fumbling to drop a coin in the slot, pulled the control level all the way over.

Twenty minutes later, the *Starduster* hovered for a moment over Aurora, then shimmered and vanished as it went into subspace.

OCTOBER 2, 435th Year GALACTIC ERA

The *Starduster* materialized just outside the atmosphere of the planet Elysia, and fluttered erratically downward, like a wounded bird. A hundred feet from the surface, the ship hesitated, shuddered throughout her length, then dropped like a plummet, crashing heavily into a grove of trees.

For Tee there was a long period of blessed darkness, of peace, of nonremembering, then his mind clawed upward toward consciousness. The fear and uncertainty were with him again—nagging, nibbling, gnawing at his reason.

He fought to close his mind and drift back down into the darkness of peace and forgetting, but contrarily the past marched in review before his consciousness. The twin worlds of Thole revolving about each other as he fled down the shallow ravine before the creeping wall of lava, while the ancient mountain grunted and belched, and coughed up its insides. The terrible pull of the uncharted black star as it tugged at the feeble *Starduster*. The enervating heat and humidity of perpetually cloudy Thymis. Pyramids of gleaming penryx crystals piled high as mountains, and Yule Larson towering above the landscape, draining gargantuan rainbows at a single gulp; striding like Paul Bunyan across the land in mile-long strides and kicking over the pyramids of crystals, laughing uproariously at the sport. And Jenner, grinning idiotically, pointing a thick finger at him and repeating over and over: "Out of their jurisdiction! Nothing to fear! Nothing to fear! Nothing to fear! Noth—"

"Stop it! Stop it!" cried Tee, and a brilliant burst of light like a thousand skyrockets seemed to go off in his head. He shrieked like an animal in agony, then fell back sobbing, bathed in perspiration.

Something cool touched his forehead and he pulled away

violently, then as his head cleared he opened his eyes slowly. A blur of shadows and light shimmering indistinctly, then suddenly like the picture on a visiphone the blurs coalesced and formed a clear image, and everything was normal again, the fear still hovering close, but pushed back for the time being.

A girl stood before him smiling rather uncertainly. The sweetness and cleanness of that smile after his recent ordeal washed over his tortured mind like a cooling astringent, and he smiled gratefully up at her. She put a cool palm on his forehead and as she started to withdraw it he clutched it in an emaciated fist and mumbled indistinctly through cracked dry lips.

She smiled down at him and smoothed back his damp hair. She pulled up a chair beside the bed and continued to stroke his hair until his eyes closed in sleep.

He awoke ravenous and thirsty, but lay quietly for a time, luxuriating in the feel of the clean soft sheets. He was in a simply but tastefully decorated room. Three of the walls were made of transparent glass, and the warm golden rays of a type G sun bathed the room. Outside he could seee green rolling meadowland, broken here and there by sylvan groves. A brilliantly colored bird swooped down and preened itself for a moment, then raised its head and flooded the silence with melody. Faintly from a grove of trees came an answering treble. The songbird cocked its head to the side, listening, then swooped upward on wings of flashing color. A small squirrellike creature bounded nervously up to the transparent wall and sat on its haunches, surveying the room with bright beady eyes. As Tee's ears attuned themselves he was suddenly aware of chirpings, trebles, clear-pitched whistles, and from somewhere in the depths of the grove, a deep-pitched ga-rooph, ga-roomph.

A chubby little man with a round face and alert twinkling eyes entered the room. He seemed to radiate happiness and contentment. ''Well, I see the patient's finally come around,'' he said cheerfully.

''What happened?'' asked Tee.

''Your ship crashed just beyond that grove.''

Tee clutched at him. ''The ship! How bad is it?''

''I think you were in worse shape than your ship. **You**

must have had it under control almost to the end, though how you stayed conscious with space fever is beyond me.''

"Space fever? So that's it. I remember getting sick and light-headed, and just before I passed out I flipped out of subspace and the automatic finder, of course, took the ship to the nearest planet. I must have landed by reflex action. I sure don't remember anything about it.''

"Well,'' the man laughed, ''I *have* seen better landings, but not when the pilot had a temperature of one-o-five. Anyway, you're safe now. Welcome to Elysia.''

There it was again. Safe! Safe! Tee raised up, then fell back weakly.

"Is anything wrong?'' asked the little man, alarmed.

"N . . . nothing, I just . . . nothing!''

The man was looking at him questioningly.

"Elysia,'' mused Tee. ''I seem to remember an old old myth brought from the original Earth.'' He waved toward the sylvan setting, outside.

The little man smiled. ''Yes, the old settlers named our planet well.'' He caught himself. ''Oh, I'm sorry; I'm Dr. Chensi. This is my home.''

Tee smiled. ''Well, at least you'll have to admit I showed good judgment crashing next to a doctor's house.'' Then more seriously, ''Thanks, doc, thanks for everything.''

"My degrees aren't in medicine,'' replied Dr. Chensi. "I'm afraid I had little to do with your recovery. My daughter's the one who nursed you. Oh, here she is now.'' He raised his voice. ''Come in, Lara.''

Since Dr. Chensi was using the only chair she sat down on the edge of the bed.

"Here,'' said the doctor teasingly, ''what kind of nurse are you, mussing up your patient's bed?''

She pouted prettily. ''He's *my* patient.'' Then, looking down at Tee with a smile, ''You'll be up and around in no time now.''

"Time!'' cried Tee, raising up. *"What's the date? I've got to know!''*

"You've been delirious for two weeks,'' answered the doctor. ''Another two weeks of convalescence and you ought to be as good as new.''

"But two weeks, I can't—''

"Can't leave before then anyway," replied the doctor calmly. "I knew you'd want your ship repaired, so I had it hauled to the port. Won't be ready for two more weeks. So you might as well relax."

Tee bit his lip, and clenched his fists to keep from trembling. It was a moment before he could trust himself to speak without a quaver in his voice. "Nothing else I can do, I guess. Thanks, anyway. And by the way, there's enough credits in the ship's safe to pay for the repairs, I'm sure."

"I think we should start the patient walking tomorrow," said Lara, in a mock-professional voice. She punched the ends of Tee's pillow. "Now you'd better get some sleep. You're still very weak, you know."

The days that followed were like an idyll for Tee. With Lara he wandered through the parklike wooded groves. They sat near shaded pools and ate wild berries while she told him stories of the founding of Elysia. They held hands and ran exuberantly across the grassy meadows, and waded like children in the clear brooks.

A thousand times, a word, an endearing term, sprang to his lips, and each time the fear clamped his tongue in a vise of steel. A thousand times he wanted to touch her, feel the silkiness of her hair, the warmth of her lips, but each time the fear and uncertainty stood between them like twin specters of doom, pointing and saying, "Fool! Why torture yourself?"

In the daytime when Lara was with him it wasn't so bad, but at night the fear and uncertainty crowded to the fore and blanked out everything else. It was then he prayed for the courage to kill himself, and despised the weakness that made him draw back from the thought. If only he could stop thinking. Make his mind a blank. But that was death, and death was what he feared. How long ago was it when he'd first realized that hope was an illusion, a false god that smiled and lied, and held out vain promises only to prolong the torture?

Then one day the word came that his ship was repaired. As though the word were a catalyst the terrible fear overwhelmed him, drowning out every other thought, and he knew he had to leave. When he had no means of leaving the planet he could partially close off his dread and wait resignedly. But now that the ship was ready, every moment he remained was an agony.

He led Lara to their favorite spot by a quiet pool. She looked radiant, and smiled to herself, as though at a secret. He steeled himself and finally blurted out, "Lara, I'm leaving tomorrow." He hesitated and bit his lip. "And . . . thanks for everything."

"Thanks?" She choked on the words.

"I'm sorry—" he trailed off, lamely.

"But . . . but I thought—" She looked down.

He reached out and gently touched her cheek. "Can't you see I *want* to stay?" he pleaded.

"Then why? Why?" She was crying now.

"I . . . I just can't. It's no good." He stood up.

She reached out and caught his hand. "Then take me with you. I've heard you at night pacing in your room. I don't know what it is that drives you on and on, but if space is what you want, let me go with you. I can help you, darling, You'll see. And some day when you grow tired of space, we can come back to Elysia." She was babbling now.

He pulled roughly away. "No! It's no good. I'm—If only I *could* stay." He brushed her hair softly with his palm, and as she reached out toward him he turned and walked swiftly toward the house, pitying and hating himself by turn, while Lara sat forlornly by the pool looking after him.

He began to sweat before he reached the house, and his knees began to tremble so he had to stop for a moment, to keep his balance. Determinedly he started forward again and continued on past the house to the highway that wound by half a kilometer away. There he hailed a passing ground car and rode to the spaceport, where a few judiciously distributed credits facilitated his immediate clearance. Before the ship had even left the atmosphere he rammed in the subspace control.

MAY 4, 437th Year GALACTIC ERA

Tantalus lay far out on a spiral arm, well away from the main stream of traffic that flowed through the galaxy. It was a fair planet boasting an equable climate, at least in the tropic zone. But as yet the population was small, consisting mostly of administrative officials who served their alloted time and thankfully returned to their home planets closer to the center of population.

Tee entered the towering building and after consulting a wall directory stepped into the antigrav chute and was whisked high up into the heart of the building. He stepped out before a plain door and as he advanced the center panel fluoresced briefly with the printed legend "GALACTIC PRISON AUTHORITY, Ary Mefford, Administrator for Tantalus."

He hesitated for a moment, then squaring his shoulders, stepped forward, and as he crossed the beam the door swung open before him. The gray-haired man sitting at the desk studying a paper looked up and smiled politely. He indicated a chair with a nod, then bent his head again. After a moment he shoved the paper aside and looked questioningly at Tee.

"I want to give myself up," blurted Tee.

"I'm the administrator for Hades," said the man calmly. "I think you want the *local* authorities."

"You don't understand. I escaped from Hades."

"No one escapes from Hades," replied the administrator.

"*I* escaped!" insisted Tee. "Ten years ago. You can check. I'm tired of running. I want to go back."

"This is most unusual," said the administrator in a disturbed voice. He looked unbelievingly at Tee. "*Ten years ago*, you say?"

"*Yes! Yes!* And I'm ready to go back, before it's too late. Can't you understand?"

The administrator shook his head pityingly. "It's already too late. I'm sorry." He bent his his head guiltily and began to fumble with the papers on his desk.

Tee started to say something, but the administrator raised his head and said slowly, "It was too late the day you left Hades. Nothing I can do." He looked down again. Tee turned and slowly walked out the door. The administrator didn't look up.

As Tee walked aimlessly down the deserted corridor, his footsteps echoed hollowly like a dirge. A line from an old poem sprang to his mind: "We are the dead, row on row we lie—" He was the dead, but still he chased the chimera of hope, yet knowing in his heart it was hopeless.

JUNE 11, 437th Year GALACTIC ERA

The *Starduster*, pocked and pitted from innumerable collisions with dust particles, sped out and out. The close-packed suns of the central hub lay far behind. Here at the rim of the galaxy the stars lay scattered, separated by vast distances. A gaunt hollow-eyed figure sat in the observation bubble staring half hopefully, half despairingly at the unimaginable depths beyond the rim.

JUNE 12, 437th year GALACTIC ERA

On and on past the thinning stars raced the patient electronic bloodhound; invisible, irreversible, indestructible; slowly, but inexorably accelerating. It flashed by the planet Damocles at multiples of the speed of light, and sensing the proximity of the prey on which it was homed, spurted into the intergalactic depths after the receding ship, intent on meshing with and thereby distorting the encephalograph pattern of its target. It was quite mindless, and the final pattern its meshing would create would be something quite strange, and not very human.

Safe Harbor

Donald Wismer

I set up Wave's Refuge to reflect, in various ways, my own need for separation from the oppressions of the urbania to the south. I built a baker's dozen of cabins, each out of sight of the others on the backside of a rocky dune or behind a clump of popples, just the loft windows peeking over at the sea. The wood I trucked in on flatbed truck, for I did not want to lay a chain saw on the white pine stands that were left from the last round of lumbering. A local foundation man laid concrete piers for me, and I built the frame on top of them, and insulated between the nine-inch floor joists and six-inch studs with a layer of six-mil poly stapled and taped all around the inside. I let the outside breathe through Tyvek paper and laid long, wide lapboards partly on top of one another, like shingling a roof, up the cabin sides. Then I laid the roof in ceramic tile, most unusual as far down east as I was. I gave each cabin its own twenty-foot dug well and septic and gray water fields, and ran electricity in via underground cable, with some heavy-duty plastic batteries for backup.

The wood heaters presented something of a dilemma. I had to have them or the rustic flavor of the Refuge would be compromised, yet I did not want combustion within such airtight walls despite each cabin's air-to-air heat exchanger. I finally found a Danish unit that offered outside air intake coupled with a reasonably tight glass front. There were more efficient heaters, but it didn't take much to warm up those cabins, and in fact I heard some complaints when tenants had to get up in the middle of the night to let cold air in.

We, my wife and son and daughter and I, lived in the 130-year-old year-round house that had been the only structure on the acreage. It directly faced the ocean, unlike the cabins, and it was higher, on a sort of minor bluff with white pine on three sides. There was scarcely a day that we didn't hear the wind, sighing or growling or shuddering past the house, off the sea.

I advertised in the online *New Yorker*, and in a few travel bulletin boards around the eastern seaboard. In the summer I offered standard Maine fare, but I kept my rates high to discourage any casual drop-ins. In the winter I was the only open camp for fifty miles either side, and that was the unusual thing that I advertised. Solitude barely says it. I offered business people a place where they would feel truly cut off from everything outside. I offered a place with no visitors at all, no telephones, no cellular radio, no television, no interference from the outside save what the traveler might bring in on his or her own, nothing except standard satellite surveillance. Where car makers offered sexual power rather than transportation, I offered peace and quiet rather than lodging. I had had no idea if the approach would work, but it did, at least enough for us to get by, and that was our intention in the first place, and the costly piece of land was being paid for.

I was aware that Fairchild was in some way unusual almost from the first. Let me give the credit where it belongs, namely my daughter, who spotted the scar behind his ear. Fairchild was a slender, wiry sort, whiplash-strong. He came in from Bangor by human-driven chauffeured limosine, of all things; that must have cost a fortune. He had a reservation, and I had four empty cabins that week and looked forward to the money. It had been one of those snow-drought winters, and the limo had no trouble floating in on the ice glaze that lay over the dirt track that is our road, even without satlink control.

When Fairchild climbed out and looked around, I saw in him the stiffness of tension, as if he were expecting some kind of assault, from where I couldn't imagine. My daughter, Sam, was ten at the time, and was past the visitor to the back of the vehicle even before the chauffeur was. Nevertheless, she had time to see the scar with that uncanny attention for detail that she has. She didn't say anything about it then, just set herself to lifting what she could out of the hatch and laying it in a neat row along the snow-swept path.

Fairchild shook my hand and we exchanged names. His light brown eyes scarcely looked at me. Instead they cast over the wild expanse of bay that our house faced. The wind was easy that day, and even so there were whitecaps aplenty. Far across, the headland was shrouded in spray from the full force of the Atlantic, beating in from the south. The bay itself was only partly protected, and when the wind was right we felt a pounding nearly as direct as the headland itself.

Fairchild said nothing; he just looked. Just how impressed he was, I couldn't tell, but I had never yet met anyone who could look with detachment at that tossed, violent winter sea. But I was distracted then, by my daughter and the chauffeur. They were hoisting an airchair out of the back of the cab.

I had suspected a companion. Many of my clients, both men and women, brought at least one other person along, married or not I did not make it my business to know. Others came alone, though, the true partisans of solitude, and wrote books or sketched or strolled, parka-shrouded, along the beach when the wind was down. These latter were my most satisfied customers; I could have set up on the moon and offered the same thing, and they would have come back again and again.

That Fairchild had a companion had been obvious from the bulk of his luggage. The limo was not something normally found around Bangor, another sign of the cost of its trip here, and every square inch of the back must have been crammed with the things that Fairchild brought with him. That his companion was handicapped, though, was unusual. When they had the airchair set up, Sam and the cabbie moved forward to help the person out of the cab, but Fairchild waved them away and did it himself.

What he bundled out of the cab in gentle arms was a woman. She was in her mid-thirties, as far as I could tell. She had thin blond hair, cut short, and a squarish face with alert gray eyes that smiled almost all the time. Swaddled as she was in winter wear, I could see nothing abnormal about her legs, just that they hung as loose as wind socks. Moving up to her, I introduced myself and Sam, and she shook my hand with a strikingly strong grip and told us that she was Abigail Townsend, and that she was delighted to be here.

The chauffeur spun his vehicle around and sped away, the limo raising particles of snow from its cushion of air. He had shifted from manual to satellite control before he was fairly down the hill, and was already reclining his seat as the machine disappeared around the first curve.

Sam and I brought our guests to their cabin. It was a quarter-mile hike along a path beaten by our old-fashioned treaded snowmobile. Ms. Townsend handled her airchair with consummate ease, whisking ahead of us, then pivoting around as she asked with her eyes if this or that cabin was theirs. Fairchild strode along behind her. He carried a gigantic backpack. When I pressed on him that luggage delivery was one of the services of the management, he waved it away and told me that he'd carry every last item in himself. I protested, and he insisted, and being the paying guest, he won.

There was a fire going in the cabin, of course, and Ms. Townsend expressed glowing-eyed delight at everything she saw. Fairchild shucked off the pack and looked around, satisfaction on his face. Again we offered to help him, and he shooed us off as if we were panhandlers on a city street.

"He doesn't have a bug," Sam told me when we were back inside our own house.

"What?" I asked absently. We were in our large kitchen, and my attention was on the coffee that my wife was pouring out, while the baby crawled around underneath the spigot and threatened to receive a scalding drop or two.

"His bug is gone," Sam said. She was sitting on one of the barstools that we used for many of our catch-as-catch-can meals. "There's just a spider scar there. And so is hers."

My wife looked at me, and I looked at her. She was a tall, solid woman, as steady as the shore itself.

"A spider scar, like in the movies?" she said.

"Yes," my daughter said. "Maybe he's an international spy, or archfiend criminal."

I smiled. "You don't have to be an archfiend not to have a bug," I said. "I read that about half of one percent don't have them. Their bodies won't tolerate them."

"I read," said my wife, "the same article. It also said that a lot of those people bribe doctors with incredible bucks to get them to take the bugs out.''

''Lots of criminals take them out,'' Sam said, chewing on the heel of some home-ground bread.

''But they don't have spider scars,'' I said. ''They don't want people to know.''

''Spider scars are a status symbol in some circles,'' my wife said. ''They prove you're rich enough and independent enough and attended to enough that you don't care whether the satellite knows where you are or not.''

''Not with criminals,'' I said.

''Suppose something happens to them,'' Sam went on. ''Suppose they suffocate or oh-dee on drugs or something. The satellite wouldn't know. We might not find them for days.''

''And suppose they really are on the run from the cops,'' my wife said, smiling.

''Yeah!'' Sam said. My son drooled on the floor and hauled himself to his feet by my wife's pants.

Fairchild settled in easily. The second day he pointed to the stack of split ash and maple that sat outside his cabin and said: ''Where do you get that?''

''I have a woodlot about a mile from here,'' I told him. ''Mixed growth, forty acres more or less. I cut down enough every year and let them cure sitting on their own branches. Then the next fall I chain-saw them and haul them over here.''

His tanned face was turned toward the sea.

''I brought an ax. Would you mind if I split some?''

Well, of course I didn't mind. The ''ax'' he had turned out to be a light single-headed one that any Mainer would have used only for limbing. He had a sure, savage stroke, as if he were pounding at some worry and beating it to death. I hauled up a cart full of unsplit logs and let him have them. In a few minutes he had his fur-lined coat off and was sweating freely in the fifteen-degree heat.

That seemed to hold him for a few days. I went over to the constable's office one evening, riding on the moonless cold air. Eldon Hodgdon was sitting alone in his easy chair, as he always is that time of night, watching his old color television with dull placitude. He roused himself enough to get interested about the spider scars.

"If they're illegals, we'll find out soon enough," he said, hefting himself out of the chair and moving over to his unit. He spoke to it and it looked at his retinas and let him into the police databases where I could not go. At home I had tried the social news files, but there was no Fairchild in there that made any sense, and no Abigail Townsend either.

"Nothing under those names," Eldon said after talking it over with his machine for a while. "Not necessarily illegal, though. Nothing says a man has to go by his right name all the time. You say they have a pile of money?"

"Seems like it."

Eldon scratched his chin. "Maybe if you describe them. The machine'll tell me if anyone close is wanted anywhere."

"I've got something better than that," I said, and I went to the truck and fetched the ax, which Fairchild had left sticking in the butt end of a log.

Eldon lifted the prints and ran them through the machine. A moment later he whistled.

"They're registered, all right. I never did see the like, though. The machine won't release anything on them; they're classified higher than a kite."

"Well, who are they?" I asked irritably. "Foreign diplomats? CIA spies? Android robots?"

Hodgdon chuckled. "None of the above, most likely. But I get a sense from the machine that these are people to leave alone. There're a few families at the very top that you can't ever get nothing on, and by top I mean a few of the billionaires and all of the trillionaires."

The first thing that really jarred me was when Fairchild phoned me over the intercabin line that same night and asked me to shut off their electricity.

"But why?" I asked. I was almost getting used to the spider scar thing, but this was still bizarre enough to get me to wondering. "What will you use for light? How will you cook?"

"I've brought in some kerosene lamps," his uncannily calm voice came over the wire. "We've been cooking on the woodstove."

I almost said, "That's a wood heater, not a stove," but figured it wouldn't help any.

By this time my wife and Sam were hanging around me listening. The baby was in his mother's arms, nursing for dear life.

"Listen, Mr. Fairchild," I began, trying to keep the annoyance out of my voice. "I'm not sure that you realize that your cabin is superinsulated. Combustion sources are serious pollutants. If I cut off your power, you're air-to-air heat exchanger will cut out, and you won't have enough ventilation to turn a sliced apple brown."

"We've already worked that out," he said. "We've got a window cracked. Now I want the power off." It wasn't said harshly, nor angrily, nor with any emotion that I could hear, but it was as definite as bedrock and as hard.

I turned the power off.

I went over there the next day and knocked on the cabin door. It was one of the warmest days so far that winter, and for a change, nearly windless. At the house, the only heat we were needing was coming in through the windows.

Abigail Townsend opened the door. That startled me, though it shouldn't have. Again I saw that heart-stopping smile.

"Won't you come in, Mr. Deniston," she said.

"Seth," I said, and stepped inside. Her airchair, with its armrests off for inside traveling, slid aside. Fairchild looked up from some papers he was working on at the pedestal table.

"Are you folks doing all right?" I began to ask, but he cut me off.

"Your daughter was here earlier. I caught her peeking in the window. I want it stopped."

That caught me by surprise. Sam had hardly a disobedient streak in her, so it took me a moment to realize where her mind must have been. But Abigail said it first.

"I think she thinks we're international smugglers of some sort, Weston," she said. "Would you like some coffee, Mr. Deniston?"

"Seth," I said.

"Smugglers?" Fairchild said, turning his strong face toward his companion.

"I'd better explain," I said, and I told them about Sam and

the spider scars, and the romantic tripe that television made of them.

Fairchild touched behind his ear.

"It is none of her business where this came from or why we're here. I hope that you'll make it clear to her," he said stiffly.

"Indeed." I was getting somewhat stiff too.

"Weston, she's just a little girl thinking and hoping she's got an adventure here," Abigail told him.

I echoed that and apologized for her. I told them that she would be over herself to make her own apology.

"There's no need," Abigail said.

"It's something she has to do," I said. "But I run this place and it's my job to ask," I continued. "I don't know much about it, but what would either of you do if you got in an accident or took sick? No one would be monitoring you. You wouldn't get help until someone else noticed what was happening."

"Do you think anyone is monitoring you?" Fairchild demanded. His gorge seemed to be rising now.

"Of course," I answered, puzzled. "If I get in physical trouble, the bug knows it and the satellite therefore knows it, and they come and get me out."

"And if you get lost in the woods or run away with someone's wife, the satellite can find you among a million trees or a million people," he sneered. Sneered. It was the first overt expression I had seen on his face.

"No one is monitoring you, Deniston. You think about it," he said. "It's some damned computer that's watching you. It's watching the sixteen billion people, and it can pay attention to each and every one because it's bigger and faster and smarter than we. Did you ever think about that?"

The spirit of the argument was rising in me now. I never could resist arguing, especially when the assumptions were something all normal people I knew shared, and the conclusions too.

"Who cares?" I said. "Virtually no one dies of a heart attack or any kind of sudden event anymore, except for accidents in remote places, like those lobstermen. We're safer, and I think we feel it and are calmer now than ever before."

"Riots in Bangladesh, food lines in Dallas, famine in the Sahara, war in Tibet. Fast service here, though," he said.

"For heaven's sake, Fairchild, I don't understand where you're coming from," I said, pushing a little. "Things are coming under control now for the first time in man's memory. The MITI computers and their network satellites just plain do a better job than we ever did ourselves."

"Coffee," Abigail said, and placed it down in front of me. I noticed that I was sitting on a barstool, hands gripping the edge of that pedestal table like two lobster claws.

"The point is that they say that people control those machines, but I don't believe it," Fairchild said, his voice subsiding toward his usual calm, seeming in inverse relationship to mine, which it probably was—the unconscious pattern of a lifetime, the damper that kept his emotionality at bay. "What I believe is that the computers themselves are in charge; wasn't that the point of the fifth generation in the first place?"

"So what?" I began, getting really heated now. "What if it's computers, and who cares if anyone admits it or not? The world is still better off than it was before. Hardly anyone talks about nuclear war anymore, for example. That's an incredible piece of progress."

"In either case, we humans have delivered our souls to those machines," Fairchild said. "Do you suppose people are, in fact, still in charge? It's just an illusion, because such people make all their decisions from information gathered, analyzed, and supplied by the machines. Either the machines are directly in control, or indirectly, and either way it's the same thing."

"Is that why you're here, fleeing the evolution of the new life form superseding the old?" I kept the sarcasm in my voice, deliberate and biting. He didn't react at all.

Abigail Townsend looked at me mutely, some kind of plea in her face. I stayed for a few minutes more, drinking the coffee and arguing, and getting nowhere.

I thought about it on the way back home. I had never had such a discussion with a tenant, and I wasn't at all sure it was a good idea. Something had come of it, though. I still didn't know who they were, but I had now a faint sense of why they were here, although I couldn't seem to reason it entirely out from their point of view. If they were after some kind of computer-free primitivism, how could they imagine that they'd find it in an exclusive camp on the coast of Maine?

I forgot how rich they probably were. One time I was in Newport, not Maine's but Rhode Island's, and walked along the renovated Cliff Walk. The great mansions of the Vanderbilts and Mellons and others were there, the incredible fifty-room palaces with their porticos and colonnades, buttresses and towers and gables and manicured lawns, one after another on land worth a million dollars a square foot.

Those mansions in Newport were their summer cottages. That was how they roughed it.

I went home and gave Sam holy hell.

The next day Fairchild came strolling by with Ms. Townsend riding on a cushion of air alongside. She gave me her usual smile that left me kind of dazed despite myself. He looked toward me, the cold pale brown of his eyes somehow inside, not paying much attention outside.

He pointed at the bay.

"I'd like to take Abigail fishing out there," he said.

"What?" exploded out of me before I could stop it. Then I caught my breath and said: "I'm sorry, Mr. Fairchild. It's just that anything smaller than a lobster boat wouldn't last a minute out there. Look at it."

The wind was up that day, and the bay had scattered chunks of ice in it that it heaved up and down and sometimes ground together. The water was slate-gray, and the sky lowery. Up here on the tree-lined bluff, we could hear the sea growling, a sentient angry kind of thing, as vicious as anything on the planet.

"I see lobster pots," he said mildly, some expression coming into his eyes.

"Yes, some of the boys drag them when it's calm enough," I admitted grudgingly. "But you need years behind you to get the feel of the waves and weather; they change faster than a flea's sneeze, faster than the satellite ever knows. My rec boats are hauled out; most everyone's are, except the diehard fishermen that live on what they bring in. We always lose some of them every year, despite the bugs; you spend a few minutes in that kind of water and you're dead.''

"I could hire an airboat," he said then, mostly to himself. "That would ride over the surface."

"The wind would blow it right up on shore," I said, "or if you're really unlucky, right out to sea. Of course," I needled him, "the satellite would be monitoring the boat and the Coast Guard would bring you back in."

"But that would defeat the purpose," he said, still talking to himself. Abigail Townsend was looking up at him, her smile gone for the moment.

"I beg your pardon," I said.

Ms. Townsend glanced at me and seemed about to speak, but Fairchild suddenly spun around and headed back toward their cabin. "It's something I'll put off for now," he said, again more to himself than anyone else.

I found out later that he had walked almost eleven miles a few days later, up the blunt peninsula and away from the Refuge, and asked three different lobstermen to take him and Ms. Townsend out. None of them would do it at first; they had insurance problems enough. He offered them money beyond their dreams. The first two put him off, said they'd think about it; if they were caught, it would mean the end of their life-style, and money was not necessarily enough to risk it. The third one, Hovey I think it was, had been divorced twice, and said he'd come by the first calm day, that he wouldn't chance his license if the sea was running hard. But the weather was bad that week. Fairchild had to be satisfied with that. As it happened, it was not to be.

Eight days later, the morning broke with the sky in turmoil and the sea oily and colorless. The monitor woke me up and I listened to the NOAA satellite report on mandatory. A storm was on its way, and there was a 30 percent chance it would miss us.

I thought I knew everything about what a big storm could do. Every year had its storms, but the big ones only came around once in a while, with unpredictable savagery. There had been a tremendous one in 1952, and again in 1960, 1961, 1972, and 1978, and we were overdue. In 1938 half the trees in Maine had gone down. The 1978 storm had changed parts of the coastline beyond recognition. Sometimes they were associated with hurricanes, but often they just came out of nowhere and hit too suddenly to get an official name.

If it was going to hit, it would do it in thirteen hours. I set about getting the Refuge as ready as I could.

First I sent the wife and kids inland to her sister's in Wytopitlock. Sam didn't like that; she wanted to stay with me where the action was.

At the same time I told my ten tenants what they would have to do. I had reservations inland at a motel in Hampden, and I let them know that they were being evicted from the Refuge, though of course the Hampden costs were on me.

Fairchild, by the way, took the news without the faintest flicker of expression. Abigail looked concerned, but had nothing to say, leaving it all to him.

A few hours later as I was helping the tenants climb aboard the automated airbus I had called in, I realized that the group was short. Neither Fairchild nor Abigail was with them.

I told the bus computer to stand by and ran over to the cabin. The wind was rising already, and I could hear the sea pounding savagely behind the rocks. I had seen the barometer reading a little earlier, and that, even more than the sea and the waxen sky, had scared me. And on top of it all, it was cold, five degrees Fahrenheit with an awesome windchill. I could hear that wind howling like wolves, ready to eat the land alive.

Fairchild answered the door. I saw that he had split shakes off of the logs and nailed them over the windows of the little cabin. He seemed burning from an inner fire; his hand shook just a little as he let me in the cabin.

"You've got to get out," I said. I then saw Abigail, resting on the lower cot across the room. She was leaning on one elbow, looking at me with those eyes. Even then, I saw something in their shattering grayness that I didn't think I wanted to see. And I knew that it might not be there at all.

"You've got to go," I said, addressing them both. "NOAA's best guess is that it will be at least as bad as '78, and then every building on this part of the coast was leveled flat and blown away."

Fairchild's eyes darted around the room.

"I think that you underestimate the quality you've built here," he said, his voice under that same uncanny control.

"I appreciate the compliment, but you've got to go. It's not a matter of choice anymore. The storm and high tide are going to hit at the same time. Even if the dunes stand up to it, the sea will come around and between them and flood everything in sight. You won't have a chance if that happens; your only chance is to get out now."

"If," Fairchild said. I had known the moment the word left my mouth that it was the worst thing I could have said.

"Think of Ms. Townsend," I said desperately. I turned to her. "Abigail, tell him. I don't think that airchair could fight the wind even now, and it's going to get much worse."

In some way, we had reached a crisis point. I think it was reflected in the fact that I had used her first name for the first time. Fairchild looked at her, and I looked at her, and we waited. It wasn't so much that she held their lives in her hands. Instead it was Fairchild that she held there, in a figurative way, his ego and the structure of his world, built around his relationship with her and his fantasies about how the world was and how it should be. He sensed it quite directly, I think; I didn't, and I was very conscious of the muffled moan of the wind outside, and the bus full of people who were my responsibility.

"Weston and I stay, if that's his wish," she said at last.

I threw up my hands.

"I'll be back," I told them.

It took me seven hours to get the rest of them settled in Hampden, a trip that normally took an hour and a half each way. It wasn't getting there that was hard, it was getting back. I had left the airbus at the motel and taken a rental back, and the wind blew me all over the road, and five or six times I wondered if the satellite knew what it was doing. The snow was driving hard now, and I kept seeing cars off in the ditch, and I passed a number of rescue vehicles, heavy enough to resist the wind as it was so far, very busy vehicles indeed. The satlink kept warning me to get inside somewhere. At length, when the car was turning right onto the tertiary road that led to the Refuge, it ordered the car off the road to the nearest house, which it alerted to receive me. I killed the engine and went under the hood and ripped the satlink controller wires away from the car's computer box. Someday

262 *Donald Wismer*

they'll find a way to seal the whole innards of a car away from knowledgeable meddlers like me, but they haven't yet. No doubt the satellite was yelling at Eldon Hodgdon about me already, but unless he was just around the corner, I had plenty of time.

I took control and drove past the last turnoff, which went fifty feet back to Quentin Harold's place behind a high hill, and headed downslope into the pocket beyond which a gradual rise would take me home.

It took me only a few minutes to pass through the low place, with salt marshes on either side, that marked the boundary of Wave's Refuge. There was a vicious crosswind at the lowest point, with no trees on either side, just marshland, and the aircar skittered to one side and I thought I was going to lose her. Then it recovered and I gunned her back onto the roadbed and crossed into the Refuge.

I parked the aircar next to the garage and strode up the path to the house. I saw that some of the popples were down, but I'd expected that. They were fast-growing trees, weak of wood and root. Around the house itself, the white pines still stood.

Then I topped the rise and the wind hit me, and I saw the sea.

God! I hope never to see it that way again, savagely beautiful and deadly as an erupting volcano.

It was a sea of white, like the foaming of a rabid dog, whitecaps breaking into scud, moving faster than I had ever seen them, hitting the shore as if they expected to go right on through. High tide was still two hours away, and even then the little that I could see told me that the water was far beyond the highest tide I had ever heard of. The wind was blowing the water into the open mouth of the bay, and, reinforced by the tides—we weren't that far from the Bay of Fundy, which has the highest tides on earth—it was piling up like sand against a cliff, only this cliff was just a low rock-and-sand coast. I looked out toward the headland across the bay, but there was no way I could see that far. The air was gray with spray, the sea white and gray, with the immense bass sound of the crashing waves underlying the howling of the wind.

I struggled against the tangible wall of wind and reached

the door to the house. I fetched out the keys to the old tire-driven truck, which had been made back when manual or satellite control was still a matter of choice. I left the house door hooked open to keep the air pressure inside about the same as it was outside.

As I climbed off the bluff, heading to the garage below, I looked back, and the spray seemed to part for a moment, as if the wind were piling up somewhere waiting to burst an invisible dam. At that moment I should have been able to see the headland, but I couldn't. It was gone. There were just waves where it had been.

The rented aircar, which was a cheap subcompact, wouldn't have stood a chance, but the old truck rode on wheels, and it was a heavy machine. I pulled it out of the garage, and it stood stolidly against the wind, scarcely rocking as the gusts hit it again and again and again. I put it in park and, leaving the engine running, started out for Fairchild's cabin.

Just then, I caught a snatch of sound like another motor, and looked around and saw Eldon Hodgdon pull up. His police aircar was heavier than most, but I don't think that it could have survived if it weren't for the bluff on which the house stood. I fought the wind the other way and reached the aircar's window.

"What the hell's wrong with you?" Eldon demanded. "I got a summons on you off the satellite, and here you are taking a walk. You get yourself in that truck of yours and you follow along behind. I got lots of coast to cover and no time to screw around with you."

His beefy face was red, and it wasn't the wind. I guess he was that way with everybody.

"I've still got a tenant in one of the cabins," I said.

His face turned a shade deeper. "You don't either. The satellite says you're the only one closer than . . . Wait. You mean the folks with the spiders on them?"

We fought our way to the cabin and pounded on the door. After a moment, it opened silently and we crowded in.

"Mister, you and your lady put on them parkas and come along," Hodgdon said without preamble. He almost had to shout, the wind was so loud, even with the door shut, surrounded by six inches of superinsulation.

Fairchild was standing there, arms folded, backside leaning

against the heavy pine table. I looked for Abigail, and found her again on the lower bed, propped on an elbow. Our eyes met, and I smiled slightly. She looked away.

"We're not leaving," Fairchild was saying. I noticed that his fists, at the ends of his folded arms, were clenched so tight that they were white underneath the expensive tan.

"You leave or we'll drag you out," said Hodgdon. "I've got a dozen more places to check, and the worst of it isn't here yet."

"You'll drag no one, Officer," said Fairchild. "This is a tight cabin, protected by the rock dune. We'll be perfectly safe here. You go let that satellite tell you what to do. I make the decisions here."

For the first time, Eldon hesitated. I could see that he was wanting to flatten the handsome, smug face in front of him, though I had a notion that it wouldn't be so easy to do. But Eldon was a politician, among other things. He had tried to find out about these two, and hadn't been able to, and that made him cautious.

"Listen here," he said, trying reason. "You've got a lady that can't walk, and this stretch of beach is going to get flooded out, you mark my words. I might not be able to make it back here if you get in trouble later. Deniston tells me you ripped out the cabin's radio; now, if those scars mean anything, how the hell will I know if you're in trouble or not? It's my job to get you out right now."

"We're staying," Fairchild said, his eyes as bright as agates. "If anything happens, we'll walk out."

"Don't be a fool!" I said then. "Quentin Harold's place is three miles down the road. Abigail's airchair wouldn't make it ten feet."

Fairchild looked around. The cabin, stout as it was, rattled here and there as the wind, even enervated by the dune, shook and pounded it mercilessly.

"We've got light and warmth, and food, and water," he said. You could hear the shrill satisfaction in his voice. "We need nothing and no one."

"Abigail . . . " I said, stretching a hand out to her. Hodgdon shot an odd look at me.

"No," she said.

We forced the door open against the wind and left them there.

"Damn fools," Eldon said when he was inside his vehicle. I had my head almost entirely inside his window so as to hear what he was saying. "There'll be hell to pay when this gets out."

"Why should it get out?" I asked him. "They don't have bugs. The satellite thinks we're the only ones here."

Hodgdon grunted. "You get in that truck and come along," he said. "I've got stops to make, and I'm not waiting for you, I don't care what the damn satellite says. You get on up to Quentin's and wait there; with that big hill between him and the sea, you'll be safe enough."

He drove off then. I went back to the house and gathered together all the papers I couldn't afford to lose; the wife had taken the larger valuables with her when she left. A few more popples were down, and one of the pines, and I had thought I wouldn't make it to the house, when I felt the wind. I couldn't even see the sea now. The snow was heavy and sticking almost nowhere; instead it drove in blasting, confused gusts along with the wind, like a sandblaster.

When I came back to the truck, I looked along the path toward the cabin. It was their own damn decision, and yet I wanted to go down there and club them outside. Instead I climbed into the truck, and it clashed its gears as the satellite trundled it forward down the road. I passed the rented aircar, barely glancing at it. It was the last I would ever see of it.

Whiteout. The truck was turning into Quentin's drive when it hit. I had seen one before, such blank whiteness of snow and light that you couldn't see past a foot in front of your face. This one was intermittent. For a moment, an extra big gust of snow would rise up and you couldn't see a thing, and then it would pass and there was visibility for maybe ten feet ahead. It was getting dark, and that didn't help at all.

The satlink said that seawater was coming inland all along the coast. High tide was nearly upon us, and with it the worst of the storm. Most houses had plastic battery backup, so power outages weren't so important as they once were. But houses exposed to that wind would be in trouble.

When I reached the turnaround in front of Quentin's dark

brown, vertical frame house, I just sat there as the engine
turned itself off. Abigail was in my mind, of course. I felt
sorry enough for Fairchild and his obsessions. But she was
caught in a web. If he hadn't been there, I had no doubt that
she would have come along readily enough with Eldon and
me. He wouldn't have come whether she had or not.

"You all right, Seth?" the satlink suddenly relayed. I saw
Quentin Harold's bearded face, peering out of his front-room
window.

"Yeah," I said, and then: "I'm going back." I reached
over and switched the truck to manual, and started the engine.

"Don't be crazy!" Quentin said. "What can you save, a
TV or two?" Of course he didn't know about the two people,
any more than the satellite did. "There're a couple of people
drowned already down east. Stay here, Seth. Nothing's worth
it."

But something was worth it. I would tie Fairchild up in a
gunny sack if I had to. I was going to get Abigail Townsend
off that beach.

When I turned onto the road, I had a lot of trouble with the
whiteout. If I hadn't known the road so well, every tree and
bounder on either side, I would have ended up in the woods.
If I had tried the satlink, it would have tried to turn me
around and head back to Quentin's. As it was, I couldn't tell
the road from the ditches on either side. I couldn't decide if
the truck lights were helping or hurting; I left them on. It was
like crawling through a sea of white molasses.

A long time later I drove down into the pocket. I felt the
truck lurch, and steered a little left. Then the view ahead of
me opened up; the wind across the salt marshes was so fierce,
it was driving the snow in a straight line, which gave more
visibility than the confused swirling of the whiteout. I saw,
and I gasped.

The road was gone. The ocean had risen over the marshes
and consumed them. The road began again across thirty feet
of violent water, rising up toward the Refuge farther ahead.

I turned the satlink on long enough to ask the satellite how
deep the water ran, but as sophisticated as the machine was, that
was something it couldn't perceive. But it was at least three feet
deep, deep enough to drown the truck's engine.

I leaped out of the cab and ran down to the edge of the

water. The wind was like a living thing, wrapping me in its powerful hands and trying to lift me into the air and fling me aside like another droplet of spray. I had heard of people being blown off mountains by incredibly strong winds, and for the first time I believed that it could happen. The snow sandblasted me, and wrapped as I was in various layers of wool and down, I felt that wind knifing into my skin and knew that it wouldn't take long before I would freeze to death.

For a moment I stood there in an agony of indecision. To enter that water was madness, and yet to stay on this side of it was to abandon Abigail to a death that I now believed was almost certain.

I never had to make that decision; perhaps it was better that way. For I looked up, and saw something moving toward me through the water.

It was Fairchild, and he was carrying Abigail in his arms. They were already halfway across, and I could not believe that he was still upright in the face of that awful storm. The water tore at him, nearly touching her body as he strove to hold it high. I could only imagine the terrible coldness that was eating at him, with the wind only a minor factor now as the coldest water on the eastern seaboard ripped into and past him like a sluice.

I couldn't tell if he saw me or not. His wiry body, whiplash-strong as I have said, plodded forward, step by step. What unbelievable strength that man had; I truly believe that if it weren't for the water itself holding him down, he would have been blown aloft at the center of the airstream, Abigail and all. As it was, he reached the middle of the water and passed it, rising now out of it, faltering for a moment as a particularly violent gust hit, then forging onward. I stepped a few inches into the water and held my hands out to take Abigail. He stepped sideways and walked up onto the snow, still holding her. I couldn't tell if she was alive or dead.

"Why are you here?" he said harshly, standing there, the wind buffeting him, not looking at me, water already freezing up and down the parka that he wore.

I saw that I could increase his paranoia, reinforce his fear that other forces were constantly violating him, or I could give him something to make him feel left alone and in control. In doing the latter, I realized, I was placing myself in the same role that Abigail herself filled, day in and day out.

"For the Refuge," I answered, looking away. "The minute it lets up, I'm going in."

He stood there for a long minute, clothes freezing to his body. I saw that his arms were trembling. Then he nodded, stiffly; he just stood there, as if uncertain what to do.

"Get in the cab and warm up," I said offhandedly. "We'll all go back in together."

Still he swayed there, and then finally his voice came again, the muted power in it beginning to show the strain.

"That truck of yours—it has a satlink?"

"Of course, but . . ."

And abruptly, he began walking forward into the storm.

I waited as long as I dared, long enough for him to make it down to Harold's, then I turned the truck around and drove, as slowly as I could. Even so I almost missed them in the uncertain glare of the headlights, an irregular lump on the road being rapidly covered by snow. I pulled them one by one into the truck, and then, with relief, let the satlink take me through the whiteout to Quentin Harold's driveway.

I touched her face, and she opened her eyes and looked at me. The shocking, deep, intelligent grayness hit me, and I felt it all the way down. She saw, and smiled her gentlest, saddest smile.

"The loft blew off," she said, before I had a chance to speak. "I don't think there's a cabin anymore. Most of the dune was gone by the time we started out."

"Never mind," I said, as gently as I knew how. I looked at her in silence, and something must have showed in my eyes, because she looked away.

"Why do you let this kind of thing happen?" I asked her then.

She seemed to reflect, lost in thoughts as incomprehensible to me as a cat's.

"Because I love him," she said at last, looking me again in the eyes, and finally I saw the source of the sadness, the great, kind, empathetic sweetness of her, and I turned away, embarrassed that I was so exposed when I did not hope to be, had never thought or wanted to be.

"And because I am his anchor," her voice said, coming at me. "As long as he loves me, he can't go off the end."

"No, I see that," I said, my face still averted. I wanted no more of this; I never wanted it in the first place.

"I don't think you do," she said. "Love is only the half of it." She stopped for a moment, and then said quietly: "Six years ago he bought me one of those auto/manual cars, the last year you could get them, and he switched it to manual and took me down the controlled highway between D.C. and Baltimore. And he was looking at me, the way he always looked at me. Too long. The car hit the back of a controlled car ahead of us and went off the edge. It hurt me." She reflected a little, and I could feel the pain of the man in her, but of her own bitterness and pain there was nothing, and I was looking for it.

And so he tries to prove his competence, I thought, every way he can. And she knows that if she left him, he would fly apart, like a boiler, under too much pressure, pricked by a bullet. And yet, if she stayed with him, he would test himself, one test more demanding than the other, and the day had to come when he made up one last test, and failed. And if she were still with him then, they would both go down together, *folie à deux*.

"Let it end here," I told her then, knowing that she would grasp what I meant. "Tell him he's proved it; he doesn't need the satellites. He made it here, all by himself, with you in his arms, and blacked out. Tell him that."

"It might work, for a few days," she said to me, her eyes looking directly into mine now, bravery and defiance in them. She was telling me that her decisions were made. She was telling me the way it was.

"The other part is the airchair," she said. "Did you ever think about someone like me without it?"

I let the silence hang, the fire popping and crackling in the air. It hung a long time.

He thought about it, I'll bet. I'll bet his mind approached it constantly, and sheered away, again, and again.

The airchair was necessary. He loved her. It was completely utterly necessary. But it was a machine. It was technology.

He couldn't get away from it.

* * *

Fairchild wasn't that badly off. He thawed out quickly. The storm died out after a while. Seventy-three people had died from Delaware to Nova Scotia. The bugs had led rescuers to snowbound cars and furnaces gone out and woodstove fires, but that was later. During the storm, the wind had blown rescue vehicles into trees and hills and buildings, and the powdery swirling snow got into intakes and choked off engines. Fifteen of the dead had been rescuers themselves.

Wave's Refuge was mostly gone. The house, roofless, still stood, but all the cabins had been swept away. Most of the white pines were down. We found pieces of the cabins a mile and a half inland.

After the storm was over, Fairchild and Abigail called up a private, piloted copter and flew to Bangor, where they boarded a Lear jet, also piloted, and flew away. We never did find out who they were, and that was very hard on our neighbors, who knew everyone else's business, even if they never interfered in it. I think of her, and him, once in a while, and every time I scan the online obituaries I look for short blond hair and gray eyes and a square face, and a brown-haired, light-brown-eyed man, whiplash-strong.

Weston Fairchild. Some might call him a hero. Man against technology, that sort of thing, the stuff of which empires are built and fortunes made. But it seems to me that real heroes are ordinary people who react extraordinarily to some crisis. They don't push their way into places where they then have no choice but to practice heroics. And they surely don't drag someone else with them. Maybe in the cotton-batting comfort of the future, when satellites and MITI computers save mankind from itself everywhere, in everything, people will point to the likes of Weston Fairchild with nostalgia, and trace his spirit back to the movers and shakers of history. They'll forget that many of those movers and shakers were surrounded by corpses. Movers don't always move in the right direction.

Our direction now is surveillance. War, crime, and human suffering are lessening. Most people don't think much about it, but those that do seem happy enough.

As for me, here on the coast of Maine, I will build again. Storms such as that hit Maine now and again; it's part of living here, and the satellites give us ample warning, and insurance is available. The wife and kids and I are content. I intend it so. We are happy here, and I aim to keep it that way. Anything that might threaten it, I will put aside.

Examination Day

Henry Slesar

The Jordans never spoke of the exam, not until their son,
Dickie, was twelve years old. It was on his birthday that Mrs.
Jordan first mentioned the subject in his presence, and the
anxious manner of her speech caused her husband to answer
sharply.

"Forget about it," he said. "He'll do all right."

They were at the breakfast table, and the boy looked up
from his plate curiously. He was an alert-eyed youngster,
with flat blond hair and a quick, nervous manner. He didn't
understand what the sudden tension was about, but he did
know that today was his birthday, and he wanted harmony
above all. Somewhere in the little apartment there were
wrapped, beribboned packages waiting to be opened, and in
the tiny wall kitchen something warm and sweet was being
prepared in the automatic stove. He wanted the day to be
happy, and the moistness of his mother's eyes, the scowl on
his father's face, spoiled the mood of fluttering expectation
with which he had greeted the morning.

"What exam?" he asked.

His mother looked at the tablecloth. "It's just a sort of
government intelligence test they give children at the age of
twelve. You'll be getting it next week. It's nothing to worry
about."

"You mean a test like in school?"

"Something like that," his father said, getting up from the
table. "Go read your comic books, Dickie."

The boy rose and wandered toward that part of the living

272

room which had been "his" corner since infancy. He fingered the topmost comic of the stack, but seemed uninterested in the colorful squares of fast-paced action. He wandered toward the window and peered gloomily out at the veil of mist.

"Why did it have to rain *today*?" he said. "Why couldn't it rain tomorrow?"

His father, now slumped into an armchair with the government newspaper, rattled the sheets in vexation. "Because it just did, that's all. Rain makes the grass grow."

"Why, dad?"

"Because it does, that's all."

Dickie puckered his brow. "What makes it green, though? The grass?"

"Nobody knows," his father snapped, then immediately regretted his abruptness.

Later in the day, it was birthday time again. His mother beamed as she handed over the gaily colored packages, and even his father managed a grin and a rumple of the hair. He kissed his mother and shook hands gravely with his father. Then the birthday cake was brought forth and the ceremonies concluded.

An hour later, seated by the window, he watched the sun force its way between the clouds.

"Dad," he said, "how far away is the sun?"

"Five thousand miles," his father said.

Dick sat at the breakfast table and again saw moisture in his mother's eyes. He didn't connect her tears with the exam until his father suddenly brought the subject to light again.

"Well, Dickie," he said with a manly frown, "you've got an appointment today."

"I know, dad. I hope—"

"Now, it's nothing to worry about. Thousands of children take this test every day. The government wants to know how smart you are, Dickie. That's all there is to it."

"I get good marks in school," he said hesitantly.

"This is different. This is a—special kind of test. They give you this stuff to drink, you see, and then you go into a room where there's a sort of machine—"

"What stuff to drink?" Dickie said.

"It's nothing. It tastes like peppermint. It's just to make sure you answer the questions truthfully. Not that the government thinks you won't tell the truth, but this stuff makes *sure*."

Dickie's face showed puzzlement and a touch of fright. He looked at his mother, and she composed her face into a misty smile.

"Everything will be all right," she said.

"Of course it will," his father agreed. "You're a good boy, Dickie; you'll make out fine. Then we'll come home and celebrate. All right?"

"Yes, sir," Dickie said.

They entered the Governmental Educational Building fifteen minutes before the appointed hour. They crossed the marble floors of the great pillared lobby, passed beneath an archway and entered an automatic elevator that brought them to the fourth floor.

There was a young man wearing an insignialess tunic, seated at a polished desk in front of room 404. He held a clipboard in his hand, checked the list to the *J*s and permitted the Jordans to enter.

The room was as cold and official as a courtroom, with long benches flanking metal tables. There were several fathers and sons already there, and a thin-lipped woman with cropped black hair was passing out sheets of paper.

Mr. Jordan filled out the form and returned it to the clerk. Then he told Dickie, "It won't be long now. When they call your name, you just go through the doorway at that end of the room." He indicated the portal with his finger.

A concealed loudspeaker crackled and called off the first name. Dickie saw a boy leave his father's side reluctantly and walk slowly toward the door.

At five minutes of eleven, they called the name of Jordan.

"Good luck, son," his father said without looking at him. "I'll call for you when the test is over."

Dickie walked to the door and turned the knob. The room inside was dim, and he could barely make out the features of the gray-tunicked attendant.

"Sit down," the man said softly. He indicated a high stool beside his desk. "Your name's Richard Jordan?"

"Yes, sir."

"Your classification number is 600-115. Drink this, Richard."

He lifted a plastic cup from the desk and handed it to the boy. The liquid inside had the consistency of buttermilk, tasted only vaguely of the promised peppermint. Dickie downed it and handed the man the empty cup.

He sat in silence, feeling drowsy, while the man wrote busily on a sheet of paper. Then the attendant looked at his watch and rose to stand only inches from Dickie's face. He unclipped a penlike object from the pocket of his tunic and flashed a tiny light into the boy's eyes.

"All right," he said. "Come with me, Richard."

He led Dickie to the end of the room, where a single wooden armchair faced a multidialed computing machine. There was a microphone on the left arm of the chair, and when the boy sat down, he found its pinpoint head conveniently at his mouth.

"Now just relax, Richard. You'll be asked some questions, and you think them over carefully. Then give your answers into the microphone. The machine will take care of the rest."

"Yes, sir."

"I'll leave you alone now. Whenever you want to start, just say 'ready' into the microphone."

"Yes, sir."

The man squeezed his shoulder and left.

Dickie said, "Ready."

Lights appeared on the machine, and a mechanism whirred. A voice said:

"Complete this sequence. One, four, seven, ten . . ."

Mr. and Mrs. Jordan were in the living room, not speaking, not even speculating.

It was almost four o'clock when the telephone rang. The woman tried to reach it first, but her husband was quicker.

"Mr. Jordan?"

The voice was clipped, a brisk, official voice.

"Yes, speaking."

"This is the Government Educational Service. Your son, Richard M. Jordan, Classification 600-115, has completed the government examination. We regret to inform you that his intelligence quotient has exceeded the government regulation, according to Rule 84, Section 5, of the New Code.''

Across the room, the woman cried out, knowing nothing except the emotion she read on her husband's face.

"You may specify by telephone," the voice droned on, "whether you wish his body interred by the government or would prefer a private burial place. The fee for government burial is ten dollars."

The Cruel Equations

Robert Sheckley

After landing on Regulus V, the men of the Yarmolinsky Expedition made camp and activated PR-22-0134, their perimeter robot, whom they called Max. The robot was a voice-activated, bipedal mechanism whose function was to guard the camp against the depredations of aliens, in the event that aliens were ever encountered. Max had originally been a regulation gun-metal gray, but on the interminable outward trip they had repainted him a baby blue. Max stood exactly four feet high. The men of the expedition had come to think of him as a kindly, reasonable little metal man—a ferrous gnome, a miniature Tin Woodman of Oz.

They were wrong, of course. Their robot had none of the qualities which they projected onto him. PR-22-0134 was no more reasonable than a McCormick harvester, no more kindly than an automated steel mill. Morally, he might be compared to a turbine or a radio, but not to anything human. PR-22-0134's only human attribute was potentiality.

Little Max, baby blue with red eyes, circled the perimeter of the camp, his sensors alert. Captain Beatty and Lieutenant James took off in the hoverjet for a week of exploration. They left Lieutenant Halloran to mind the store.

Halloran was a short, stocky man with a barrel chest and bandy legs. He was cheerful, freckled, tough, profane, and resourceful. He ate lunch and acknowledged a radio check from the exploring team. Then he unfolded a canvas chair and sat back to enjoy the scenery.

Regulus V was a pretty nice place, if you happened to be

an admirer of desolation. A superheated landscape of rock, gravel, and lava stretched on all sides. There were some birds that looked like sparrows and some animals that looked like coyotes. A few cacti scratched out a bare living.

Halloran pulled himself to his feet. "Max! I'm going to take a look outside the perimeter. You'll be in charge while I'm gone."

The robot stopped patrolling. "Yes sir, I will be in charge."

"You will not allow any aliens to come busting in; especially the two-headed kind with their feet on backwards."

"Very well, sir." Max had no sense of humor when it came to aliens. "Do you have the password, Mr. Halloran?"

"I got it, Max. How about you?"

"I have it, sir."

"OK. See you later." Halloran left the camp.

After examining the real estate for an hour and finding nothing of interest, Halloran came back. He was pleased to see PR-22-0134 patrolling along the perimeter. It meant that everything was all right.

"Hi there, Max," he called. "Any messages for me?"

"Halt," the robot said. "Give the password."

"Cut the comedy, Max. I'm in no mood for—"

"*HALT!*" the robot shouted, as Halloran was about to cross the perimeter.

Halloran came to an abrupt stop. Max's photoelectric eyes had flared, and a soft double click announced that his primary armament was activated. Halloran decided to proceed with caution.

"I am halted. My name is Halloran. OK now, Maxie?"

"Give the password, please."

" 'Bluebells,' " Halloran said. "Now, if you don't mind—"

"Do not cross the perimeter," the robot said. "Your password is incorrect."

"The hell it is. I gave it to you myself."

"That was the previous password."

"Previous? You're out of your semi-solid mind," Halloran said. " 'Bluebells' is the only password, and you didn't get any new one because there isn't any new one. Unless . . ."

The robot waited. Halloran considered the unpleasant thought from various angles, and at last put words to it.

"Unless Captain Beatty gave you a new password before he left. Is *that* what happened?"

"Yes," the robot said.

"I should have thought of it," Halloran said. He grinned, but he was annoyed. There had been slipups like this before. But there had always been someone inside the camp to correct them.

Still, there was nothing to worry about. When you came right down to it, the situation was more than a little funny. And it could be resolved with just a modicum of reason.

Halloran was assuming, of course, that PR robots posess a modicum of reason.

"Max," Halloran said, "I see how it probably happened. Captain Beatty probably gave you a new password. But he failed to tell me about it. I then compounded his error by neglecting to check on the password situation before I left the perimeter."

The robot made no comment. Halloran went on. "The mistake, in any case, is easily corrected."

"I sincerely hope so," the robot said.

"Of course it is," Halloran said, a little less confidently. "The captain and I follow a set procedure in these matters. When he gives you a password, he also transmits it to me orally. But, just in case there is any lapse—like now—he also writes it down."

"Does he?" the robot asked.

"Yes, he does," Halloran said. "Always. Invariably. Which includes this time too, I hope. Do you see that tent behind you?"

The robot swiveled one sensor, keeping the other fixed on Halloran. "I see it."

"OK. Inside the tent, there is a table. On the table is a gray metal clipboard."

"Correct," Max said.

"Fine! Now then, there is a sheet of paper in the clipboard. On it is a list of vital data—emergency radio frequencies, that sort of thing. On the top of the paper, circled in red, is the current password."

The robot extended and focused his sensor, then retracted it. He said to Halloran, "What you say is true, but irrelevent.

I am concerned only with your knowledge of the actual password, not its location. If you can state the password, I must let you into the camp. If not, I must keep you out.''

"This is insane!" Halloran shouted. "Max, you legalistic idiot, it's *me*, Halloran, and you damned well know it! We've been together since the day you were activated! Now will you please stop playing Horatius at the bridge and let me in?''

"Your resemblance to Mr. Halloran *is* uncanny," the robot admitted. "But I am neither equipped nor empowered to conduct identity tests; nor am I permitted to act on the basis of my perceptions. The only proof I can accept is the password itself.''

Halloran fought down his rage. In a conversational tone he said, "Max, old buddy, it sounds like you're implying that I'm an alien.''

"Since you do not have the password," Max said, "I must proceed on that assumption.''

"Max!" Halloran shouted, stepping forward, "for Christ's sake!''

"Do not approach the perimeter!" the robot said, his sensors flaring. "Whoever or whatever you are, stand back!''

"All right, I'm standing back," Halloran said quickly. "Don't get so nervous.''

He backed away from the perimeter and waited until the robot's sensors had gone quiescent. Then he sat down on a rock. He had some serious thinking to do.

It was almost noon in Regulus's thousand-hour day. The twin suns hung overhead, distorted white blobs in a dead white sky. They moved sluggishly above a dark granite landscape, slow-motion juggernauts who destroyed what they touched.

An occasional bird soared in weary circles through the dry fiery air. A few small animals crept from shadow to shadow. A creature that looked like a wolverine gnawed at a tent peg, and was ignored by a small blue robot. A man sat on a rock and watched the robot.

Halloran, already feeling the effects of exposure and thirst, was trying to understand his situation and to plan a way out of it.

He wanted water. Soon he would need water. Not long after that, he would die for lack of water.

There was no known source of potable water within walking distance, except in the camp.

There was plenty of water in the camp. But he couldn't get to it past the robot.

Beatty and James would routinely try to contact him in three days, but they would probably not be alarmed if he didn't reply. Short-wave reception was erratic, even on Earth. They would try again in the evening and again the next day. Failing to raise him then, they would come back.

Call it four Earth days, then. How long could he go without water?

The answer depended on his rate of water loss. When he had sustained a total liquid loss of between ten and fifteen percent of his body weight, he would go into shock. This could happen with disastrous suddenness. Bedouin tribesmen, separated from their supplies, had been known to succumb in twenty-four hours. Stranded motorists in the American Southwest, trying to walk out of the Baker or Mojave Desert, sometimes didn't last out the day.

Regulus V was as hot as the Kalahari, and had less humidity than Death Valley. A day on Regulus stretched for just under a thousand Earth hours. It was noon, he had five hundred hours of unremitting sunshine ahead of him without shelter or shade.

How long could he last? One earth day. Two, at the most optimistic estimate.

Forget about Beatty and James. He had to get water from the camp, and he had to get it fast.

That meant he had to find a way past the robot.

He decided to try logic. "Max, you must know that I, Halloran, left the camp and that I, Halloran, returned an hour later, and that it is I, Halloran, now standing in front of you without the password."

"The probabilities are very strongly in favor of your interpretation," the robot admitted.

"Well, then—"

"But I cannot act on probabilities, or even near-certainties. After all, I have been created for the express purpose of dealing with aliens, despite the extremely low probability that I will ever meet one."

"Can you at least give me a canteen of water?"

"No. That would be against orders."

"When did you ever get orders about giving out water?"

"I didn't, not specifically. But the conclusion flows from my primary directive. I am not supposed to aid or assist aliens."

Halloran then said a great many things, very rapidly and in a loud voice. His statements were pungently and idiomatically Terran; but Max ignored them since they were abusive, tendentious, and entirely without merit.

After a while, the alien who called himself Halloran moved out of sight behind a pile of rocks.

After some minutes, a creature sauntered out from behind a pile of rocks, whistling.

"Hello there, Max," the creature said.

"Hello, Mr. Halloran," the robot replied.

Halloran stopped ten feet away from the perimeter. "Well," he said, "I've been looking around, but there's not much to see. Anything happen here while I've been gone?"

"Yes, sir," Max said. "An alien tried to enter the camp."

Halloran raised both eyebrows. "Is that a fact?"

"Indeed it is, sir."

"What did this alien look like?"

"He looked very much like you, Mr. Halloran."

"God in heaven!" Halloran exclaimed. "How did you know he was *not* me?"

"Because he tried to enter the camp without giving the password. That, of course, the real Mr. Halloran would never do."

"Exactly so," Halloran said. "Good work, Maxie. We'll have to keep our eyes open for that fellow."

"Yes, sir. Thank you, sir."

Halloran nodded casually. He was pleased with himself. He had figured out that Max, by the very terms of his construction, would have to deal with each encounter as unique, and to dispose of it according to its immediate merits. This had to be so, since Max was not permitted to reason on the basis of prior experiences.

Max had built-in biases. He assumed that Earthmen always have the password. He assumed that aliens never have the password, but always try to enter the camp. Therefore, a creature who did not try to enter the camp must be presumed to be free of the alien camp-entering compulsion, and therefore to be an Earthman, until proven otherwise.

Halloran thought that was pretty good reasoning for a man who had lost several percent of his body fluids. Now he had to hope that the rest of his plan would work as well.

"Max," he said, "during my inspection, I made one rather disturbing discovery."

"Sir?"

"I found that we are camped on the edge of a fault in this planet's crust. The lines of the schism are unmistakable; they make the San Andreas Fault look like a hairline fracture."

"Sounds bad, sir. Is there much risk?"

"You bet your tin ass there's much risk. And much risk means much work. You and I, Maxie, are going to shift the entire camp about two miles due west. Immediately! So pick up the canteens and follow me."

"Yes, sir," Max said. "As soon as you release me."

"OK, I release you," Halloran said. "Hurry up!"

"I can't," the robot said. "You must release me by giving the current password and stating that it is canceled. Then I'll be able to stop guarding this particular perimeter."

"There's no time for formalities," Halloran said tightly. "The new password is 'whitefish.' Get moving, Max, I just felt a tremor."

"I didn't feel anything."

"Why should you?" Halloran snapped. "You're just a PR robot, not an Earthman with special training and finely attuned sensory apparatus. Damn, there it goes again! You must have felt it that time!"

"I think I did feel it!"

"Then get moving!"

"Mr. Halloran, I can't! It is physically impossible for me to leave this perimeter without a formal release! Please, sir, release me!"

"Don't get so excited," Halloran said. "On second thought, we're going to leave the camp right here."

"But the earthquake—"

"I've just made a new calculation. We've got more time than I had thought. I'm going to take another look around."

Halloran moved behind the rocks, out of the robot's sight. His heart was beating heavily, and the blood in his veins felt thick and sluggish. Bright spots were dancing between his eyes. He diagnosed an incipient sunstroke, and forced himself to sit very quietly in a patch of shade.

The endless day stretched on. The amorphous white blob of the double suns crept an inch toward the horizon. PR-22-0134 guarded his perimeter.

A breeze sprang up, turned into half a gale, and blew sand against Max's unblinking sensors. The robot trudged on, keeping to an exact circle. The wind died down and a figure appeared among the rocks some twenty yards away. Someone was watching him: was it Halloran, or the alien? Max refused to speculate. He guarded his perimeter.

A small creature like a coyote darted out of the desert and ran a zigzag course almost under Max's feet. A large bird dived down in pursuit. There was a thin, high scream and blood was splashed against one of the tents. The bird flapped heavily into the air with something writhing in its claws.

Max paid no attention to this. He was watching a humanoid creature stagger toward him out of the rocks.

The creature stopped. "Good day, Mr. Halloran," Max said at once. "I feel that I should mention, sir, that you show definite signs of dehydration. That is the condition which leads to shock, unconsciousness, and death, unless attended to promptly."

"Shut up," Halloran said, in a husky, heat-parched voice.

"Very well, Mr. Halloran."

"And stop calling me Mr. Halloran."

"Why should I do that, sir?"

"Because I am not Halloran. I am an alien."

"Indeed?" the robot said.

"Yes, indeed. Do you doubt my word?"

"Well, your mere unsupported statement—"

"Never mind, I'll give you proof. *I do not know the password.* Is that proof enough?"

When the robot still hesitated, Halloran said, "Look, Mr. Halloran told me that I should remind you of your own fundamental definitions, which are the criteria by which you perform your job. To wit: an Earthman is a sentient creature who knows the password; an alien is a sentient creature who does not know the password.''

"Yes," the robot said reluctantly, "knowledge of the password is my yardstick. But still, I sense something wrong. Suppose you're lying to me?"

"If I'm lying, then I must be an Earthman who knows the password," Halloran explained. "In which case, there's no danger. But you know that I'm not lying, because you know that no Earthman would lie about the password.''

"I don't know if I can assume that."

"You must. No Earthman wants to appear as an alien, does he?"

"Of course not."

"And a password is the only certain differentiation between a human and an alien?"

"Yes."

"Then the case is proven."

"I'm still not sure," Max said, and Halloran realized that the robot was reluctant to receive instruction from an alien, even if the alien was only trying to prove that he was an alien.

He waited. After a while, Max said, "All right, I agree that you are an alien. Accordingly, I refuse to let you into the camp."

"I'm not asking you to let me in. The point is, I am Halloran's prisoner, and you know what that means."

The robot blinked his sensors rapidly. "I don't know what that means."

"It means," Halloran said, "that you must follow Halloran's orders concerning me. His orders are that I must be detained within the perimeter of the camp, and must not be released unless he gives specific orders to that effect."

Max cried, "Mr. Halloran knows that I can't let you into the camp!"

"Of course! But Halloran is telling you to *imprison* me in the camp, which is an entirely different matter."

"Is it, really?"

"It certainly is! You must know that Earthmen *always* imprison aliens who try to break into their camp!"

"I seem to have heard something to that effect," Max

said. "Still, I cannot allow you in. But I can guard you here, just in front of the camp."

"That's not very good," Halloran said sulkily.

"I'm sorry, but it's the best I can do."

"Oh, very well," Halloran said, sitting down on the sand. "I am your prisoner, then."

"Yes."

"Then give me a drink of water."

"I am not allowed—"

"Damn it, you certainly know that alien prisoners are to be treated with the courtesy appropriate to their rank and are to be given the necessities of life according to the Geneva Convention and other international protocols."

"Yes, I've heard about that," Max said. "What is your rank?"

"Jamisdar, senior grade. My serial number is 12278031. And I need water immediately, because I'll die without it."

Max thought for several seconds. At last he said, "I will give you water. But only after Mr. Halloran has had water."

"Surely there's enough for both of us?" Halloran asked, trying to smile in a winning manner.

"That," Max said firmly, "is for Mr. Halloran to decide."

"All right," Halloran said, getting to his feet.

"Wait! Stop! Where are you going?"

"Just behind those rocks," Halloran said. "It's time for my noon prayer, which I must do in utter privacy."

"But what if you escape?"

"What would be the use?" Halloran asked, walking off. "Halloran would simply capture me again."

"True, true, the man's a genius," the robot muttered.

Very little time passed. Suddenly, Halloran came out of the rocks.

"Mr. Halloran?" Max asked.

"That's me," Halloran said cheerfully. "Did my prisoner get here OK?"

"Yes, sir. He's over there in the rocks, praying."

"No harm in that," Halloran said. "Listen, Max, when he comes out again, make sure he gets some water."

"I'll be glad to. After you have had your water, sir."

"Hell, I'm not even thirsty. Just see that the poor damned alien gets some."

"I can't, not until I've seen you drink your fill. The state of dehydration I mentioned, sir, is now more advanced. You are not far from collapse. I insist and I implore you—drink!"

"All right, stop nagging, get me a canteen."

"Oh, sir!"

"Eh? What's the matter?"

"You know I can't leave my post here on the perimeter."

"Why in hell can't you?"

"It's against orders. And also, because there's an alien behind those rocks."

"I'll keep watch for you, Max old boy, and you fetch a canteen like a good boy."

"It's good of you to offer, sir, but I can't allow that. I am a PR robot, constructed for the sole purpose of guarding the camp. I must not turn that responsibility over to anyone else, not even an Earthman or another PR robot, until the password is given and I am relieved of duty."

"Yeah, yeah," Halloran muttered. "Any place I start, it still comes out zero." Painfully he dragged himself behind the rocks.

"What's the matter?" the robot asked. "What did I say?" There was no answer.

"Mr. Halloran? Jamisdar Alien?"

Still no answer. Max continued to guard his perimeter.

Halloran was tired. His throat hurt from talking with a stupid robot, and his body hurt all over from the endless blows of the double sun. He had gone beyond sunburn; he was blackened, crusted over, a roast turkey of a man. Pain, thirst, and fatigue dominated him, leaving no room for any emotion except anger.

He was furious at himself for being caught in so absurd a situation, for letting himself be killed so casually. ("Halloran? Oh, yes, he didn't know the password, poor devil, and he died of exposure not fifty yards from water and shelter. Sad, strange, funny sort of end. . . .")

It was anger that kept him going now, that enabled him to review his situation and to search for a way into the camp.

He had convinced the robot that he was an Earthman. Then he had convinced the robot that he was an alien. Both approaches had failed when it came to the crucial issue of entry into the camp.

What was there left to try now?

He rolled over and stared up into the glowing white sky. Black specks moved across his line of vision. Hallucination? No, birds were circling. They were ignoring their usual diet of coyotes, waiting for the collapse of something really tasty, a walking banquet. . . .

Halloran forced himself to sit upright. Now, he told himself, I must review the situation and search for a loophole.

From Max's viewpoint, all sentient creatures who possess the password are Earthmen; all sentient creatures who do not possess the password are aliens.

Which means . . .

Means what? For a second, Halloran thought he had stumbled on to the key to the puzzle. But he was having difficulty concentrating. The birds were circling lower. One of the coyotes had come out and was sniffing at his shoes.

Forget all that. Concentrate. Become a practical automatologist.

Really, when you get right down to it, Max is *stupid*. He wasn't designed to detect frauds, except in the most limited capacity. His criteria are—archaic. Like that story about how Plato defined man as a featherless biped, and Diogenes the Cynic produced a plucked chicken which he maintained fitted the definition. Plato thereupon changed his definition to state that man was a featherless biped with broad nails.

But what has that got to do with Max?

Halloran shook his head savagely, trying to force himself to concentrate. But all he could see was Plato's man—a six-foot chicken without a feather on his body, but with broad fingernails.

Max was vulnerable. He had to be! Unlike Plato, he couldn't change his mind. Max was stuck with his definitions, and with their logical consequences. . . .

"Well, I'll be damned," Halloran said. "I do believe I have figured a way."

He tried to think it through, but found he wasn't able. He simply had to try it, and win or lose on the result. "Max," he said softly, "one plucked chicken is coming up. Or rather, one unplucked chicken. Put *that* in your cosmology and smoke it!''

He wasn't sure what he meant, but he knew what he was going to do.

Captain Beatty and Lieutenant James returned to the camp at the end of three Earth days. They found Halloran unconscious and delirious, a victim of dehydration and sunstroke. He raved about how Plato had tried to keep him out of the camp, and how Halloran had transformed himself into a six-foot chicken without broad fingernails, thus getting the best of the learned philosopher and his robot buddy.

Max had given him water, wrapped his body in wet blankets, and had produced black shade out of a double sheet of plastic. Halloran would recover in a day or two.

He had written a note before passing out: *No password couldn't get back in tell factory install emergency bypass in PR robots*.

Beatty couldn't make any sense out of Halloran, so he questioned Max. He heard about Halloran's trip of inspection and the various aliens who looked exactly like him, and what they said and what Halloran said. Obviously, these were all increasingly desperate attempts on Halloran's part to get back into the camp.

"But what happened after that?" Beatty asked. "How did he finally get in?"

"He didn't 'get in,' " Max said. "He simply *was* in at one point."

"But how did he get past you?"

"He didn't! That would have been quite impossible. Mr. Halloran simply *was* inside the camp."

"I don't understand," Beatty said.

"Quite frankly, sir, I don't either. I'm afraid that only Mr. Halloran can answer your question."

"It'll be a while before Halloran talks to anyone," Beatty said. "Still, if he figured out a way, I suppose I can, too."

Beatty and James both tried, but they couldn't come up with the answer. They weren't desperate enough or angry enough, and they weren't even thinking along the right lines. To understand how Halloran had gotten in, it was necessary to view the final course of events from Max's viewpoint.

* * *

Heat, wind, birds, rock, suns, sand. I disregard the irrelevant. I guard the camp perimeter against aliens.

Now something is coming toward me, out of the rocks, out of the desert. It is a large creature, it has hair hanging over its face, it creeps on four limbs.

I challenge. It snarls at me. I challenge again, in a more premptory manner, I switch on my armament, I threaten. The creature growls and keeps on crawling toward the camp.

I consult my definitions in order to produce an appropriate response.

I know that humans and aliens are both classes of sentient creature characterized by intelligence, which is expressed through the faculty of speech. This faculty is invariably employed to respond to my challenges.

Humans always answer correctly when asked the password.

Aliens always answer incorrectly when asked the password.

Both aliens and humans always answer—correctly or incorrectly—when asked the password.

Since this is invariably so, I must assume that any creature which does *not* answer my challenge is *unable* to answer, and can be ignored.

Birds and reptiles can be ignored. This large beast which crawls past me can also be ignored. I pay no attention to the creature; but I keep my sensors at extended alert, because Mr. Halloran is somewhere out in the desert. There is also an alien out there, a Jamisdar.

But what is this? It is Mr. Halloran, miraculously back in the camp, groaning, suffering from dehydration and sunstroke. The beast who crept past me is gone without trace, and the Jamisdar is presumably still praying in the rocks. . . .

Animal Lover

Stephen R. Donaldson

1

I was standing in front of Elizabeth's cage when the hum behind my right ear told me Inspector Morganstark wanted to see me. I was a little surprised, but I didn't show it. I was trained not to show it. I tongued one of the small switches set against my back teeth and said, "I copy. Be there in half an hour." I had to talk out loud if I wanted the receivers and tape decks back at the Bureau to hear me. The transceiver implanted in my mastoid process wasn't sensitive enough to pick up my voice if I whispered (or else the monitors would've spent a hell of a lot of time just listening to me breathe and swallow). But I was the only one in the area, so I didn't have to worry about being overheard.

After I acknowledged the Inspector's call, I stayed in front of Elizabeth's cage for a few more minutes. It wasn't that I had any objection to being called in, even though this was supposed to be my day off. And it certainly wasn't that I was having a particularly good time where I was. I don't like zoos. Not that this wasn't a nice place—for people, anyway. There were clean walks and drinking fountains, and plenty of signs describing the animals. But for the animals . . .

Well, take Elizabeth, for example. When I brought her in a couple months ago, she was the prettiest cougar I'd ever seen. She had those intense eyes only real hunters have, a delicate face, and her whiskers were absolutely magnificent. But now her eyes were dull, didn't seem to focus on anything. Her pacing was spongy instead of tight; sometimes she even scraped her toes because she didn't lift her feet high enough. And her whiskers had been trimmed short by the zoo keepers—probably because some great cats in zoos keep trying to push their faces between the bars, and some bastards who go to zoos like to pull whiskers, just to show how brave they are. In that cage, Elizabeth was just another shabby animal going to waste.

That raises the questions of why I put her there in the first place. Well, what else could I do? Leave her to starve when she was a cub? Turn her over to the breeders after I found her, so she could grow up and go through the same thing that killed her mother? Raise her in my apartment until she got so big and feisty she might tear my throat out? Let her go somewhere—with her not knowing how to hunt for food, and the people in the area likely to go after her with demolition grenades?

No, the zoo was the only choice I had. I didn't like it much.

Back when I was a kid, I used to say that someday I was going to be rich enough to build a real zoo. The kind of zoo they had thirty or forty years ago, where the animals lived in what they called a "natural habitat." But by now I know I'm not going to be rich. And all those good old zoos are gone. They were turned into hunting preserves when the demand for "sport" got high enough. These days, the only animals that find their ways into zoos at all are the ones that are too broken to be hunters—or the ones that are just naturally harmless. With exceptions like Elizabeth every once in a while.

I suppose the reason I didn't leave right away was the same reason I visited Elizabeth in the first place—and Emily and John, too. I was hoping she'd give some sign that she recognized me. Fat chance. She was a cougar—she wasn't sentimental enough to be grateful. Anyway, zoos aren't exactly conducive to sentimentality in animals of prey. Even Emily, the coyote, had finally forgotten me. (And John, the bald eagle, was too stupid for sentiment. He looked like he'd already forgotten everything he'd ever known.) No, I was the only sentimental one of the bunch. It made me late getting to the Bureau.

But I wasn't thinking about that when I arrived. I was thinking about my work. A trip to the zoo always makes me notice certain things about the duty room where all the Special Agents and Inspectors in our Division have their desks. Here we were in the year 2011—men had walked on Mars, microwave stations were being built to transmit solar power, marijuana and car racing were so important they were subsidized by the government—but the rooms where men and women like me did their paperwork still looked like the squadrooms I'd seen in old movies when I was a kid.

There were no windows. The dust and butts in the corners were so old they were starting to fossilize. The desks (all of them littered with paper that seemed to have fallen from the ceiling) were so close together we could smell each other working, sweating because we were tired of doing reports, or because we were sick of the fact that we never seemed to make a dent in the crime rate, or because we were afraid. Or because we were different. It was like one big cage. Even the ID clipped to the lapel of my jacket, identifying me as *Special Agent Sam Browne*, looked more like a zoo label than anything else.

I hadn't worked there long, as years go, but already I was glad every time Inspector Morganstark sent me out in the field. About the only difference the past forty years had made in the atmosphere of the Bureau was that everything was grimmer now. Special Agents didn't work on trivial crimes like prostitution, gambling, missing persons, because they were too busy with kidnapping, terrorism, murder, gang warfare. And they worked alone, because there weren't enough of us to go around.

The real changes were hidden. The room next door was even bigger than this one, and it was full to the ceiling with computer banks and programmers. And in the room next to that were the transmitters and tape decks that monitored Agents in the field. Because the Special Agents had been altered, too.

But philosophy (or physiology, depending on the point of view) is like sentiment, and I was already late. Before I had even reached my desk, the Inspector spotted me from across the room and shouted, "Browne!" He didn't sound in any

mood to be kept waiting, so I just ignored all the new paper
on my desk and went into his office.

I closed the door and stood waiting for him to decide
whether he wanted to chew me out or not. Not that I had any
particular objection to being chewed out. I liked Inspector
Morganstark, even when he was mad at me. He was a
sawed-off man with a receding hairline, and during his years
in the Bureau his eyes had turned bleak and tired. He always
looked harassed—and probably he was. He was the only
Inspector in the Division who was sometimes human enough,
or stubborn enough, anyway, to ignore the computers. He
played his hunches sometimes, and sometimes his hunches
got him in trouble. I liked him for that. It was worth being
roasted once in a while to work for him.

He was sitting with his elbows on his desk, clutching a file
with both hands as if it was trying to get away from him. It
was a pretty thin file, by Bureau standards—it's hard to shut
computers off once they get started. He didn't look up at me,
which is usually a bad sign; but his expression wasn't angry.
It was "something-about-this-isn't-right-and-I-don't-like-it."
All of a sudden, I wanted that case. So I took a chance and
sat down in front of his desk. Trying to show off my self-
confidence—of which I didn't have a hell of a lot. After two
years as a Special Agent, I was still the rookie under Inspector Morganstark. So far he'd never given me anything to do
that wasn't basically routine.

After a minute, he put down the file and looked at me. His
eyes weren't angry, either. They were worried. He clamped
his hands behind his head and leaned back in his chair. Then
he said, "You were at the zoo?"

That was another reason I liked him. He took my pets
seriously. Made me feel less like a piece of equipment.
"Yes," I said. For the sake of looking competent, I didn't
smile.

"How many have you got there now?"

"Three. I took Elizabeth in a couple of months ago."

"How's she doing?"

I shrugged. "Fair. It never takes them very long to lose
spirit—once they're caged up."

His eyes studied me a minute longer. Then he said, "That's
why I want you for this assignment. You know about ani-

mals. You know about hunting. You won't jump to the wrong conclusions.''

Well, I was no hunter but I knew what he meant. I was familiar with hunting preserves. That was where I got John and Emily and Elizabeth. Sort of a hobby. Whenever I get a chance (like when I'm on leave), I go to preserves. I pay my way in like anybody else—take my chances like anybody else. But I don't have any guns, and I'm not trying to kill anything. I'm hunting for cubs like Elizabeth—young that are left to die when their mothers are shot or trapped. When I find them, I smuggle them out of the preserves, and raise them myself as long as I can, and then give them to the zoo.

Sometimes I don't find them in time. And sometimes when I find them they've already been crippled by careless shots or traps. Them I kill. Like I say, I'm sentimental.

But I didn't know what the Inspector meant about jumping to the wrong conclusions. I put a question on my face and waited, until he said, ''Ever hear of the Sharon's Point Hunting Preserve?''

''No. But there are a lot of preserves. Next to car racing, hunting preserves are the most popular—''

He cut me off. He sat forward and poked the file accusingly with one finger. ''People get killed there.''

I didn't say anything to that. People get killed at all hunting preserves. That's what they're for. Since crime became the top-priority problem in this country about twenty years ago, the government has spent a lot of money on it. A *lot* of money. On ''law enforcement'' and prisons, of course. On drugs like marijuana that pacify people. But also on every conceivable way of giving people some kind of noncriminal outlet for their hostility.

Racing, for instance. With government subsidies, there isn't a man or woman in the country so poor they can't afford to get in a hot car and slam it around a track. The important thing, according to the social scientists, is to give people a chance to do something violent at the risk of their lives. Both violence and risk have to be real for catharsis to take place. With all the population and economic pressure people are under, they have to have some way to let off steam. Keep them from becoming criminals out of simple boredom and frustration and perversity.

So we have hunting preserves. Wilderness areas are sealed off and stocked with all manner of dangerous beasts and then hunters are turned loose in them—alone, of course—to kill everything they can while trying to stay alive. Everyone who has a yen to see the warm blood run can take a rifle and go pit himself, or at least his firepower, against various assortments of great cats, wolves, wildebeests, grizzly bears, whatever.

It's almost as popular as racing. People like the illusion of "kill or be killed." They slaughter animals as fast as the breeders can supply them. (Some people use poisoned darts and dumdum bullets. Some people even try to sneak lasers into the preserves, but that is strictly not allowed. Private citizens are strictly not allowed to have lasers at all.) It's all very therapeutic. And it's all very messy. Slow deaths and crippling outnumber clean kills twenty to one, and not enough hunters get killed to suit me. But I suppose it's better than war. At least we aren't trying to do the same thing to the Chinese.

The Inspector said, "You're thinking, 'Horray for the lions and tigers.' "

I shrugged again. "Sharon's Point must be popular."

"I wouldn't know," he said acidly. "They don't get Federal money, so they don't have to file preserve-use figures. All I get is death certificates." This time, he touched the file with his fingertips as if it were delicate or dangerous. "Since Sharon's Point opened, twenty months ago, forty-five people have been killed."

Involuntarily, I said, "Sonofabitch!" Which probably didn't make me sound a whole lot more competent. But I was surprised. Forty-five! I knew of preserves that hadn't lost forty-five people in five years. Most hunters don't like to be in all *that* much danger.

"It's getting worse, too," Inspector Morganstark went on. "Ten in the first ten months. Fifteen in the next five. Twenty in the last five."

"They're very popular," I muttered.

"Which is strange," he said, "since they don't advertise."

"You mean they rely on word-of-mouth?" That implied several things, but the first one that occurred to me was, "What have they got that's so special?"

"You mean besides forty-five dead?" the Inspector growled. "They get more complaints than any other preserve in the country." That didn't seem to make sense, but he explained it. "Complaints from the families. They don't get the bodies back."

Well, that was special—sort of. I'd never heard of a preserve that didn't send the bodies to the next of kin. "What happens to them?"

"Cremated. At Sharon's Point. The complaints say that spouses have to sign a release before the hunters can go there. A custom some of the spouses don't like. But what they really don't like is that their husbands or wives are cremated right away. The spouses don't even get to see the bodies. All they get is notification and a death certificate." He looked at me sharply. "This is not against the law. All the releases were signed in advance."

I thought for a minute, then said something noncommittal. "What kind of hunters were they?"

The Inspector frowned bleakly. "The best. Most of them shouldn't be dead." He took a readout from the file and tossed it across the desk at me. "Take a look."

The readout was a computer summary of the forty-five dead. All were wealthy, but only 26.67% had acquired their money themselves. 73.33% had inherited it or married it. 82.2% had bright financial futures. 91.1% were experienced hunters, and of those 65.9% had reputations of being exceptionally skilled. 84.4% had traveled extensively around the world in search of "game"—the more dangerous the better.

"Maybe the animals are experienced too," I said.

The Inspector didn't laugh. I went on reading.

At the bottom of the sheet was an interesting piece of information: 75.56% of the people on this list had known at least five other people on the list; 0.00% had known none of the others.

I handed the readout back to Inspector Morganstark. "Word-of-mouth for sure. It's like a club." Something important was going on at the Sharon's Point Hunting Preserve, and I wanted to know what it was. Trying to sound casual, I asked, "What does the computer recommend?"

He looked at the ceiling. "It says to forget the whole thing. That damn machine can't even understand why I bother to ask it questions about this. No law broken. Death rate irrelevant. I asked for a secondary recommendation, and it suggested I talk to some other computer.''

I watched him carefully. "But you're not going to forget it."

He threw up his hands. "Me forget it? Do I look like a man who has that much common sense? You know perfectly well I'm not going to forget it."

"Why not?"

It seemed like a reasonable question to me, but the Inspector waved it aside. "In fact," he went on in a steadier tone, "I'm assigning it to you. I want you out there tomorrow."

I started to say something, but he stopped me. He was looking straight at me, and I knew he was going to tell me something that was important to him. "I'm giving it to you," he said, "because I'm worried about you. Not because you're a rookie and this case is trivial. It is not trivial. I can feel it—right here." He put his hand over the bulge of his skull behind his right ear, as if his hunches came from the transceiver in his mastoid process. Then he sighed. "That's part of it, I suppose. I know you won't go off the deep end on this, if I'm wrong. Just because people are getting killed, you won't go all righteous on me and try to get Sharon's Point shut down. You won't make up charges against them just because their death rate is too high. You'll be cheering for the animals.

"But on top of that," he went on so I didn't have a chance to interrupt, "I want you to do this because I think you need it. I don't have to tell you you're not comfortable being a Special Agent. You're not comfortable with all that fancy equipment we put in you. All the adjustment tests indicate a deep-seated reluctance to accept yourself. You need a case that'll let you find out what you can do."

"Inspector," I said carefully, "I'm a big boy now. I'm here of my own free will. You're not sending me out on this just because you want me to adjust. Why don't you tell me why you decided to ignore the computer?"

He was watching me like I'd just suggested some kind of unnatural act. But I knew that look. It meant he was angry about something, and he was about to admit it to both of us for the first time. Abruptly, he picked up the file and shoved it at me in disgust. "The last person on that list of dead is Nick Kolcsz. He was a Special Agent."

A Special Agent. That told me something, but not enough. I didn't know Kolcsz. He must have had money, but I wanted more than that. I gave the Inspector's temper another nudge. "What was he doing there?"

He jumped to his feet to make shouting easier. "How the hell should I know?" Like all good men in the Bureau, he took the death of an Agent personally. "He was on leave! His goddam transceiver was off!" Then with a jerk he sat down again. After a minute, all his anger was gone and he was just tired. "I presume he went there for the hunting, just like the rest of them. You know as well as I do we don't monitor Agents on leave. Even Agents need privacy once in a while. We didn't even know he was dead until his wife filed a complaint because they didn't let her see his body.

"Never mind the security leak—all that metal in his ashes. What scares me"—now there was something like fear in his bleak eyes—"is that we hadn't turned off his power pack. We never do that—not just for a leave. He should have been safe. Wild elephants shouldn't have been able to hurt him."

I knew what he meant. Nick Kolcsz was a cyborg. Like me. Whatever killed him was more dangerous than that.

2

Well, yes—a cyborg. But it isn't everything it's cracked up to be. People these days make the mistake of thinking Special Agents are "super" somehow. This comes from the old movies, where cyborgs were always super-fast and super-strong. They were loaded with weaponry. They had built-in computers to do things like think for them. They were slightly more human than robots.

Maybe someday. Right now no one has the technology for that kind of thing. I mean the medical technology. For lots of reasons, medicine hasn't made much progress in the last twenty years. What with all the population trouble we have, the science of "saving lives" doesn't seem as valuable as it used to. And then there were the genetic riots of 1989, which ended up shutting down whole research centers.

No, what I have in the way of equipment is a transceiver in the mastoid process behind my right ear, so that I'm always in contact with the Bureau; thin, practically weightless plastene struts along my legs and arms and spine, so I'm pretty hard to cripple (in theory, anyway); and a nuclear power pack implanted in my chest so its shielding protects my heart as well. The power pack runs my transceiver. It also runs the hypersonic blaster built into the palm of my left hand.

This has it disadvantages. I can hardly flex the first knuckles of that hand, so the hand itself doesn't have a whole lot it can do. And the blaster is covered by a latex membrane (looks just like skin) that burns away every time I use it, so I always have to carry replacements. But there are advantages, too—sort of. I can kill people at twenty-five meters, and stun them at fifty. I can tear holes in concrete walls, if I can get close enough.

That was what the Inspector was talking about when he said I hadn't adjusted. I can't get used to the fact that I can kill my friends just by pushing my tongue against one of my back teeth in a certain way. So I tend not to have very many friends.

Anyway, being a cyborg wasn't much comfort on this assignment. That was all I had going for me—exactly the same equipment that hadn't saved Nick Kolcsz. And he'd had something I didn't have—something that also hadn't saved him. He'd known what he was getting into. He'd been an experienced hunter, and he'd known three other people on that list of dead. (He must've known some of the survivors, too. Or known of them through friends. How else could he have known the place was dangerous?) Maybe that was why he went to Sharon's Point—to do some private research to find out what happened to those dead hunters.

Unfortunately, that didn't give me the option of going to one of his friends and asking what Kolcsz had known. The people who benefit (if that's the right word) from an exclusive arrangement don't have much reason to trust outsiders (like me). And they certainly weren't going to reveal knowing about anything illegal to a Special Agent. That would hurt themselves as well as Sharon's Point.

But I didn't like the idea of facing whatever killed Kolcsz without more data. So I started to do some digging.

I got information of a sort by checking out the preserve's registration, but it didn't help much. Registration meant only that the Federal inspector had approved Sharon's Point's equipment. And inspection only covers two things: fencing and medical facilities.

Every hunting preserve is required to insure that its animals can't get loose, and to staff a small clinic to treat injured customers (never mind the crippled animals). The inspector verified that Sharon's Point had these things. It perimeter (roughly 133 km.) was appropriately fenced. Its facilities included a very well-equipped surgery and dispensary; and a veterinary hospital (which surprised me); *and* a cremator—supposedly for getting rid of animals too badly wounded to be treated.

Other information was slim. The preserve itself contained about 1,100 square km. of forests, swamps, hills, meadows. It was owned and run by a man named Fritz Ushre. Its staff consisted of one surgeon (a Dr. Avid Paracels) and a half-dozen handlers for the animals.

But one item was conspicuously absent: the name of the breeder. Most hunting preserves get their animals by contract with one of three or four big breeding firms. Sharon's Point's registration didn't name one. It didn't name any source for its animals at all, which made me think maybe the people who went hunting there weren't hunting animals.

People hunting people? That's as illegal as hell. But it might explain the high death rate. Mere lions and baboons (even rabid baboons in packs) don't kill forty-five hunters at an exclusive preserve in twenty months. I was beginning to understand why the Inspector was willing to defy the computer on this assignment.

I went to the programmers and got a readout on the death certificates. All had been signed by "Avid Paracels, M.D." All specified "normal" hunting-preserve causes of death (the usual combinations of injury and exposure, in addition to outright killing), but the type of animal involved was never identified.

That bothered me. This time I had the computers read out everything they had on Fritz Ushre and Avid Paracels.

Ushre's file was small. Things like age, marital status, blood type aside, it contained only a sketchy résumé of his past employment. Twenty years of perfectly acceptable work as an engineer in various electronics firms. Then he inherited some land. He promptly quit his job, and two years later he opened up Sharon's Point. Now (according to his bank statements) he was in the process of getting rich. That told me just about nothing. I already knew Sharon's Point was popular.

But the file on Avid Paracels, Ph.D., M.D., F.A.C.S., was something else. It was full of stuff. Apparently at one time Dr. Paracels had held a high security clearance because of some research he was doing, so the Bureau had studied him down to his toenails. That produced reams of data, most of it pointless, but it didn't take me long to find the real goodies. After which (as my mother used to say) I could've been knocked over with a shovel. Avid Paracels was one of the victims of the genetic riots of 1989.

This is basically what happened. In 1989 one of the newspapers broke the story that a team of biologists (including the distinguished Avid Paracels) working under a massive Federal grant had achieved a major breakthrough in what they called "recombinant DNA research"—"genetic engineering," to ignorant sods like me. They'd mastered the techniques of raising animals with altered genes. Now they were beginning to experiment with human embryos. Their goal, according to the newspaper, was to attempt "minor improvements" in the human being—"cat" eyes, for instance, or prehensile toes.

So what happened? Riots is what happened. Which in itself wasn't unusual. By 1989, crime and whatnot, social unrest of all kinds, had already become the biggest single threat to the country, but the government still hadn't faced up to the problem. So riots and other types of violence used to start up for any reason at all: higher fuel prices, higher food costs, higher rents. In other words (according to the social scientists), the level of general public aggression had reached crisis proportions. Nobody had any acceptable outlets for anger, so whenever people were able to identify a grievance they went bananas.

That newspaper article triggered the great-granddaddy of all riots. There was a lot of screaming about "the sanctity of human life," but I suppose the main thing was that the idea of a "superior human being" was pretty threatening to most people. So scientists and Congressmen were attacked in the streets. Three government buildings were wrecked (including a post office—God knows why). Seven apartment complexes were wrecked. One hundred thirty-seven stores were looted and wrecked. The recombinant DNA research program was wrecked. And a handful of careers went down the drain. Because this riot was too big to be put down. The cops (Special Agents) would have had to kill too many people. So the President himself set about appeasing the rioters—which led, naturally enough, to our present policy of trying to appease violence itself.

Avid Paracels was one of the men who went down the drain. I guess he was lucky not to lose his medical license. He certainly never got the chance to do any more research.

Well, that didn't prove anything, but it sure made me curious. People who lose high positions have been known to become somewhat vague about matters of legality. So that gave me a place to start when I went to Sharon's Point. Maybe if I was lucky I could even get out of pretending to go hunting in the preserve itself.

So I was feeling like I knew what I was doing (which probably should've told me I was in trouble already) when I left the duty room to go arrange for transportation and money. But it didn't last. Along the way I got one of those hot flashes, like an inspiration or a premonition. So when I was done with Accounting I went back to the computers and asked for a readout on any unsolved crimes in the area around Sharon's Point. The answer gave my so-called self-confidence a jolt.

Sharon's Point was only 80 km. from the Procureton Arsenal, where a lot of old munitions (mostly from the '60s and '70s) were stored. Two years ago, someone had broken into Procureton (God knows how) and helped himself to a few odds and ends—like fifty M-16 rifles (along with five thousand loaded clips), a hundred .22 Magnum automatic handguns (and another five thousand clips), five hundred hand grenades, and more than five hundred antipersonnel mines of various types. Enough to supply a good-sized street mob.

Which made no sense at all. Any street mob these days—or terrorist organization, or heist gang, for that matter—that tried to use obsolete weaponry like M-16s would get cut to shreds in minutes by cops using laser cannons. And who else would want the damn stuff?

I didn't believe I was going to find any animals at Sharon's Point at all. Just hunters picking one another off.

Before I went home, I spent an hour down in the range, practicing with my blaster. Just to be sure it worked.

The next morning early I went to Supply and got myself some "rich" clothes, along with a bunch of hunting gear. Then I went to Weapons and checked out an old Winchester .30–06 carbine that looked to me like the kind of rifle a "true" (eccentric) sportsman might use—takes a degree of skill, and fires plain old lead slugs instead of hypodarts or fragmentation bullets—sort of a way of giving the "game" a chance. After that I checked the tape decks to be sure they had me on active status. Then I went to Sharon's Point.

I took the chute from D.C. to St. Louis (actually, it's an electrostatic shuttle, but it's called "the chute" because the early designs reminded some romantic of the old logging chutes in the Northwest), but after that I had to rent a car. Which was appropriate, since I was supposed to be rich. Only the rich can afford cars these days—and Special Agents on assignment (fuel prices being what they are, the only time most people see the inside of a car is at a subsidized track). But I didn't enjoy it much. Never mind that I'm not much of a driver (I haven't exactly had a lot of practice). It was raining like hades in St. Louis, and I had to drive 300 km. through the back hills of Missouri as if I was swimming. That slowed me down so much I didn't get near Sharon's Point until after dark.

I stopped for the night at the village of Sharon's Point, which was about 5 km. shy of the preserve. It was a dismal little town, too far from anywhere to have anything going for it. But it did have one motel. When I splashed my way through the rain and mud and went dripping into the lobby, I found that one motel was doing very well for itself. It was as plush as any motel I'd ever seen. And expensive. The receptionist didn't even blush when she told me the place cost a thousand dollars a night.

So it was obvious this motel didn't get its business from local people and tourists. Probably it catered to the hunters who came to and went from the preserve. *I* might've blushed if I hadn't come prepared to handle situations like this. I had a special credit card Accounting had given me. Made me look rich without saying anything about where I got my money. I checked in as if I did this kind of thing every day. The receptionist sent my stuff to my room, and I went into the bar.

Hoping there might be another hunter or two around. But except for the bartender the place was empty. So I perched myself on one of the barstools and tried to find out if the bartender liked to talk.

He did. I guess he didn't get a lot of opportunity. Probably people who didn't mind paying a thousand dollars a night for a room didn't turn up too often. Once he got started, I didn't think I would be able to stop him from telling me everything he knew.

Which wasn't a whole lot more than I already knew—about the preserve, anyway. The people who went there had money. They threw their weight around. They liked to drink—before and after hunting. But maybe half of them didn't stop by to celebrate on their way home. After a while I asked him what kind of trophies the ones that did stop by got.

"Funny thing about that," he said. "They don't bring anything back. Don't even talk about what they got. I used to do some hunting when I was a kid, and I never met a hunter who didn't like to show off what he shot. I've seen grown men act like God Almighty when they dinged a rabbit. But not here. 'Course''—he smiled—''I never went hunting in a place as pricey as Sharon's Point.''

But I wasn't thinking about the money. I was thinking about forty-five bodies. That was something even rich hunters wouldn't brag about. Probably those trophies had bullet holes in them.

3

I promised myself I was going to find out about those "trophies." One way or another. It wasn't that I was feeling confident. Right then I don't think I even knew what confidence was. No, it was that confidence didn't matter anymore. I couldn't afford to worry about it. This case was too serious.

When I was sure I was the only guest, I gave up the idea of getting any more information that night. There was no cure for it—I was going to have to go up to the preserve and bluff my way along until I got the answers I needed. Not a comforting thought. When I went to bed, I spent a long time listening to the rain before I fell asleep.

In the morning it was still raining, but that didn't seem like a good enough reason to postpone what I had to do. So I spent a while in the bathroom, running the shower to cover the sound of my voice while I talked to the tape decks in the Bureau (via microwave relays in St. Louis, Indianapolis, Pittsburgh, and God knows where else). Then I had breakfast, and went and got soaked running through the rain out to my car.

The drive to the preserve was slow because of the rain. The road wound up and down hills between walls of dark trees that seemed to be crouching there, waiting for me, but I didn't see anything else until my car began picking its way up a long slope toward the outbuildings of Sharon's Point.

They sat below the crest of a long transverse ridge that blocked everything beyond it from sight. Right ahead of me was a large squat complex; that was probably where the offices and medical facilities were. To the right was a long building like a barracks that probably housed the animal handlers. On the left was the landing area. Three doughnut-shaped open-cockpit hovercraft stood there. (Most hunting preserves used hovercraft for jobs like inspecting the fences and looking for missing hunters.) They were covered by styrene sheets against the rain.

And behind all this, stretching along the ridge like the promise of something deadly, was the fence. It looked gray and bitter against the black clouds and the rain. The chain steel was at least five meters high, curved inward and viciously barbed along the top to keep certain kinds of animals from being able to climb out. But it didn't make me feel safe. Whatever was in there had killed forty-five people. Five meters of fence was either inadequate or irrelevant.

More for my own benefit than for Inspector Morganstark's, I said into my transceiver, "Relinquish all hope, ye who enter here." Then I drove up to the squat building, parked as close as I could get to a door marked OFFICE, and ran through the rain as if I couldn't wait to take on Sharon's Point single-handedly.

I rushed into the office, pulled the door shut behind me—and almost fell on my face. Pain as keen as steel went through my head like a drill from somewhere behind my right ear. For an instant I was blind and deaf with pain, and my knees were bending under me.

It was coming from my mastoid process.

Some kind of power feedback in my transceiver.

It felt like one of the monitors back at the Bureau was trying to kill me.

I knew that wasn't it; but right then I didn't care what it was. I tongued the switch to cut off transmission. And, shoving out one leg, caught myself with a jerk before I fell.

It was over. The pain disappeared. Just like that.

I was woozy with relief. There was a ringing in my ears that made it hard for me to keep my balance. Seconds passed before I could focus well enough to look around. Not think—just look.

I was in a bare office, a place with no frills, not even any curtains on the windows to keep out the dankness of the rain. I was almost in reach of a long counter.

Behind the counter stood a man. He was tall and fat—not overweight-fat, but bloated-fat, as if he was stuffing himself to feed some grotesque appetite. He had the face of a boar, the cunning and malicious eyes of a boar, and he was looking at me as if he was trying to decide where to use his tusks. But his voice was suave and kind. "Are you all right?" he asked. "What happened?"

With a lurch, my brain started working again.

Power feedback. Something had caused a feedback in my transceiver. Must've been some kind of electronic jamming device. The government used jammers for security—a way of screening secret meetings. To protect against people like me.

Sharon's Point was using a security screen.

What were they trying to hide?

But that was secondary. I had a more immediate problem. The fat man had been watching me when the jammer hit. He'd seen my reaction. He would know I had a transceiver in my skull. Unless I did something about it. Fast.

He hadn't even blinked. "What happened?"

I was sweating. My hands were trembling. But I looked him straight in the eye and said, "It'll pass. I'll be all right in a minute."

Nothing could've been kinder than the way he asked, "What is the matter?"

"Just a spasm," I said straight at him. "Comes and goes. Brain tumor. Inoperable. I'll be dead in six months. That's why I'm here."

"Ah," he said without moving. "That is why you are here." His pudgy hands were folded and resting on his gut. "I understand." If he was suspicious of me, he didn't let it ruffle his composure. "I understand perfectly."

"I don't like hospitals," I said sternly, just to show him I was back in control of myself.

"Naturally not," he assented. "You have come to the right place, Mr. . . . ?"

"Browne," I said. "Sam Browne."

"Mr. Browne." He filed my name away with a nod. Gave me the uncomfortable impression he was never going to forget it. "We have what you want here." For the first time, I saw him blink. Then he said, "How did you hear of us, Mr. Browne?"

I was prepared for that. I mentioned a couple names off the preserve's list of dead, and followed them up by saying squarely, "You must be Ushre."

He nodded again. "I am Fritz Ushre." He said it the same way he might've said, "I am the President of the United States." Nothing diffident about him.

Trying to match him, I said, "Tell me about it."

His boar eyes didn't waver, but he didn't answer me directly. Instead, he said, "Mr. Browne, we generally ask our patrons for payment in advance. Our standard fee is for a week's hunting. Forty thousand dollars."

I certainly did admire his composure. He was better at it than I was. I felt my face react before I could stop it. Forty—! Well, so much for acting like I was rich. It was all I could do to keep from cursing myself out loud.

"We run a costly operation," he said. He was as smooth as stainless steel. "Our facilities are the best. And we breed our own animals. That way, we are able to maintain the quality of what we offer. But for that reason we are required to have veterinary as well as medical facilities. Since we receive no Federal money—and submit to no Federal inspections''—he couldn't have sounded less like he was threatening me—''we cannot afford to be wasteful.''

He might've gone on—not apologizing, just tactfully getting rid of me—but I cut him off. "Better be worth it," I said with all the toughness I could manage. "I didn't get where I am throwing my money away." At the same time, I took out my credit card and set it down with a snap on the counter.

"Your satisfaction is guaranteed." Ushre inspected my card briefly, then asked, "Will one week suffice, Mr. Browne?"

"For a start."

"I understand," he said as if he understood me completely. Then he turned away for a minute while he ran my card through his accounting computer. The ac-computer verified my credit due and printed out a receipt that Ushre presented to me for validation. After I'd pressed my thumbprint onto the identiplate, he returned my card and filed the receipt in an ac-computer.

In the meantime, I did some glancing around, trying nonchalantly (I hoped I looked nonchalant) to spot the jammer. But I didn't find it. In fact, as an investigator I was getting nowhere fast. If I didn't start finding things out soon, I was going to have real trouble explaining that forty-thousand-dollar bill to Accounting. Not to mention staying alive.

So when Ushre turned back to me, I said, "I don't want to start in the rain. I'll come back tomorrow. But while I'm here I want to look at your facilities." It wasn't much, but it was the best I could do without giving away that I really didn't know those two dead men I'd mentioned. I was supposed to know what I was doing; I couldn't very well just ask him right out what kind of animals he had. Or didn't have.

Ushre put a sheaf of papers down on the counter in front of me, and said again, "I understand." The way he said things like that was beginning to make my scalp itch. "Once you have completed these forms, I will ask Dr. Paracels to show you around."

I said, "Fine," and started to fill out the forms. I didn't worry too much about what I was signing. Except for the one that had to do with cremating my body, they were pretty much standard releases—so that Sharon's Point wouldn't be liable for anything that might happen to me. The disposal-of-the-body form I read more carefully than the others, but it didn't tell me anything I didn't already know. And by the time I was done, Dr. Avid Paracels had come into the office.

I studied him as Ushre introduced us. I would've been interested to meet him anytime, but right then I was particularly keen. I knew more about him than I did about Ushre—which meant that for me he was the key to Sharon's Point.

He was tall and gaunt—next to Ushre he was outright emaciated. Scrawny and stooped, as if the better part of him had been chipped away by a long series of personal catastrophes. And he looked a good bit more than thirty years older than I was. His face was gray, like the face of a man with a terminal disease, and the skin stretched from his cheekbones to his jaw as if it was too small for his skull. His eyes were hidden most of the time beneath his thick, ragged eyebrows, but when I caught a glimpse of them they looked as dead as plastene. I would've thought he was a cadaver if he wasn't standing up and wearing a white coat. If he hadn't licked his lips once when he first saw me. Just the tip of his tongue circled his lips that once—not like he was hungry, but instead like he was wondering in an abstract way whether I might turn out to be tasty. Something about that little pink gesture in that gray face made me feel cold all of a sudden. For a second I felt like I knew what he was really thinking. He was wondering how he was going to be able to use me. And how I was going to die. Maybe not in that order.

"Dr. Paracels," I said. I was wondering if he or Ushre knew there was sweat running down the small of my back.

"I won't show you where we do our breeding," he said in a petulant way that surprised me, "or my animal hospital." The whine of his voice sounded almost deliberate, like he was trying to sound pathetic.

"We never show our patrons those facilities," Ushre added smoothly. "There is an element of surprise in what we offer." He blinked again. The rareness of that movement emphasized the cunning and malice of his eyes. "We believe that it improves the sport. Most of our patrons agree."

"But you can see my clinic," Paracels added impatiently.

"This way." He didn't wait for me. He turned around and went out the inner door of the office.

Ushre's eyes never left my face. "A brilliant surgeon, Dr. Paracels. We are fortunate to have him."

I shrugged. The way I was feeling right then, there didn't seem to be anything else I could do. Then I went after the good doctor.

That door opened into a wide corridor running through the complex. I caught a glimpse of Paracels going through a set of double doors at the end of the corridor, but there were other doors along the hall, and they were tempting. They might lead me to Ushre's records—and Ushre's records might tell me what I needed to know about Sharon's Point. But this was no time for taking risks. I couldn't very well tell Ushre when he caught me that I'd blundered onto his records by mistake—assuming I even found them. So I went straight to the double doors and pushed my way into the surgery.

The registration inspector was right: Sharon's Point was very well equipped. There were several examination and treatment rooms (including x-ray, oxygen, and ophthalmological equipment), a half-dozen beds, a pharmacy that looked more than adequate (maybe a lot more than adequate), and an operating theater that reminded me of the place where I was made into a cyborg.

That was where I caught up with Paracels. In his whining voice (was he really that full of self-pity?), he described the main features of the place. He assumed I'd want to know how he could do effective surgery alone there, and that was what he told me.

Well, his equipment was certainly compact and flexible, but what really interested me was that he had a surgical laser. (I didn't ask him if he had a license for it. His license was hanging right there on the wall.) That wasn't common at all, especially in a small clinic like this. A surgical laser is very specialized equipment. These days they're used for things like eye surgery and lobotomies. And making cyborgs. But a while back (twenty-two years) they were used in genetic engineering.

The whole idea made my skin crawl. There was something menacing about it. As innocently as I could, I asked Paracels the nastiest question I could think of. "Do you save any lives here, Doctor?"

That was all it took to make him stop whining. All at once he was so bitter I half expected him to begin foaming at the mouth. "What're you," he spat, "some kind of bleeding heart? The men who come here know they might get killed. I do everything for them that any doctor could do. You think I have all this stuff just for the hell of it?"

I was surprised to find I believed him. I believed he did everything he could to save every life that ended up on his operating table. He was a doctor, wasn't he? If he was killing people, he was doing it some other way.

4

Well, maybe I was being naive. I didn't know yet. But I figured I'd already learned everything Paracels and Ushre were likely to tell me of their own free will. I told them I'd be back bright and early the next morning, and then I left.

The rain was easing, so I didn't get too wet on the way back to my car, but that didn't make me feel any better. There was no doubt about it: I was outclassed. Ushre and Paracels had given away practically nothing. They'd come up with neat plausible stories to cover strange things like their vet hospital and their independence from the usual animal breeders. In fact, they'd explained away everything except their policy of cremating their dead hunters—and that was something I couldn't challenge them on without showing off my ignorance. Maybe they had even spotted me for what I was. And I'd gotten nothing out of them except a cold sweat. I had an unfamiliar itch to use my blaster; I wanted to raze that whole building, clinic and all. When I reactivated my transmitter, I felt like telling Inspector Morganstark to pull me off the case and send in someone who knew what he was doing.

But I didn't. Instead I acted just like a good Special Agent is supposed to. I spent the drive back to town talking to the tape decks, telling them the whole story. If nothing else, I'd accomplished something by finding out Sharon's Point ran a security screen. That would tell the Inspector his hunch was right.

I didn't have any doubt his hunch was right. Something stank at that preserve. In different ways, Ushre and Paracels reminded me of maneaters. They had acquired a taste for blood. Human blood. In the back of my head a loud voice was shouting that Sharon's Point used genetically altered people for "game." No wonder Paracels looked so sick. The M.D. in him was dying of outrage.

So I didn't tell Inspector Morganstark to pull me off the case. I did what I was supposed to do. I went back to the motel and spent the afternoon acting like a rich man who was eager to go hunting. I turned in early after supper, to get plenty of rest. I asked the desk to call me at 6 A.M. With the shower running, I told the tape decks what I was going to do.

When midnight came, and the sky blew clear for the first time in two days, I climbed out a window and went back to the preserve on foot.

I wasn't exactly loaded down with equipment. I left my .30–06 and all my rich-hunter gear back at the motel. But I figured I didn't need it. After all, I was a cyborg. Besides, I had a needle flash and a small set of electromagnetic lockpicks and jimmies. I had a good sense of direction. I wasn't afraid of the dark.

And I had my personal good-luck piece. It way an old Gerber hunting knife that used to be my father's. It was balanced for throwing (which I was better at than using a rifle anyway), and its edges near the hilt were serrated, so it was good for cutting things like rope. I'd taken it with me on all my visits to hunting preserves, and once or twice it had kept me alive. It was what I used when I had to kill some poor animal crippled by a trap of a bad shot. Now I wore it hidden under my clothes at the small of my back. Made me feel a little more self-confident.

I was on my way to try to sneak a look at a few things. Like Paracels's vet hospital and breeding pens. And Ushre's records. I really didn't want to just walk into the preserve in the morning and find out what I was up against the hard way. Better to take my chances in the dark.

I reached the preserve in about an hour and hunched down in the brush beside the road to plan what I was going to do.

All the lights in the barracks and office complex were out, but there was a bright pink freon bulb burning next to the landing area and the hovercraft. I was tempted to put it out, just to make myself feel safer. But I figured that would be like announcing to Sharon's Point I was there, so I left it alone.

The barracks I decided to leave alone, too. Maybe that wasn't where the handlers lived—maybe that was where Paracels kept his animals. But if it was living quarters, I was going to look pretty silly when I got caught breaking in there. Better not to take that chance.

So I concentrated on the office building. Using the shadow of the barracks for cover, I crept around until I was in back of the complex, between it and the fence. There, about where I figured the vet facilities ought to be, I found a door that suited me. I wanted to look at that clinic. No matter what Ushre said, it sounded to me like a grand place to engineer "game." I tongued off my transmitter so I wouldn't run into that jammer again and set about trying to open the door without setting off any alarms.

One of my picks opened the lock easily enough. But I didn't crack the door more than a few cm. In the light of my needle flash, the corridor beyond looked harmless enough, but I didn't trust it. I took a lockpick and returned it to react to magnetic-field scanners (the most common security system these days). Then I slipped it through the crack of the door. If it met a scanner field, I'd feel resistance in the air—before I tripped the alarm (in theory, anyway).

Isn't technology wonderful? (Said the cyborg.) My pick didn't meet any resistance. After a minute or two of deep breathing, I opened the door enough to step into the complex. Then I closed it behind me and leaned against it.

I checked the corridor with my flash, but didn't learn anything except that I had several doors to choose from. Holding the pick in front of me like some kind of magic wand, I started to move, half expecting the pick to start bucking in my hand and all hell to break loose.

But it didn't. I got to the first door and opened it. And found floor-cleaning equipment—electrostatic sweepers and whatnot. The night was cool—the building was cool—but I was sweating.

The next door was a linen closet. The next was a bathroom.

I gritted my teeth, trying to keep from talking out loud. Telling the tape decks what I was doing was already an old habit.

The next door was the one I wanted. It put me in a large room that smelled like a lab.

I shut the door behind me, too, and spent a long time just standing there, making sure I wasn't making any noise. Then I broadened the beam of my flash and spread it around the room.

Definitely a laboratory. At this end there were four large worktables covered with equipment: burners, microscopes, glassine apparatus of all kinds—I couldn't identify half that stuff. I couldn't identify the chemicals ranked along the shelves on this wall or figure out what was in the specimen bottles on the opposite side of the room (What the hell did Paracels need all this for?) But there was one thing I could identify.

A surgical laser.

It was so fancy it made the one in the surgery look like a toy.

When I saw it, something deep down in my chest started to shiver.

And that was only half the room. The other half was something else. When I was done checking over the lab equipment, I scanned the far end, and spotted the cremator.

It was set into the wall like a giant surgical sterilizer, but I knew what it was. I'd seen cremators before. This was just the largest one I'd ever come across. It looked big enough to hold a grizzly. Which was strange, because hunting preserves didn't usually have animals that size. Too expensive to replace.

But almost immediately I saw something stranger. In front of the cremator stood a gurney that looked like a hospital cart. On it was a body, covered with a sheet. From what I could see, it looked like the body of a man.

I didn't run over to it. Instead, I forced myself to locate all the doors into the lab. There were four—two opposite each other at each end of the room. So no matter what I did I was going to have to turn my back on at least one of them.

But there was nothing I could do about that. I went to the door across from me and put my ear to it for a long minute, listening as hard as I knew how, trying to tell if anything was happening on the other side. Then I went to the other two doors and did the same thing. But all I heard was the thudding of my heart. If Sharon's Point was using sound-sensor alarms instead of field scanners, I was in big trouble.

I didn't hear anything. But still my nerves were strung as tight as a cat's as I went over to the gurney. I think I was holding my breath.

Under the sheet I found a dead man. He was naked, and I could see the bullet holes in his chest as plain as day. There were a lot of them. Too many. He looked as if he'd walked into a machine gun. But it must have happened a while ago. His skin was cold, and he was stiff, and there was no blood.

Now I understood why Ushre and Paracels needed a cremator. They couldn't very well send bodies to the next of kin looking like this.

For a minute I just stood there, thinking I was right, Sharon's Point used people instead of animals, people hunting people.

Then all the lights in the lab came on, and I almost collapsed in surprise and panic.

Avid Paracels stood in the doorway where I'd entered the lab. His hand was still on the light switch. He didn't look like he'd even been to bed. He was still wearing his white coat, as if it was the most natural thing in the world for him to be up in his lab at 1 A.M. Well, maybe it was. Somehow that kind of light made him look solider, even more dangerous.

And he wasn't surprised. Not him. He was looking right at me as if we were both keeping some kind of appointment.

For the first couple heartbeats I couldn't seem to think anything except, Well, so much for technology. They have some other kind of alarm system.

Then Paracels started talking. His thin old voice sounded almost smug. "Ushre spotted you right away," he said. "We knew you would come back tonight. You're investigating us."

For some strange reason, that statement made me feel better. My pick hadn't failed me after all. My equipment was still reliable. Maybe I was better adjusted to being a cyborg than I thought. Paracels was obviously unarmed—and I had my blaster. There was no way on God's green earth he could stop me from using it. My pulse actually began to feel like it was getting back to normal.

"So what happens now?" I asked. I was trying for bravado. Special Agents are supposed to be brave. "Are you going to kill me?"

Paracels's mood seemed to change by the second. Now he was bitter again. "I answered that question this morning," he snapped. "I'm a doctor. I don't take lives."

I shrugged, then gestured toward the gurney. "That's probably a real comfort to him." I wanted to goad the good doctor.

But he didn't seem to hear me. Already he was back to smug. "A good specimen." He smirked. "His genes should be very useful."

"He's dead," I said. "What good're dead genes?"

Paracels almost smiled. "Parts of him aren't dead yet. Did you know that? Some part of him won't die for two more days. After that we'll burn him." The tip of his tongue came out and drew a neat line of saliva around his lips.

Probably that should've warned me. But I was concentrating on him the wrong way. I was watching him as if he was the only thing I had to worry about. I didn't hear the door open behind me at all. All I heard was one last quick step. Then something hit the back of my head and switched off the world.

5

Which just goes to show that being a cyborg isn't everything it's cracked up to be. Cyborgs are in trouble as soon as they do start adjusting to what they are. They don't rely on themselves anymore—they rely on their equipment. Then when they're in a situation where they need something besides a blaster, they don't have it.

Two years ago there wasn't a man or animal that could sneak up behind me. The hunting preserves taught me how to watch my back. The animals didn't know I was on their side, and they were hungry. I had to watch my back to stay alive. Apparently not any more. Now I was Sam Browne, Special—

Agent—cyborg—hotshot. As far as I could tell, I was as good as dead.

My hands were taped behind my back, and I was lying on my face in something that used to be mud before it dried, and the sun was slowly cooking me. When I cranked my eyes open, all I could see was brush a few cm. from my nose. A long time seemed to pass before I could get up the strength to focus my eyes and lift my head. Then I saw I was lying on a dirt path that ran through a field of low bushes. Beyond the bushes were trees.

All around me there was a faint smell of blood. My blood. From the back of my head.

Which hurt like a sonofabitch. I put my face back down in the dirt. I would've done some cursing, but I didn't have the strength. I knew what had happened.

Ushre and Paracels had trussed me up and dropped me off in the middle of their preserve. Smelling like blood. They weren't going to kill me—not them. I was just going to be another one of their dead hunters.

Well, at least I was going to find out who was hunting what (or whom) around here.

Minutes passed before I mustered enough energy to find out if my legs were taped, too. They weren't. How very sporting. I wondered if it was Ushre's idea or Paracels's.

That hit on the head must've scrambled my brains (the pain was scrambling them for sure). I spent what felt like ages trying to figure out who was responsible for leaving my legs free, when I should've been pulling myself together. Getting to my feet. Trying to find some water to wash off the blood. Thinking about staying alive. More time passed before I remembered I had a transceiver in my skull. I could call for help.

Help would take time. Probably it wouldn't come fast enough to save me. But I could at least call for it. It would guarantee that Sharon's Point got shut down. Ushre and Paracels would get murder one—mandatory death sentence. I could at least call.

My tongue felt like a sponge in my mouth, but I concentrated hard, and managed to find the transmission switch. Then I tried to talk. That took longer. I had to swallow several times to work up enough saliva to make a sound. But finally I did it. Out loud I said one of the Bureau's emergency code words.

Nothing happened.

Something was supposed to happen. That word was supposed to trigger the automatic monitors in the tape room. The monitors were supposed to put the duty room on emergency status. Instantly. Inspector Morganstark (or whoever was in charge) was supposed to come running. He was supposed to start talking to me (well, not actually talking—my equipment didn't receive voices. Only a modulated hum. But I knew how to read that hum). My transceiver was supposed to hum.

It didn't.

I waited, and it still didn't. I said my code word again, and it still didn't. I said all the code words, and it still didn't. I swore at it until I ran out of strength. Nothing.

Which told me (when I recovered enough to do more thinking) that my transceiver wasn't working. Wonderful. Maybe that hit on the head had broken it. Or maybe—

I made sure my right hand was behind my left. Then I tongued the switch that was supposed to fire my blaster.

Again nothing.

Twisting my right hand, I used those fingers to probe my left palm. My blaster was intact. The concealing membrane was still in place. The thing should've worked.

I was absolutely as good as dead.

Those bastards (probably Ushre, the electronics engineer) had found out how to turn off my power pack. They had turned me off.

That made a nasty kind of sense. Ushre and Paracels had already cremated one Special Agent. Probably that was where they had gotten their information. Kolcsz's power pack wouldn't have melted. With the thing right there in his hand, Ushre would've had an easy time making a magnetic probe to turn it off. All he had to do was experiment until he got it right.

What didn't make sense was the way I felt about it. Here I was, a disabled cyborg with his hands taped behind him, lying on his face in a hunting preserve that had already killed forty-five people—forty-six counting the man in Paracels's lab—and all of a sudden I began to feel like I knew what to do. I didn't feel turned off: I felt as if I was coming back to life. Strength began coming back into my muscles. My brain was clearing. I was getting ready to move.

I was going to make Ushre and Paracels pay for this.

Those bastards were so goddam self-confident, they hadn't even bothered to search me. I still had my knife. It was right there—my hands were resting on it.

What did they think the Bureau was going to do when the monitors found out my transceiver was dead? Just sit there on its ass and let Sharon's Point go its merry way?

I started to move, tried to get up. Which was something I should've done a long time ago. Or maybe it wouldn't have made any difference. That didn't matter now. By the time I got to my knees, it was already too late. I was in trouble.

Big trouble.

A rabbit came out of the brush a meter down the path from me. I thought he was a rabbit—he looked like a rabbit. An ordinary long-eared jackrabbit. Male—the males are a lot bigger than the females. Then he didn't look like a rabbit. His jaws were too big; he had the kind of jaws a dog has. His front paws were too broad and strong.

What the hell?

In his jaws he held a hand grenade, carrying it by the ring of the pin.

He didn't waste any time. He put the grenade down on the path and braced his paws on it. With a jerk of his head, he pulled the pin. Then he dashed back into the bushes.

I just kneeled there and stared at the damn thing. For the longest time all I could do was stare at it and think: That's a live grenade. They got it from the Procureton Arsenal.

In the back of my head a desperate voice was screaming: Move it, you sonofabitch!

I moved. Lurched to my feet, took a step toward the grenade, kicked it away from me. It skidded down the path. I didn't wait to see how far it went. I ran about two steps into the brush and threw myself flat. Any cover was better than nothing.

I landed hard, but that didn't matter. One second after I hit the ground, the grenade went off. It made a crumping noise like a demolition ram hitting concrete. Cast-iron fragments went ripping through the brush in all directions.

None of them hit me.

But it wasn't over. There were more explosions. A line of detonations came pounding up the path from where the grenade went off. The fourth one was so close the concussion flipped me over in the brush, and dirt rained on me. There were three more before the blasting stopped.

After that, the air was as quiet as a grave.

I didn't move for a long time. I stayed where I was, trying to act like I was dead and buried. I didn't risk even a twitch until I was sure my smell was covered by all the gelignite in the air. Then I pulled up the back of my shirt and slipped out my knife.

Getting my hands free was awkward, but the serrated edges of the blade helped, and I didn't cut myself more than a little bit. When I had the tape off, I eased up onto my hands and knees. Then I spent more time just listening, listening hard, trying to remember how I used to listen two years ago, before I got in the habit of depending on equipment.

I was in luck. There was a slow breeze. It was blowing past me across the path—which meant anything upwind couldn't smell me, and anything downwind would get too much gelignite to know I was there. So I was covered—sort of.

I crawled forward to take a look at the path.

The line of shallow craters—spaced about a half-dozen meters apart—told me what had happened. Antipersonnel mines. A string of them wired together buried in the path. The grenade set one of them off, and they all went up. The nearest one would have killed me if it hadn't been buried so deep. Fortunately the blast went upward instead of out to the sides.

I wiped the sweat out of my eyes and lay down where I was to do a little thinking.

A rabbit that wasn't a rabbit. A genetically altered rabbit, armed with munitions from the Procureton Arsenal.

No wonder Ushre and Paracels raised their own animals—the genes had to be altered when the animal was an embryo. No wonder they had a vet hospital. And a cremator. No wonder they kept their breeding pens secret. No wonder their rates were so high. No wonder they wanted to keep their clientele exclusive.

No wonder they wanted me dead.

All of a sudden, their confidence didn't surprise me anymore.

I didn't even consider moving from where I was. I wasn't ready. I wanted more information. I was as sure as hell rabbits weren't the only animals in the Sharon's Point Hunting Preserve. I figured those explosions would bring some of the others to me.

I was right sooner than I expected. By the time I had myself reasonably well hidden in the brush, I heard the soft flop of heavy paws coming down the path. Almost at once, two dogs were trotting by. At least they should've been dogs. They were big brown boxers, and at first glance the only thing unusual about them was they carried sacks slung over their shoulders.

But they stopped at the farthest mine crater, and I got a better look. Their shoulders were too broad and square, and instead of front paws they had hands—chimp hands, except for the strong claws.

They shrugged off their sacks, nosed them open. Took out half a dozen or so mines.

Working together with all the efficiency in the world, they put new mines in the old craters. They wired the mines together and attached the wires to a flat gray box that must have been the arming switch. They hid the wires and the box in the brush along the path (fortunately on the opposite side from me—I didn't want to try to fight them off). Then they filled in the craters, packing them down until just the vaguest discoloration of the dirt gave away where the mines were. When that was done, one of them armed the mines.

A minute later, they went gamboling away through the brush. They were actually playing with each other, jumping and rolling together as they made their way toward the far line of trees.

Fifteen minutes ago they'd tried to kill me. They'd just finished setting a trap to kill someone else. Now they were playing.

Which didn't have anything to do with them, of course. They were just dogs. They had new shoulders and new hands—and probably new brains (setting mines seemed a little bit much for ordinary boxers to me)—but they were just dogs. They didn't know what they were doing.

Ushre and Paracels knew.

All of a sudden, I was tired of being cautious. I was mad,

and I didn't want to do any more waiting around. My sense of direction told me those dogs were going the same way I wanted to go: toward the front gate of the preserve. When they were out of sight, I got up into a crouch. I scanned the field to make sure there was nothing around me. Then I dove over the path, somersaulted to my feet, and started to run. Covering the same ground the dogs did. They hadn't been blown up, so I figured I wouldn't be either. Everything ahead of me was upwind, so except for the noise nothing in those trees would know I was coming. I didn't make much noise.

In two minutes, I was into the trees and hiding under a rotten old log.

The air was a lot cooler in the shade, and I spent a little while just recovering from the heat of the sun and letting my eyes get used to the dimmer light. And listening. I couldn't tell much at first because I was breathing so hard, but before long I was able to get my hearing adjusted to the breeze and the woods. After that, I relaxed enough to figure out exactly what I meant to do.

I meant to get at Ushre and Paracels.

Fine. I wanted to do that. There was only one problem. First I had to stay alive.

If I wanted to stay alive, I had to have water. Wash the blood off. If I could smell me this easily, it was a sure bet every animal within fifty meters could, too.

I started hunting for a tree I could climb—a tree tall enough to give me a view out over these woods.

It took me half an hour because I was being so cautious, but finally I found what I needed. A tall straight ash. It didn't have any branches for the first six meters or so, but a tree nearby had fallen into it and stuck there, caught leaning in the lowest branches. By risking my neck, and not thinking too hard about what I was doing, I was able to shinny up that leaning trunk and climb into the ash.

With my left hand the way it was, I didn't have much of a grip, and I learned quickly enough that I wasn't going to be able to climb as high as I wanted. But just when I figured I'd gone about as far as I could go, I got lucky.

I spotted a stream. It was a couple of km. away past a meadow and another line of trees, cutting across between me and the front gate. Looked like exactly what I needed. If I could just get to it.

I didn't waste time worrying. I took a minute to fix the territory in my mind. Then I started back down the trunk.

My ears must've been improving. Before I was halfway to the ground (which I couldn't see because the leaves and branches were so thick), I heard something heading toward me through the trees.

Judging by the sound, whatever it was wasn't in any hurry, just moving across the branches in a leisurely way. But it was coming close. Too close.

I straddled a branch with my back to the trunk and braced my hands on the wood in front of me, and froze. I couldn't reach my knife that way, but I didn't want to. I couldn't picture myself doing any knife-fighting in a tree.

I barely got set in time. Three seconds later, there was a thrashing above me in the next tree over, and then a monkey landed maybe four meters away from me on the same branch.

He was a normal howler monkey—normal for Sharon's Point. Sturdy gray body, pitch-black face with deep gleaming eyes; a good bit bigger and stronger than a chimp. But he had those wide square shoulders, and hands that were too broad. He had a knapsack on his back.

And he was carrying an M-16 by the handle on top of the barrel.

He wasn't looking for me. He was just wandering. He was lonely. Howler monkeys live in packs; in his dumb instinctive way, he was probably looking for company—without knowing what he was looking for. He might've gone right on by without noticing me.

But when he hit the branch, the lurch made me move. Just a few cm.—but that was enough. It caught his attention. I should've had my eyes shut, but it was too late for that now. The howler knew I had eyes—he knew I was alive. In about five seconds he was going to know I smelled like blood.

He took the M-16 in both hands, tucked the stock into his shoulder, wrapped a finger around the trigger.

I stared back at him and didn't move a muscle.

What else could I do? I couldn't reach him—and if I could, I couldn't move fast enough to keep him from pulling the trigger. He'd cut me to pieces before I touched him. I wanted to plead with him, Don't shoot. I'm no threat to you. But he wouldn't understand. He was just a monkey. He would just shoot me.

I was so scared and angry I was afraid I was going to do something stupid. But I didn't. I just stared and didn't move.

The howler was curious. He kept his M-16 aimed at my chest, but he didn't shoot. I could detect no malice or cunning in his face. Slowly he came closer to me. He wanted to see what I was.

He was going to smell my blood soon, but I had to wait. I had to let him get close enough.

He kept coming. From four meters to three. To two. I thought I was going to scream. The muzzle of that rifle was lined up on my chest. It was all I could do to keep from looking at it, keep myself staring straight at the howler without blinking.

One meter.

Very, very slowly, I closed my eyes. See, howler. I'm no threat. I'm not even afraid. I'm going to sleep. How can you be afraid of me?

But he was going to be afraid of me. He was going to smell my blood.

I counted two heartbeats with my eyes closed. Then I moved.

With my right foot braced on the trunk under me, I swung my left leg hard, kicked it over the top of the branch. I felt a heavy jolt through my knee as I hit the howler.

Right then, he started to fire. I heard the rapid metal stuttering of the M-16 on automatic, heard .22 slugs slashing through the leaves. But I must have knocked him off balance. In that first fraction of a second, none of the slugs got me.

Then my kick carried me off the branch. I was falling.

I went crashing down through the leaves with M-16 fire swarming after me like hornets.

Three or four meters later, a stiff limb caught me across the chest. I saw it just in time, got my arms over it and grabbed it as it hit. That stopped me with a jerk that almost tore my arms off.

I wasn't breathing anymore, the impact knocked all the air out of me. But I didn't worry about it. I craned my neck, trying to see what the monkey was doing.

He was right above me on his branch, looking right at me. From there he couldn't have missed me to save his life.

But he wasn't firing. As slowly as if he had all the time in the world, he was taking the clip out of his rifle. He threw it away and reached back into his knapsack to get another one.

If I'd had a handgun or even a blaster, I could have shot him dead. He didn't even seem to know he was in danger, that it was dangerous for him to expose himself like that.

I didn't wait around for him to finish. Instead I swung my legs under the branch and let myself fall again.

This time I got lucky. For a second. My feet landed square on another branch. That steadied me, but I didn't try to stop. I took a running step down onto another branch, then jumped for another one.

That was the end of my luck. I lost my balance and fell. Probably would have broken my leg if I hadn't had those plastene struts along the bones. But I didn't have time to worry about that, either. I wasn't any more than ten meters off the ground now. There was only one branch left between me and a broken back, and it was practically out of reach.

Not quite. I got both hands on it.

But I couldn't grip with my left. The whip of my weight tore my right loose. I landed flat on my back at the base of the tree.

I didn't feel like the fall kicked the air out of me—I couldn't remember the last time I did any breathng anyway. But the impact didn't help my head much. I went blind for a while, and there was a long crashing noise in my ears, as if the only thing I was able to hear, was ever going to hear, was the sound of myself hitting the ground. I felt like I'd landed hard enough to bury myself. But I fought it. I needed air. Needed to see.

That howler probably had me lined up in his sights already.

I fought it.

Got my eyes back first. Felt like hours, but probably didn't take more than five seconds. I wanted to look up into the tree, try to locate the monkey, but something else snagged my attention.

A coughing noise.

It wasn't coming from me. I wasn't breathing at all. It was coming from somewhere off to my left.

I didn't have to turn my head much to look in that direction. It was practically no trouble at all. But right away I wished I hadn't done it.

I saw a brown bear. A big brown bear. He must've been ten meters or more away, and he was down on all fours, but he looked huge. Too huge. I couldn't fight anything like that. I couldn't even breathe.

He was staring at me. Must've seen me fall. Now he was trying to decide what to do. Probably trying to decide whether to claw my throat out or bite my face off. The only reason he hadn't done anything yet was that I wasn't moving.

But I couldn't keep that up. I absolutely couldn't help myself. I needed air. A spasm of carbon-dioxide poisoning clutched my chest, made me twitch. When I finally took a breath, I made a whooping noise I couldn't control.

Which told the bear everything he wanted to know about me. With a roar that might have made me panic if I hadn't already been more dead than alive, he reared up onto his hind legs, and I got a look at what Paracels had done to him.

He had hands instead of forepaws. Paracels certainly liked hands. They were good for handling weapons. The bear's hands were so humanlike I was sure Paracels must have got them from one of the dead hunters. They looked too small for the bear. I couldn't figure out how he was able to walk on them. But of course that wasn't too much of a problem for a bear. They were big enough for what Paracels had in mind.

Against his belly the bear had a furry pouch like a kangaroo's. As he reared up, he arched both hands into his pouch. When he brought them out again, he had an automatic in each fist. A pair of .22 Magnums.

He was going to blow my head off.

There was nothing I could do about it.

I had to do something about it. I didn't want to die. I was too mad to die.

Whatever it was I was going to do, I had about half a second to do it in. The bear hadn't cocked his automatics. It would take him half a second to pull the trigger far enough to get off his first shot—and that one wouldn't be very accurate. After that, the recoil of each shot would cock the gun for him. He'd be able to shoot faster and more accurately.

I flipped to my feet, then jumped backward, putting the tree between him and me.

I was too slow. He was firing before I reached my feet. But his first shots were wild, and after that I was moving. As I jerked backward, one of his bullets licked a shallow furrow across my chest. Then I was behind the tree. A half-dozen slugs chewed into the trunk, too fast for me to count them. He had ten rounds in each gun. I was stuck until he had to reload.

Before I had time to even wonder what I was going to do, the howler opened fire.

He was above me, perched on the leaning dead tree. He must've been there when I started to move.

With all that lead flying around, he took aim at the thing that was most dangerous to him and opened up.

Damn near cut the bear in half.

Nothing bothered his aim, and his target was stationary. In three seconds he emptied an entire clip into the bear's guts.

He didn't move from where he was. He looked absolutely tame, like a monkey in a zoo. Nothing could have looked tamer than he did as he sat there taking out his spent clip, throwing it away, reaching into his knapsack for a fresh one.

That was the end of him. His blast had knocked the bear backward until the bear was sitting on the ground with his hind legs stretched out in front of him, looking as human as any animal in the world. He was bleeding to death; he'd be dead in ten seconds. But bears generally are stubborn and bloody-minded, and this one was no exception. Before he died, he raised his guns and blew the howler away.

I didn't spend any time congratulating myself for being alive. All that shooting was going to draw other animals, and I was in no shape to face them. I was bleeding from that bullet furrow, the back of my head, and a half-dozen other cuts and scrapes. And the parts of me that weren't bleeding were too bruised to be much good. I turned and shambled away as quietly as I could in the direction of the stream.

I didn't get far. Reaction set in, and I had to hide myself in the best cover I could find and just be sick for a while.

Sick with anger.

I was starting to see the pattern of this preserve. These animals were nothing but cannon fodder. They were as deadly

as could be—and at the same time they were so tame they
didn't know how to run away. That's right: *tame*. Because of
their training.

Genetic alteration wasn't enough. First the animals had to
be taught how to use their strange appendages. Then they had
to be taught how to use their weapons, and finally they had to
be taught not to use their weapons on their trainers or on each
other. That mix-up between the bear and the howler was an
accident; the bear just happened to be shooting too close to
the monkey. They had to be taught not to attack each other
every chance they got. Paracels probably boosted their brain-
power, but they still had to be taught. Otherwise they'd just
butcher each other. Dogs and rabbits, bears and dogs—they
don't usually leave each other alone.

With one hand, Paracels gave them guns, mines, grenades;
with the other, he took away their instincts for flight, self-
preservation, even feeding themselves. They were crippled
worse than a cyborg with his power turned off. They were
deadly—but they were still crippled. Probably Paracels or
Ushre or any of the handlers could walk the preserve end to
end without being in any danger.

That was why I was so mad.

Somebody had to stop those bastards.

I wanted that somebody to be me.

I knew how to do it now. I understood what was happening
in this preserve. I knew how it worked; I knew how to get out
of it. Sharon's Point was unnatural in more ways than one.
Maybe I could take advantage of one of those ways. If I
could just find what I needed.

If I was going to do it, I had to do it now. Noon was
already past, and I had to find what I was looking for before
evening. And before some animal hunted me down. I stank of
blood.

My muscles were queasy, but I made them carry me.
Sweating and trembling, I did my damnedest to sneak through
the woods toward the stream without giving myself away.

It wasn't easy, but after what I'd been through, nothing
could be easy. I spent a while looking for tracks—and even
that was hard. After all the rain, the ground was still soft
enough to hold tracks, but I had trouble getting my eyes

focused enough to see them. Sweat made all my scrapes and
wounds feel like they were on fire.

But the only absolutely miserable trouble I had was crossing the meadow. Never mind the danger of exposing myself
out in the open. I was worried about mines. And rabbits with
hand grenades. I had to stay low, pick my way with terrible
care. I had to keep off bare ground, and grass that was too
thin (grass with a mine under it was likely to be thin), and
grass that was too thick (rabbits might be hiding there). For a
while I didn't think I was ever going to make it.

After that, the outcome was out of my hands. I was
attacked again. At the last second, my ears warned me: I
heard something cutting across the breeze. I fell to the side—
and a hawk went whizzing past where my head had been. I
didn't get a very good look at it, but there was something
strange about its talons. They looked a lot like fangs.

A hawk with poisoned talons?

It circled above me and poised for another dive, but I
didn't wait around for it. A rabbit with a grenade probably
couldn't hit a running target. And if I touched a mine, I was
better off moving fast—or so I told myself. I ran like hell for
the line of trees between me and the stream.

The hawk's next dive was the worst. I misjudged it. If I
hadn't tripped, the bird would have had me. But the next time
I was more careful. It didn't get within a meter of me.

Then I reached the trees. I stopped there, froze as well as I
could and still gasp for breath. After a while the hawk went
barking away in frustration.

When I got up the nerve to move again, I scanned the area
for animals. Didn't spot any. But on the ground I found what
looked like a set of deer tracks. I didn't even try to think
about what kind of alterations Paracels might have made in a
deer. I didn't want to know. They were like the few tracks I'd
seen back in the woods; they came toward me from the left
and went away to the right. Downstream.

That was what I wanted to know. If I was wrong, I was
dead.

I didn't wait much longer—just long enough to choose
where I was going to put my feet. Then I went down to the
stream. There was a small pool nearby, and I slid into it until
I was completely submerged.

I stayed there for the better part of an hour. Spent a while just soaking—lying in the pool with my face barely out of water—trying to get back my strength. Then with my knife I cut away my clothes wherever I was hurt. But I didn't use the cloth for bandages; I had other ideas. After my wounds had bled clean and the bleeding had stopped, I eased partway out of the water and set about covering myself with mud.

I didn't want to look like a man and smell like blood; I wanted to look and smell like mud. The mud under the banks was just right—it was thick and black, and it dried fast. When I was done, my eyes, mouth, and hands were the only parts of me that weren't caked with mud.

The solution wasn't perfect, but mud was the best camouflage I was likely to find. And it would keep me from bleeding some more, at least for a while. As soon as I felt up to it, I started to work my way downstream along the bank.

My luck held. Nothing was following my track out of the woods. Probably all that blood around the dead bear and monkey was enough to cover me, keep any other animals from recognizing the man-blood smell and nosing around after me. But other than that I was in as much trouble as ever. I wasn't exactly strong on my feet. And I was running out of time. I had to find what I was looking for before evening. Before the animals came down to the stream to drink.

Before feeding time.

I didn't know how far I had to go, or even if I was going in the right direction. And I didn't like being out in the open. So I pushed myself pretty hard until I got out of the meadow. But when the stream ran back into some woods, I had to be more careful. I suppose I should have been grateful I didn't have to make my way through a swamp, but I wasn't. I was too busy trying to watch for everything and still keep going. Half the time I had to fight myself to stay alert. And half the time I had to fight myself to move at all.

But I found what I was looking for in time. For once I was right. It was just exactly where it should have been.

In a clearing in the trees. The woods around it were thick and tall, so it would be hard to spot—except from the air. Paracels and Ushre certainly didn't want their hunters to do what I was doing. The stream ran along one edge. And the bottom had been leveled. So a hovercraft could land.

Except for the landing area, the clearing was practically crowded with feeding troughs of all kinds.

Probably there were several places like this around the preserve. Sharon's Point needed them to survive. The animals were trained not to hunt each other. But that kind of training wouldn't last very long if they got hungry. Animals can't be trained to just let themselves starve. So Ushre and Parcels had to feed their animals. Regularly. At places like this.

Now the only question remaining was how soon the 'craft would come. It had to come—most of the troughs were empty. But if it came late—if the clearing had time to fill up before it got here—I wouldn't have a chance.

But it wasn't going to do me any good to worry about it. I worked my way around the clearing to where the woods were closest to the landing area. Then I picked a tree with bark about the same color as my mud, sat down against it, and tried to get some rest.

What I got was lucky—one last piece of luck to save my hide. Sunset was still a good quarter of an hour away when I began to hear the big fan of the 'craft whirring in the distance.

I didn't move. I wasn't all that lucky. Some animals were already in the clearing. A big whitetail buck was drinking at the stream, and a hawk was perched on one of the troughs. Out of the corner of my eye I could see two boxers (probably the same two I'd seen before) sitting and waiting, their tongues hanging out, not more than a dozen meters off to my left. Hidden where I was, I was practically invisible. But if I moved, I was finished.

At least there weren't very many of them. Yet.

I almost sighed out loud when the 'craft came skidding past the treetops. Gently it lined itself up and settled down onto the landing area.

Now time was all against me. Every animal in this sector of the preserve had heard the 'craft coming, and most of them would already be on their way to supper. But I couldn't just run down to the 'craft and ask for a ride. If the handler didn't shoot me himself, he'd take off, leaving me to the mercy of the animals. I gripped myself and didn't move.

The handler was taking his own sweet time.

As he moved around in the cockpit, I saw he was wearing a heavy gray jumpsuit. Probably all the handlers—as well as

Ushre and Paracels when they worked with the animals—wore the same uniform. It provided good protection, and the animals could recognize it. Furthermore it probably had a characteristic smell the animals had been taught to associate with food and friends. So the man was pretty much safe. The animals weren't going to turn on him.

Finally he started heaving sacks and bales out onto the ground: hay and grain for the deer, chow for the dogs, fruit for the monkey—things like that. When he was finished emptying his cockpit, he jumped out of the 'craft to put the food in the troughs.

I still waited. I waited until the dogs ran out into the clearing. I waited until the hawk snatched a piece of meat and flew away. I waited until the handler picked up a sack of grain and carried it off toward some of the troughs farthest away from the 'craft (and me).

Then I ran.

The buck saw me right away and jumped back. But the dogs didn't. The man didn't. He was looking at the buck. I was halfway to the 'craft before the dogs spotted me.

After that, it was a race. I had momentum and a headstart; the boxers had speed. They didn't even waste time barking; they just came right for me.

They were too fast. They were going to beat me.

In the last three meters, they were between me and the 'craft. The closest one sprang at me, and the other was right behind.

I ducked to the side, slipped the first dog past my shoulder. I could hear his jaws snap as he went by, but he missed.

The second dog I chopped as hard as I could across the side of the head with the edge of my left fist. The weight of my blaster gave that hand a little extra clout. I must have stunned him, because he fell and was slow getting up.

I saw that out of the corner of my eye. By the time I finished my swing, I was already sprinting toward the 'craft again. It wasn't more than three running steps away. But I could hear the first dog coming at me again. I took one of those steps, then hit the dirt.

The boxer went over and cracked into the bulging side of the 'craft.

Two seconds later, I was in the cockpit.

The handler had a late start, but once he got going, he didn't waste any time. When I landed in the cockpit, he was barely five meters away. I knew how to fly a hovercraft, and he'd made it easy for me—he'd left it idling. All I had to do was rev up the fan and tighten the wind convector until I lifted off. But he was jumping at me by the time I started to rise. He got his hands on the edge of the cockpit. Then I yanked him up into the air.

The jerk took his feet out from under him, so he was just hanging there by his hands.

Just to be sure he'd be safe, I rubbed a hand along the arm of his jumpsuit, then smelled my hand. It smelled like creosote.

I leveled off at about three meters. Before he could heave himself up into the cockpit, I banged his hands a couple of times with my heavy left fist. He fell and hit the ground pretty hard.

But a second later he was on his feet and yelling at me. "Stop!" he shouted. "Come back!" He sounded desperate. "You don't know what you're doing!"

"You'll be all right," I shouted back. "You can walk out of here by tomorrow morning. Just don' step on any mines."

"No!" he cried, and for a second he sounded so terrified I almost went back for him. "You don't know Ushre! You don't know what he'll do! He's crazy!"

But I thought I had a pretty good idea what Fritz Ushre was capable of. It didn't surprise me at all to hear someone say he was crazy—even someone who worked for him. And I didn't want the handler along with me. He'd get in my way.

I left him. I gunned the 'craft up over the trees and sent it skimming in the direction of the front gate. Going to give Ushre and Paracels what I owed them.

6

But I didn't let myself think about that. I was mad enough already. I didn't want to get all livid and careless. I wanted to be calm and quick and precise. More dangerous than anything Paracels ever made—or ever even dreamed about making. Because I was doing something that was too important to have room for miscalculations.

Well, important to me, anyway. Probably nobody in the world but me (and Morganstark) gave a rusty damn what was happening at Sharon's Point—just as long as the animals didn't get loose. But that's what Special Agents are for. To care about things like this, so other people don't have to.

But I didn't have to talk myself into anything; I knew what I was going to do. The big thing I had to worry about was the lousy shape I was in. I was giddy with hunger and woozy with fatigue and queasy with pain, and I kept having bad patches where I couldn't seem to make the 'craft fly straight, or even level.

The darkness didn't improve my flying any. The sun went down right after I left the clearing, and by the time I was halfway to the front gate evening had turned into night. I suppose I should've been grateful for the cover: when I finally got to the gate, my bad flying probably wouldn't attract any attention. But I wasn't feeling grateful about much of anything right then. In the dark I had to fly by my instruments, and I wasn't doing a very good job of it. Direction I could handle (sort of), and I already had enough altitude to get me over the hills. But the little green dial that showed the artificial horizon seemed to have a life of its own; it wouldn't sit still long enough for me to get it into focus. I spent the whole trip yawing back and forth like a drunk.

But I made it. My aim wasn't too good (when I finally spotted the bright pink freon bulb at the landing area, it was way the hell off to my left), but it was good enough. I went skidding over there until I was sitting almost on top of the light, but then I took a couple minutes to scan the area before I put the 'craft down.

I suppose what I should've done was not land there at all. I should've just gone until I got someplace where I could call the Bureau for help. But I figured if I did that Ushre and Paracels would get away. They'd know something was wrong when their hovercraft didn't come back, and they'd be on the run before the Bureau could do anything about it. Then the Bureau would be hunting them for days—and I'd miss out on the finish of my own assignment. I wasn't about to let that happen.

So I took a good look below me before I landed. Both the other 'craft were there (they must've had shorter feeding

336 Stephen R. Donaldson

runs), but nobody was standing around outside—at least not where I could see them. Most of the windows of the barracks showed light, but the office complex was dark—except for the front office and the laboratory wing.

Ushre and Paracels.

If they stayed where they were, I could go in after them, get them out to the 'craft—take them into St. Louis myself. If I caught them by surprise. And didn't run into anybody else. And didn't crack up trying to fly the 300 km. to St. Louis.

I didn't even worry about it. I put the 'craft down as gently as I could and threw it into idle. Before the fan even had time to slow down, I jumped out of the cockpit and went pelting as fast as I could go toward the front office.

Yanked open the door, jumped inside, shut it behind me. Stopped.

Fritz Ushre was standing behind the counter. He must have been doing some work with his ac-computer; he had the console in front of him. His face was white, and his little boar eyes were staring at me as if I'd just come back from the dead. He didn't even twitch—he looked paralyzed with surprise and fear.

"Fritz Ushre," I said with my own particular brand of malice, "you're under arrest for murder, attempted murder, and conspiracy." Then, just because it felt good, I went on, "You have the right to remain silent. If you choose to speak, anything you say can and will be used against you in a court of law. You have the right to be represented by an attorney. If you can't afford one—"

He wasn't listening. There was a struggle going on in his face that didn't have anything to do with what I was saying. For once, he looked too surprised to be cunning, too beaten to be malicious. He was trying to fight it, but he wasn't getting anywhere. He was trying to find a way out, a way to get rid of me, save himself, and there wasn't any. Sharon's Point was dead, and he knew it.

Or maybe it wasn't. Maybe there was a way out. All of a sudden the struggle was over. He met my eyes, and the expression on his face was more naked and terrible than anything he'd ever let me see before. It was hunger. And glee.

He looked down. Reached for something under the counter.

I was already moving, throwing myself at him. I got my hands on the edge of the counter, vaulted over it, hit him square in the chest with both heels.

He smacked against the wall behind him, bounced back, stumbled to his knees. I fell beside him. But I was up before he could move. In almost the same movement, I got my knife out and pressed the point against the side of his fat neck. "If you make a sound," I said, panting, "I'll bleed you right here."

He didn't act like he heard me. He was coughing for air. And laughing.

Quickly, I looked around behind the counter to find what he'd been reaching for.

For a second I couldn't figure it out. There was an M-16 lying on a shelf off to one side, but that wasn't it—he hadn't been reaching in that direction.

Then I saw it. A small gray box built into the counter near where he'd been standing. It wasn't much—just a big red button and a little red light. The little red light was on.

Right then, I realized I was hearing something. Something so high-pitched it was almost inaudible. Something keen and carrying.

I'd heard something like it before, but at first I couldn't remember where. Then I had it.

An animal whistle.

It was pitched almost out of the range of human hearing, but probably there wasn't an animal in 10 km. that couldn't hear it. Or didn't know what it meant.

I put my knife away and picked up the M-16. I didn't have time to be scrupulous; I cocked it and pointed it at Ushre's head. "Turn it off," I said.

He was just laughing now. Laughing softly. "You cannot turn it off. Once it has been activated, nothing can stop it."

I got out my knife again, tore the box out of the counter, cut the wires. He was right. The red light went off, but the sound didn't stop.

"What does it do?"

He was absolutely shaking with suppressed hilarity. "Guess!"

I jabbed him with the muzzle of the M-16. "What does it do?"

He didn't stop shaking. But he turned to look at me. His eyes were bright and wild and mad. "You will not shoot me." He almost giggled. "You are not the type."

Well, he was right about that, too. I wasn't even thinking about killing him. I wanted information. I made a huge effort to sound reasonable. "Tell me anyway. I can't stop it, so why not?"

"Ah," he sighed. He liked that idea. "May I stand?"

I let him get to his feet.

"Much better," he said. "Thank you, Mr. Browne."

After that, I don't think I could've stopped him from telling me. He enjoyed it too much. He was manic with glee. Some sharp appetite maybe he didn't even know he had was about to get fed.

"Dr. Paracels may be old and unbalanced," he said, "but he is brilliant in his way. And he has a taste for revenge. He has developed his genetic techniques to the point of precise control.

"As you may know, Mr. Browne, all animals may be conditioned to perform certain actions upon certain signals— even human animals. The more complex the brain of the animal, the more complex the actions which may be conditioned into it—but also the more complex and difficult the conditioning process. For human animals, the difficulty of the process is often prohibitive."

He relished what he was saying so much he was practically slobbering. I wanted to scream with frustration, but I forced the impulse down. I had to hear what he was saying, needed to hear it all.

"Dr. Paracels—bless his retributive old heart—has learned how to increase animal brain capacity enough to make possible a very gratifying level of conditioning without increasing it enough to make conditioning unduly difficult. That provides the basis for the way in which we train our animals. But it serves one other purpose also.

"Each of our animals has been keyed to that sound." He gestured happily at the air. "They have been conditioned to respond to that sound in a certain way. With violence, Mr. Browne!" He was bubbling over with laughter. "But not against each other. Oh no—that would never do. They have

been conditioned to attack humans, Mr. Browne—to come to
the source of the sound and then attack.

"Even our handlers are not immune. This conditioning
overrides all other training. Only Dr. Paracels and myself are
safe. All our animals have been imprinted with our voices, so
that even in their most violent frenzies they will recognize us.
And obey us, Mr. Browne. Obey us!"

I was shaking as bad as he was, but for different reasons.
"So what?" I demanded. "They can't get past the fence."

"Past the fence?" Ushre was ecstatic. "You fool! The gate
is open! It opened automatically when I pressed the button."

So finally I knew what that handler back in the preserve
had been so scared about. Ushre was letting the animals out.
Out to terrorize the countryside until God knew how many
people were killed trying to hunt them down. Or just trying to
get away from them. Or even just sitting at home minding
their own business.

I had to stop those animals.

With just an M-16? Fat chance!

But I had to try. I was a Special Agent, wasn't I? This was
my job. I'd signed up for it of my own free will.

I rammed the muzzle of the M-16 hard into Ushre's stomach. He doubled over. I grabbed his collar and yanked his
head up again.

"Listen to me," I said very softly. "I didn't used to be the
type to shoot people in cold blood, but I am now. I'm mad
enough to do it now. Get moving."

I made him believe me. When I gave him a shove, he went
where I wanted him to go. Toward the front door.

He opened it, and we went out together into the night.

I could see the front gates clearly in the light from the
landing area. He was absolutely right. They were open.

I was already too late to close them. A dark crowd of
animals was already coming out of the preserve. They bris-
tled with weapons. They didn't hurry, didn't make any noise,
didn't get in each other's way. And more came over the ridge
every second, moving like they were on their way out of Fritz
Ushre's private hell. In the darkness they looked practically
numberless. For one dizzy second I couldn't believe Ushre
and Paracels had had time to engineer so many helpless
creatures individually. But of course they'd been working at

it for years. Sharon's Point must have been almost completely
stocked when they opened for business. And since then they'd
had twenty months to alter and raise even more animals.

I had to move fast. I had one gamble left, and if it didn't
work I was just going to be the first on a long list of people
who were going to die.

I gave Ushre a shove that sent him stumbling forward.

Out in front of that surging crowd. Between them and the
road.

Before he could try to get away, I caught up with him,
grabbed his elbow, jabbed the M-16 into his ribs. "Now, Mr.
Ushre," I said through my teeth. "You're going to tell them
to go back. Back through the gates. They'll obey you."
When he didn't respond, I gouged him viciously. "Tell
them!"

Well, it was a good idea. Worth a try. It might even have
worked—if I could've controlled Ushre. But he was out of
control. He was crazy for blood now, completely bananas.

"Tell them to go back?" he cried with a laugh. "Are you
joking?" There was blood in his voice—blood and power.
"These beasts are mine! Mine! My will commands them!
They will rain bloodshed upon the country! They will destroy
you, and all people like you. I will teach you what hunting
truly means, Mr. Browne!" He made my name sound like a
deadly insult. "I will teach you to understand death!"

"You'll go first!" I shouted, trying to cut through his
madness. "I'll blow you to pieces where you stand."

"You will not!"

He was faster than I expected. Much faster. With one
quick swing of his massive arm, he smacked me to the
ground.

"Kill him!" he howled at the animals. He was waving his
fists as if he was conducting an orchestra of butchery. "Kill
them all!"

A monkey near the front of the crowd fired, and all of a
sudden Ushre's hell erupted.

All the animals that had clear space in front of them started
shooting at once. M-16 and .22 Magnum fire shattered the
air; bullets screamed wildly in all directions. The night was
full of thunder and death. I couldn't understand why I wasn't
being hit.

Then I saw why.

Two thin beams of ruby-red light were slashing back and forth across the front of that dark surge of animals. The animals weren't shooting at me. They were firing back at those beams.

Laser cannon!

I spotted one of them in the woods off to one side of the landing area. The other was blazing away from a window of the barracks.

They were cutting the animals to shreds. Flesh and blood can't stand up against laser cannon, no matter what kind of genes it has. Monkeys and bears were throwing sheets of lead back at the beams, but they were in each other's way, and most of their shooting was wild. And the people operating the cannon were shielded. It was just slaughter, that's all.

Because the animals couldn't run away. They didn't know how. They were conditioned. They reminded me of a tame dog that can't even try to avoid an angry master. But instead of cringing they were shooting.

The outcome wasn't any kind of sure thing. The animals were getting cut down by the dozens—but all they needed was a few hand grenades, or maybe a couple mines in the right places, and that would be the end of the cannon. And the dogs, for one, didn't have to be told what to do. Already they were trying to get through the fire with mines in their jaws. The lasers had to draw in their aim to get the dogs, and that gave the other animals time to spread out, get out of direct range of the lasers.

It was going to be a long, bloody battle. And I was lying in the dirt right in the middle of it. I didn't know how I was going to live through it.

I don't know how Ushre lasted even that long. He was on his feet, wasn't even trying to avoid getting hit. But nothing touched him. There must've been a charm of madness on his life. Roaring and laughing, he was on his way to the hover-craft. A minute later he climbed into the one I had so conveniently left idling.

I wanted to run after him, but I didn't get the chance. Before I could move, a rabbit went scrambling past and practically hit me in the face with a live grenade.

I didn't stop to think about it. I didn't have time to ask

342 Stephen R. Donaldson

myself what I was doing. I didn't want to ask. All those dogs
and deer and rabbits and God knows what else were getting
butchered, and I'd already gone more than a little bit crazy
myself.

I picked up the grenade and threw it. Watched it land
beside Ushre in the cockpit of the craft.

Blow him apart.

The 'craft would've gone up in flames if it hadn't been
built around a power pack like the one that wasn't doing me
any good.

I just turned my back on it.

The next minute, a man came running out of the barracks.
He dodged frantically toward me, firing his blaster in front of
him as he ran. Then he landed on his stomach beside me.

Morganstark.

"You all right?" he panted. He had to stop blasting to
talk, but he started up again right away.

"Yes!" I shouted to make myself heard. "Where did you
come from?"

"Your transceiver went off!" he shouted back. "Did you
think I was going to just sit on my hands and wait for your
death certificate?" He fired a couple bursts, then added,
"We've got the handlers tied up in the barracks, but there's
one missing. Who was that you just blew up?"

I didn't tell him. I didn't have time. I didn't want Paracels
to get away.

What I wanted was to tell Morganstark to stop the killing. I
was going wild, seeing all those animals die. But I didn't say
anything about it. What choice did Morganstark have? Let
Paracels's fine creations go and wreak havoc around the
countryside? No, I was going to have to live with all this
blood. It was my doing as much as anybody else's. If I'd
done my job right, Ushre would never have gotten a chance
to push that button. If I'd killed him right away. Or if I
hadn't confronted him at all. If I'd let that handler back in the
preserve tell me what he was afraid of.

"Get those gates shut!" I yelled at Morganstark. "I'm
going after Paracels!"

He didn't have a chance to stop me. I was already on my
feet, running and dodging toward the office door.

I took the M-16 with me. I thought it was about time Dr. Avid Paracels had one of these things pointed at him.

7

I don't know how I made it. I was moving low and fast—I wasn't very easy to see, much less hit. And I had only about twenty meters to go. But the air was alive with fire. Bullets were ripping all around me. Morganstark and his men were answering with lasers and blasters. Ushre must not have been the only one with a charm on him. Five seconds later, I dove through the open doorway, and there wasn't a mark on me. Nothing new, anyway.

Inside the complex, I didn't slow down. It was a sure thing Paracels knew what was happening—he could hear the noise if nothing else. So he'd be trying to make some kind of escape. I had to stop him before he got out into the night. He was the only one left who could stop the slaughter.

But I was probably too late. He'd had plenty of time to disappear; it wouldn't take much at night in these hills. I ran like a crazy man down the corridor toward the surgery—like I wasn't exhausted and hurt and sick, and didn't even know what fear was. Slammed into the clinic, scanned it. But Paracles wasn't there. I went on, hunting for a way into the lab wing.

A couple of corridors took me in the right direction. Then I was in one of those spots where I had several doors to choose from and no way to tell which was right. Again. But now I was going things by instinct—things I couldn't have done if I'd been thinking about them. I knew where I was in the building and had a relative idea where the lab was. I went straight to one of the doors, stopped. Touched the knob carefully.

It was unlocked.

I threw it open and stormed in.

He was there.

I'd come in through a door near the cremator. He was across the room from me, standing beside the lab tables. He didn't look like he'd even changed his clothes since last night—he didn't look like he had enough life in him to make the effort. In the bright white lights he looked like death. He should not have even been able to stand up, looking like that. But he was standing up. He was moving around. He wasn't hurrying, but he wasn't wasting any time, either. He was packing lab equipment into a big black satchel.

He glanced at me when I came in, but he didn't stop what he was doing. Taking everything he could fit in his bag.

I had the M-16 tucked under my right elbow and braced with my left hand. My index finger was on the trigger. Not the best shooting position, but I wasn't likely to miss at this range.

"They're getting butchered," I said. My voice shook, but I couldn't help it. "You're going to stop it. You're going to tell me how to shut down that goddam whistle. Then you're going to go out there with me, and you're going to order them back into the preserve."

Paracels glanced at me again, but didn't stop what he was doing.

"You're going to do it *now!*"

He almost smiled. "Or else?" Every time I saw him he seemed to have a different voice. Now he sounded calm and confident, like a man who'd finally arrived at a victory he'd been working toward for years, and he was mocking me.

"Or else," I hissed at him, trying to make him feel my anger, "I'll drag you out there and let them shoot you themselves."

"I don't think so." I wasn't making any kind of dent in him. He surprised me when he went on. "But part of that I was going to do anyway. I don't want too many of my animals killed." He moved to the far wall, flipped something that looked like a light switch. All at once, the high-pitched pressure of the whistles burst like a bubble and was gone.

Then he really did smile—a grin that looked as if he'd learned it from Ushre. "Ushre probably told you it couldn't be shut off. And you believed him." He shook his head. "He wanted to make it that way. But I made him put a switch in here. He isn't very farsighted."

"Wasn't," I said. I don't know why. I didn't have any intention of bandying words with Dr. Avid Paracels. But something changed for me when the whistle stopped. I lost a lot of my urgency. Now the animals would stop coming, and

Morganstark would be able to get the gates closed. Soon the killing would be over. All at once I realized how tired I was. I hurt everywhere.

And there was something else. Something about the good doctor didn't fit. I had a loaded M-16 aimed right at him. He didn't have any business being so sure of himself. I said, "He's dead. I killed him." Trying to shake his confidence.

It didn't work. He had something going for him I didn't know about—something made him immune to me. All he did was shrug and say, "I'm not surprised. He wasn't very stable."

He was so calm about it I wanted to start shooting at him. But I didn't. I didn't want to kill him. I wanted to make him talk. It took a real effort, but I asked him as casually as I could, "Did you know what you were getting into when you started doing business with him?"

"Did I know?" He snorted. "I counted on it. I knew I could handle him. He was perfect for me. He offered me exactly what I was looking for—a chance to do some research." For an instant there was something in his eyes that almost looked like a spark of life. "And a chance to pay a few debts."

"The genetic riots," I said. "You lost your job."

"I lost my career!" All of a sudden he was mad, furious. "I lost my whole future! My life! I was on my way to things you couldn't even imagine. Recombinant DNA was just the beginning, just the first step. By now I would have been able to synthesize genes. I would've been making supermen! Think about it. Geniuses smart enough to run the country decently for a change. Smart enough to crack the speed of light. Smart enough to create life. A whole generation of people that were immune to disease. People who could adapt to whatever in food or climate the future holds. Astronauts who didn't need pressure suits. I could have done it!"

"But there were riots," I said softly.

"They should have been put down. The government should have shot anybody who objected. What I was doing was too important.

"But they didn't. They blamed the riots on me. They said I violated the sanctity of life. They sent me out in disgrace. By the time they were finished, I couldn't get a legitimate research grant to save my life."

"That's why you want revenge," I said. Keep talking, Paracels. Tell me what I need to know.

"Retribution." He loved the sound of that word. "When I'm done, they're going to beg me to let them give me whatever I want."

I tried to steer him where I wanted him to go. "How're you going to accomplish that? So far all you've done is kill a few hunters. That isn't exactly going to topple the government."

"Ah"—he grinned again—"but this is just the beginning. In about two minutes, I'm going to leave here. They won't be able to find me—they won't know where I've gone. By the time they find out, I'll be ready for them."

I shook my head. "I don't understand."

"Of course you don't understand!" He was triumphant. "You spent the whole day in my preserve and you still don't understand. You aren't able to understand."

I was afraid he was going to stop then, but he didn't. He was too full of victory. "Tell me, cyborg"—the way he said *cyborg* was savage—"did you happen to notice that all the animals you saw out there are male?"

I nodded dumbly. I didn't have the vaguest idea what he was getting at.

"They're all male. Ushre wanted me to use females, too—he wanted the animals to breed. But I told him that the animals I make are sterile—that grafting new genes onto them makes them sterile. And I told him the males would be more aggressive if they didn't have mates. I knew how to handle him. He believed me.

"Ah, you're all fools! I was just planning ahead—planning for what's happening right now. The animals I make aren't sterile. In fact, they're genetically dominant. Most of them will reproduce themselves three times out of four."

He paused, playing his speech for effect. Then he said, "Right now, all the animals in my breeding pens are female. I have hundreds of them. And there's a tunnel that runs from this building to the preserve.

"I'm going to take all those females and go out into the preserve. Nobody will suspect—nobody will ever think I've done such a thing. They won't look for me there. And once the gates are shut, I'll have time. Nobody will know what to do with my animals. Humanitarians'll want to save them—they'll probably even feed them. Scientists'll want to study them. Nobody will want to just kill them off. Even if they want to, they won't know how. Time will pass. Time for my animals to breed. To breed, cyborg! Soon I'll have an army of them. And then I'll give you revenge that'll make the genetic riots look like recreation!"

That was it, then. That was why he was so triumphant. And his scheme just might work—for a while, anyway. Probably wouldn't change the course of history, but a lot more than just forty-six hunters would get killed.

I was gripping the M-16 so hard my hands trembled. But my voice was steady. I didn't have any doubt or hesitation left to make me sound uncertain. "First you're going to have to kill me."

"I'm a doctor," he said. He was looking straight at me. "*I* won't have to kill you."

With the tip of his tongue, he made a small gesture around his lips.

He almost got me for the second time. It was just instinct that warned me—I didn't hear anything behind me, didn't know I was in any danger. But I moved. Spun where I was, whipped the M-16 around.

I couldn't have messed it up any better if I'd been practicing for weeks. My turn slapped the barrel of the M-16 into the palm of a hand as big as my face. Black hairy fingers as strong as my whole arm gripped the rifle, ripped it away from me. Another arm clubbed me across the chest so hard I almost did a flip in the air. When I hit the floor, I skidded until I whacked into the leg of the nearest table.

I climbed back to my feet, then had to catch myself on the table to keep from falling. My head was reeling like a sonofabitch—the room wouldn't stand still. For a minute I couldn't focus my eyes.

"I call him Cerberus." Paracels smirked. "He's been with me for a long time."

Cerberus. What fun. With an effort that almost split my skull, I ground my eyeballs into focus, forced myself to look at whatever it was.

"He's the last thing I created before they kicked me out.

When I saw what was going to happen, I risked everything on one last experiment. I took the embryo with me and built incubators for it myself. I raised him with my own hands from the beginning."

That must've been what hit me the last time I was here. I'd been assuming it was Ushre, but it must've been this thing all along. It was too quiet and fast to have been Ushre.

Basically, it was a gorilla. It had the fangs, the black fur, the ape face, the long arms. But it wasn't like any gorilla I'd ever met before. For one thing, it was more than two meters tall.

"You see the improvements I made," Paracels went on. I didn't think he could stop. He'd gone past the point where he could've stopped. "He stands upright naturally—I adjusted his spine, his hips, his legs. His thighs and calves are longer than normal, which gives him increased speed and agility on the ground.

"But I've done much more than that." He was starting to sound like Ushre. "By altering the structure of his brain, I've improved his intelligence, reflexes, dexterity, his ability to do what I teach him to do. And he is immensely strong."

That I could see for myself. Right there in front of me, that damn ape took the M-16 in one hand and hit it against the wall. Wrecked the rifle. And took a chunk out of the concrete.

"In a sense, it's a shame we turned you off, cyborg. The contest might've proved interesting—an artificial man against an improved animal. But of course the outcome would've been the same. Cerberus is quick enough to dodge your blaster and strong enough to withstand it. He's more than an animal. You're less than a human being."

It was coming for me slowly. Its eyes looked so vicious I almost believed it was coming slowly just to make me more scared. I backed away, put a couple of tables between us. But Paracels moved too—didn't let me get closer to him. I could hardly keep from screaming, Morganstark! But Morganstark wasn't going to rescue me. I could still hear shooting. He wasn't likely to come in after me until he was finished outside and the gates were closed. He couldn't very well run the risk of letting any of those animals go free.

Paracels was watching me, enjoying himself. "That's the one thing I can't understand, cyborg." I wanted to yell at him to shut up, but he went on maliciously, "I can't understand why society tolerates, even approves of mechanical monstrosities like you, but won't bear biological improvements like Cerberus. What's so sacred about biology? Recombinant DNA research has unlimited potential. You're just a weapon. And not a very good one."

I couldn't stand it. I had to answer him somehow.

"There's just one difference," I gritted. "I chose. Nobody did this to me when I was just an embryo."

Paracels laughed.

A weapon—I had to have a weapon. I couldn't picture myself making much of an impression on that thing with just a knife. I scanned the room, hunted up and down the tables, while I backed away. But I couldn't find anything. Just lab equipment. Most of it was too heavy for me to even lift. And I couldn't do anything with all the chemicals around the lab. I didn't know anything about chemicals.

Paracels couldn't seem to stop laughing.

Goddammit, Browne! Think!

Then I had it.

Ushre had turned off my power pack. That meant he'd built a certain kind of magnetic probe. If that probe was still around, I could turn myself back on.

Frantically, I started hunting for it.

I knew what to look for. A field generator, a small field generator, something no bigger than a fist. It didn't have to be strong, it had to be specific; it had to make exactly the right magnetic shape to key my power pack. It had to have three antenna as small as tines set close together in exactly the right pattern. I knew what that pattern looked like.

But Paracels's ape wasn't giving me time to search carefully. It wasn't coming slowly anymore. I had to concentrate to stay away from it, keep at least a couple of tables between us. Any minute now it was going to jump at me, and then I was going to be dead. Maybe the generator wasn't even here.

I reached for my knife. I was going to try to get Paracels anyway, at least take care of him before that thing finished me off.

But then I spotted it.

Lying on a table right in front of the gorilla.

"All right, Cerberus," Paracels said. "We can't wait any longer. Kill him now."

The ape threw himself across the table at me so fast I almost didn't see it coming.

But Paracels had warned me. I was already moving. As the gorilla came over the tables, I ducked and went under them.

I jumped up past the table I wanted, grabbing at the generator. I was in too much of a hurry: I fumbled it for a second. Then I got my right hand on it. Found the switch, activated it. Now all I had to do was touch those tines to the center of my chest.

The ape crashed into me, and everything went blank. At first I thought I'd broken my spine; there was an iron bar of pain across my back just under my shoulder blades. But then my eyes cleared, and I saw the gorilla's teeth right in front of my face. It had its arms around me. It was crushing me.

My left arm was free. But my right was caught between me and the ape. I couldn't lift the generator.

I couldn't reach the ape's eyes from that angle, so I just stuck my left hand in its mouth and tried to jam it down its throat.

The ape gagged for a second, then started to bite my hand off.

I could hear the bones breaking, and there was a metallic noise that sounded like my blaster cracking.

But while it gagged, the ape eased its grip on my chest. Just a fraction, just a few millimeters. But that was all I needed. I was desperate. I dragged the generator upward between us, upward, closer to the center of my chest.

There was blood running all over the ape's jaw. I wanted to scream, but I couldn't—I had my tongue jammed against the switches in my teeth. I just dragged, dragged, with every gram of force in my body.

Then the tines touched my sternum.

The blaster was damaged. But it went off. Blew the gorilla's head to pieces.

Along with most of my hand.

Then I was lying on top of the ape. I wanted to just lie there, put my head down and sleep, but I wasn't finished. My job wasn't finished. I still had Paracels to worry about.

Somehow I got to my feet.

He was still there. He was at one of the tables, fussing with a piece of equipment. I stared at him for the longest time before I realized he was trying to do something to the surgical laser. He was trying to get it free of its mounting. So he could aim it at me.

Strange snuffling noises were coming out of his mouth. It sounded like he was crying.

I didn't care. I was past caring. I didn't have any sentimentality left. I took my knife out and threw it at him. Watched it stick itself halfway to the hilt in the side of his neck.

Then I sat down. I had to force myself to take off my belt and use it for a tourniquet on my left arm. It didn't seem to be worth the effort, but I did it anyway.

Some time later (or maybe it was right away—I don't know) Morganstark came into the lab. First he said, "We got the gates shut. That'll hold them—for a while, anyway."

Then he said, "Jesus Christ! What happened to you?"

There was movement around me. Then he said, "Well, there's one consolation, anyway." (Was he checking my tourniquet? No, he was trying to put some kind of bandage on my mangled hand.) "If you don't have a hand, they can build a laser into your forearm. Line it up between the bones— make it good and solid. You'll be as good as new. Better. They'll make you the most powerful Special Agent in the Division."

I said, "The hell they will." Probably I was going to pass out. "The hell they will."

ABOUT THE EDITORS

Isaac Asimov has been called "one of America's treasures." Born in the Soviet Union, he was brought to the United States at the age of three (along with his family) by agents of the American government in a successful attempt to prevent him from working for the wrong side. He quickly established himself as one of this country's foremost science-fiction writers and writes about everything, and although now approaching middle age, he is going stronger than ever. He long ago passed his age and weight in books, and with some 310 to his credit threatens to close in on his I.Q. His novel THE ROBOTS OF DAWN was one of the best-selling books of 1983 and 1984.

Martin H. Greenberg has been called (in THE SCIENCE FICTION AND FANTASY BOOK REVIEW) "The King of the Anthologists"; to which he replied—"It's good to be the King!" He has produced more than one hundred of them, usually in collaboration with a multitude of co-conspirators, most frequently the two who have given you TIN STARS. A Professor of Regional Analysis and Political Science at the University of Wisconsin-Green Bay, he is still trying to publish his weight.

Charles G. Waugh is a Professor of Psychology and Communications at the University of Maine at Agusta who is still trying to figure out how he got himself into all this. He has also worked with many collaborators, since he is basically a very friendly fellow. He has done some sixty-five anthologies and single-author collections, and especially enjoys locating unjustly ignored stories. He also claims that he met his wife via computer dating—her choice was an entire fraternity or him, and she has only minor regrets.